NEW DOC IN MAPLE RIDGE

Dr. Bob Bell

Non Nocere Press

D1523327

This book is dedicated to all primary care health professionals who provide the foundation for a healthier community.

And to our grandchildren who inspire us to improve everything.

CONTENTS

Title Page

Copyright

Dedication

Endorsements

Chapter 1: Arrival in Maple Ridge   1

Chapter 2: The Civic Luncheon   12

Chapter 3: Meeting Lawrence   17

Chapter 4: Esther   25

Chapter 5: Sharon   30

Chapter 6: Piper Forceps   36

Chapter 7: Tony   47

Chapter 8: The Silent Auction   54

Chapter 9: Intimidation   64

Chapter 10: Learning About Linda   68

Chapter 11: Salmon with Salsa   73

Chapter 12: The Diagnosis   82

Chapter 13: Visiting the Hospital   87

Chapter 14: ER Surge   90

Chapter 15: The Back Nine   95

Chapter 16: Geothermal Waters   98

Chapter 17: Hot Springs   101

Chapter 18: The Black Hole   104

Chapter 19: Sunday Night at the Office   109

Chapter 20: HQ   113

Chapter 21: Counterattack   123

Chapter 22: RICO   128

Chapter 23: Linda meets Ben   134

Chapter 24: Standard Operating Procedure   142

Chapter 25: Two Missing Years   145

Chapter 26: Special Forces Operational Detachment   151
Alpha

Chapter 27: Dixie gang   163

Chapter 28: PTSD   175

Chapter 29: Little Rock   183

Chapter 30: Tommy's transcript   190

Chapter 31: Saddling Up   194

Chapter 32: Tony's transcript   196

Chapter 33: Tactics   199

Chapter 34: Falling in Love   204

Chapter 35: Sarah is Puzzled   211

Chapter 36: Gabriel Ponders   217

Chapter 37: Trusting Your Life   219

Chapter 38: The Start of Ben's Plan   224

Chapter 39: Gabriel's Thoughts   229

Chapter 40: Going South and Going East   232

Chapter 41: Migrating Discs   235

Chapter 42: Biloxi   241

Chapter 43: Making the Case   247

Chapter 44: Gabriel's Arrest   251

Chapter 45: The Offer   260

Chapter 46: Saving Gabriel   266

Chapter 47: Visiting Hours   271

Chapter 48: Maple Ridge   283

About The Author   291

Books By This Author   295

Hope you enjoy this gift from my.

Best wishes,

Rob

ENDORSEMENTS

New Doc in Maple Ridge is a wild ride that takes the reader from a small-town ER to the battlefields of Afghanistan, to the underworld, to the courtroom, with high-spirited stops along the way in the bedroom. A real page-turner, grounded in the unparalleled, extensive experiences of Dr. Bob Bell. *Deb Matthews, PhD, Former Ontario Minister of Health*

After decades performing life-saving surgery as an elite surgeon, Dr. Bob Bell uses his surgeon's attention to detail to craft a brilliant story populated by some of the most extraordinary characters you will ever encounter! I dare you to put this book down once you have started the remarkable journey with Dr. Ed Brinkley. *Paul Alofs, Author of "Passion Capital"*

Surgeon, hospital CEO, and provincial deputy health minister-....Dr. Bob Bell has done it all, so no surprise that his new novel is steeped in medical authenticity. The tension builds from the first page, when the new doctor in town saves a boy from choking on a peanut. Whether it's treating a mobster's STD, or reliving military action in Afghanistan, you feel that you are right there. *Phillip Crawley, CEO/Publisher of The Globe and Mail*

Dr. Bob Bell has written a barn burner of a novel that reads like James Patterson at his best but with an expert medical thread throughout reflecting his preeminence as a surgeon. Terrific read. *Robert Prichard, President Emeritus, University of Toronto*

Dr. Bob Bell has written another medical thriller pitting 'good vs. evil'. There is much more to the "new doc" than originally meets the eye....as there is to the quiet Arkansas town of Maple Ridge. Dr. Bob's views on issues ranging from health-care delivery models to wealth inequality, race relations, and medical class-action law suits make this book not only a good read, but also a catalyst for reflection on some of the most pressing social issues of our time. *Keith Ambachtsheer, Former Chair PMH Foundation, Global Pension Expert, Philanthropist & Author.*

New Doc in Maple Ridge is a riveting, suspenseful story with fascinating characters with whom you can't help but become attached. While subtly touching on the delivery of healthcare, it is a thrilling story of exceptional individuals who take on the mob to protect their community and themselves. *Gord Nixon, Business Leader*

Dr. Bell writes with an intuitive insight that only someone who's been there and done that can. The depth of character development in this story reflects his wide experience in the real-life worlds of medicine and management. Medicine is drama – life and death. This book depicts that drama at its best. *David Patchell-Evans, Founder & CEO, GoodLife Fitness*

Rarely does one read a thriller to learn about modern health-care. But Dr. Bob Bell, in this terrific page turner, skillfully combines an irresistible story, with cutting edge medicine. What an enjoyable read! *Dr. Richard Reznick, Surgeon & Health System Leader*

Dr Bob Bell has written an engaging book about a doctor. Bell uses some interesting insights into modern medical technology and public health policy to create a fast moving organized crime story set in the U.S. south. A surprising plot with enough twists that, once starting to read, it's hard to put down. *Ian Delaney, Business Leader & Philanthropist*

The topic of healthcare system performance is on everyone's mind today. ***New Doc in Maple Ridge*** discusses this important issue in the context of a page-turning thriller that both teaches and entertains. ***Lionel Robins, Former Chair Princess Margaret Cancer Foundation & Philanthropist***

Through the eyes of a war hero, Dr. Bob Bell does a masterful job of creating a page-turning thriller that exposes the raw underbelly of today's society - corporate greed, violence, corruption, mental illness, systemic inequity, and the atrocities of war. Yet, as the intriguing plot unfolds, it is impossible to miss the message that courage, perseverance, creativity, and love give us all hope that a better future might be in our reach. ***John Bowey, Former Chair Princess Margaret Cancer Foundation***

Dr. Bob Bell has created a cunning story of a doctor suffering from PTSD entering the fray of a small-town medical system intent on providing a more personalized medical approach to his patients. Mob violence, the horrors of war, romance, and the effects of medical innovations are described with keen insight. This book has been written by a well-respected doctor. It is a treat for the reader to be exposed to his depth of knowledge and expertise through these entertaining pages. ***John Mulvihill, Former Chair University Health Network Board***

What a great read! From small town USA to the war zone in Afghanistan, Dr. Bob Bell takes his readers on an adventure that makes it impossible to put this book down! ***Dr. Dhun Noria, Former Trustee University Health Network & Health System Leader***

Dr. Bob Bell packs it all into the story of Dr. Ed Brinkley. Health care, drama and romance move this story at a fast pace, and ***New Doc in Maple Ridge*** satisfies with a great conclusion. ***Rita Burak, Former Trustee University Health Network***

There is lots to enjoy and unravel in this medico-legal-military mixture. Set in a small town in the southern US, Bob has managed to give us a good thriller and a slice of modern life at the same time. *Eileen Mercier, Former Trustee University Health Network*

Bell is a master storyteller who captures the reader's attention with engaging characters and an intriguing plot. His unique insight into the world of healthcare imbues his writing with wit and realism. *Emily Musing, Healthcare Leader*

Dr. Bob Bell has done it again with a scintillating medical thriller. *New Doc in Maple Ridge* is a page turner with several important messages. *Don Johnson, Business Leader, Philanthropist & Author.*

In Dr. Bob Bell's latest medical thriller, a decorated and skilled physician yearns for a change of pace, practice and relationships in a charming small town. The new doc quickly learns of the town's dark secrets and in dealing with its sinister underworld, his own buried secrets are resurfaced. I was rooting for the heroes vs. villains throughout this book and enjoyed the evidence of Dr. Bell's knowledge and experience leading to a climax that only he could write! *Lori Marshall, Health System Leader*

This second novel by Dr. Bob Bell is an engaging thriller, with a plot that weaves its way through small town medicine, domestic abuse, romance, organized crime and flashbacks that plague a physician on his return from a tour of duty in Afghanistan. From the young doctor who moves to a small-town hospital in Arkansas to practice a new style of medicine, to the lawyer that he becomes romantically involved with, to his patient that is suffering from spousal abuse, to her gangster husband that terrorizes all three, this story is a real page turner.

Lawrence Bloomberg, Business Leader & Philanthropist

This novel has it all: health care reform, covert military action, a class action lawsuit, modern tech wizardry, an inside look at organized crime and a beautiful love story. Exciting, informative, and highly entertaining. A classic "must read". *Dr Michael A Baker, Former UHN Physician-in-Chief*

Dr. Brinkley's commitment to starting a new life after the deep and debilitating traumas of war, is rattled by gangsters, enabled by intense loyalty of military colleagues, and fueled by passionate love. A story of courage, intrigue, and triumph! *Mary Jo Haddad, Health System Leader*

It was a fun and easy read. Great storytelling, lots of action, a few twists, and all set against an intriguing medical backdrop. *Matt Anderson, Health System Leader*

Once I started the book, I couldn't put it down. It was a great read with intrigue, romance, heroes both real and inspirational, and an invitation to imagine life in a small town where global challenges are tackled. *Ralph Shedletsky, Executive & Board Advisor*

A compelling, intricate, and intelligent storyline that weaves the author's deep knowledge of medicine and health care delivery with the social and criminal elements of small-town America. It has you rooting for the hero's success in love and life as he navigates difficult, sometimes life-threatening situations--- fixating you from the start! *Debbie Fisher, Health System Leader*

From small town America to the battlefields of Afghanistan, Dr. Bob Bell weaves a tale that pits love and loyalty against cruelty and corruption. Whether firefights, court room battles, or medical emergencies, action packed drama, with layers of ethical overtones, commands your attention to the last ironic line. A great read. **Dr. *Chris Paige, Health Research Leader***

A must read for the holidays. This medical thriller takes you from the heroics in a small-town ER in Arkansas to the battle field in Afghanistan. One piece of advice, don't start reading it before bedtime unless you plan to sleep in the next morning. After the first three chapters, you can't put the book down and have to finish reading it. **Dr. *Charlie Chan, Medical Leader***

New Doc in Maple Ridge is an engaging story of Dr. Brinkley, a physician and new comer in Maple Ridge Arkansas. The doctor is starting his new chapter after military service, guarding a deep secret. The small town has its secrets too. The story blends intrigue and medicine, clearly written by a physician who understands practice and explores how a doctor from outside fits into a small community and a local medical culture. Enjoyed the read! **Dr. *Wendy Levinson, Health System Leader***

A page-turner from the beginning that weaves together medical drama, romance, war trauma and crime. All against a backdrop of a broken health system and the people struggling to change it. A great read! **Dr. *Michael Schull, Health System Leader***

Dr. Bob Bell captures the human dynamics of a new doctor settling into a community but also tackles social issues through the eye of an experienced healthcare leader. The Arkansas setting and the characters in Maple Ridge come to life in this page turner. **New Doc in Maple Ridge** provides a realistic glimpse into the American healthcare as well as a very compelling story. **Tom Wellner, Health System Leader**

A gripping page turner from beginning to end. ***New Doc in Maple Ridge*** takes the reader on a thrilling adventure from the wilds of Afghanistan to a small town in Arkansas. Something for everyone – a must read. *Virginia McLaughlin, Health System Leader & Philanthropist*

Another enjoyable read from Dr. Bob Bell that seamlessly weaves his medical knowledge with his story telling prowess! *Tom Ehrlich, Business Leader & Philanthropist*

Dr. Bob Bell brings all his experience as a family physician, world renowned surgeon and senior health care administrator to bear in this medical thriller. From the backstory to the action and the unexpected denouement, you will be intrigued from start to finish. **Dr.** *Charles Catton, Medical Leader*

In this fast paced and explosive novel Dr. Ed Brinkley is trying to make a personal and professional transition from war zone combatant and life saver to small town hospital physician. Little does he know that intrigue, danger, and romance await him and that the new battlefield he has been thrust into can be just as deadly as the one he left behind. *Bruce McKelvey, Business leader*

Dr. Bob Bell does it again…. he has crafted a riveting medical thriller that keeps the reader captivated from the first page through to the dramatic and ingenious finale. *Catherine Booth, Information Management Leader*

New Doc in Maple Ridge provides " stories within stories" to create multiple plots involving much suspense!! These stories were intriguing and filled with mystery, thus keeping me on the edge of my seat throughout the entire book. I was kept in suspense as to how these "stories" would turn out. It's going to be a best seller! *Ronald P. Schlegel, O.C., Healthcare Leader & Philanthropist*

Dr Bob Bell was a transformative leader as hospital CEO and Deputy Minister. And he is now writing transformative fiction.

You must read *New Doc in Maple Ridge*!! *Leo Goldhar, Philanthropist*

A clever assimilation of intriguing story lines with alluring characters that keep the reader engaged and excited to witness the next twist in this dynamic plot. This is a unique novel with broad appeal to a wide range of readers who get a thrill from mystery, suspense and a resulting love story. *Jeff Mainland, Healthcare Leader*

Bell weaves his unique experience in the medical world into the complex machinations of organized crime creating a great read with many page turning twists and turns! An adventure laced with medical eye openers*Graham Scott, Strategist & Healthcare Consultant*

Another fast paced and enjoyable read from Dr. Bob Bell, with a few twists! Great to see primary care profiled so positively. *Dr. David Price, Family Physician & Health System Leader*

This book offers a fast-paced drama that weaves together medical expertise, crime-busting technology and insight on a range of topical issues from confronting combat casualties to litigating faulty medical devices. *Dr. Pauline Pariser, Family Physician & Health System Leader*

Dr. Bob Bell has taken his deep knowledge of clinical care and health systems to shine a light on the unique position of primary care. In Dr. Ed Brinkley, he has created a brilliant character who is the kind of generalist that our health systems need - someone who can put the needs of patients first while still attending to the success of the whole community. *Dr. Sarah Newbery, Family Physician and Health System Leader*

Dr. Robert Bell writes a riveting tale of medicine, murder and Machiavellian tactics that will keep the reader enthralled from start to finish. His detailed research and his deep knowledge of medicine is evident and makes the story truly compelling. *Dr. Mohamed Alarakhia, Family Physician & Health System Leader*

It really was a page turner! The combination of romance, medicine, corruption, and special ops shouts out for a film treatment! I liked the way the action moved along quickly. **Dr.** *Howard Abrams, Medical Leader*

Dr. Bob Bell's latest work offers a smart, fast paced plot with compelling characters and unpredictable twists and turns. His medical knowledge always adds a layer of credibility to an otherwise tall tale! *Cindy Morton, Health System Leader*

A truly enjoyable and intriguing read from start to finish. Small town dynamics, organized crime and medical emergencies are wound around the life of a recently transplanted physician - whose skills go far beyond those of the average medical practitioner! *Dr. Barry McLellan, Health System Leader*

New Doc in Maple Ridge is a snappy page turner. The action of Grisham with the health-system insights of Gawande. *Dr. Andy Smith, Surgeon & Health System Leader*

An intriguing adventure in which good people take a stand against organized crime. Great characters and action-packed. And love the way Dr. Bell has woven social commentary and healthcare reform concepts into the story. *Dr. Tim Rutledge, Health System Leader*

New Doc in Maple Ridge introduces us to Dr. Ed Brinkley, a former military trauma surgeon restarting his life in a small town in after a horrific deployment in Afghanistan. Dr. Bob Bell uses insights derived from his career to craft a tale involving the life of a family physician that becomes very complicated. It is a fun read which is at once a crime story, an action movie screenplay, and a romance novel. *Rob MacIsaac, Health System Leader*

Dr. Bob Bell's second book is a powerful, fast paced story of a veteran military surgeon intent on establishing a new life in a community where he finds not only love and a new approach to his profession but also a significant intrusion by organized crime. This is a thrilling portrayal of good people thrust into an undercurrent of illegal activity that leaves the reader wanting to read on to the next chapter. *New Doc in Maple Ridge* should be on everyone's reading list! *Mark Rochon, Healthcare Leader & Consultant*

Bell has written a page turner! I couldn't put it down—finished it in one sitting. Dr Ed Brinkley is the medical world's answer to Jack Ryan. Can't wait for the netflix series. *Will Falk, Health System Leader*

Dr. Bob Bell's latest novel *New Doc in Maple Ridge* is a gripping page turner that ranges in scope from fighting the Taliban Afghanistan to the mob in Arkansas all the while wrapping in a tender romance. It's a great tale! *Peter M. Jacobsen, Attorney*

This book is a fun read. The story moves along quickly and has very engaging characters. Making the book particularly special is that it packages together aspects of human relationships, organized crime, special forces military, medical practice, cybersecurity and class action lawsuits. *Tom Closson, Health System Leader*

New Doc in Maple Ridge is a wonderful read - fast moving, intensely engaging, and with a terrific story line. As compelling is the way that Dr Bell weaves in medical information that fits perfectly with the overall story and that is incredibly interesting and educational. This could only have been written by a medical doctor - and a worldly one with a great imagination like Dr Bell. *Stephen Bear, Business Leader*

New Doc in Maple Ridge not only provides the reader with an action packed, page-turning thriller. It also speaks to advances in medical technology and innovation in healthcare in general. This is a best seller than you can learn from as well as enjoy. *Dr. Peter Ferguson, Professor & Chair of Orthopaedic Surgery*

A compelling and intriguing medical thriller. Dr. Bob Bell weaves his health care and human experience into the fabric of this book. The well-written and detailed work holds the reader's attention from the first page to last and is a very satisfying read. With proceeds from this novel supporting community research in primary care, Dr. Bell continues his legacy a transformer of health care. *Dr. Joel Werier, Surgeon & Health System Leader*

A thrilling read that is captivating, heart-warming, with unexpected twists – a real page-turner! Dr. Bell has become a masterful story-teller! *Dr. Fei-Fei Liu, Health System Leader*

New Doc in Maple Ridge is a modern day suspense of finding renewed purpose and love with intriguing twists and turns. This engaging novel provides accurate learnings for an inspiring vision for primary healthcare and the role of the legal system in protecting the public's interests. *Ron Noble, Health System Leader*

New Doc in Maple Ridge has compelling, nuanced characters, multiple beautifully interwoven story lines, explores the personal consequences of covert operations, delves into what is good and what is bad about medicine today, and has a shocking ending that I did not see coming. *Dr. Barry Rubin, Surgeon & Health System Leader.*

This is a great read. I wondered how Dr. Bob Bell could create widespread interest in new models of healthcare. He achieves this by deftly weaving the relevant factors of population health, high risk patients, traditional physician practices, and government policy, into a fast paced, intriguing 'page turner' with a very engaging storyline. *Dr. David Pichora , Surgeon & Health System Leader*

New Doc in Maple Ridge is an entertaining read. The characters are well developed and the story develops at a rapid pace that will keep you turning pages in anticipation. *Dr. Phil Hooper, Surgeon & Health System Leader*

New Doc in Maple Ridge is a twisting, page turning thriller that includes real healthcare situations in a compelling story that follows engaging characters through professional complexity, danger and romance. A must read. *Dr. Thierry Mesana, Surgeon & Health System Leader*

An intriguing story of medical practice, criminal gang violence and romance in a small southern town. A great read and difficult to put down. *Dr. Bill Orovan, Surgeon & Health System Leader*

This is an exciting medical thriller which will keep you wanting for more. Bob Bell brings his deep knowledge of medicine and intertwines it with life in small town USA. I would highly recommend this to anyone looking for an exciting multi-faceted thriller. *Dr. Nizar Mohamed, Surgeon & Health System Leader*

Although I have known Dr. Bob Bell as a master surgeon, healthcare leader and mentor, I am now equally amazed by his skills as an author. This medical thriller kept me glued to the pages till the end. *Dr. Stephen Gallay, Surgeon & Health System Leader*

By seamlessly integrating a "Bond"-like adventure with the medico-legal disparities that plague US healthcare, Dr. Bell succeeds in allowing his readers to conceptualize the unfortunate realities our patients face though an engrossing and entertaining story. Once I started, I couldn't put it down! *Dr. Sabrena Noria, Surgeon & Health System Leader*

I just read *New Doc in Maple Ridge* by Bob Bell. The chapter called *Piper Forceps* got this obstetrician's heart beating! Through his hero he puts a story and faces to the problems of US primary care, but then touches on criminal conspiracies, class action lawsuits, spousal abuse, Afghan military action, and "a doctor's innate tendency to judge himself harshly when things do not go well". Highly addictive, in a non-opioid way! *Dr. David Rouselle, Obstetrician & Health System Leader*

Action packed story. It has medical and non- medical components and is a very good read. *George Enns, Former Corporate Headhunter*

A brilliant military doctor, a lawyer, the mob and special forces. What could possibly go wrong? Dr. Bob Bell has written an entertaining story with a bit of education about both medicine and life in a small town in the south. *Kevin Empey, Health System Leader*

This book has it all— Love, idealism, commitment. Doctors fighting for medical welfare and care for all!... A winner! *David Goldstein, Philanthropist*

Another Great Read! Dr. Bob Bell's second novel *New Doc in Maple Ridge* takes the reader on a journey from war-torn Afghanistan to a medical practice in a small town in Arkansas. This is an action packed story with unexpected and exciting twists and turns. *Ruth Gopaul, Assistant to Four UHN CEO's*

A fantastic read that is highly entertaining cover to cover. Dr. Bob Bell is an excellent story teller, there is no end to his many talents. I can't wait for the movie! *Kim Baker, Health System Leader*

From Afghanistan to Arkansas this is a thoroughly enjoyable read from start to finish with something for everyone. The author weaves a compelling story line with engaging and Interesting characters, and a plot that draws the reader in with unexpected twists and turns. *Ken Deane, Health System Leader*

New Doc in Maple Ridge is a well-written, suspenseful novel that I had trouble putting down. Couldn't wait to get back to it as it had all the elements of a good story: well developed characters in a contemporary setting facing very topical issues. *Sal Badali, Not-for-Profit Search Consultant.*

This hard-hitting saga strikes its points in a hurry, hastily marrying spine-tingling thuggery with sizzling passion - both unfolding inside progressive medicine's inherent competitive skepticism. In this COVID era of inbound PTSD, we can learn from this protagonist. The only problem with this book is that it ends. Hopefully a sequel is in the works. *Ronnie Gavsie, Health System Leader*

Dr. Bob Bell weaves a story of intrigue through the main characters of Dr. Ed and lawyer Linda. This journey takes the reader through human struggles of war, love, trauma, and crime. Will they defeat the criminals? Will their idyllic medical and legal models of caring for the poorest and sickest prevail? An interesting read! *Sarah Downey, Health System Leader*

Not your usual medical thriller. Cybersecurity, organized crime, unconditional love. It's a great story!! *Rocco Gerace, MD, Health System Leader*

A thoroughly enjoyable read. It's a combination of intrigue, peppered with some life lessons and some great reflections about what we could do to make our primary health care system better. *Jo-anne Marr, Health System Leader*

Is Dr Bob Bell a one-hit wonder? ABSOLUTELY NOT!! *New Doc in Maple Ridge* is another best seller from Dr Bell. I love the way he combines his medical knowledge, romance and intrigue into a captivating "can't put the book down" book. *Lisa Benvenuto, Assistant to four Deputy Ministers of Health*

New Doc in Maple Ridge holds many surprising twists and turns as it takes us on a journey into health care, power, love and the lasting effects that war has on those who survive. I thoroughly enjoyed every chapter! *Chris Power, Health System Leader*

SUSPENSEFUL! An exciting medical drama full of corruption, covert missions and romance. It's a real page turner! *Linda Haslam-Stroud, Health System Leader*

A very enjoyable read. A good mix of criminal activity, suspense/thriller with a little romance thrown in. I highly recommend this book. *Paul Cullen, Business Leader*

New Doc in Maple Ridge is a thrilling and intriguing read, informed by the insights and real-world experiences of Dr. Bob Bell. With proceeds supporting the UHN Foundation for community research in primary care, this novel is especially timely and relevant in today's health care environment. *Tracy MacCharles, Former Ontario Cabinet Minister*

Dr. Bob Bell's new thriller reads like a John Grisham novel. A fast, frantic page turner and a perfect tonic to escape on the cottage docks. *Elmer Kim, Business Leader*

Dr. Bell is back with another fast paced medical thriller. Ed Brinkley is a recently retired military trauma physician who seeks a quieter life and practice in a small city in Arkansas and, instead, finds professional challenge, violent mobsters and romance. Propelled by completely believable characters, **New Doc in Maple Ridge** is an exciting ride. **David Steele, Attorney**

Dr. Bob Bell tells a great story! He skillfully develops his characters as they uncover the layers of society living and working in Maple Ridge, and brings the reader to a startling climax. **Krista Sereno, Health System Assistant**

After a career in surgery and health system leadership, Dr. Bob Bell has created a page-turner that reveals insights on creating a new primary care practice in a small town with unexpected romance and criminal elements to be confronted. **Dr. Walter Wodchis, Health System Research Leader**

This book encapsulates the experience of Primary Care Physicians as seen through the eyes of a Doctor. Transported to a small community somewhere deep in the southern United States you learn to value the critical role Primary Care Physicians play in contributing to their patient's care and to the health of a community. Learning about the trauma physicians experienced during the war in Afghanistan strengthened the lead character's appeal. A must read!!! **Kim Bellissimo, Health System Leader**

Dr. Bob Bell brings his decades of experience as a frontline surgeon and health system guru to this captivating medical thriller. Through his eyes, New Doc in Maple Ridge expertly pulls back the layers of a small town filled with crime, intrigue, and a brewing showdown. **Elliot Pobjoy, Health System Leader**

New Doc in Maple Ridge is a perfect mix of crime and medical intrigue, with a splash of romance! Dr. Bob Bell has created strong, memorable characters that his readers will love and make for a satisfying read from the first to the last page. *Lynn Guerriero, Health System Leader*

New Doc in Maple Ridge has it all - glimpses into the US healthcare system, military tours in Afghanistan, the impacts of greed and corruption, and of course a healthy dose of romance! An intriguing read that was hard to put down! *Heather Sulkers, Systems Leader*

New Doc in Maple Ridge merges medical, legal, technology and military operations with detailed FBI and local police enforcement protocols to create a compelling story of criminal intrigue, personal relationships, suspense, and romance. This is a must read and superbly enjoyable. *Paul Sulkers, Health Systems Leader*

The New Doc in Maple Ridge tackles multiple issues in a seamless way. It is the perfect blend of medicine, politics, romance, action, and intrigue. *Dr. Rhonda Collins, Health System Leader*

Dr. Ed Brinkley brings his hidden talents and surgical precision to protecting his patients, his loved ones, his healthcare teams and his community. Ed's loyalty to both his current teams and his past colleagues is unparalleled and as you turn every page, you will be rooting for this modern-day hero who is guided by his compassion, experience and heart. *Dr. Val Grdisa, Health System Leader*

This is a very engaging book. The insights into the medical field were honest and refreshing. I enjoyed the events that happened and watched as the characters developed. Great book. *Wendy Gilmour, Health System Leader*

A doctor, a soldier, a lover. But why is this man of mystery hiding his past? A must read for those who believe in altruism and sticking up to those that threaten a better society. *Garth Matheson, Health System Leader*

Dr. Ed Brinkley's journey through small town Arkansas pulls you into a truly immersive understanding of the challenges and joys of the life of a primary care physician coupled with an edge of your seat thriller! *Shiran Isaacksz, Health System Leader*

Barring breaks for eating & sleeping I could not put down New Doc in Maple Ridge until I finished. Exciting suspenseful riveting & an ending that only Dr. Bob Bell could imagine. *Fred Levy, CPA, Business Leader*

CHAPTER 1: ARRIVAL
IN MAPLE RIDGE

Sitting just outside the ER exam room, Dr. Ed Brinkley could sense the emergency doctor's growing concern as he tried to treat the young boy's asthma. Ed felt his own mouth dry with apprehension as the child's breathing became more and more labored.

"How long has he had asthma?" the doctor asked the child's mother. She shook her head in confusion. "He's never had this before, Doc. He was out in the yard playing and came in wheezing and moaning. It's just getting worse and worse."

Ed watched as the middle-aged physician coaxed the distressed boy to breathe in asthma medication through an inhaler mask. The kid looked about five years of age. He was fighting and kept pulling the mask off his face. He could barely speak with hoarse wheezing choking him as he required more and more effort to breathe. "I can't breathe. Get that thing offa me."

His mother was trying to convince her son to use the mask. "William, you gotta listen to the doctor and breathe in that medicine. That medicine's gonna help you breathe."

It was clear to Ed that this child was in real trouble. The emergency doc was also realizing that he needed help. He called to the nurses at the ER front desk. "Get me respiratory therapy and anesthesia stat." A nurse at the desk relayed the order which was immediately broadcast over the hospital speaker system three times.

"Anesthesia and RT to ER stat."

1

The phone on the reception desk rang seconds later and the message was passed back to the doctor. "Anesthesia and RT are tied up in ICU for at least ten minutes. No one can come until the next case is done in the OR."

Ed knew that he should not get involved before he was officially registered on staff. But this situation was deteriorating rapidly, and he knew that this boy did not have asthma.

Leaving his seat, Ed gingerly entered the ER and quietly addressed the doctor. "Do you mind if I take a look? I have some experience with airway problems like this."

He showed his visitor's pass to the nonplussed physician, "I'm Dr. Ed Brinkley. I was just appointed to staff at the hospital. I'm here to see Dr. Stanton."

Then, observing the child's deteriorating condition, he lost all hesitancy as his training and experience took control. He turned to the nurse. "We need an IV for this kid right now."

Ed knew that asthma makes a wheezing noise when a child is trying to breathe out through narrowed, constricted air passages in the lungs. The noise this child was making was higher pitched and increased when he was breathing in. His condition sounded similar to asthma but is called stridor in medical books. That sound told Ed that something was wrong with this kid's airway – the term doctors use to name the large tubes like the trachea that move air from the throat to the lungs.

The ER doc was happy to have any help but unwilling to give up on his diagnosis. "If he would only cooperate and breathe in the asthma meds through the mask his wheezing would improve."

Ed shook his head. "It sounds more like stridor than wheezing to me."

He asked the nurse who was now starting the intra-venous in the child's arm, "Do we have an Ear, Nose & Throat doctor in the hospital?"

The nurse shook her head. "The ENT guys come in for consults and to operate but there is no one in the hospital right now."

Ed called to the desk. "Phone ENT in the office and tell them we have a kid with a likely foreign body obstruction. We need more help here. Call a code blue, get an intubation tray and a rigid bronch set ready."

The team in the ER responded rapidly, gathering equipment and making calls. Two nurses joined their colleague already looking after William. But just as rapidly as the code blue call went out over the PA, the struggling child stopped fighting and then just stopped breathing. They were losing him.

Ed turned to the nurse who had just taped down the IV line. "We need to sedate him before we intubate. Give him 30 milligrams of propofol slow push."

As the nurse injected the anesthetic agent through William's IV line, Ed tried breathing for him using a mask and ventilator bag. It was difficult to push air into his lungs and he immediately asked for a laryngoscope device to put a plastic tube into his lungs. As Ed lifted William's jaw forward with the laryngoscope and looked down his throat at the boy's vocal cords, the reason for the emergency instantly became evident.

"Gimme a grasping forceps please." Ed's eyes were fixed on the child's vocal cords as the nurse placed the narrow grasping instrument in his right hand. Neither Ed, nor the child, nor anyone else in the exam room was breathing.

Holding the laryngoscope motionless in his left hand, Ed reached down William's throat with the instrument in his right hand and gently grasped the peanut from the side of the vocal cords where it had been obstructing the flow of air. Nearly in unison the doctors and nurses gasped as they watched Ed slowly pull the nut out of William's throat.

William's mother exclaimed. "Oh my God, where did he get that? I would never have let him run around if I knew he had a nut."

Having removed the obstruction, Ed released the grasping forceps, took a small tube from the nurse and slipped it through the child's swollen vocal cords to ensure airway control. But as the rapid acting propofol sedative drug wore off,

3

William started breathing deeply and began to buck against the irritating tube in his throat.

Telling the nurse to keep another dose of anesthesia drug handy in case reinsertion became necessary, Ed cautiously removed the tube. As the tube slid out, William's stridor noises were gone, and he seemed to be breathing normally. The small group watching the child with rapt attention exhaled together.

The call for anesthesia and respiratory therapy was suddenly answered as three individuals raced into the ER exam room. Ed recognized one of them from his picture on the hospital website as Dr. Bill Stanton, the hospital's chief doctor.

Looking around the room, Ed cleared his throat sheepishly. "I guess that I should introduce myself. My name is Dr. Ed Brinkley, and I am due to start on staff at the hospital in the next couple of days. I was here to meet with Dr. Stanton and thought that I might help Dr..." at this point he quickly glanced at the name tag of his future colleague, "Dr. Appleton manage this airway foreign body that was causing some difficulty for William."

Appleton stared at the new doctor, and then smiled and offered his hand. "Ed, thank you. I missed the diagnosis. Thank God you picked it up and got that peanut out before it went into the trachea."

Ed nodded in agreement. "Yeah, it was a big peanut – I guess that's why it didn't get through the vocal cords. If it had gone through the cords down into the trachea it would have been a lot harder to remove."

William's mother grabbed on to Ed's arm. "Thank you so much, Doctor. You saved my boy's life."

"Ma'am you know this is a team thing. We are all happy that William is doing better. Just keep him away from peanuts when he's playing."

The kid was obviously improving and there was really little for the team to do other than observe his status and ensure that his vocal cords did not swell. The anesthetist left to go back to the OR and the respiratory therapist gave William a mask with humidified air which he now readily accepted. Ed turned to Dr. Appleton. "Sorry for the drama, Doc. Nice to meet you, I look forward to working with you."

Appleton smiled back. "Quite a start to your Maple Ridge practice, Ed. Welcome to town."

Ed looked over at Stanton. "I'm here to see you Dr. Stanton. Apologies for the delay."

Bill Stanton shook his head slowly. "Welcome Dr. Brinkley." He turned to the door out of the small exam room extending his arm. "Come on back to my office. I hope this introduction to Maple Ridge does not mean that you are going to be a source of constant excitement for our little hospital."

****

Twenty minutes earlier Ed had arrived at the reception desk of Maple Ridge Hospital Emergency Department and greeted the receptionist. "My name is Dr. Ed Brinkley, and I am here to see Dr. Bill Stanton. He told me to find the emergency department reception when I arrived and that you would notify him that I am here."

The woman behind reception smiled with welcome and nodded. "Dr. Stanton told me that you would be coming Dr. Brinkley. I think that you are a few minutes early. His office is across the main room of the ER and just down that right corridor." She rotated her chair to show him the direction. "There is a chair just outside the ER if you want to wait there. He should be back from his rounds in ten or fifteen minutes."

She wrote "Dr. Brinkley" on a sticky tag marked VISITOR and told Ed to apply it to his coat. With his identification settled Brinkley wandered through the ER and settled just outside the department in the corridor that led to Dr. Stanton's office.

Ed had not yet met Dr. Stanton, but they had been exchanging messages. The new doctor had just arrived in Maple Ridge, Arkansas and would start working in the Maple Ridge clinic in the next few days. The family practice clinic was owned by the hospital, and part of Ed's responsibilities would include working in this ER and looking after the clinic's hospitalized patients admitted through the ER.

Ed was coming to Maple Ridge because he liked the way that Arkansas was reorganizing its medical care. It was one of the first states to start a new model of primary care where general practitioners accepted responsibility for more complex patients.

Medicare was calling it the "patient medical home." Ed had read about the medical home concept and thought the idea could help the country's struggling healthcare system.

He knew that in most places, complex patients were looked after by multiple specialists with nobody in charge of the overall patient. The patient had different specialists for their heart disease, diabetes, arthritis and depression but no one was coordinating the impact of all this medical treatment on the entire person. The new concept was that the medical home General Practitioner or GP would serve as the quarterback for all of a patient's treatments.

Ed also liked how this system would allow him to serve the community. He would be looking after sicker people with the medical home team in his office and trying to keep them out of the hospital. By also working on the hospital wards and in the ER, Ed felt that he would be making the overall system more efficient.

Of course, this was really all conjecture. He had just arrived in Maple Ridge yesterday and checked into a furnished rental apartment that he had organized online. That morning he had taken a leisurely walk around the historic center of town to get oriented to his new home. On his way to meet Dr. Stanton he had enjoyed walking along the prominent cliff that gave the town its name overlooking the river that divided Maple Ridge into east and west sides.

Now, having started his ER practice with some drama, Ed followed Dr. Stanton down the corridor to his office. After a full day walking around town, then standing on his right leg forcefully while looking down William's throat, he knew that his limp was probably more apparent than usual as he followed Stanton.

Entering Stanton's small office, Ed sat across from the chief's desk. As Chief of Staff, Dr. Stanton was in charge of organizing all medical services in the hospital and was responsible for the facility's quality of care. He seemed to be in early middle age, balding and starting to show a paunch. His important role in the hospital did not qualify him for a prestigious office. The two doctors could touch all four walls from their chairs. Ed instinctively liked the lack of pretension that the small office suggested about his new boss.

"First of all, welcome to Maple Ridge, Ed. You mentioned that you were planning on renting a place. Has that worked out okay?" While Ed nodded, Stanton rubbed his jaw in contemplation while looking at the newcomer thoughtfully, his chair reclining slightly. Then he leaned forward decisively, resting his forearms on his desk.

"Ed, I think you just demonstrated what we are trying to accomplish with this new model of physician care. American medicine has been really successful at developing specialty care, but we have forgotten the value of the generalist – the doctor who is able to serve a variety of patient needs." He continued looking at his newest staff member carefully.

"With this new funding from Medicare, some practices in Arkansas are trying to change back to the way medicine used to be practiced – where your doctor knew everything about you and didn't consign your various ailing organs to different specialists to look after." Stanton leaned back again to place his fist over the junction of his generous belly and chest to show where the organs lived.

"And we also are looking for docs like yourself who want to work in both the clinic and the hospital, attending in the ER and looking after patients who are admitted." He pointed at Ed as the example of what he was describing. "When someone gets admitted to hospital today, you may get good care, but when you leave the hospital, it can be like falling off a cliff. Your doc outside the hospital doesn't know what went on when you were admitted." He shook his head sadly thinking about how medicine had changed.

Ed didn't refute Dr. Stanton but truthfully couldn't offer much proof for the chief's argument either. This was a new approach for him, even though theoretically it sounded right. He had been doing something very different in his own practice for the past ten years.

Ed knew that it was time for him to change – he needed to start over. And looking after sick people with all their problems, whether they were in the clinic, in the ER or in the hospital, there was something about that continuity of care that appealed to him.

Stanton motioned back to the ER down the hall. "Ed, that was really something special you did back there, thinking about an airway obstruction in that kid and removing the peanut. Did you look after a lot of kids in the army?"

It was hard for Ed to explain everything that he had been responsible for in his last job. Stationed in one of the more remote and dangerous parts of Afghanistan, his primary responsibility had been to the soldiers in his unit – especially when they were on assignment in the field.

But there was no other health care practitioner for many miles around. When word got out that the Americans had a doctor, the local people streamed to the clinic that Ed established on base.

With help from a couple of army medics, he looked after whoever showed up when the medical team was in camp. The team would deliver babies, provide vaccinations, and generally diagnose and treat the Afghans in the local area. Looking after the locals kept Ed busy and engaged in practicing medicine.

His bosses supported Ed in this activity as long as he was ready at any time to do his primary job looking after soldiers in combat. In addition to improving the Americans' reputation with the locals, treating the Afghans who flocked to the camp also afforded an opportunity to gather intelligence about Taliban activities in the region. Ed had facility with languages and became reasonably conversant in the local Pashto dialect to help the intel guys understand what was being said in his clinic.

He broke away from his brief recollection of a former life. "Dr. Stanton, I guess that my practice with local Afghans was part of the 'winning hearts and minds' approach that we sometimes adopted in Afghanistan. And for me, it helped me to maintain my skills and gave a sense of reality to what we were doing in the country."

Stanton looked up from his desk and smiled. "Well Ed, word is going to get around about what you did here today in the ER. Not everyone in the community believes in what I am promoting – that docs can work both in the clinic and the hospital. I am glad that you met Appleton. He's a fulltime ER doc and Peter would probably be one of the doubters. But he appreciated your help today and he'll tell others."

Ed nodded. Having colleagues who would be interested in his practice was a new concept. He had been working as a very solitary practitioner in recent years. That was part of the reason that he had chosen Maple Ridge to start over. He needed to work like a normal doctor in a normal town.

Ed noticed that Stanton had attached some stickies to the resume on his desk. "I have to say that management here at the hospital and clinic is delighted that you have decided to come to Maple Ridge. This is a true-blue American town and all of us have tremendous respect for people who served in the military." He nodded firmly in emphasis and picked up the file.

"Your resume is remarkable, but I have to say that we were a little surprised that you chose our hospital rather than a trauma center, with all your training and experience."

The newcomer took a deep breath. "Let's just say that I am looking for a change. Trauma surgery is rewarding but it's probably better suited to younger surgeons. I am looking for a practice that I can enjoy in a town where I can think of settling down. When I saw your ad, the concept of the patient medical home was very appealing to me."

"Well, your resume is very special," said Stanton. "The only thing that worried us a bit was the two-year gap after you left the military. I know that it's common for people to take a bit of a break between jobs. But two years seems like a long time."

"Is there a question about that, Dr. Stanton?"

"Well, we were wondering just what you were doing these past two years."

There was only so much Ed could say. He knew that Bill Stanton could never understand, and much of his experience was classified by the military. And his work with Dr. Romulus was so recent and so intense. Ed was not ready to discuss what he had been through.

"Dr. Stanton, I had a health problem when I left the forces. I needed some treatment and I got it. It took a bit longer than I initially expected. But you will see a letter in my file from my doctor, Dr. Romulus, who attests to the fact that I am very ready to take on this practice. He had no hesitation in clearing me for the role."

"Yeah, I read Dr. Romulus's report and he offers strong support. He just does not say what he was treating you for."

Ed nodded his head slowly, looking very directly in Stanton's eyes. "That is correct. It really is my business. And there are classified military issues that I cannot discuss."

"I suppose that Dr. Romulus is unlikely to tell me if I call him?" Stanton was persistent. Ed knew that he needed to shut this down.

"He will simply tell you that I am ready to get back to practice. Dr. Stanton, if there is a problem appointing me to staff with what you know today, maybe we should both reconsider whether I am the right guy for the job."

Stanton closed the dossier on his desk, smiled and stood to conclude the meeting. "Okay, Doc, welcome to Maple Ridge. You certainly got off to a fast start today. Thanks for helping out with that kid. I'm glad you were around."

As he stood, Stanton's text messaging pinged. He looked discouraged as he read the message, but then his face lit up with an idea. "Ed you can start your time here in Maple Ridge by doing me a big favor. Tomorrow there's a Civic Luncheon to celebrate work the service clubs are doing to help the hospital. I had arranged a couple of docs to attend the lunch and they have now both cancelled on me."

He smiled convincingly. "Your schedule will still be light. Do me a favor and come to the event. My office will provide you with details. It'll give me a chance to introduce you to some people in our community."

Ed knew that Stanton would guess that he probably hated this kind of thing. But he couldn't say that he was too busy at this point of his Maple Ridge practice. The two doctors shook hands and Ed walked out of Stanton's small office. As he left the hospital through the emergency department, several of the nurses smiled as he passed, and he could hear quiet conversation behind his back.

Ed understood how fast stories spread in hospitals. He realized that the whole organization would soon know that Dr. Brinkley had arrived in Maple Ridge.

CHAPTER 2: THE CIVIC LUNCHEON

Linda Davis knew that her sophisticated friends back east would think that she was a boring hometown girl if they saw her working the room before the Civic Luncheon.

But, when you were born in the place where you are now a business leader, and your family has lived here for more than one hundred and fifty years, there are things that you must do. Twice a year, one of the three service clubs in town took a turn organizing a lunch where all the club leaders got together. Each club then tried to outdo the others bragging about progress on its projects. And everyone would notice if Linda missed the event.

Eleven years ago, when she took over the law firm following her dad's accident, she was invited to join a service club as the first woman member. Four years later, she was made president of the club and shortly after took on the chairman's role for the Civic Luncheon. And now that her firm had become such a vital part of Maple Ridge's business world, she was committed to supporting the town's institutions.

She had arrived a few minutes early in the hotel ballroom where the event was always held and was standing by the entrance door schmoozing when a man arrived that she didn't recognize. Tall, lean, early graying short hair, great blue eyes. He looked around the room but did not seem to know anyone.

She watched as he examined the seating list beside reception and then sat at his assigned place gazing at his cell phone.

Checking name cards on the table, Linda saw his name was Dr. Ed Brinkley. And he was seated next to her at the table her firm had purchased for the luncheon.

Linda walked over to Bill Stanton who was standing in a corner lecturing business folks on why better technology was needed at the hospital. As she approached him, she thought to herself that Bill was one of the people who maintained the vitality of this community. His commitment to the hospital and his constant efforts to keep the facility up to date were essential to people believing that this was a town that they could rely on.

Linda gave Bill a hug and air kissed the surprised doctor. They went back to elementary school together and had dated in high school. But Bill was way too serious for Linda. As a younger woman, Linda had cultivated an occasionally unfortunate taste for bad boys. Bill was definitely one of the good guys.

"Bill, there is a Dr. Ed Brinkley sitting next to me at lunch. I don't know him. Do you have any idea who he is?"

Bill either smiled or smirked. "Linda, Linda, Linda. I was assigned by the Lions to put the seating plan together for this lunch. I am trying to convince Dr. Ed that Maple Ridge is where he should settle down, so I seated him next to you. You now owe me." He put his arm around her shoulders and gave her a good-guy squeeze.

"Who is he? And why do I owe you?"

"Well, he is new to town, single, and has already demonstrated that he is one helluva doctor. We need more people like this guy. And as Maple Ridge's most prominent single woman, I thought that you were just the right person to welcome him."

"What's so special about him?"

"Well, he hadn't even started on staff yet, he literally had just arrived in Maple Ridge, and he comes to the ER to meet me and recognizes some kid has gotten a peanut stuck in his throat and removes it when the ER doc had missed the diagnosis. We have lots of specialists in town who would have failed that test." Bill was serious as usual.

"Where is he from?" Linda was curious, this guy did sound interesting. She knew a little about doctors from her law practice and they usually didn't exceed expectations.

"His last job was in Afghanistan as a military trauma surgeon. But that was a few years ago. He's really a bit of a mystery but we are lucky to have him."

"Thanks, Bill. I'll see what I can do to interest him in staying in the Ridge." She gave Bill a smile and sauntered to her table, anticipating that Dr. Special would remember who Linda Davis was when he saw her approaching.

Linda's adherence to her regular workout remained an indulgence in her days that were largely focused on solving other people's problems. No matter how impossible her daily schedule, she reserved forty-five minutes for cardio and weights, not as a ritual but rather as a commitment to herself.

And it showed. The red dress that she put on that morning stretched with elastic fiber as she closed the zip and she was pleased to see that the resulting contour was smooth and slender. On Linda Davis this dress deserved to be seen.

She strolled toward the doctor with a brilliant smile that emphasized the town's southern hospitality. "You must be Dr. Brinkley. I have heard so much about you. My name is Linda Davis." He rose immediately from his chair like a gentleman. Linda noticed the tailored suit. He looked fit.

"Linda, nice to meet you. According to our name cards we are sitting next to each other. I've just arrived in Maple Ridge. Can you give me some orientation to what I need to know about this lunch?"

God, Linda thought, *he sounds like he's asking for a military briefing.*

"Sure Ed. Bill Stanton told me that you are new to town, and I think he wanted me to explain what's going on here. This lunch is held every six months and allows the three service clubs in the Ridge to brag about their projects." She lifted her arms and rotated her hands around the room for emphasis, showing off the dress.

"As you will learn from three interminable speeches today, the clubs are always raising money for the hospital. We like to get doctors to come to this luncheon and tell us we are doing a great job and are appreciated." She looked at him directly, intrigued by those blue eyes.

"Your task today, Dr. Brinkley, is to listen like you are interested and appear ever so grateful for what the clubs are doing for the hospital." Linda was standing close to him, but his eyes stayed on her face.

"And what about you, Linda? Are you a fundraiser at the hospital?"

She felt herself bristle. Of course, this arrogant doctor would think any woman at the luncheon would be a blonde bimbo who raised money for the hospital by gushing over guys with money. She was preparing to leave him with a sharp comment that he would learn soon enough what she did in this town.

Then she quickly reconsidered. The best-looking women in the room were, as always, the hospital fundraisers. So maybe his question wasn't so insulting after all. She decided to stay with him for now. And enjoy looking at him.

"I am the managing partner of the biggest law firm in Arkansas. We happen to be located in the Ridge because my family settled here before the war between the states, and I haven't yet found a reason to move us."

Linda was amused that this new doc still hadn't lowered his gaze. Her knee was extending just a bit through the subtle slit in the front of her frock, but Ed continued staring straight into her eyes without dropping his gaze.

I guess it's always eyes front and center in the military, she thought to herself.

"What kind of law does your firm practice, Linda?"

Just then, the host for the luncheon asked everyone to take their seats to begin the event and other guests came to join the table. Ed circled the table greeting their tablemates and then held out Linda's chair while she sat. She found his manners pleasing. Not what she would necessarily expect from a doctor or a soldier.

The luncheon was as boring as Linda had come to expect. One club's president was enthusiastic about the new hospital angiography equipment his club had raised money to purchase and another speech described the procurement of great new hospital beds that prevented pressure sores. The final speaker went through a PowerPoint presentation showing endless architectural drawings for planned renovations of the emergency department.

After hearing about the three service projects and applauding each one in turn, the meeting broke up into a few minutes of networking. As usual, Linda's various suppliers and contractors made a beeline for her table. She could see Ed watching in amusement as they formed a line to chat with her.

After introducing himself to the three speakers and complimenting them on their presentations, Ed was starting to leave when Linda broke away from her petitioners to intercept him.

"Lovely to meet you, Ed. I want to find out more about what brings you to the Ridge. Our firm is hosting an event to benefit the local orchestra in the next few weeks. I will make sure that you get an invitation."

"Thanks, Linda. I want to hear more about your firm."

And then to Linda's considerable surprise, he took her right hand in both of his and leaned forward to murmur close to her ear, "I am really pleased to have met you, Linda. That is a great dress by the way," before walking out the door.

CHAPTER 3: MEETING LAWRENCE

The day after the Civic Luncheon, Ed was scheduled to meet his new colleagues in the Maple Ridge clinic. His few belongings had been settled into the apartment that he had chosen at walking distance to the hospital and the clinic. At five p.m. the clinic schedule was winding down and Ed was invited to meet his new partners after work.

Maple Ridge was a medium-sized Arkansas town of about fifty thousand people. There were three medical clinics in town and Ed's new workplace was the largest, with eighteen full time doctors. Some of the clinic's younger physicians had practices similar to Ed's, with work in the hospital as well as the office.

This was Ed's second walk to the hospital neighborhood from his apartment, and he enjoyed taking an indirect route that provided a stroll along the ridge overlooking the river. The river generally ran southeast from the Rockies to its junction with the Mississippi, but in this stretch it curved due south and bisected the town from north to south. It had historically provided local plantations with transportation to the Mississippi for the cotton that grew in the deep, well-drained soil surrounding Maple Ridge. That rich soil had developed over many thousands of years as the river overflowed its banks during the spring runoff, leaving sediment on its banks upstream and downstream from Maple Ridge. Ed had read that the combination of rich soil and the navigable river resulted in the town's settlement and incorporation about twenty years before the start of the Civil War.

The ridge overlooking the river kept the eastern side of the town high and dry. The maple forests that covered the ridge provided green canopies for the east side boulevards lined with classic southern homes. These traditional houses surrounded the historic town center, which had been redeveloped while maintaining the town's heritage charm.

Ed enjoyed strolling through the town center on his way to the river walk. The central six blocks had been carefully restored by local businesses, with attractive cobblestone sidewalks, planters and plenty of benches, which were popular with older folks meeting friends as they took a break from shopping. Ed noticed that the street level of this attractive neighborhood was lined with coffee shops, food stores and restaurants as well as upscale retail establishments.

The sidewalks were generally covered by the second stories of buildings extending out toward the street providing shelter from rain and shade from the sun. These second story overhangs were finished with gingerbread trim that contributed to the sense of old-world charm.

Most of the buildings in the city center were three or four stories in height, with either offices or apartments sitting on top of the retail level. Ed had noticed a large parking lot and garage at the periphery of the town center that obviated the need for street parking. The resulting lack of automobiles provided more room for people to walk and enjoy their surroundings.

Leaving the town center, it was a short six-block stroll to the east side of the river. A lovely river walk had been built along the top of the ridge, with several sheltered lookouts that provided views of the water below.

One railway and two traffic bridges crossed the river. As Ed wandered along the river towards the clinic, he could see that the opposite western shore was much less appealing for homeowners. There was a long levee that ran along the river's edge, but he understood that a hundred-year flood had recently been happening every five years and the levee had been frequently breached in multiple places.

Many of the properties close to the river on the western, levee side were derelict and deserted after the flooding. Neighborhoods further back from the river were densely populated. Ed had learned that the western, lower side of town housed the Black community, which he understood comprised about half of Maple Ridge's population.

The hospital, the small state college, the county courthouse, and most of the professional offices in town were located on the east side of the river up on the ridge. The best residential areas were south of the hospital on the east side, situated on broad, maple lined streets with some fronting on the narrow parkway that paralleled the ridge. The rental accommodation was mainly north of the hospital and Ed had arranged a unit in a nondescript neighborhood that allowed him to walk to work and easily access the town center.

He looked forward to eventually organizing a car to drive along the Ridge just north of town, where ante-bellum plantations with stunning views over the river had apparently been restored. Two miles north, the ridge rapidly declined in height until it was just above the level of the river. Past that point, the river curved back west with both banks level. Along the entire river, the dramatic cliff at Maple Ridge was unique.

Ed's physiotherapists had emphasized that constant walking was important for rebuilding his leg. He had been following the therapists' advice, walking around Maple Ridge most of the day both sight-seeing and learning where to find food, dry cleaning, and other staples of a single man's life.

Now, his leg was tiring. He knew that he was limping when he arrived at the clinic and decided to go in the rear entrance to avoid hobbling across the waiting room in front of the receptionists.

As he entered through the back door unannounced, he could hear voices coming from a room that staff were using for a break.

"I heard he was in the ER two days ago and saved a kid's life takin' a peanut out of his throat. I am pretty sure that he's single and the girls in the ER say he is very cool under pressure and sexy as hell. I can't wait for him to start here. I bet some of our girls and patients are going to be droolin' over him."

Ed knew that he could not go out the back door and reenter at this point. Leaning back toward the rear entrance, he called out, "Hello, is this the clinic entrance? This is Dr. Brinkley, and I am a bit lost."

Laughter broke out in the staff room and a tall, mildly flustered Black woman came into the corridor. "Hi, Dr. Brinkley, I am Esther Hightower, nurse in charge for the clinic. Welcome to Maple Ridge and to our office. I think your new partners are waiting for you in the boardroom."

Walking down the hall observed from behind by the staff who had been discussing him, Ed entered a small boardroom where about a dozen doctors were chatting. Ed noticed that all but two of the doctors were white. He had seen as he passed the staff room that most of the office staff were Black.

A woman sitting at the head of the table stood as Ed entered and came around the table with a smile to shake his hand.

"Hi, I am Suzanne Fortis. You must be Dr. Brinkley. Dr. Lawrence Skalbane is our chief and would normally be here to greet you, but he's in the ER today and will be a few minutes late. Please join us with a coffee until Lawrence gets here."

Ed introduced himself to the other docs at the table who generally seemed a bit younger than him. Getting out of the military, Ed had been approaching forty and he was now past that significant milestone.

Ed had just poured a coffee when an older doctor walked in. It was the chief of the clinic, Dr. Lawrence Skalbane, who had just finished his ER shift. Ed had emailed the clinic chief, several weeks prior to arrival, expressing his pleasure at joining the clinic team and asking a few questions about routine clinic operations. He was surprised to receive a curt response saying that these issues would be discussed when he arrived. As it turned out, the tone of that email was an accurate indication of the greeting that Ed was about to receive.

"Nice to meet you, Dr. Brinkley." The look on Dr. Skalbane's face did not match the welcome in his words. He was staring at Ed with open suspicion.

He took the seat at the head of the table next to Dr. Fortis. "Well Brinkley, the whole ER is talking about your arrival." He looked significantly around to his colleagues and continued.

"Dr. Brinkley came into the ER to meet with Bill Stanton. Peter Appleton was looking after a child, and it sounds like for some reason, Dr. Brinkley just moved in and took over the kid's care."

He turned to look at Ed without evidence of a welcoming smile. "We have a strong tradition of collegiality between doctors in Maple Ridge, Dr. Brinkley, and some of the docs in the hospital think that you violated that spirit of working together."

Ed remained silent. There was not much to say in his defense that wouldn't criticize Dr. Appleton. He could say that he took over because Appleton had missed the diagnosis and was allowing a peanut to kill a child. However, Ed quickly figured that he would hear about that statement for a long time to come. Skalbane had already made up his mind that Ed had treated his colleague with arrogant disrespect.

Ed decided that the only safe response was the time-honored approach to complimenting the team and speaking to the good outcome. "Dr. Skalbane, I was pleased with how the team worked together in diagnosing the cause of the boy's symptoms and providing a successful treatment plan." The words felt like molasses coming out of his mouth, but he figured this was the best strategy for the time being.

Dr. Suzanne Fortis looked concerned. "What happened in the ER, Lawrence? Those of us working in clinic today haven't heard anything about this."

Skalbane looked around the table. "Let's just say that our new recruit here did not make any friends on his first visit to the ER. I heard that he pushed Peter Appleton out of the way when he was caring for a child and treated Peter in a very disdainful fashion."

Suzanne sounded puzzled. "I was speaking to Peter about one of my patients that he admitted at end of his shift, and he did not seem upset. Are you sure about this, Lawrence?"

Skalbane looked at the ceiling, pursing his lips. "The case will be reviewed, and we will all look at that review. But I would say that for now, Dr. Brinkley has introduced himself as someone whose collegial attitude bears watching."

Looking around the room, Ed had the sense that most of his new partners were embarrassed by Skalbane's comments, so he decided against rising to his bait. "Well, thanks for letting me know that Dr. Appleton is upset, Lawrence. I will make sure that I find him and apologize. I pride myself on being a team player. I would hate to get a bad rep before I even start working with you folks."

Dr. Fortis was looking sympathetic to Ed's cause and a couple of other docs nodded with his words. But Skalbane would not give up.

"You know Dr. Brinkley, hospital management oversees recruitment to the medical staff of this clinic, and they don't tell us much about a new recruit until he or she arrives. That has caused problems for us in the past when management fails to recognize that someone is not going to be a good fit in our group.

"All we have heard about you, Dr. Brinkley, is that you left the army at least two years ago. Can you at least commit to your new partners that you will provide us with a resume, so we know where you are coming from?"

Suzanne Fortis interrupted. "Lawrence, I think that you are verging on being impolite. I am sure that Dr. Brinkley will provide us with his resume in due time. Is that fair, Dr. Brinkley?"

"Yes, of course. I wasn't aware that management in the hospital failed to share my dossier with you. I have nothing to hide and it's appropriate that you know what experiences a new partner is bringing to your clinic." This was turning into an inquisition rather than the meet and greet that Ed had expected.

He was, however, pleased to see smiles on the faces of most of the docs sitting around the table. Lawrence Skalbane continued to appear grumpy, but Ed was starting to think that this was probably his customary facial expression.

Ed decided the best course was to change the subject. "One thing that I want to ask you about is enrollment of chronically ill patients. I am very interested in this patient medical home model that Arkansas is developing to look after chronically ill patients. It sounds like an important innovation. Do you have a waiting list for these patients? Do I need to announce that I want to take on this sort of practice?"

Smiles were renewed around the table. Dr. Suzanne Fortis responded while nodding. "We generally agree that this is an interesting new approach to take and most of us are enrolling patients with chronic conditions in the medical home model."

Her voice then took on a different tone. "You don't need to worry about attracting these patients, Ed. There are more chronically unwell patients in this jurisdiction, especially in the Medicaid population, than we could all possibly care for. In fact, we need to be careful not to put too much strain on our overall practice by taking on too many of these people."

Suzanne continued and it was clear to Ed that he was getting advice that she expected him to follow. "Remember, on the days when you are in the hospital or away on a course or vacation, the on-call doctor for the group needs to cover urgent patients from your practice. So, when you accept care for a complex patient, we are really all accepting responsibility for that patient's care."

Lawrence Skalbane could not resist. "We expect you to share the load here, Dr. Brinkley. It's easy to accept these patients onto your roster and then expect your partners to look after them."

Lawrence was getting under Ed's skin, but he decided to keep it mellow. "I can assure you, Lawrence, that I am the kinda guy who carries his share of the load. I have never been accused of shirking responsibility and have no anticipation that will change now." He looked at his new partners. Some seemed bored and ready to leave. Others seemed embarrassed by the welcome Dr. Lawrence Skalbane had provided for their new colleague.

"Who do I speak to about enrollment in my practice?"

Suzanne suggested that Ed should come with her to meet the Head Nurse, Esther Hightower, whom he had already encountered briefly. Ed bid farewell to his new colleagues including the charming Lawrence Skalbane.

Suzanne shook her head as they left the boardroom. "Thanks for not getting upset with Lawrence. He really inherited his job as chief of the clinic because nobody else wanted to do it and he is obviously the most senior guy. Although the title sounds grandiose, there is really very little that goes with the job. Esther does all the real work, and she is lovely. Recently Lawrence has been so difficult to deal with that she comes to me with issues as often as she does to Dr. Skalbane."

CHAPTER 4: ESTHER

Suzanne Fortis brought Ed to Esther Hightower's office just as she was finishing the wrap-up from the afternoon clinic. Ed smiled at the nurse as they settled onto chairs in her little office. "Nice to meet you, Esther. Can I call you Esther? I understand that you are the go-to person about how the clinic works."

Esther appreciated his politeness. Not always what she experienced from her doctors.

Esther was a tall and proud woman. Proud of her accomplishments and proud of who she had become. Although the doctors in the clinic thought they controlled the facility, Esther knew that it was her clinic. Most of the doctors were transient players pursuing their careers, whereas Esther embodied the commitment to the community that the clinic represented for Maple Ridge.

"I started working at this clinic as a nursing assistant when it opened twenty-five years ago. I got my nursing degree at night and now I've been in charge of the clinic for the last fifteen years. So, yeah, I know this place pretty well." He was listening with interest, nodding his head.

"I appreciate you coming to see me so soon, Dr. Brinkley. I am hearing a lot about you already." She grinned at him a bit shyly.

He smiled back, "So, what are you hearing?" Esther liked his warmth. He had very blue eyes and they crinkled when he smiled.

"When you are born and raised in this town and when you

have been around this place and the hospital as long as me, you get tightly embedded into the grapevine. I heard that the girls in the ER were pretty impressed with you day before yesterday and that you were real nice to that boy William and his momma.

"I also saw when you came in the back way and overheard the girls gossiping about you – you didn't embarrass them. And then I heard just now from Suzanne that you took the usual nonsense from Dr. Skalbane, and you were a grown-up and just held your tongue."

Esther saw the new doc was still half smiling so she continued. "I don't know if you have noticed Dr. Brinkley, but a lot of doctors are not that grown up. It's funny with the amount of learning you have to do. You would think that doctors would learn maturity along the way with all their other education, but my observation is that maturity is not necessarily a common trait in your colleagues." She knew that she was being a bit forward, but for some reason she felt that she could trust this man.

Ed smiled at the nurse. "Esther, I guess you are assuming that this is a confidential conversation?"

"Oh, I will just deny it if you tell anybody what I say", and Esther burst into a long laugh.

"Unlike your colleagues, Doctor, I *have* seen your resume and I am so pleased that you have decided to come to Maple Ridge. You have some incredible experience that I am sure we will take advantage of. One of my nephews was in Desert Storm and I have huge respect for our men and women who serve." Esther had noticed his limp and wondered what he had been through.

"Thanks, Esther. I appreciate that. Could you tell me what my practice will look like and how it's going to grow?"

"Well, we have two waiting lists." Esther reached into her desk and lifted out several lists of potential patients for the clinic. "As you know from the advertisement you responded to, two doctors have left the clinic in the past eighteen months and the other docs in the group have been providing coverage to their patients. I would think that you should gradually take on about nine hundred of those people onto your roster." Ed could tell that he was listening to a knowledgeable voice about how the clinic worked.

"Most of those patients will be pretty healthy. There are young women with families, and they will need obstetrical care and their kids will attend for well-baby and child care. And seniors. Most of these people will be covered by workplace insurance or Medicare plus their own private insurance."

Ed continued to listen closely. "The other group of patients are on our chronically ill wait list, and they are mostly Medicaid patients. The new medical home government program is encouraging us to care for more of those patients by offering a pretty generous roster fee for taking them on rather than just a fee for every visit.

"The roster fee is a lump sum we get paid whether the patient sees the doctor or not. This encourages us to reach out and try and improve their health at home rather than waiting to see them in the office after they get sick."

Esther's voice indicated her enthusiasm about this new model of care. "We are using part of the roster funds to hire more nurses and other staff to help the doctors look after those people with more complex needs. The new staff are calling patients at home and seeing them between doctor's regular visits to make sure they understand how they can look after themselves better."

She paused, wondering whether she should explain further and decided that she should trust this doctor, even though she had just met him. "You know Dr. Brinkley, you and your colleagues do best in sorting through a patient's problems, making diagnoses and prescribing treatment. But I have always thought that nurses do a better job of ensuring the patient understands what they are supposed to do to improve their health and helping them achieve their goals. And this program allows us to hire nurses to play that role." Esther was watching

Ed carefully while she made this statement. She was pleased to see the new doc nodding in agreement.

Esther knew that the next part was important for him to understand, especially to get along with his partners.

"I was pleased reading your application to join the clinic that this type of practice is what attracted you to Arkansas. I would suggest though that you start off slowly, taking no more than about four hundred people onto your roster from that wait list for complex patients. They require a lot more care. And if you take too many, your partners will complain that you are over-loading the practice and that you will overwhelm the nurses and other staff we have hired for the medical home."

She could see that he was listening carefully. *Unusual,* she thought. *Usually, doctors paid lip service to what she suggested, but this guy really seems to be paying attention.*

"Esther," Ed said, "I hope to work a day a week in the ER and will be covering some of our group's hospitalized patients who get admitted through the ER. I assume most days I will see those patients in hospital before and after office hours. I also want to deliver babies. Does that make sense with the numbers of patients you are recommending?"

"Absolutely Dr. Brinkley. You will have a busy roster with thirteen hundred patients including four hundred of those complex folks. But reading your application and resume, I think that you like to be busy, am I right?"

"Yeah, I have come to Maple Ridge to work, that's for sure." He smiled and his eyes crinkled again.

Ed leaned forward. "Thanks for your advice, Esther." He was slowly nodding his head. "I will follow exactly what you sug-gest. I assume that with this kind of practice it will take me about a year to enroll the thirteen hundred patients you are suggesting. Do you think that there are enough patients wait-ing for a doctor to allow me to achieve a list that quickly?"

She reached forward and took both his hands in hers and chuckled. "Dr. Brinkley, when Maple Ridge hears how cute you are, and how nice you are, we are going to have to beat them off with a stick at the front door." And then she started laughing again.

CHAPTER 5: SHARON

Four weeks after starting in the clinic, Ed's office practice was keeping him busy. Esther made sure that the receptionists booked extra time for him to see new patients. His practice grew quickly, with about one third complex patients and the remainder comprised of healthier patients left behind when their former doctors had moved on.

The more complex patients suffered from multiple conditions with heart failure, diabetes, lung disease, arthritis, depression, and high blood pressure as their most common ailments. But of course, it was unusual to see only one of these conditions in a single patient. Usually, they presented with at least three chronic illnesses, with diabetes, high blood pressure and arthritis the most common trifecta.

And for most of these patients, these conditions were additive in their complexity. Ed would see a fifty-four year-old man who was one hundred pounds overweight with diabetes, high blood pressure and knee arthritis. Ed would describe the importance of diabetic sugar control and tell him that normalizing his high blood pressure was essential since diabetics had a higher risk of stroke or heart attack if their blood pressure was elevated.

That conversation would lead to the need for an exercise plan that could include walking, biking, or jogging, which would all be painful and difficult due to the knee arthritis. Of course, carrying one hundred pounds of extra weight would rapidly wear out an artificial joint, making the patient a poor candidate for a knee replacement to treat the knee arthritis pain.

Most of the chronic disease patients were on Medicaid because they either did not have a job, or they had insufficient income to pay for private health insurance and no insurance from their work. Patients who made more income tended to be insured under Obamacare if they did not have workplace insurance.

Those Obamacare people seemed vulnerable. They needed to reapply to the state exchange for health insurance every year, and the insurance companies often changed their plans annually, making continued coverage complex and confusing. Companies frequently increased their premiums once the patient was enrolled, especially in low-income areas since insurers had discovered that poor folks were expensive to care for. Although Obamacare was a great idea, lots of people were still falling through its cracks as the program got started.

The other group of people joining Ed's practice were generally healthier people with good health insurance provided by their employers.

The medical home model seemed promising for the more complex patients. On first meeting with these people, Ed would go over their various ailments and history with a nurse. They would then develop a team appropriate for the patient's particular health problems. If the patient had diabetes a dietician would teach them about the impact of diet on their blood sugar. If they suffered from depression a social worker could help them to better manage their mood. Basically, the team would be customized to suit the patient's illness profile.

Although it initially might seem like an expensive way to treat poorly insured people, the model was based on the premise that this team-based care would keep patients with chronic illnesses out of the hospital. One hospital admission could cost hundreds of thousands of dollars. If the medical home model of care reduced just a few hospitalizations each year for complex patients, it would readily pay for hiring extra staff with money left over.

Ed could already observe that the nurses' phone calls to patients to check on their home blood pressure measurements or their daily sugar test was having an impact on the patients' management of their long-term illnesses and reducing the risk of hospital admission.

On this morning Ed had six new clinic patients booked from nine to noon. The first patient had been cared for by the group over the past year after her prior doctor left the clinic. Her name was Sharon Malto, and her appearance was unusual for the socially conservative town of Maple Ridge. At nine in the morning, she was dressed in a tight-fitting dress with a revealing neckline. She was wearing dramatic jewelry and noticeable perfume. Despite this provocative appearance she seemed quite shy in meeting her new doctor.

Sharon's son was with her and he behaved aggressively, occasionally punching his mother in the leg. Sharon appeared intimidated by her four-year-old and did not discipline or correct him. She was wearing long sleeves, but when the sleeves slipped up Ed saw bruises on both forearms. Watching her trying to manage her son, Ed sensed that there was a story behind Sharon's demeanor.

After a general discussion of her health, he asked Sharon why she was here to see him. She mentioned that she had been feeling very edgy lately and was having trouble sleeping. Her previous doctor had provided her with sleeping pills, and she wanted a new prescription to help her sleep.

Ed wondered whether she was feeling anxious during the day as well. Her eyes turned down and she said under her breath, "This is shit. I just want some pills."

Ed responded, "Mrs. Malto giving you sleeping pills without talking about whether you are generally anxious is pretty short sighted. As time passes the sleeping pills will stop working. Relying on pills to deal with anxiousness without treating the cause is really bad practice."

She did not seem convinced. "What do I need to do to get some pills?"

"Well, we can talk about managing your sleep better by dealing with your anxiety. I would recommend a program of talk therapy where you work with me and one of our team to recognize the sources of your anxiety and manage them in a healthier, more proactive way. We have a six-week course here at the clinic to help you learn techniques for reducing anxiety."

She was staring at the floor. Ed continued. "Sharon, eighty per cent of people with anxiety say that they feel much better after a six-week or in some cases a twelve-week course. In addition to the weekly sessions with a social worker, we also set you up with access to online tools to help you recognize and deal with stress."

"Doc, I already know the cause of my stress and he is not going away with any course or online app."

"Are you referring to your son, Sharon?" She shook her head "no" and leaned over, ruffling her boy's hair affectionately. Her eyes were still locked on the floor.

Ed guessed, "Your husband?"

With that Sharon started to weep quietly, still looking down. Taking a Kleenex from her purse, she carefully dabbed her eyes. "Yeah, I guess so."

"Does he hit or grab you sometimes?" Ed asked, remembering the bruises on her arm.

"Sometimes." No eye contact at all. She pulled her son onto her lap. He had noticed her tears, but his mother's distress did not seem to surprise him.

"Would your husband come in to discuss your marriage, Sharon? Can we think about family counseling for the two of you?"

"He would never agree to counseling. He just tells me if I acted like a decent wife, he wouldn't need to get mad with me." Briefly lifting her eyes to Ed's, there was a flash of anger.

Ed realized that he was in the deep end pretty fast with Sharon. "Sharon, I don't know you that well yet, but it sounds like this might be a dangerous situation for you and your son."

"No, he'd never hurt his little Tony. This is his pride and joy."

She messed her son's hair again. This time the boy irritably pushed her hand away.

"You know there are safe houses where you can go Sharon, shelters that can protect you if there is physical abuse happening."

"Doc, listen to me. There is no shelter in this state that is going to protect me against Tony Malto if I try and leave him. I just need something to help me to calm down and live with it, that's all. You know, Doc, I can get downers anywhere, it's not hard. I just like to get a prescription, so I know what I am taking is legitimate and safe."

"Sharon, I'll give you two weeks supply of something to help you sleep. But I want you to promise to come back in two weeks. I want to spend some more time talking about what is making you upset and thinking about how we could get your husband engaged for some therapy."

Ed looked at her boy. "One approach is that we could talk to him about what his son is learning. I am sure that your husband would not want his son to grow up like a gangster thinking that it's okay to hit women." He had entered the prescription in the computer on his desk and handed her the print-out.

Sharon looked at her doctor suspiciously as she took the prescription and checked her make-up in a pocket mirror as she dried her eyes. "You don't understand nothin' Doc. But yeah, I'll make another appointment to get a new prescription and sit and talk to you in two weeks." And with that she bent over in front of him to pick up her handbag, providing a view of her impressive cleavage.

"Come on Tony. Mummy's got her pills. Let's go home." And with that she strode out of the exam room with a pronounced roll to her full and tightly clothed buttocks. Sharon Malto was quite a show.

As Sharon left, Ed went looking for Esther, who had become his primary source of local intel. He had already learned that she was both a great nurse and a reliable source of information about the practice, various patients, and the larger world of

Maple Ridge.

"Esther, I just met a woman named Sharon Malto. There's not much in her record except she occasionally gets sleeping pills. But it seemed to me like there may be a strong backstory happening – maybe with her husband – that I should understand. Do you know her at all?"

Esther grunted. "She's a tricky one, Ed. Married to Tony Malto, a local guy whose family has been running at the edge of the law for a long time. His daddy and his two uncles spent some time in jail, but Tony has either stayed out of trouble or more likely he is smarter about keepin' the police happy than his elders were."

"I think that he may be dangerous, Dr. Ed. Rumors have it he is tied in with the Dixie Gang down in the Gulf, and those guys are known to be bad news. If I were you, I would think carefully about whether it's a good idea to have his wife in your practice."

"Thanks Esther, that sounds like great advice." But as he went back to his office to complete the computer record of her visit, he remembered the bruises on Sharon's arms as well as her spontaneous tears. There was no question this woman needed help.

CHAPTER 6: PIPER FORCEPS

E d was enjoying delivering babies for his clinic group. Maple Ridge was a young community and there were plenty of pregnant women and children. This was a part of the practice that appealed to the newest doctor in town.

Although he did not have formal training in labor and delivery, Ed had learned a lot on the job in Helmand province in Afghanistan. British forces had initially been assigned to Helmand as part of the international team committed to pushing back the Taliban insurgents and restoring Afghanistan from its status as a rogue state. The Brits originally were responsible for Helmand, the Canadians had Kandahar, and the Americans had responsibility for most of the rest of the country as well as providing logistics and backup to their allies.

After the President increased the deployment of American troops in 2010, Ed's Special Forces team was assigned to Helmand province to take over some of the clandestine duties from the British SAS forces that had been operating out of Bastion airbase. Despite the usual jostling and teasing, they got along well with the Brits, and everyone was disappointed when the British troops eventually left.

Helmand province was largely desert with irrigated farmland surrounding the Helmand River. The region was the world's primary opium producer. The local people had a long history of resisting invaders that began with Alexander the Great, continued with Genghis Khan, included Russian conquerors and now Americans who were supporting the government in Kabul.

By the time Ed's Special Forces team entered Helmand, their adversaries included Taliban fighters and local warlords as well as drug dealers. This southern province was recognized as the most dangerous region of Afghanistan. Ed's team established a forward base in a Taliban-dominated area of the province. Basically, the Taliban owned the area at night, but the Afghans tried to benefit from the presence of the American doctor's clinic during the day.

The Special Forces troops were extremely fit and rarely needed attention until combat assignments started. To keep up skills between assignments, Ed and his medical team served as healthcare providers for the region and that healthcare had a major focus on obstetrics.

As the only surgeon in the region, Ed was the designated Caesarian section provider for the clinic. He had performed a few C-sections during surgical training, and the operation itself was pretty straightforward. His ability to offer C-section proved useful during their early days in Helmand when the typical obstetrical patient would be a young, teenaged mother in her second or third day of obstructed labor. In the US, these patients would have received sections hours or days earlier. If Caesarian section were not available, these two children (the teenaged mother and baby would both be considered children at home) could die.

But months after starting this surgical maternity practice, Ed learned from the team's local translators that a C-section might not be the best solution for these young women.

Misinformation had spread through the local communities that 'cutting out the baby' was accompanied by removal of the uterus and that the woman delivered by Caesarian would be sterile thereafter. Most obstructed labor occurred in first time mothers and women in this part of the world were expected to bear multiple children. Women with a Caesarian scar were therefore considered sterile and damaged. They might then be deserted by their husbands and families, putting both mother and baby at risk of deprivation.

Learning this unique social circumstance motivated Ed to become more expert at non-surgical assisted delivery. The team medics were committed to making this practice work and begged, borrowed, and stole fetal monitoring and anesthesia equipment, as well as labor induction drugs. Their base became the place to go for obstructed labor in Helmand province. If he was not in the field with his troops, Ed would be present at most of these difficult deliveries. C-section was sometimes needed, but the team tried whenever possible to achieve a vaginal delivery using forceps or vacuum assistance when necessary.

With this practice in Helmand, Ed developed extensive experience in difficult deliveries. Women in normal labor never came to the military base. They were managed by local midwives who had received traditional training in their villages. The young age of many of the mothers and the fact that so many of them were malnourished and weakened from their pregnancy meant that the team saw quite a few patients who could not deliver their babies without medical assistance.

Despite the tension associated with managing difficult pregnancies and deliveries, Ed enjoyed this part of his Afghanistan practice. He knew that if his team did not help, these women and their babies might not survive. And nothing gratifies a doctor more than the smile of a new mum as she meets her newborn for the first time.

In Maple Ridge, labor and delivery were, of course, infinitely safer. Mothers generally received high quality prenatal care and the hospital birthing facilities and staff were first rate. All difficult labors were managed by obstetricians as well as the majority of normal deliveries. However, some patients wanted to be delivered by their clinic GP's as long as they could immediately access specialist care if needed. In Ed's clinic group, five doctors including Ed did routine deliveries at the hospital.

Most of their clinic partners who chose not to do deliveries followed their patients until close to term when they would transfer them to their colleagues that did deliveries or, if the patient preferred, refer them to an obstetrician. The five docs who did deliveries took turns with weekend call for the group.

This call service was usually not too busy, with two or three normal deliveries most weekends. Ed had covered two weekends on call before the Sunday when he again found himself causing some excitement at the hospital.

Chloe Smallman and her husband were both from well-established Maple Ridge families. She had been followed during her pregnancy by one of Ed's partners who did not do deliveries and was about to see an obstetrician in referral when her water ruptured at thirty-seven weeks.

Ed met her for the first time in the labor room. On examination, he was concerned that her cervix was widely dilated, and that she felt like pushing. Normally that would be fine. At thirty-seven weeks the baby would be considered nearly full term and not at risk for complications from premature delivery. However, Chloe's clinic doctor had missed the fact that this first baby was a breech presentation.

Ed knew that about three to four per cent of babies are breech at delivery. He knew that with breech presentation, the baby's bum is facing down rather than the baby's head. The newborn's buttocks are narrower than the baby's head and the bum can get out through a birth canal that has not been fully opened by passage of the head. When that happens, the head can get stuck in the birth canal because the baby's skull is broader than its buttocks.

Normally the bigger head goes through the birth canal first and stretches the mum's pelvic ligaments while gradually compressing the baby's flexible skull bones to allow the head to fit through the pelvis. With a breech birth, that gradual moulding of the head and pelvis doesn't happen because the smaller buttocks are leading the way. This can lead to terrible problems, especially with a first baby when the mother's birth canal has not been contoured by a previous delivery.

Ed knew that if the baby's head gets stuck with the baby three quarters delivered, it could be a medical disaster that can result in injury to the newborn. The umbilical cord that provides oxygenated blood to the baby's brain is caught between the mother's pelvic bones and the baby's head. If oxygen supply is reduced by prolonged compression of the cord, irreversible brain damage can occur.

Ed understood that when a first baby is recognized as breech in the last few weeks of pregnancy, the woman should always be referred to an obstetrician specialist. Generally, the obstetrician would book the patient for an elective C-section to avoid the risks associated with vaginal breech delivery.

Unfortunately, in Chloe's case, the doctor in Ed's clinic had not recognized the breech presentation during prenatal checks. Ed was now facing the risky situation where the head might get stuck during vaginal delivery.

Chloe needed an urgent C-section. However, the obstetrician on call was just scrubbing to do an emergency section for a baby in distress that needed immediate delivery.

Assessing the situation he was suddenly facing on an otherwise peaceful Sunday morning, it was obvious to Ed that the child in distress had priority over Chloe's baby. At present Chloe's baby had a good heart rate and was showing no signs of problems. However, Ed also recognized that Chloe and her baby might quickly get into real trouble in the next few minutes.

Ed joined Chloe's nurse in wheeling Chloe into a delivery room. Based on his experience in Afghanistan, Ed wondered whether he should suggest to the obstetrician that he should just go ahead and start a C-section for Chloe while the specialist attended to the other baby. However, the specialist had never met him, and this would be against medical protocol since Ed did not have hospital privileges to do that operation. He decided it would be better just to wait with Chloe and pray that her baby stayed put until the obstetrician completed the emergency section.

Unfortunately, Chloe and her baby had other ideas. Just as Ed and the nurses transferred her onto the delivery table to examine her, there was a sudden gush of amniotic fluid as the baby's bum came rushing out, followed by the legs rapidly delivering. Ed looked at the nurse. They both knew that he was going to need to deliver this baby girl one way or another.

Reaching under the baby's tummy Ed pulled down a length of umbilical cord so that the cord would not tighten and restrain the baby's progress. It was crucial that the cord could continue to supply blood to the brain until the baby's head emerged and she could breathe for herself.

Chloe was pushing hard now, and Ed felt under the baby's chest to sweep the left arm and then the right arm down. So far so good. But then, just as he had feared, with all but the baby's head delivered, everything stopped.

The nurses in the Maple Ridge case room were experienced, and another colleague immediately joined Chloe's nurse. She had opened the instruments for breech delivery that included metal Piper forceps which are specially designed to assist in delivering a breech baby's head. The new nurse passed the forceps over to Ed while quietly whispering, "I sure hope that you know how to use these forceps, Doc." Chloe's original nurse was now holding the baby's body wrapped in a surgical towel, supporting the child suspended from her head which remained trapped in the birth canal.

Chloe's husband was still outside the delivery room. Chloe was bearing up well and was not aware of the risk to her baby. There had been no time to provide her with an epidural for pain control, but she was pushing hard with contractions to try and deliver her first baby.

Ed's thinking slowed down as he recalled the one time that he had used the Piper forceps to deliver a breech baby in Afghanistan. In America this was a very unusual situation – the use of Piper forceps had been basically replaced by Caesarian section. The breech delivery in Afghanistan had given Ed some very anxious moments, but Mum and babe came through it in good shape. He said a silent prayer that he would achieve a similar outcome now for Chloe and her child.

He crouched down on one knee between Chloe's legs, which were supported by the foot stirrups on the table. Trying to sound more confident than he felt, Ed said to Chloe, "We are going to help your baby's head to deliver, Chloe. I want you to stop pushing while I put these forceps in to help you push the head out."

With help from the nurse reaching over Chloe's legs to hold the baby, Ed exposed the baby's mouth and suctioned mucous out to reduce the risk of the baby aspirating fluid into her lungs.

He then bent close to the floor and slid in the first limb of the Piper forceps between the baby's head and the vaginal wall and then the second. He linked the two sides of the forceps together and kept the handle low like he had learned from the video he had watched before using the instrument for the first time in Afghanistan.

"Ok Chloe, with the next few contractions I want you to push and give us a baby."

He directed the second nurse standing over Chloe's stomach to place her hand on the back of the baby's head. "When Chloe pushes, I want you want to press the back of the head down to keep the baby's neck flexed."

Chloe was an absolute trooper. As she moaned and pushed, Ed gently pulled the baby's head down toward the floor. There was very little forward motion that he could detect, and he felt a chill of desperation starting up his spine. The two nurses looked at each other wordlessly.

This was exactly the situation that could result in a stuck and damaged baby. If the baby were not delivered soon, the blood supply through the cord to the baby's brain would be at risk. The nurses and Ed all knew it.

The nurse holding the baby's body repeated suctioning of the little bit of mouth that could be seen. And then Chloe began to bear down on the next contraction.

As Chloe pushed, Ed again pulled to the floor and the nurse standing beside Chloe's tummy pushed on the back of the baby's head. And then, thank God, Ed could feel the head start coming. It moved a centimeter or two further down the birth canal and Ed could suddenly see the baby's nose. He pulled the cord further down and said to Chloe, "On the next contraction we are going to have a baby if you push just as hard as you can."

Moments later, Ed heard the door open behind him and the obstetrician arrived, instructing the nurses, "OK, we're ready for the breech section. Let's get her into the OR."

But just at that moment the next contraction started and, slick as can be, Chloe pushed, Ed pulled with the forceps and suddenly the baby was out and screaming.

"She's a beautiful little girl, Chloe. You'll have her in just a moment."

The nurses divided the cord and measured the baby while Ed sewed up a small vaginal tear. The baby was bright pink one minute after delivery and starting to suckle by the time that he finished the stitching.

The nurses had brought Chloe's husband into the delivery room to meet his daughter. Just as Ed was starting to compliment the parents on their newborn, he felt a hand on his arm. It was the obstetrician, Dr. Jim Downir and he did not look happy.

"What the hell happened here? Why didn't I know about this breech in advance?"

"Well, nice to meet you, Dr. Downir, I believe." Ed had heard his name mentioned by the delivery room staff. "My name is Ed Brinkley, and I am on call for the clinic's deliveries this weekend."

"Brinkley, I don't know where you are from, but this is not the way that we deal with breeches at this hospital."

Ed took a big breath. He was getting tired of people in this hospital telling him that he had done something wrong after just saving a life. He was about to respond when one of the nurses that had assisted with the delivery put an arm around each of the two doctors' waists and pushed them out into the hallway through the case room door.

"You two need to take this outside away from Mum and Dad. And Jim, before you say another word, when was the last time that you delivered the after-coming head of a breech with Pipers? Dr. Brinkley here just did a textbook job. He doesn't need you preaching all over him."

These two had clearly worked together in the case room for some time and Ed decided that he would best just remain silent.

"Julia, you know that we don't use Piper forceps any longer. We schedule C-sections for first-time breeches and avoid this cowboy stuff with forceps."

"Now Jim Downir, you listen to me. We didn't know this girl was breech until we examined her on arrival. That's not on Dr. Ed. It was one of his colleagues that missed the breech in the office during prenatal care. Her waters had broken, she was fully dilated, and she was pushing. You were tied up with the section for fetal distress and by the time we moved Chloe into the case room the breech and legs had delivered." She paused for a breath.

"And I know if Ed here hadn't used those forceps as well as he did, that baby would have been another twenty minutes getting delivered and would have been cold and blue instead of pink and warm."

The obstetrician leaned back against the wall and looked at Ed. "It sure looks like Julia is a fan of yours Ed. Where the hell did you learn to use those damn Piper forceps? I haven't used them in twenty years."

Ed explained a little bit about his obstetrical practice in Helmand province and could see Jim and Julia's eyes widening. "You were doing C-sections and forceps deliveries in the desert on Afghan women?"

"Well, not exactly in the desert. We were in a military hospital tent."

"Are you planning on doing C-sections for your clinic patients here in Maple Ridge?"

And now Ed could not resist laughing. As he started laughing, the doors to the case room opened and Chloe, her baby and husband came wheeling out. The baby was pink and gorgeous. Chloe grasped Ed's arm to stop the stretcher as she passed him. "Thank you so much, Doctor. Things were so hectic; I didn't catch your name."

"Brinkley. Ed Brinkley."

"Thank you so much Dr. Ed. We don't really have a name for her yet 'cause she's a few weeks early." Chloe paused, thinking. "Would you mind if we called her Edwina after you?"

Ed saw Chloe's husband gasp and grimace. He smiled and winked broadly at the new father.

"Ah, I wouldn't go with Edwina, if I were you, Chloe. I am very honored that you would think of me but give it a day or two to think about a name. Edwina – I just would not go there." Her husband fist pumped the doctor with gratitude as the stretcher rolled by.

Ed turned back to the obstetrician. "Jim, I enjoy delivering babies but have no intention of doing C-sections here in Maple Ridge. I will probably not even use forceps if you guys are around. But today was a kinda special case. We couldn't just stand there doing nothing and waiting while you did the emergency section. We needed to do something to help that kid and thank God it turned out okay." Ed lifted his hands in gratitude.

"Ed, are you one of these new medical home docs who are working in the clinics and the hospital? I've heard Bill Stanton talking about you guys and I thought it sounded like a load of BS. But if you guys are all as good as Julia thinks you are, then maybe Bill has the right idea."

"Yeah, I am working with Bill on the medical home model Jim. I'll look forward to working with you."

"Well, Ed, I'd offer to buy you a drink, but we're both on call for the weekend, so I guess it'll have to wait. Julia, how many cases are in now?"

Julia and Jim returned to the case room. But as the door was closing, Julia stuck her head out.

"Great job, Doc. That was something I haven't seen in a long time. I don't think I want to see it again soon, but well done."

CHAPTER 7: TONY

By six weeks after his arrival in the Ridge, Ed's practice had settled into a busy routine which he found both enjoyable and stimulating. Each day started with him making rounds on clinic patients in the hospital who had been admitted through emergency.

About once a week Ed would take an eight or twelve-hour shift in the Maple Ridge Emergency Room. Occasionally the doctor on call in emergency would also ask him to help out, after hours, if emergency was extra busy. Ed lived close by the hospital, and as a single guy, his ER partners knew that he might be available if they needed help. His willingness to help smoothed over any concern that Ed's colleagues might have about his interaction with Peter Appleton when he first arrived in town.

In the clinic, at least half of Ed's patients were new to him each day as he built his practice. Ed rapidly developed new respect for the challenge of sorting through the issues that patients bring to their first appointment with a new doctor. A patient's main health complaint was often amplified or disguised by opinions from friends or family as well as Dr. Google. One day in the office, Ed had spent twenty minutes convincing a patient with mild eczema on the legs that he did not have an underactive thyroid that a website suggested could be linked to leg skin changes. Meeting a new patient was like a detective exercise of sorting fact from fiction.

Ed recognized the wealth gap that separated the clinic's well-insured patients and the Medicaid ones. However, as he settled into town, Ed was also sensing a consistent level of background apprehension that united many citizens of Maple Ridge.

The precarious existence of Medicaid patients was understandable. If they worked, their income was generally incompatible with a living wage, even though housing and living costs were relatively inexpensive in Maple Ridge.

It was understandable that these patients considered life to be risky and unstable. However, Ed found this sense of anxiety extended across reasonably well-insured patients in his practice as well. Blue-collar workers had seen their job opportunities shrink as good middle class factory jobs were eliminated by companies moving away or adopting automation. White-collar jobs were also always at risk from outsourcing and technology.

Ed soon learned that the auto parts industry was making a comeback in Arkansas and providing some opportunity for minimally skilled workers. However, Arkansas was a right-to-work state, and legislation made it challenging to start up unions in factories. The lack of unions decreased job security for these factory workers who were often hired as part-time or contract workers. These contract jobs rarely provided health insurance.

Even if their work provided health coverage, an important contributor to anxiety in both blue-collar and white-collar workers was the way health insurance was tied to employment. Ed frequently heard from anxious patients that fear of losing their family's health coverage was a major factor related to their worried mood.

Ed was also surprised by the number of people in his practice who were addicted to pain killers and was increasingly disturbed by the number of opioid overdoses that he was seeing in the emergency department. He was starting to believe that this widespread dependency on pain killers had as much to do with dulling chronic anxiety as dealing with chronic pain.

Ed became acquainted with the concept of 'deaths of despair,' especially in middle-aged men in Maple Ridge. These men had been left behind by the economic challenges of globalization and automation and could no longer support their families with their limited skills. Too often these men resorted to drugs and/or alcohol to deal with depression or anxiety, and too often this substance abuse could prove fatal.

This morning Ed was booked to see six new patients in the office. He was starting out to the waiting room to call his first patient when he heard a commotion at the reception desk. Three large men were telling the receptionist that one of them needed to be seen immediately. Ed wandered over to the desk. "Can I help?"

"Yeah Doc, you gotta see me right away. I got business to do." This came from a large, suntanned man impressively decked out in heavy neck jewelry and some dramatic tattoos.

The receptionist was flustered. "There is one patient ahead of Mr. Malto, Doctor, but she is still with the nursing team. You can see Mr. Malto now if you wish."

"C'mon Doc, I know you're new, you don't gotta lot of stuff happenin'. I gotta get goin' and I gotta see you fast."

"Make sure you take good care of him, Doc." This came from one of the two heavyset men accompanying Mr. Malto. Ed examined the two companions. The verbal one had paler skin but like his colleagues, his shirt was opened three buttons, and he had lots of neck bling and tats.

"Mr. Malto, follow me in here, please." He led him into his exam room. "How can I help?"

"You look after my wife now, right Doc? Sharon Malto? She told me you hassled her about takin' sleepin' pills but gave her some anyway. Listen, I want her to get pills from you instead of gettin' them on the street. God knows what you get when you buy from junkies." He was shaking his head fiercely and held a clenched fist in front of him to emphasize what he wanted Ed to do for his wife.

"You're Sharon's husband, Mr. Malto?"

"Yeah, Doc, you met her, so you know she's gorgeous and

she's all mine. Me and Tony Junior and her are a big happy family."

"Tony – can I call you Tony?" The big man shrugged in response. "I would love to talk with you and Sharon about why she thinks that she needs sleeping pills. But she needs to be here and agree to that discussion. I can't talk about her without her permission." Having now met Sharon's husband for all of about three minutes, Ed could understand Sharon's reluctance to accept his offer of family counseling.

"Yeah, yeah, I get it Doc. That's not why I'm here. I'm pretty sure I got the clap again. I was away on a business trip with the boys three weeks ago and we got ourselves a few party girls and now I'm dripping again like the last time I got it."

Ed nodded. "Okay, Mr. Malto let's have a look." Tony dropped his trousers and demonstrated drainage typical of gonorrhea. Ed took swabs from Tony's penis and told him to bend over so he could take a swab from his rectum.

"Hey Doc, you don't need that. I'm not that kinda guy. What are you thinkin'?"

"Tony it's routine to take swabs from the rectum and throat. If you want me to treat you, please bend over."

"Hey, who do you think you're talking to?"

"A guy with the clap, Tony, just a guy with the clap." Reluctantly, Tony let Ed take the swabs. And then he stepped a foot closer to the doctor, so he was literally in his face.

"Ok Doc, look, I need you to stay quiet about this and figure out a way to treat Sharon without tellin' her what I got. I really need this favor from you. She gets pissed when I go out with party girls, and I don't need her naggin' right now."

Ed looked at Tony carefully, standing inches from his face. "Tony – I think you know that's not the way this works. First of all, I am required by law to report this infection to the Department of Health. If I don't report it then they will come to talk to you when they see this swab is growing gonorrhea. They will ask about your sex contacts, and they will ask Sharon if she is having any symptoms."

Ed continued to talk despite Tony's presence inches away from him. "Have you had sex with Sharon since you were away and got this infection?"

Tony puffed up a little. "You seen Sharon, Doc. I have sex with her whenever she ain't bitchin' about something. Yeah, we done it at least ten times since I got back."

"Okay, she needs treatment for sure. Two potential ways to go. The best way is that you tell her I need to see her about something. Maybe, you just man up and tell her the truth. Otherwise just tell her that you were seeing me, and I told you that I needed to see her."

Now Ed brought up his hand literally an inch from Tony's nose, holding up his index finger. "I am going to give you an antibiotic injection plus some pills that you will take right now that will hopefully fix you up. Do not have sex with Sharon until she is treated and I confirm that you are both cured."

"What the hell are you going to tell her when she comes in?" Providing medical advice with Tony trying to intimidate him was becoming tiresome. Ed turned away to sit at the computer and started typing in Tony's prescription for the clinic nurses.

"I will tell her that she needs treatment based on what I am treating you for. And I will take swabs from her like I took from you prior to treatment."

Tony stepped closer to the doctor yet again. His cologne did not smell cheap, but it was inescapable in the small exam room. "And what if she asks if it's the clap? This ain't the first time I had it, Doc."

Ed lifted his hands upright at chest height. "I will tell her the truth. If these cultures are positive for gonorrhea, I will tell her that I am prescribing for her based on her history of having sex with you, Tony."

"You said somethin' about another option?"

"Yeah, you can go to the Public Health clinic. They have a program to treat spouses with the partner coming in for the injection and pills. But they will definitely make sure that she knows why she is being treated."

Tony turned away and paced in a small circle around the room, his agitation apparent. "Oh, if I do that, she'll know right away what's going on." He stopped pacing and as Ed stood up from the computer he again stepped deep into the doctor's personal space. "Look Doc, understand I gotta have a favor. You gotta do me a solid and get her treated without her knowing what it's for. Maybe tell her it's a urine infection or somethin'. The last guy here did me a solid. I don't know what he told Sharon, but he got her treated and she didn't know it was for clap."

Ed snorted. "I don't think many doctors would do that Tony. Lying to your patient about treatment is malpractice."

Tony paused for a moment and then leaned forward. If it were possible, he was now even more threatening. "Doc I said I needed a favor. Ask around. If you do a favor for Tony Malto, he will be grateful and that's a good thing. If you don't do him a favor, then he'll get pissed and that's not so good."

Ed leaned over to lift the printed record of Tony's prescription off the printer and give it to him. "Tony, I am going to ignore that you seem to be threatening me. Our nurses are going to give you an injection and some pills which you will take right now. Tell Sharon to come and see me and I will break the news gently. I think maybe you two could use some counseling anyway. Maybe we should take advantage of this infection and talk about a change in the way your marriage works. I could see you both together."

And then Ed reminded him. "And Tony, if you don't tell her to come in, either me or the public health nurse will contact her once we have these cultures back."

Tony took the prescription from Ed with a face like thunder. "Thanks a fuckin' lot, Doc. I just asked you a favor and you just told me to go fuck myself. This ain't over."

Tony left the office, slamming the door and muttering, "Fuckin' change in the way my marriage works. Who the fuck does he think he is?"

The receptionist was terrified as he stomped to the desk and roared at her. "The nurse is gonna give me a shot. Where is she?" The receptionist nervously motioned him into to the clinic room behind her desk where the nurse was preparing the treatment Ed had ordered.

Tony's paler skinned companion looked back at Ed as Tony charged out of the office. "You just made Tony mad, Doc," he growled, "That's not so smart". And then he and his silent colleague sat back down to wait for their boss.

As Ed turned to his next patient, Esther Hightower came over from behind the reception where she was organizing the nursing schedule. "Let me guess, was that Sharon's husband?"

"It sure was, Esther."

She shook her head. "Doctor Ed, I don't know him personally but like I told you before, the word on the street is that Mr. Malto may be a pretty bad guy. Are you sure that you want to look after that family?"

To her surprise, Ed grinned. "I don't think that they are likely to go away if you tell them that I don't want to see them anymore, Esther. Tony will probably cool down. If he doesn't, we will just have to deal with it." Then he walked over to his next patient in the waiting room.

"Mrs. Flannery, sorry to keep you waiting. And sorry for all the commotion." Mrs. Flannery was a frail elderly patient who had been upset by Tony's drama. "Come on in my office with me."

Ed looked over his shoulder at Esther and smiled. She was puzzled by his lack of concern about Tony. But then again, she didn't know much about his previous practice.

CHAPTER 8: THE SILENT AUCTION

As she anticipated the crowd starting to gather this beautiful night on the Ridge, Linda Davis realized how much she had come to enjoy these evenings raising money for the arts. Her law firm sponsored at least one major fundraising event each year for the Maple Ridge orchestra. She found it a pleasure to make her home available for a good cause and also enjoy an orchestral evening outdoors. Linda was proud that her company was the first in town to start this kind of fundraiser. Now several of the professional firms in town held similar evenings to support the art gallery or the orchestra. But of course, Linda liked to believe that hers was the best event, as well as being the first.

Linda always scheduled the evening in late spring before it became too hot to sit outside and she was pleased to show off her spring gardens at the event. Her family had owned this property since before the Civil War and it definitely had the finest views of the river. It was located less than a mile north of town, not at the highest elevation of the Ridge but at the point where the river curved around a shoal, giving a sweeping view of the water below.

If the evening was blessed with fine weather as they were expecting tonight, then a delicious meal and great music over the river in the spring moonlight could be terribly romantic. Linda recalled some fun and passion from a few of these evenings. There was that evening with the Dutch guest conductor and the night that the commodity trader from Chicago had surprised her by flying in on his private jet for the evening.

And tonight, Linda was considering starting a new romantic interest. She had invited the new doctor in town to sit at her table and she was looking forward to getting to know him.

In a small town like Maple Ridge with a limited number of professionals, there are no secrets and a very efficient grapevine. Linda had heard how this new doctor had saved the life of young Chloe Smallman's baby – amazing that child could be a mother already – and had just heard that the doctor had faced down Tony Malto over something, that Tony had left his office angry, and that the new doctor hadn't broken a sweat.

This Dr. Brinkley sounded an interesting character – and she liked what she had seen at the Civic Luncheon a few weeks before.

Linda had tried to find out more from Bill Stanton about the doctor's military service prior to coming to Maple Ridge, but it sounded pretty hushed up. He had been in Afghanistan for an ungodly long period of time. Linda had noticed that he had a limp that might have been from a war injury. But apart from that, he was a bit of a mystery man and Linda had a penchant for mysteries in good-looking men.

Linda had dressed carefully for the occasion. She did not want to appear too flirty. After all, it was her company's evening and she needed to remind the town who ran the state's biggest law firm. So she selected a well-tailored blazer over a tight, spaghetti-strapped blouse and a soft, silk skirt that ended just above the knee. She knew that as the evening wore on the blazer would probably come off and that she might even hike the skirt's waist band under the blouse just like the high school girls did. The doctor's comment about Linda's red dress at the end of the Civic Luncheon still stuck with her. If he was going to notice what she was wearing, then Linda was going to make sure that she was wearing something notable.

She completed the outfit with stilettos. The party would be on the patio away from the river most of the evening and if she ended up walking across the lawns to look down on the river with the doctor, she would probably need to take the shoes off.

But Linda liked the height and the drama afforded by the heels.

They were lucky with the weather on this early May evening. The temperature was in the mid-seventies, humidity was low and there were no clouds to hide a nearly full moon. The tables were set on the patio facing toward the river. Tents were available if it rained but it looked like her guests would be dining under the stars.

Linda was proud of her home. She had spent a small fortune updating it while preserving its Southern charm, and she enjoyed showing it off.

As she checked the final arrangements and prepared to welcome her first guests, Linda was pleased to hear the string quartet starting to play. They would entertain during the cocktail hour and dinner. Then the chamber orchestra would take over following dinner and would play through dessert and liqueurs.

Linda's satisfaction was enhanced by learning that the orchestra had sold more than three hundred tickets at $5,000 each for the performance. Her law firm was covering all expenses so that the orchestra would clear the full one and a half million in ticket sales from the evening. That would cover operating expenses for the fall season. The orchestra would also benefit from various events at the dinner, including a silent auction.

As guests started arriving for the cocktail hour, Linda busied herself as hostess. All her suppliers and contractors were expected to be there, of course. Law firms that the Davis firm contracted to do work, their IT suppliers, commercial real estate people, the financing group, bankers, accountants – the Davis firm created a lot of business in Maple Ridge, and all the leaders of those companies were here tonight with their partners or dates. Linda also encouraged all her suppliers to lean on their suppliers as well. Tonight, they were setting a record for both attendance and the donation to a good cause.

While she welcomed guests and kibitzed with the growing crowd, Linda kept her eye out for Dr. Brinkley and was delighted when she saw him striding up the walk in a dress uniform, looking like a very effective recruitment poster.

He headed straight for her. "I hope that you don't mind the uniform, Linda. I forgot all my suits are at the cleaner. I am having trouble getting used to having a life where I need a suit occasionally. I was glad that I have this dress uniform and that I am still allowed to wear it."

"Doctor, I must say that you look dashing," she replied. "I am even happier now that I sat you at my table. That uniform is going to make our table stand out!"

Before she knew it, the cocktail hour had ended and staff were directing guests to their assigned seating. Linda walked up to the stage and was handed a microphone as the quartet paused their performance.

"Friends, welcome and thanks for joining the members of our Davis firm family on this beautiful evening to celebrate the arts in Maple Ridge. We are blessed with great music this evening, with fine spring weather and with wonderful company.

"On behalf of the orchestra and our firm, thank you for your generosity in coming tonight. You all know how important these musicians are to the life of our community. And remember, generosity does not end with the purchase of your dinner ticket."

She pointed to tables set up behind the dining area. "There is a wonderful silent auction tonight with items displayed on those tables behind you. And you have an opportunity to make an entirely tax-deductible donation to the orchestra at that booth across the patio. Finally, there a few tickets left for the fall/winter orchestral season. You can purchase a ticket tonight that promises you a wonderful season of beautiful music."

Lifting her left hand in welcome, Linda wished her guests good appetite. "And now, I will ask our quartet to strike up, ask the wait staff to start serving and invite you to join me in enjoying the evening, the great food and this wonderful music."

With perfect timing the quartet launched into the Spring

movement of Vivaldi's *Four Seasons* and servers appeared at the tables. Linda wandered across the patio greeting guests as she returned to her seat where Ed immediately stood and held the chair out for her.

"Nicely said, Linda. You are a great hostess and quite a fund-raiser. And you look simply stunning this evening."

Linda appreciated having this gracious doctor sitting beside her. She had seated a senior partner from Maple Ridge's second largest law firm, the mayor, and a city counsellor along with their spouses at their table. But with Ed at the table, the talk naturally turned to the state of Maple Ridge's medical facilities.

Ed politely complimented the town and its support of the hospital and clinic. And then someone asked if he'd had any surprises on arriving in Maple Ridge. Ed thought for a moment and then said something that gave Linda pause.

"Surprised, yes, I am a bit surprised about the mood I am finding here in Maple Ridge. I left to go overseas on various assignments quite a few years ago. At that time, we were reeling from 9/11, but there was no problem that this country could not solve if our people put their minds to it.

"The Cold War was over, and we had won. We were headed off to Afghanistan and the Middle East to avenge the attack on our homeland and we were confident that we would win."

He looked around the table, perhaps to gauge whether anyone would be insulted by what he said next. "And now I feel that sense of purpose and confidence has somehow been eroded by an atmosphere of general unease. That things are somehow unfair. The use of opioids in our community is alarming, and it sometimes seems that people are using drugs to get over the sense that life is ... well, I guess that the best word I can use is precarious. I am especially surprised at middle-aged men. Life just seems precarious for so many men that I am meeting, and I guess that I am surprised by that."

Linda knew exactly what he meant. Maple Ridge certainly had poverty issues and disadvantaged folks. There was still a marked divide between the white community on this high side of the river and the Black community that was historically located on the lower marshy side. But unemployment was lower than Linda remembered it, and people were buying more new boats and trucks than they ever had before.

However, people just seemed anxious that they were getting more and more in debt to afford the lifestyles they wanted. And the difference between the top one per cent and the beleaguered middle class seemed to be increasing every year. Linda also reflected on what Ed had mentioned about men. She could imagine that with competition from women and younger people in the workplace, middle-aged men could certainly be feeling squeezed and vulnerable.

Ed's comments came at the end of dinner when plates were being collected prior to the orchestra starting. One of the staff announced that the silent auction would be over in ten minutes, and Ed excused himself. He looked very dapper in his dress blues, and Linda's eyes and other women's eyes followed him as he stepped off to the auction exhibits. Then a couple of colleagues sat down to talk shop and Linda lost track of time.

Before she knew it, the conductor was taking applause as he made his way to the podium and Ed was sitting back down beside her.

Linda pulled him close with an arm linked into his and asked, "Did you find anything interesting on the auction table, Doctor?"

His response surprised her. "Linda, I purchased a couple of items that I hope I can interest you in. The first is for a romantic dinner in a spot that I know that you will really enjoy. And, if that works out, I also bought a weekend golfing/spa package to Hot Springs for one of the new boutique hotels. Depending on how our dinner goes, perhaps I can try and convince you to come golfing in Hot Springs with me?" Then he turned to listen to the orchestra leaving Linda in her seat with her mouth slightly open.

****

Linda had helped with the selection of music by the conductor and normally she would have just relaxed enjoying listening under the stars. But now Ed's words were echoing in her imagination. As she listened to the orchestra, she was surprised at how this doctor was affecting her.

At the end of the evening, the line of people coming to thank Linda and say goodnight seemed endless and she was sure that Ed would have left. But Linda was pleased to see him hanging around talking to their tablemates and then going deep into conversation with a gentleman who seemed to be thanking Ed at great length.

As she finished with her well-wishers, Ed's conversation was also breaking up and Linda realized that the man thanking Ed was Bob Smallman, Chloe's father-in-law, who was a lawyer in town. Bob had learned that the man who had delivered his new granddaughter was at the dinner and was taking the opportunity to express his appreciation.

Ed looked across the patio, pointed to Linda, then to his chest and back to her. Linda nodded her head 'yes' and made the universal sign for a drink which he caught with a wink. As he headed off for the bar Linda slipped off her blazer and surreptitiously hiked her skirt an inch under the blouse.

Returning with two glasses of red wine, Ed stopped and looked appreciatively.

"I must say, Linda, that you certainly know how to dress for the occasion. What do you say we enjoy this nightcap overlooking the river?"

"We will need to walk across my lawn to get to the chairs overlooking the river. I will either need to take off these shoes or lean on you to keep my heels out of the grass."

"Those shoes deserve to be worn, Linda. Not only can I support you across that lawn, but I figure, if need be, I'll just pick you up and carry you. But then people might talk. Here, take my arm."

Linda leaned on his arm and relaxed her body against him

at the same time. She could feel the definition in his arm muscles. He was a sinewy, strong guy and she enjoyed supporting herself against him. They made it to the chairs overlooking the river and Ed watched as Linda crossed her legs and twirled her shoe.

"So this is your family home, huh?"

"Yes, my family came here shortly before the Civil War, and if I had children, who knows, our family might be here for generations to come. But my mum died young, and my dad was killed in an accident just after I joined the firm. I am an only child, and it looks like the Davis family influence on Maple Ridge may be in its final generation."

"No cousins?"

"Dad had a sister, but she moved away to St. Louis. Her husband is on faculty at the University there and they are childless. I am the last Ridge Davis – so I need to leave a legacy."

Ed leaned forward. "Well, Linda, from the little bit I have learned about you, you have redefined legal practice in this state. I've heard that your firm is the number one class action firm from here to Chicago."

Linda nodded. "Yeah, we have had some luck and capitalized on it. I kind of fell into our first class action case about eight years ago. We launched a suit claiming overtime for casual workers against the big retailer that is headquartered here in the state. That turned into a national success story, and we made a lot of money for the workers and a lot of money for my firm when it settled."

He was listening with interest, so Linda continued. "And I learned that it is advantageous to run national class action lawsuits from right here in Maple Ridge. We have more than three hundred people working at the firm now, and you saw tonight how many other folks in town rely on us for work. We also have collaborators across the country that we can call on when needed."

Linda paused for a moment taking in the view of the moon over the river. "But the most important assets we have are our paralegals who sign up and manage the clients. They live out of suitcases, crisscrossing the country collecting clients whenever we learn about a group that might have a claim. Those women – ninety per cent of them are women – are the keys to our success and we take very good care of them."

Ed was sitting back listening to her. Then, he suddenly leaned forward, seeming very earnest. "Linda, it's getting late, and I really appreciate the invitation tonight and the lovely evening. Now, please don't think that there is any obligation on your part. But, as I mentioned earlier, I purchased two items at the silent auction.

"The first event is a bit ironic in that I think you may have donated it along with the catering service that provided the meal tonight. It's a dinner for two right here on your estate overlooking the river. If you would agree, I would love to have you join me for dinner so that I can hear about your family's history here at Maple Ridge. This would be a wonderful spot to learn more about you."

He paused, looked at the beautiful moon and then pressed on. "And then, please don't think that I am being sleazy – I promise to be a total gentleman – I also purchased a weekend for two in Hot Springs and would be delighted to have you join me on that weekend."

Ed's blue eyes were luminous in the moonlight and Linda thought that she would go away just about anywhere with him at this very moment. "Linda, I want to start playing golf again, so I bought the weekend spa and golf package. I used to play but have been away from the game for a long time. I thought that it might be fun to visit Hot Springs to restart my frustration with the game of golf. What do you think? Do you ever golf?"

Linda did not need long to answer. "I would love to go, Ed. I haven't been to the Hot Springs in years, and I understand that they have some interesting new boutique hotels. My dad introduced me to golf when I was a kid and there are a couple of courses in Hot Springs that I used to really enjoy playing."

Ed remembered his well-constructed plan and reminded her. "Before you commit to a weekend, let's have a dinner together here, which I will totally organize. That will give you a chance to consider the weekend trip after you check me out over a meal." And while he said this, his face turned from earnest to a smile that crinkled his eyes.

Linda thought to herself again that this dinner date better get set soon. The idea of a weekend away was intriguing and she hoped that he did not take his pledge of being a gentleman too seriously.

They arose from the riverside chairs and headed back across the lawn to where Linda's car and driver were always available. "Can I offer you a lift?"

"No thank you, Linda. I am going to walk and clear my head. It's a beautiful evening." And then he turned back to her.

"Linda, I know I am free next weekend. It may be too soon for your schedule, but how about I arrange the dinner for Saturday or Sunday evening?"

Linda frowned. She was planning to spend the next weekend working with her litigation partners from Maryland. She knew that they would be working intensely from Friday evening onward. She had booked a room at a local restaurant for her team and the visitors to get to know each other better Saturday night. But then her face lit up.

"I am going to be working all next weekend with my partners from Maryland. But I think that I could get away Sunday evening for dinner with you. I will probably need to return to the office after dinner, but let's plan for Sunday. It'll be fun, and I will need a break by then. And I do like that caterer's salmon with salsa," she concluded with a smile.

Ed reached out and grasped her hands in his. "So, next Sunday evening is a date. Leave everything up to me." And then he headed down her driveway with a buoyant step in his limp as Linda watched his dress blues fade into the night.

CHAPTER 9: INTIMIDATION

Tommy Lawsen was reflecting on the past couple of days as he described to Billy the orders he had received from Tony Malto.

"After we was in that fancy doctor's office," he told Billy as they walked out to Billy's car, "Tony told me that damn doc refused to do Tony a favor and maybe we needed to teach him a lesson. I knew it was about Sharon, and – keep it to yourself, huh, Billy – Tony got the clap when we was away."

Tommy shook his head. "I know, I know, it seems strange Tony is always playin' around on Sharon. Sharon is one of the hottest girls I know and they gotta little boy together. But I guess Tony just needs some variety is all and you can't blame a guy for that." Billy nodded in agreement.

Tommy went on. "We was all down on the Gulf 'cause Tony had business with Gabriel and Gabe and his boys always like to party after business and that's where Tony got the clap. It was just business is all, and the doc shoulda knowed he coulda done Tony a solid by helping him out with Sharon. When she gets pissed, she can be a real pistol and that doc shoulda helped Tony for sure."

As they drove, Tommy described what Tony had ordered them to do. "Tony figures maybe it ain't too late and we can convince the doc it would be best to think again and help Tony out. I checked him out and most days he walks home about now from his office to the crappy apartment he lives in. It's about six blocks from the clinic to his apartment and part of the walk is on this long, quiet street with only a couple of houses. I figure this would be a good place to convince that doctor to think again about helpin' Tony out."

They parked on the side of the long, quiet street. Billy stayed behind the wheel. They were both armed.

Tommy let Billy know what Tony wanted. "Tony told me that we could scare the shit outta him and maybe touch him up a bit, but not go too far with really rough stuff. With both of us showin' we is carryin' and meanin' business, I figure the guy will be beggin' for us to get Tony to come back to his office so he can help him out."

Tommy went on to his colleague. "I heard this doc was military and maybe that makes him tough or somethin'. But he won't be packin' coming back from work and he looks like a skinny shit to me. Maybe he was tough when he was surrounded by Marines but there ain't gonna be no helicopters comin' to rescue him here in the Ridge."

Just then, Ed approached their parked car on his stroll home. Tommy jumped out of the passenger side and walked around the front of the car to block the doctor's path.

"Hey Doc, I wanna word with you. Remember me, I was in your fuckin' office with my friend Tony Malto? You remember me?"

Tommy thought the doc looked surprised and figured that he was going to shit his pants. He started looking around like he was going to yell for help but there was no one nearby. Tommy had noticed Ed's limp when he was walking and thought that if he tried to run, he could chase him down easy.

"Yes, I remember you. How can I help?" *Funny,* thought Tommy, *he don't sound too scared.*

"My friend Tony told me he asked you for a favor and you told him to screw himself. When you don't do a favor when Tony asks you, all his friends get pissed off. I'm here to tell you I ain't happy with you."

"What's your name? You must know that I am not going to talk about one of my patients without his consent." Asking Tommy his name told the big man that he needed to tighten the screws on this damn doctor.

"Yeah, well, fuck you. Tony gave me the say so to speak to you. He told me to show you this consent here." And he pulled his jacket open and showed Ed the nine millimeter he had tucked in his waistband.

In retrospect, he later told Billy, "I knew the doc was starting to get scared. He took a step toward me looking at the gun and then he sorta crouched and twisted away. I figured he was getting ready to run. That's when I turned to you, Billy, to tell you to get ready to drive after the guy if he ran and that's why he was able to sucker me."

He shook his head as he recounted the next moment, "He just sorta twists outta that crouch. I saw him coming at me outta the corner of my eye but then he nailed me with his fist right in the throat. It hurt like shit and I couldn't breathe or talk. I just remember bendin' over gaspin' and then he reaches inside my coat and grabs my gun. And then the pain in my fuckin' throat was so bad, and I think I just kinda passed out."

Billy told him later that the doc threw Tommy on the front of the car so Billy couldn't move the automobile without risking running over Tommy. The doc chambered a round in Tommy's nine millimeter and aimed it at Billy's face through the windshield.

Billy was struggling to get his gun out, but his belly prevented him from recovering his weapon from his waistband while sitting behind the steering wheel. Ed came around to the driver's side with Tommy lying on the hood of the car and reached in through Billy's window with Tommy's weapon inches from Billy's nose.

Ed pulled Billy's gun out of his waistband and popped out the magazine and checked that there was no round chambered. And then he ejected the round from Tommy's gun, put both magazines in his pocket, threw the guns into the bushes and turned to walk home.

Billy dragged Tommy into the car. Tommy was waking up and coughing but couldn't talk. Billy suggested going to tell

Tony what happened. Tommy knew this would make him look stupid, and he said to Billy in a hoarse whisper, "Look this is jus' between us, okay Billy? No way Tony can know the guy got the drop on me. He won't get away with that again. We'll figure out how to get him but let's just keep this between us for now."

Billy nodded. Tommy knew he was a good kid and could be trusted to keep his mouth shut. He was from Tommy's neighborhood and had just joined Tony's squad with Tommy vouching for him. As they drove away, Tommy promised his younger companion, "We're gonna figure out another way to get that prick doctor."

CHAPTER 10: LEARNING ABOUT LINDA

E d realized that making preparations for Linda's Sunday evening meal was good for him. He needed to be doing something other than work. He had been in Maple Ridge for more than two months and had been practicing medicine just about every waking hour that he was not eating, shopping for food or exercising. He was leading a boring, workaholic life, and one thing that Dr. Romulus had insisted on was that he needed to find relief from his work ethic.

So, he took an extended Wednesday lunch break to learn some new things about Maple Ridge. He enjoyed walking through the center of town a short distance from the clinic. Maple Ridge had a heritage town square with shops organized around the historic courthouse. That red brick, three-story classic building dated back to shortly after the Civil War.

The orchestra that had played at Linda's fundraiser maintained an office on the broad, shady streets that surrounded the courthouse and Ed enjoyed meeting the pleasant administrative team. They confirmed that the string quartet that Linda engaged for her dinner was available on Sunday evening and Ed retained them to play for a more intimate audience.

Three doors down Main Street he found the caterer that had provided the silent auction item he had purchased. Their store doubled as a bakery and had a large window display filled with pastries and breads facing on the town square.

Ed stopped in his tracks as he entered. The combinations of chocolate, cinnamon and assorted spices wafting through the air made his mouth water. The young woman who owned the company was a native of Maple Ridge. She was intrigued as Ed explained the purpose of his visit and told him that she had known Linda since they were kids in school.

She knew Linda's tastes and was delighted to help him with the menu. They settled on hors d'oeuvres that the caterer recommended, a lightly creamed vegetable soup followed by a terrine and then the poached salmon with salsa that Linda had mentioned to Ed. The caterer said that Linda did not usually indulge in dessert but loved crème brûlée. Ed agreed that they should have it ready for her just in case.

The caterer recommended a florist on a side street just off Main Street, and Ed ordered an extravagant array of fresh-cut flowers to be delivered in prearranged settings for late Sunday afternoon. He had noticed the care that Linda took with her gardens and figured he could not go wrong with fresh flowers. As he started to leave the florist, a thought stopped him, and he turned back to order a large basket of rose petals.

Finally, he entered a fine wine store back on Main. Ed remembered that Linda might need to work after dinner but determined that he would provide a selection of appropriate wines. The merchant offered tastings but Ed's afternoon back in the office prevented him from trying the wines. With the proprietor's advice he ended up selecting a vintage champagne to start the evening, an elegant twelve-year-old Brunello for the soup and terrine followed by a crisp New Zealand Sauvignon Blanc for the salmon and a Canadian ice wine to accompany dessert, if Linda indulged.

Having completed his shopping around the charming town square, he returned to the caterer to confirm arrangements. She had checked the forecast for Sunday evening and reassured Ed that no rain was expected. She advised that she would set the table on the small patio where he and Linda had sat overlooking the river and Ed readily agreed.

Ed was pleased with his planning and looking forward to the evening. The most intriguing aspect, however, was the anticipation of getting to know Linda better. At the end of his Thursday afternoon clinic, he went to Esther Hightower, his usual source of Maple Ridge intelligence, to learn more about Linda.

"Well, Dr. Ed, you are setting your sights mighty high if you are interested in that young woman. Everyone has wondered for years who Linda will choose when she settles down, but that just hasn't happened yet."

Esther looked down, recalling old memories. "When she was little, Linda was known around town as a tomboy and a daddy's girl. Her momma died young from breast cancer I believe, and she grew up playing with her daddy on the tennis court and the golf course and then she went away to Harvard and Yale. We were all surprised when she came back to the Ridge after law school to join her poppa's law firm. We thought that she would stay back east after graduation, but we were happy when she came home.

"And then her poppa got killed in an accident and everyone figured that Linda would pull up stakes and go back east. Come to think about it, there was something about Tony Malto's family and that accident. I just don't remember exactly what was said."

Esther continued her reminiscence, shaking her head from side to side as she remembered. "When Linda stayed with her daddy's firm after he was gone, we all thought that she would finish it off – nobody wanted a woman lawyer back then – but she just worked her butt off." She looked over at Ed.

"And then she starts something called a class action for all them poor people, most of them Black women, who were working crazy hours without gettin' paid right for that big box store. Damn if she doesn't win and get them all kinds of money for overtime they shoulda been paid."

Esther was smiling at the memory of that legal victory for her hometown. "And her firm made out real well too, and that's been good for this town. I hear Linda's law firm does this class action stuff now for the whole country, and I've seen her interviewed on television saying she plans on staying in the

Ridge." Her smile broadened.

"God bless her, she says that people here are smart, and they know when a bunch of little guys are getting screwed by a big company, and they know how to help. She must have more than two hundred paralegals workin' for her who trained at the local college. I've heard they go around the country finding people who need help and signing them up for Linda."

Esther looked up at Ed. "I heard say that she has been courted by lots of big law firms in Chicago, New York and Washington who want her to move her business to their towns, and she keeps on saying that her family comes from Maple Ridge, and this is where she's gonna stay."

Ed broke in. "Esther, has she ever been married? Does she have anyone? She is a very attractive woman."

Esther looked at Ed obliquely, tilting her head back and slowly rubbing her chin. "Well now, Dr. Ed, people used to gossip about Linda and say that maybe she played around too much in the old days. I remember some very spicy stories about her and a baseball player and then a pro quarterback and about her and a movie star. And when she was becoming a famous lawyer, a couple of men who were supposed to be very rich flew in here on their private jets and all. I guess some interesting people have come to Maple Ridge because of Linda Davis – but I wouldn't be one of those people who gossip."

"Ah, c'mon Esther, tell me what you do know."

"Well, I think people would say that Miss Linda has had quite a few beaux. And way back, some of them maybe were not the most reliable kinda guys. I know when she was in high school – now that goes back a long way – she was dating the Arkansas quarterback. And of course he was cheating on her like all quarterbacks cheat on their girls and everyone knew he broke her heart. But she was just a kid then.

"I heard rumors that when she was away for university she ran in a pretty wild crowd. You even sometimes saw her in the magazines every once in a while. I know that Miss Linda caused her poor daddy a lot of grief with her social life and all. After all, this is a small and pretty conservative town and people talk.

"And then when her daddy died and she took over the firm, she became more discreet, I guess you would say. But we would hear rumors about how she was dating rich guys. Or one time she was thinking of marrying some loaded European guy, but he didn't want to live in the Ridge, and she refused to leave to live with him in Spain – I think it was Spain. Yes sir, Dr. Ed, there are lots of stories about Miss Linda."

With this intriguing information, Ed was looking forward to getting to know this interesting lady and anticipating Sunday night. He knew that Linda would be working all weekend and texted her that dinner was going to be casual dress, but he made sure that he had a fresh suit from the cleaner for Sunday afternoon and actually went out Saturday to get a new tie.

Sunday was a beautiful warm day with no rain forecasted. Ed took a taxi to Linda's place to check on preparations a couple of hours before she was due home. He met Linda's long-term housekeeper who was pleased that someone was doing something special for her boss. "That girl is jes' workin' herself to death these days. I hope you can convince her not to go back to work this evening." And she gave Ed a very suggestive grin.

CHAPTER 11: SALMON
WITH SALSA

As she was driven home from the office to join Ed for this unusual dinner at her own house, Linda put down her cell and allowed her thoughts to wander. There was something very different about this doctor she was dining with tonight. He was somehow making her feel reflective but also uneasy.

Linda knew that she had matured very quickly when her dad died in the accident. Up to that point, her future was bright but always in the future. She knew that her role in her dad's practice would always be there for her, and she enjoyed being a bit of a dilettante, learning from her dad when it interested her and enjoying herself socially when she got bored. And enjoying herself usually included a man.

Starting in high school really, she had developed a reputation around town that caused her father some distress. Maple Ridge was a very traditional, Bible Belt community where everyone knew everyone else's business. But her father gradually became more progressive in his outlook. When friends complained to him that his daughter was playing around with men too much to maintain her reputation, she heard him say when he didn't know she was listening, "Would you warn me about my daughter's reputation if she was my son?"

After his accident, she was forced to reevaluate her lifestyle from several points of view. Most important, she suddenly had responsibility for the success of her father's firm. Her legal colleagues in town probably thought that the business would fail within the year. They all told her that they would help her keep the firm going – and then tried to steal Linda's most important clients. In retrospect, Linda knew that it was in great part her stubborn reaction to predictions of her failure that drove her to work as hard as she did.

For four years Linda worked around the clock keeping her father's original business running. And then she caught a rocket with the success of the class action lawsuit that so dramatically changed the firm's reputation and fortune. Suddenly the Davis firm was a national success and Linda had new responsibility and new opportunity. Nobody had been willing to take on that case for those poor women who worked long hours for the retailer with no overtime. Linda won that case for women across the country, and also achieved a very successful financial result for the Davis firm.

But Linda found herself in her mid-thirties working incessantly with no steady companion. At the same time, her national exposure gave her access to interesting relationships that generally remained long-distance affairs. Her girlfriends from law school all lived around East Coast legal centers in Boston, New York and Washington and had managed to marry and in some cases already divorce while developing their careers. They all wondered why Linda stayed in Maple Ridge.

Sometimes she wondered the same. Linda knew that in part it was a commitment to her dad's memory and respect for her family's longevity in the community. But now, a key aspect of her loyalty to the Ridge related to how the Davis firm had grown and matured over the past few years. She was especially proud of the role of her paralegals who had developed into a major asset contributing to the success of one of the nation's premier class action legal firms.

Her team had a small-town, down-to-earth, helpful attitude that differentiated them. Linda thought that attitude definitely won clients for the Davis firm.

She realized that she had committed herself to professional success while her personal life just drifted. She knew Maple

Ridge enjoyed whispering about what they imagined to be her love life. The Davis firm was important to the town and citizens were proud that Linda was putting Maple Ridge on the map. But she knew that they also loved gossiping about her behind her back.

This Dr. Ed Brinkley had an element of intrigue to him, and by all accounts he was a great new addition to the Ridge medical community. And Linda found him just plain attractive. So she was delighted that he had started something between them with this dinner. But even though she was attracted to his sense of mystery, she was worried about how little she knew about him.

Bill Stanton had told Linda about Ed's reluctance to talk about what he had been doing prior to coming to town. And Linda found it unusual that he seemed to have such limited possessions - living in a rental apartment, walking everywhere without a car. She wondered whether he might be attracted to her wealth like a male gold digger. After all, he had seen where she lived, and she was obviously living far better than him. She did not really mind his apparent lack of wealth but found it strange for a physician.

As her driver opened the door of her car, Linda was surprised to hear violins coming from the river lookout. Walking around the house, she was delighted that the music was not recorded but provided by the same quartet that had played at her fundraiser. And they were gathered around a lovely table setting surrounded by baskets of fresh cut flowers.

She recognized one of Mozart's "Haydn" Quartets as she approached the table across the lawn, and then saw that her path was strewn with rose petals. Ed had risen from his seat and was approaching her with two glasses of champagne. He was wearing a teal suit with a lovely tie and Linda immediately appreciated the care he had taken in organizing this evening.

"Really, Doctor, rose petals on the lady's path? Isn't that a bit over the top?"

Ed smiled as she accepted one of the champagne glasses,

clinked glasses with him and took a small sip. Linda felt her delight at seeing him and these wonderful preparations subdued by the fact that she would have to go back to work with her Maryland partners this evening. She would need to limit herself with the wine.

Ed bowed deeply from the waist while sweeping his arm in front of her like a courtier. "Well, Ms. Davis, maybe these rose petals exceed usual protocols. But, when you are hosting a lovely woman at her own home, you need to do something special to make the evening memorable."

Linda turned to look at the flowers, the musicians and the lovely table setting over the river. "Well Ed, don't you worry, memorable this is."

Linda remembered that Ed had paid a considerable sum at the silent auction to host this dinner and seemed to have spared no expense in arranging the evening. Her concern about his seeming lack of worldly goods faded. She reached out, softly running her hand over his tie. "You told me casual, but you are really quite elegant this evening, Dr. Brinkley."

Linda had taken care dressing for work this morning. Her jeans were expensively faded and fit her perfectly. She had been wearing a buttoned cardigan all day in the air-conditioned office, but she removed it now in the comfortable early evening warmth and her silk camisole barely met the top of her jeans.

Ed took her hand leading her to her seat at table. "Linda, I have seen you on three occasions now and each time you are dressed perfectly for the event. Tonight, it's casual chic for al fresco dining with Mozart and you've managed it wonderfully."

They turned their chairs to face west in appreciation of the slowly sinking sun. The catering staff offered a plate of scallop canapes along with barbecued Korean duck morsels and small slices of smoked salmon on cucumber topped with caviar. The caterer had told Ed that these were Linda's favorite hors d'oeuvres.

Looking at the appetizers being offered, Linda grinned with delight and turned to her companion. "Ed, you are so sweet. You found the treats I love, how thoughtful of you."

She remembered how she liked his crinkly eyes as he smiled back at her. "I'll say again Linda, when you ask a woman for dinner at her own place, you better make sure you are serving her favorites."

And as he said this, Ed lifted Linda's hands and brushed his lips across her fingers. "I know that you may need to get back to work tonight but I am so happy to provide you with a couple hours of pampering. From what I am learning about you, you work awfully hard and probably deserve someone serving you for a change."

Linda leaned back in her chair and sighed while allowing herself another tiny sip of the champagne. "This champagne is wonderful Ed. I wish that I didn't need to go back, but unfortunately we have a long night ahead at the office. And this is just so thoughtful of you." Looking toward the slowly sinking sun, Linda turned her head through a full rotation and put her hand to the back of her neck.

The next thing she knew, Ed was standing behind her with his hands firmly placed on the top of her shoulders. "Doctor's orders, Ms. Davis. You take a few more sips of that champagne while I provide you with the acclaimed Brinkley neck rub."

As he started to gently knead her shoulders around the straps of her camisole, Linda could not help moaning. "Oh my God, Ed, that is so good." His thumbs started tracing the muscles of her neck, leaving her shoulders, and moving his hands slowly up to her head. She could feel her neck tightness magically fading away.

Her eyes were shut, and she was breathing in the rhythm of his fingers. "Do they teach you this in med school? This feels incredibly relaxing."

"The massage is actually included with the silent auction package I bought at your fundraiser. But the Brinkley technique is a little extra." With that, their soup arrived, and the quartet began a new Mozart piece.

As they slowly enjoyed their elegant meal, Ed wondered how Linda's day had gone. He mentioned that he was interested in her firm since he had learned that she was one of the major employers in Maple Ridge. But even as he led the conversation to Linda's work, Ed was mostly enjoying the delight of sitting close talking to this beautiful, intelligent, and very special woman.

With Ed's prompting and promise to provide another neck massage if she explained her firm's success, Linda started to open up about her class action work and how she had developed the national prominence that she enjoyed today. She described the risks inherent in taking on class action cases because of the expenses involved in recruiting and managing clients and paying for the legal expertise necessary for success. And she described the financial opportunity that came to her firm from contingency fees when the case was successful.

The discovery that Linda made with her first class action suit was that Maple Ridge provided her firm with a major cost advantage over lawyers located in the usual financial and legal centers. Representing hundreds or thousands of everyday people did not require the expensive facilities necessary to impress corporate clients.

She explained to Ed how she offset her financial risks by sharing costs and contingency profits with partner litigation firms. And with her help, bankers and investors in Maple Ridge had learned to syndicate funds to support her case costs with national investors.

These investors were usually paid off handsomely from contingency payments once the case closed. As the Davis firm reputation for success grew, so did the demand to invest in these syndicated funds. By now a variety of Maple Ridge businesses had benefited from the Davis firm and its class action legal work.

Linda's attachment to Maple Ridge had grown in other ways that she explained to Ed. "Everyone associates this state with landmark school desegregation, but I am afraid that separation of our two races has been an established fact in Maple Ridge forever. You've noticed I am sure that we have a Black side of town and a white side?" Ed nodded.

"Well, segregation of our professional classes has also been a long-standing tradition that I am trying to fix." Ed nodded again. He had noticed on joining the medical group that there were only two Black doctors in his clinic even though they cared for at least an equal proportion of Black patients and that the support staff was overwhelmingly Black.

Linda continued. "When we took on the big retailer in our first class action case, most of our clients were Black women. They had been turned down by all our local and regional firms and they appreciated me taking on their case. And even though I had grown up in this town, I had never really known people from our Black neighborhoods. During that case I began to appreciate the raw talent that was being locked out of our business community in Maple Ridge."

Linda took a small sip of her wine and continued. "So, when we started expanding our paralegal and legal team after that first case, I made sure that we recruited on both sides of town. Our firm started bursaries to send Black kids to college and some on to law school. I am proud of the fact that our firm now looks just like our community. And you may have noticed that our suppliers, contractors and partners are also equally drawn from both sides of Maple Ridge."

She raised her eyes to look directly at her dinner partner. "And I guess that is part of the reason that I am here in Maple Ridge. Our firm is slowly changing this town. When you get to know the town better you will see that communities on this side of the river that used to be lily white are now welcoming successful Black families. I am proud of that change and want to build on our success."

Ed looked down. "I get that, Linda. I can understand the purpose and pride in what you are doing. That sounds similar to what attracted me here as well. To try and change how we treat each other in this country. My way is through the practice I am trying to start in Maple Ridge."

Linda pushed Ed to describe what he had been doing over the past few years, but he preferred to listen to her lawyer stories and how she had achieved her national reputation. He explained that his reluctance to discuss recent experiences was because many of his activities were still classified.

He did not tell Linda that he had spent too much time putting that part of his life behind him with Dr. Romulus. He did not want to bring it back on this special evening. But it worried Linda that he was so guarded in his responses. She felt like she wanted to lower her defenses in front of this man and that feeling was clearly not being reciprocated. She could not help wondering what he was hiding.

Linda described the highlights of the case that she was working on this weekend and would soon be taking to trial in Maryland. It interested Ed because she was dealing with an innovative surgical device gone terribly wrong. Ed knew from his days in Afghanistan how new surgical techniques could benefit patients. He had plenty of experience with developing innovative surgery that had saved the lives of soldiers on the battlefield. However, no matter how proud he might be about that work, he could not really talk about it.

But listening to Linda describe the devastating impact that this failed new device had on hundreds of her clients, irritation intruded on the well-being he was enjoying with this meal. As a surgeon, he'd always understood the trust that patients placed in his profession when they signed up for an operation. Patients assumed that the surgeon's entire motivation was determined by the patient's best interests. And in this Maryland case, Linda recounted a story of surgical greed, with the doctors placing their own financial interests ahead of their patients' well-being.

As she described the case that she was working on, Linda's familiarity with complex surgery was obvious, as was her commitment to helping these injured patients. Listening to her passionate description of how she planned to right the wrong done to her clients, Ed found himself even more captivated by this lovely lawyer.

And then they were savoring the last delicious spoonful of crème brûlée. Linda checked her watch and sighed deeply. "Ah Ed, this has been so wonderful." And she reached across the table to take his hands and brought them to her lips. "I am so sorry that I must get back to the office. Thank you so much for organizing this evening."

Linda offered Ed a ride home as she returned to her office. As her driver stopped outside his apartment, Ed placed his hands on the sides of her face and kissed her gently. "Linda, remember that I have that second silent auction purchase for a golf and spa weekend in Hot Springs. Did I pass my audition tonight? Will you consider coming with me for a golf weekend?"

Linda smiled and responded. "As long as there is a Brinkley neck massage included in that package, I will be delighted to go to the Springs." She returned his kiss. "Seriously Ed, let's book that time together soon. Let me know when you can get away."

As he nodded, Linda leaned across the car, kissed him deeply and hugged him tight before he left the vehicle. They separated slowly and carefully, enjoying the closeness that had developed over one short evening.

And then she was gone, and Ed immediately felt her absence as her car drove away. Linda on the other hand felt on edge. She felt there was potential with this man, but she was concerned about his reluctance to talk about himself. She had been attracted by his sense of mystery but now found herself worried by how little she was learning about him.

She wondered about his offer to go away golfing. She fretted for a moment about getting in too deep, too fast, with someone that she knew so little about. But then her usual confidence returned. She smiled to herself, deciding that if they did visit Hot Springs, she would be focusing on much more than just the golf.

CHAPTER 12: THE DIAGNOSIS

Tony told his wife that she should go and see the doctor, so Sharon made an appointment with Dr. Brinkley. She was surprised that Tony had been nice to her in the last few days – things seemed good between them. And she was also surprised that he cared enough to ask her to go to the doctor. That just wasn't like Tony at all to care about her that way. But Tony said maybe she should go and talk to the doctor about how they were doing and stuff, so she called the office.

And it was kinda strange, but in the last week, he hadn't been pushing her for sex all the time the way he usually did. Sharon liked sex okay, but Tony didn't make it that great for her. She thought of him as a "slam, bam" kinda guy. And he always wanted oral sex and always gagged her and, as she confided in a friend, "Then he gets pissed and says that I should practice and learn how to do it better for him and that just grosses me out."

But the past week he hadn't asked for nothing.

She went into the doctor's office and Dr. Ed saw her immediately. Sharon thought to herself again that he was *kinda cute*. She felt more confidence in him than she felt in most doctors because, as she told her girlfriend, "He has a soft voice, and looks at me in the eyes instead of the boobs when I talk to him."

The doc asked her the reason for her visit. Sharon told him that Tony suggested she should come and that maybe that's a good sign that he would agree to them getting into counseling or something. And they talked about Tony a while, about how Tony traveled on business sometimes and where he went and stuff.

And then he started asking personal questions. Like whether Sharon had burning when she pees, a vaginal discharge, does she have all this kind of personal stuff. He tried to make it sound like he was just asking her general questions, but it seemed outta place to Sharon somehow.

And it was weird how he knew to ask because she had been having burning when she peed, and she was now getting up two or three times at night to go to the bathroom. And just last week she started to get a lot of discharge and thought that maybe she had yeast again except it didn't itch. And she had started feeling kinda crappy, low energy and sometimes she felt like she might have a fever.

So, she told all this to the doctor. And he said, "Sharon I want to take some cultures from your urine, from your vaginal discharge and a couple other places. And while we wait for those cultures to come back, I want to give you some antibiotics. If it's okay with you, I will ask my nurse to come in while I examine you."

And while she was lying on her back and he was taking swabs from everywhere and giving them to the nurse, she was thinking, thinking, thinking - *something's just not right.*

And then it came to her. These doctors, they never want to give you antibiotics until after they get the lab results back. It's just a waste of your time, waiting for the tests when they usually know the answer. They're just doing it to stop from being sued or something if they give you the wrong drugs.

But now this doc wanted to give me antibiotics before the tests are back. That was really weird. And the questions he asked me. It's like he knew what I had before I said anything.

And then she put it all together. Why Tony is being nice, why he doesn't want sex, why he told me to go to the doctor, why the doc asked me those personal questions.

As soon as the nurse left with the specimens Sharon demanded to know, "Doc, did Tony come in here with an infection and now you know what to give me because you got

Tony's result back already and you figure I got the same thing?"

Dr. Ed looked kinda bashful when he said, "Yes, that's right Sharon. Tony was in here and he does have an infection that I am treating. I am assuming that since you have symptoms of urine burning and vaginal discharge that you probably have the same infection. I am going to check all your results of course, but I think I already know what to treat you for."

"So, Doc, what kinda infection do I have? Or if you don't know for sure what kinda infection I have, then what infection are you treating Tony for?"

"Sharon, you know that I can't answer that question without Tony being here or giving me his consent to discuss it with you."

"Ok Doc, let me ask you a different question that you *do* have to answer. Based on everything you know right now, what are you treating me for?"

He smiled and Sharon knew she had got him, that he had to answer. "You're right Sharon, I will answer that question. I am treating you for a genitourinary infection."

"Doc you know that I have no idea what a genital urine infection is. Is it herpes, syphilis or something?"

"Are you asking me whether this is a sexually transmitted disease?"

"Yeah, of course that's what I mean."

"Yes, this is very likely an STD. It's almost certainly gonorrhea."

And that was a real shock because Sharon hadn't been with anyone except Tony in almost a year. She used to mess around a little, just to have sex that was more to her liking, but Tony got suspicious when she was seeing that college boy. Tony didn't know for sure, but he was wondering and one day he held her in his arms and squeezed her, nice at first and then a little too hard and then really hard so she could hardly breathe.

And then he said to her, "Sharon, you know how much I love you, how much you and Tony Junior mean to me. And if I ever caught a guy cheating with you, I would beat the shit out of him and then kill him and put his body in a barrel of acid. And unless you told me that he forced himself on you, Sharon, I dunno what it would mean that I would have to do to you."

After that she broke it off with the college guy and hadn't been with anyone but Tony since. Sometimes she would meet up with someone cute in a crazy place like a grocery store and he would be nice to her, and she would think about it a lot. In fact, sometimes she would just go home and pleasure herself thinking about them being nice to her. But she knew that with the way that Tony watched her, it was too dangerous to do anything more than that.

So she knew she didn't get the clap from anyone else. That only left one answer. "Doc, did I get this infection from Tony? Did he give me the clap?"

And then he did the nicest thing. She was sitting up on the examination table which was lowered after he took the cultures. And instead of standing speaking down at her, he sat down on the chair so that their eyes were at the same level. And then he took her hands in his and says, "Sharon I am sorry. Yes, I am treating you for gonorrhea and yes, you may have gotten it from Tony."

She couldn't help it. He was being so nice, she wanted to kiss him. But she knew he would never touch a girl like her because he knew that she was just a slut with the clap. Him being so nice just made her feel dirty and ugly and she just started crying.

And then he did something else that was so nice. He put his arm around her shoulders. Like he wasn't touching her in the wrong way or anything, he was just being nice and comforting her while she cried.

And his arm was so comfortable, and he was so cute, that she just kept crying for a while. But then she got all cried out and then she started getting mad.

"You know Doc, this ain't the first time. That damn Tony, this is the second time he's given me the clap and I think he gave me herpes as well. I know from before we were married that he won't use a condom – he says he can't feel it as good when he wears a rubber."

Then she remembered where he had been the last couple of months. Tony and the boys were down on the Gulf doing business with Gabriel. And when he got back, he was super horny and took her every way all the time for a couple of weeks. Being down on the Gulf must have been where he got it.

And remembering all the sex in the time when he got back, it just sickened her, and she started crying again. But this time it was mad tears. That bastard. How could he treat her like this?

CHAPTER 13: VISITING
THE HOSPITAL

Tony Malto was raging at Tommy Lawsen. Tony's face had a couple of deep scratch marks and he sounded furious.

"That bastard doctor, I can't believe what he did to me. Sharon comes home from seeing him and the bitch just attacks me. Her nails got my face, and I got this big scratch on my cheek, and she tries to knee me in the balls before I hit her the first time. And I get a little crazy and punch her a coupla times harder than I shoulda and she is lying on the floor moaning, and I am so pissed at that doctor I called you boys. We need to go to that damn doctor's office right now."

Tommy and Billy got a couple of cars and a couple more guys and they went down to the clinic to pay Ed a visit. The receptionist told Tony that he's not there and she wasn't going to say where he was until Tony slammed his fist on her desk and told her, "I gotta know where he is right now."

She told him that he had just started his emergency shift at the hospital, so Tony and the boys drove right over there. Tony went into the hospital and told the ER desk, "I need to see Brinkley right now."

Before he went into the ER, Tommy was cautioning Tony to take it easy. Tommy's voice had been hoarse, and Tony thought that he had been acting weird the last few days. Tommy told him he'd got the flu. Tony told him, "This fuckin' doctor better take it easy – he's wreckin' my marriage and nobody got the right to do that in this town."

Tony saw the security guard at the emergency edging away and figured he was going to call the cops. Tony wasn't worried because the cops in the Ridge and Tony had an understanding that if he didn't cause too much trouble, they would leave Tony alone. He had a few 'stay out of jail free cards' for favors he had done for senior officers over the past few years, covering up for them, sometimes quietly getting them stuff they wanted like girls, that kind of thing.

And he figured it was worth using a couple of those cards right now to show this fuckin' doctor who he's messin' with. He had sent Tommy to get the doc to understand what he should do but Tommy ain't done that job yet. And sometimes if you want the job done right you gotta do it yourself.

He had figured the doc would hide inside the emergency, so Tony was surprised when Brinkley came out to reception and walked right up to him. "Hello, Tony. You know that you can't come barging into the hospital like this. I can see you tomorrow in my office if its urgent, but I am the only doctor on call here right now."

Seeing him acting cool just made Tony angrier. "I don't give a shit how many doctors are here. You gotta see my wife right away today and tell her you was wrong, that my lab tests came back different than what you thought. You are fuckin' with my marriage you prick, and you gotta fix it right now."

"Tony, you know that you can't stand here and talk this way. If you don't leave, we are going to have to ask the police to have you removed."

"You just don't get who I am, do you? Those cops and me, we knowed each other forever and you just got to town, who do you think they are gonna listen to when I tell 'em this is personal, family stuff about my wife, huh?" Tony glared at Ed. He had heard that he was in the army or something but if he didn't do what Tony wanted, it was gonna be trouble for him.

"You gotta understand that in this town if you make trouble between a man and his wife, the man has some rights to get you to back off."

"Now you step outside with me, Doc, and I am going to tell you what I want you to say to my wife when you see her today and then I'm gonna take you back to your office and bring her to see you right away. Are you coming, or am I gonna have to make you come with me?"

CHAPTER 14: ER SURGE

E d thought to himself that this was really getting to be unfortunate and tedious. He had come over to the Emergency Room early without getting lunch because the place was busy, and the doc on shift wanted him to help out before Ed's shift officially started. Now his colleague was gone, and Ed was hungry, he had a waiting room full of patients, two patients waiting for him to accompany them to the ICU – and this clown wanted him to step outside so he could rough him up because his wife had learned about his venereal disease.

Ed was getting angry but decided to follow his training and try to de-escalate.

"Look Mr. Malto, I know that you are upset. I understand what is making you concerned, but this is not the right way to deal with it. I can see you and Sharon first thing in the morning in my office to talk about this. But right now, I have an Emergency Room full of patients and I simply cannot leave the ER."

"I don't give a shit about them damn patients. I am going to drag your sorry ass into my car, and we are gonna talk about what I want you to say to my wife and when you are gonna say it." Tony then pulled his jacket aside to show Ed his nine millimeter handgun. This seemed to be the standard intimidation maneuver for hoods in Maple Ridge. Ed almost laughed at him seeing his buddy Tommy standing behind him at the door to the ER.

"Tony I am going back in to see some patients and I suggest that you get out of here before the cops arrive."

With that Ed turned abruptly to head into the emergency.

He heard Tony's growl and sensed the big man rushing to grab him. He even heard Tommy Lawsen advise, "Watch out Tony, he's fuckin' slippery," delivered in a hoarse whisper.

Ed's unarmed combat training made it reasonably straight-forward for him to step aside and take Tony from behind with a pretty good choke hold while he reached around and took the nine millimeter out of his belt.

He then spun him around, keeping Tony's substantial mass between him and Tony's posse while he simultaneously cranked Tony's neck tighter with his right arm, reached across to chamber a round and aimed Tony's gun at Tommy and the gang with his left hand.

Just then, the first police squad car pulled into the Emergency Room driveway. The police saw lots of guns drawn and immediately called for backup. Ed called out to them, "Officers, I am Dr. Brinkley and I have disarmed this man. I am going to put down this weapon as long as you guys take control of this scene and make sure these other guys surrender arms as well."

With the backup call they could hear sirens approaching the hospital from every direction and within minutes there were five more cars with lights flashing in the hospital driveway. Meanwhile Ed had laid down Tony's gun and released his death grip on his neck. Like Tommy, Tony was learning that messing with Dr. Ed could leave you hoarse for a few days.

A senior officer arrived shortly after the backup squad cars. Ed suggested that he needed to get back into the ER to see a few patients or someone might die because there was no other doctor in the department. Meanwhile, the nurses had paged Dr. Stanton who was usually available to help out for an hour or so if absolutely necessary.

Ed saw a few patients in the ER with police officers watching his every move until Stanton arrived.

"Apologies Bill, if you could spell me off for half an hour, I just need to settle something with these officers."

"Ed, for God's sake, what is going on here?"

Ed shook his head. "Hard to believe, but this guy named

Tony Malto wanted to drag me out of the ER and beat me up, I think. I just told him that was impossible because I had patients to see and then the cops arrived."

"How long have you been in town, Ed?"

"Ah, I think it's been about three months, Bill."

"I think you have caused more excitement for this little hospital in those three months than we have seen in the last ten years. You go and settle with the officers but get back as soon as you can. I have a meeting on discharge planning that I need to chair upstairs in thirty minutes."

"Thanks, Bill. I don't think I will hold you up too long."

Ed had already figured that it wouldn't do much good to lay charges against Tony with the officers. Ed told them that he and Tony had a disagreement about treatment that Ed was providing for his family and that he would let bygones be bygones. Tony for his part started saying that Ed had attacked him and choked him but some of the hospital staff who had been watching the whole scene started laughing at him and yelling that he had attacked the doctor. Tony recognized that his reputation would suffer if he laid charges claiming that an unarmed emergency doc disarmed and choked him.

The police were initially questioning Tony, Tommy, and the boys about their concealed weapons but Arkansas allowed concealed carry with a permit and the boys' permits were all in order. Bottom line, without Ed complaining that Tony had threatened and attacked him, and with Tony too embarrassed to lodge a complaint that Ed had choked him, there wasn't much for the police to do.

Ed got back inside within the promised half hour and took over from Bill Stanton, who walked away muttering about the unusual performance of his newest staff member. Ed finished his shift seeing a substantial number of patients, some of whom had watched him disarm Tony Malto as he charged the doc outside the ER waiting area. These patients were impressed by Ed's hand-to-hand combat skills and wanted to discuss the event, but Ed managed to keep going and empty the waiting room before his shift ended. He figured that the Maple Ridge grapevine would spread the story of him disarming Tony Malto across town by dinner time.

That evening his cell rang and Ed was delighted to see Linda's name on the screen. "Ed, are you okay? The whole town is talking about you and Tony Malto. What the heck happened?"

Ed chuckled. "Well, Ms. Davis, it seems that not everyone in your hometown is a fan of the great healthcare that I provide."

He continued. "Mr. Malto in particular, is one very dissatisfied customer at present. And it seems in Maple Ridge that when you don't like what the doctor is suggesting you show him your nine millimeter pistol. That has happened to me twice in a week now." Ed chuckled again at the goons he was meeting.

There was a long silence at Linda's end. "For someone who has been threatened twice in the last few days, you sound pretty chipper, Ed. Are you sure that you are all right? I've had some experience with the Malto family in the past and I think they can be dangerous."

"Fortunately for me the hoods in this town so far are more fearsome looking than they are well-trained. I am just fine but there is something that you can do for me if you are willing."

"What can I do, Ed?"

"I have been checking out the new boutique hotels in Hot Springs online and the silent auction item I bought covers one that sounds very inviting. We also get a round of golf and an afternoon in the spa. What do you say we drive up this Friday evening, play golf on Saturday morning, enjoy the spa after golf, have a great meal Saturday evening and tourist around on Sunday?"

Ed continued trying to convince her. "I've never been to Hot Springs. I know its short notice, but since you were assigned by Dr. Stanton to show me the benefits of this fine community, I feel like I can impose on you for a trip to the Springs."

"So, Doctor, are you advising me to take the waters at Hot

Springs for the good of my health?"

"Yeah, that's interesting, the healing waters of Hot Springs, right? That used to be quite a thing I guess, looking at the history of the town online. Well, watching me reacquaint myself with my golf game will not be a healing experience, so hopefully the waters will make up for it."

"Playing some golf and having a spa treat – how could I say no? Especially since you bought the weekend at the silent auction I invited you to. Let's do it."

Ed was thrilled. He had worried that she might have considered the invitation as coming on too strong, too soon. And now for the final touch that would make the weekend even more memorable.

"Just one more thing, Linda. I haven't found time to get a car yet. I could go out and rent something but that will be a major downgrade for you. I know it's pathetic, but can we take that beautiful German car you get driven around in?"

There was a pause and then sarcastic laughter on the other end of the line. "Oh, you really are a smoothie, Ed Brinkley. Take a girl out of town as long as you get her wheels, huh?"

"Yeah, I know. I sound like such a loser. But driving up to the Hot Springs behind the wheel of that car will be really special." The moment the words left his lips Ed realized how stupid he sounded, and Linda immediately took him to task.

"Oh, I see Dr. Brinkley, it won't be special driving with me unless you get to drive my hot wheels, huh? I am starting to understand why Tony Malto is angry with you – you are simply outrageous." Ed started to apologize but the laughter on her end of the line started again with less sarcasm.

"Linda, I can't think of you and Tony in the same thought. Thanks for agreeing to come – and thanks for agreeing to provide the ride! You won't believe how much I am looking forward to Friday night."

CHAPTER 15: THE BACK NINE

I t really was a good time for Ed to get out of town. He and Dr. Romulus had agreed that he needed to work on his leisure life. And the night after the event with Tony Malto at the hospital, Ed had a nightmare that frightened him. That night terror reminded him of how much he had suffered over the past two years, and he was determined that he wasn't about to relapse. He knew Romulus would tell him that normal relaxation like getting back to golf would be good for his mental health, as would visiting a new place like Hot Springs.

Located to the west of Maple Ridge in the Ouachita Mountains, Hot Springs has been known for its geothermal spring water since the earliest records were kept in Arkansas. Checking out Hot Springs online, Ed learned that in the past people came from across America to bathe in the springs that were thought to have healing qualities.

The springs are the site of the oldest federal reserve lands in America, now recognized as Hot Springs National Park. The Park also preserves the original eight bathhouses that welcomed guests, including the gangster Al Capone, to the springs during the early twentieth century. As Americans became more sophisticated about healthcare, the bathhouses lost their healing attraction. But now some of them had been renovated and refurbished as boutique hotels.

And that was where Ed and Linda were headed, to a smaller hotel with forty suites, which was newly redeveloped at the periphery of the park. The hotel had access to geothermal water that served as the centerpiece for what they advertised as a "sophisticated European spa experience." Hot Springs was also known for its great golf courses and Ed had reserved a tee time for Saturday morning.

Linda picked Ed up at the clinic on Friday afternoon behind the wheel of her German sedan as promised. Linda was surprised that Ed did not have clubs and was planning to rent. This man didn't seem to own anything! Her golf bag was loaded in the trunk. As he prepared to climb in the passenger seat, Linda took Ed's arm. "Ed, I have had such a week. I could use a little snooze on the way to the Springs. Would you mind driving?"

Ed was delighted to drive her high-performance vehicle and Linda did indeed sleep all the eighty miles up the highway to Hot Springs. She woke just as they were pulling in and was pleased with the property Ed had reserved. They had adjoining rooms in the smaller hotel that had been rebuilt keeping the art deco style of the original bathhouse. After a light dinner and a nightcap they both collapsed with alarms set for their golf game.

The next morning, they met at breakfast. Linda looked terrific in a short golf skirt and a sleeveless top. She was fully recovered from the rigors of the past week and ready to golf.

And Ed discovered just how well she could golf. He hadn't played in a long time but found his game slowly coming back. Ed was longer than Linda off the tee, but she was straight down the fairway while he was spraying balls all over the course. At the turn she was six strokes ahead of Ed. Her game was conservative, and she made very few mistakes. Her drives were always in play and her short game and putting were proficient.

On the back nine Ed began to remember how to play the game and started to find the fairway. But his iron play and putting remained erratic. On the eighteenth green she was up one stroke and had a twelve-footer for a par, which she casually drained.

After a big drive and a decent approach, Ed was on in two

and had a ten-foot putt for a birdie. To his amazement, he read the green right for the first time of the day and rolled in the birdie putt to tie Linda.

Instead of shaking his hand to congratulate Ed on the putt, Linda hugged and kissed him. The hug went on and he could feel her body melting a bit. "Nice putt," she mouthed with her lips still close to his. "Your game looked great on the back nine."

Ed softly pulled her closer and told her that her game could not look better. She smiled and they walked up the hill to the clubhouse where they realized that they needed to get back to the hotel for their spa appointment.

CHAPTER 16: GEOTHERMAL WATERS

B efore they'd left for the course that morning, Linda had checked in with the spa and ensured that they had a private, "romantic" spa booking meant for couples. She realized that she was considering being less than decorous. She was troubled about how little she knew about Ed but was also excited by this man and wanted to see what she would learn about him this weekend. She decided that since they were out of town, some unrestrained behaviour would be permissible.

As she thought about the day ahead Linda's shoulders lifted, and she smiled to herself. This might just be a weekend fling, but what the heck, she hadn't had a fling in some time and maybe she could use one. She decided that she would not worry about being a bit shameless this weekend. After all, he had arranged the spa package that they were going to enjoy.

As they came down to the spa dressing room, an attractive young woman told them that she would be their hostess, handing them plush bathrobes and directing the couple to the change rooms. Ed and Linda were still in their golf gear, so it was a pleasure to take a steamy shower and return to the spa area wearing their gowns.

Their hostess was allowing geothermal water to rush into a large, two-person tub. As they prepared to enter the tub, she handed them wrap-around towels and told them that they would need to ease into the water gradually because it was extremely warm.

Linda decided that this was the moment to throw caution to

the wind. She turned away from Ed, dropped her robe and took time wrapping the towel around her.

As she turned back Ed had also dropped his robe and was wrapping the towel around his waist. Looking discreetly, Linda smiled to herself.

They then descended into the ceramic tub and initially sat on the upper level as the hostess had suggested. They had walked the course that morning and it was wonderful to let their legs relax and loosen in the geothermal liquid warmth. Linda had noticed Ed's limp increasing throughout the day and she was sure this treatment was just what the doctor needed.

And then they removed their towels and sank into the pool completely. About fifteen minutes was all they could take in the geothermal water. The hostess directed them to reapply their towels to lie on the massage table for a rough sponge massage. She and another young lady who joined them rubbed them down with soapy sponges and then sprayed them off with cool water that was wonderfully refreshing.

They then returned into a fresh hot tub for another soak to recover from the cool spray. By now they were reasonably comfortable with the mutual nakedness that was part of the "romantic" couple's spa treatment. Finally, they returned to different tables where the spa hostesses provided massages with various fragrant oils.

After two hours of this pampering they were both rejuvenated. They stepped in the spa elevator to return to their rooms in fresh bathrobes and slippers. The hostesses promised that they would arrange laundering and return of their golfing gear.

After the togetherness, it felt strange to enter separate rooms. Ed and Linda agreed that they would rest for an hour or so before going down to dinner. However, on entering her room, Linda decided that the last thing she needed was rest.

Thinking nothing ventured, nothing gained, she opened her side of the adjoining portal between their rooms and knocked on Ed's door. "Ed, there is something I need to ask you," she called through the door. He immediately opened his side. Looking down shyly, she asked him, "Is it all right if I come in?"

Their two slender bodies came together as their bathrobes dropped to the floor. He lifted her, she wrapped around him, and he began slowly, rhythmically rocking.

And then laid her carefully on the bed. As he began moving faster, she joined him and suddenly they were lying quietly on the comforter looking at each other, their faces inches apart.

His eyes were twinkling. "Linda, if this is what I get when I tie you on the 18th green, what do I get when I beat you?".

And then he started tickling Linda. As the managing partner of the biggest law firm in Arkansas, no one had tickled Linda in a long time. She started to remonstrate and that made him just tickle more.

And then they both started giggling and couldn't stop. And then she could feel him again and then they couldn't stop that either.

CHAPTER 17: HOT SPRINGS

Ed had never spent a time like he and Linda enjoyed in Hot Springs. As Saturday evening arrived, they forced themselves out of the covers and went down to the hotel dining room where they had dinner reservations.

The hotel was known for its dining room and Ed and Linda were ravenous after a relatively foodless day. Their waiter seemed to understand that their relationship was at a formative, delicate stage. He appeared when they needed his attention but generally left them alone in their private space. Although Ed knew that he had enjoyed the meal, later he could not remember what he ate. But he was very aware of sitting close to a captivating woman.

Ed understood that Maple Ridge needed to be a new start for him. He had assumed this new beginning could result in new relationships and possibly eventually a partner. But now he found himself bewitched by his intriguing dinner companion.

Having shared martinis and a bottle of Bordeaux with dinner, they returned to Ed's room a bit unsteady. Linda was leaning on Ed, and he relished supporting her. And when they arrived at the room, he continued learning about Linda.

The next morning, they woke entwined, welcoming the sun together. Thereafter they both needed food and wolfed down generous breakfasts. Dressed casually, they spent the day wandering around the historic bathhouses on a beautiful warm Hot Springs day. The National Park sustained a well-preserved record of the days when Hot Springs was an important spot in the life of the nation.

The unusual nature of this venue provided a somehow fitting backdrop for their developing closeness. The unique emotions they were both feeling seemed in keeping with this distinctive setting.

They learned about Al Capone and other gangsters enjoying the Hot Springs, discovered the role of the resort in baseball spring training and enjoyed the elaborate architecture of the restored bathhouses. Following its time in the spotlight, Hot Springs had fallen into a period of seediness and decline, but recent investments had restored its character as a center for geothermal tourism.

As they wandered slowly about the various historical exhibits, Linda and Ed shared attentive glances. They were moving gingerly, each knowing with some circumspection that they might be spinning a chrysalis of new intimacy. They were seeing Hot Springs through mutual eyes, and it was pleasant to experience this unique setting together. Linda's hands remained on Ed, holding his hands, his arms and allowing him to keep his arm around her shoulders and her waist.

In short, the day was magic. The time passed without notice.

They had agreed that they would drive back to Maple Ridge in the afternoon and Linda apologized again that she would need to meet with her team at the office at six p.m. Her class action suit in Baltimore was starting soon and her team and the Maryland litigators had been engaged in a videoconference most of Saturday and Sunday. Linda wanted to review the results of their discussions before the work week began and she was planning to meet with her team that evening.

Listening to music in the car, they chatted easily about everything and nothing on the drive home. Each felt a sense of comfort in the other's presence. After this very passionate weekend, there was no sense of regret and nothing but warm proximity.

And then they were back in Maple Ridge. Linda dropped Ed at his apartment and came around to hug him as he left the car. Her body softened against his and he could feel the passion that he had enjoyed the past two days. They separated slowly and carefully, feeling the loss as they drew apart.

Ed watched Linda's car pull away and slowly turned to enter his apartment building. But his phone rang, interrupting his progress up the stairs. It was the ICU calling.

CHAPTER 18: THE BLACK HOLE

"**D**r. Brinkley, we want to let you know that your patient Sharon Malto was admitted on Saturday. She was involved in a car accident and suffered broken ribs and a ruptured spleen. Her spleen was removed in surgery just after she was admitted. She is doing okay now post-op, but she wanted us to let you know that she is here."

Ed thanked the caller, dropped his gear and walked to the hospital to see Sharon. She was awake in the ICU, but her face was swollen, and she was clearly in pain. Tommy and a couple of Tony's guys were in the ICU waiting room and tried to stop Ed as he went in to see Sharon, but Ed walked past them without comment.

"Sharon, what the hell happened?"

Sharon motioned him closer to the head of her bed. "You know what happened, Doc. I accused Tony about giving me the clap and I scratched his face. He hit me a couple of times, but I was okay. I thought about it for a while and then we had another fight. He hit me again and then I decided that I needed to leave. I just grabbed a coat and ran down to my car.

"I could hear Tony screaming as I left that he was going to kill me." She paused, remembering what happened next.

"I was driving my little sedan when his Suburban hit my car on the driver's side, and I was smashed by the impact. I remember the airbag exploding into my abdomen. The next thing that I remember was waking up in the hospital ER and being told that I needed surgery to take out my spleen or something."

Ed squeezed Sharon's hand and told her that she was safe

now. She looked at him ironically through the facial swelling that had resulted from Tony's punches as well as the accident. "How am I ever going to be safe from him, Doc? He is gonna get to me wherever I go."

Ed got up and checked her chart. She was stable and ready to move from the ICU to the ward tomorrow. But he knew that her current medical condition was not the most pressing issue. Her husband's brutality was terrifying. He promised that he would be back to talk further with her tomorrow.

Tony's thugs were gone as Ed left the ICU. He checked on two other patients and walked down the stairs from the wards to exit the hospital. Ed was crossing the parking lot on the way home when suddenly two Suburbans blocked his progress. Tony Malto, Tommy Lawsen, and several other guys jumped out of the vehicles to surround him.

Tommy and the other boys did not have their guns in their belts. Their guns were drawn and aimed at Ed. Tony approached him with a large knife in his hand.

"Doc, you been visitin' Sharon, my wife. I don't want you seeing her no more, you bastard."

"Tony, she is my patient. That is not for you to say. Until she tells me different, I will remain her doctor."

That statement inflamed Tony and he held the knife to Ed's belly and punched him full in his face. Ed's training kicked in and he rotated his head quickly lessening the impact of the blow, but he knew that he would have a nasty bruise. The force of the punch dropped Ed to the pavement, and he went in cover-up mode but not before Tony had kicked him in the belly and tried to kick him in the head.

Ed's defensive training was fully operative. He protected his head and yelled loudly, calling for help and the police. His yelling unnerved Tony as lights went on all over the hospital and the parking lot. And Ed was a difficult target to kick while lying on the ground, rolling, and twisting. Tony tried kicking Ed again in the head, but the doctor pivoted away.

As voices came out of the hospital in response to Ed's shouting, Tony jumped back in his SUV, apparently satisfied with the damage he had already caused. Ed thought that Tony was going to run him over and he prepared to roll quickly, but Tony backed up and stopped beside Ed, lowering his window, "If you ever see her again, you are a dead man."

The Suburbans drove off and Ed assessed his injuries while he struggled to get to his feet.

His bad leg had not sustained further trauma. His cheek was sore, but he could feel that the facial bone was unbroken. He could move his jaw. It was tender, but the mandible felt intact.

However, something else felt damaged. Ed could feel a familiar deep black hole of failure and despair reopening inside him. The hole that had been patched and repaired and closed with so many months of focused work with Dr. Romulus – that hole was now suddenly gaping open and was again brimming with fear and hopelessness. Like when Ed had failed to save the lives of those men on the battlefield, he knew now that he would not be able to help Sharon.

Back then the forces and injuries challenging him on the battlefield were insurmountable, and now, Tony and his gang were overwhelming him with their power and brutality. Who did he think he was, trying to protect Sharon from Tony's aggression? Ed had seen his connection with the local police who all knew Tony. Tony had lived in Maple Ridge his entire life. Ed was a newcomer. Tony could eliminate him without a trace, and the local police would just look away.

As he struggled to stand in the parking lot, the darkness spread out from that black hole and started to control his thoughts and emotions, turning his feelings towards weakness, dread, and disappointment. It had taken him so long to control this before, to keep that darkness from dominating him. And now the despair was being recalled by Tony's violence.

Ed started moving slowly toward home and considered getting a cab or asking for a ride from hospital security. However, it did not hurt much to walk, and he turned toward his apartment, wandering slowly and aimlessly with his head and heart filled with fatigue and despondency. His attempt at starting over in Maple Ridge was clearly a failure. He started to think about just quitting and leaving his practice. How could he look after his patient with this hoodlum of a husband threatening him?

It was the weekend with Linda that started to save him from himself that night – the connection they had enjoyed for their two days together. The understanding that he was not alone – that he could feel the start of something intimate with Linda.

As Ed walked, he remembered the work that Dr. Romulus had done with him, recognizing that a single individual alone can be powerless. Ed recalled Dr. Romulus teaching him to understand his innate, self-defeating tendency to judge himself a failure if he could not right wrongs or save lives single-handed.

As he was laying on the parking lot after Tony's beating, that helpless emotion of failure associated with combat and battle-field fatalities had been retriggered.

"What a weekend." He heard himself speaking with a deep sigh to an absent audience as he walked. The wonderful weekend with Linda and then this attack from Tony. And he now fully understood the risk that Tony represented – both physically and to his carefully regained emotional balance. Linda had been right. He had underestimated this guy.

It had taken so much time and energy to put those black thoughts of failure behind him. He could feel himself balanced uncertainly on the knife edge of despair that he knew could overwhelm him if he slipped. And Ed remembered Dr. Romulus's lesson that there might be very little that he could do – either to protect Sharon from her husband or to protect himself from his feelings– while depending only on his own capabilities.

Somehow, the potential for a deep connection with Linda made him feel healthier. He did not want this to be a passing relationship; he sensed that she could bring him deeper in touch with a world that he longed to live in without compromise. It had only been two days, but he knew that there was both excitement and peace in her presence. He recognized that she was a strong and independent woman. But he also knew that he could support and respect her strength.

Having discovered Linda, this was not the time to be run out of town by Tony Malto. Nor could Ed allow Tony to continue to trigger the feelings that he had worked so long and hard to master. But who could he trust to help? He had seen the relationship Tony Malto had with the local cops. He knew that bringing assault charges against Tony with the county police was not going to protect him or his patient.

Slowly Ed remembered the lessons that he had learned from Dr. Romulus and started to realize how he could respond to Tony. He recalled that asking for help was never weakness and that his intrinsic tendency was to underestimate the willingness people had to work with him. Those remembered lessons slowly started to fill the hole. And he thought of Linda.

By the time Ed reached his small apartment, the darkness was still present, but he had the start of a plan. He called Bill Stanton to get the number of a commercial real estate broker that Bill had introduced him to. After quickly coming to agreement with the broker, his next longer call was to New York City.

Then, approaching ten p.m., Ed called retired Master Sergeant Brooke Paltrig. He was pleased and relieved that she seemed delighted to speak with him despite the lateness of the hour. Their conversation went on well past midnight and when he hung up, Ed was feeling more hopeful about his new home in Maple Ridge.

CHAPTER 19: SUNDAY
NIGHT AT THE OFFICE

D riving away from Ed on Sunday evening, Linda needed to restore her professional veneer as she headed back to the office to meet with her team. Hot Springs had been more disconcerting than the weekend fling she had expected. Returning to the firm brought Linda back to a secure place where she could expect to control the situation.

The haven afforded by her professional persona was required after this weekend. She was very unsettled by Dr. Ed Brinkley. Unsettled, at sea, and vulnerable. She knew that she might be hurt by her developing feelings for this man, but she also felt his decency. Even though it was early in their relationship, she thought that she might be able to give her heart to this man. She felt that he would treat it gently.

This was an unusual, troubling yet at the same time exhilarating feeling for Linda.

In the past, she had experienced ups and downs with men. With her mother passing away so young, Linda had no woman close to her to provide counsel, and through high school and college she developed a deserved reputation as a very social girl. It seemed so natural. She liked good-looking men and they liked her.

And she often fell for the guys who took pretty girls for granted. While she was an undergrad, it was the athletes and big names on campus who were accustomed to being pursued. And then in law school, the powerful and wealthy young lawyers and businessmen who enjoyed counselling attractive students about the career opportunities they could provide.

When she returned to the Ridge, she became more careful in her relationships, although it was not unusual for men to visit her or for Linda to occasionally leave town. Her dad covered for her. He cared for his daughter deeply and recognized that she could be independent. He hoped that Linda would settle down eventually and had accepted that she was going to be a bit of a worry to him in the meantime.

After her father's death, Linda's working world came into sudden focus. For four years she gave every moment to stabilizing the firm, convincing her dad's clients that she could look after them and then learning what they needed from her. Her social life evaporated. She rebuffed any and all overtures because she could not concentrate on anything but her practice. Most of her clients were local and Linda needed them to know that they had a serious and capable lawyer.

After the first successful class action case, she started to become known outside of Maple Ridge and outside Arkansas. As Linda resurfaced socially, she had reason to be grateful for her genes. Despite her intense work schedule, her blonde hair did not require trips to a colorist and her face remained wrinkle free despite long summers in the sun. Linda had always enjoyed sport and had maintained her workout habit, even when impossibly busy. Heads turned when Linda walked into a room. As she became well known and well off, men quickly made their way back into her life.

Linda had come close to a committed relationship on two occasions. But the last man wanted her to move to Spain where he was running a large public company. The man before him was a hedge fund operator in New York who could not see running his business from Arkansas. In the last year Linda had been dating a lawyer from Chicago but both of them had agreed several months ago that their relationship had probably progressed about as far as it was likely to go.

Linda realized that all these men had difficulty with her success and independence. They all wanted her to leave Maple

Ridge and could not understand what her home meant to her or what she was building here. But Ed seemed to understand and appreciate what she was doing.

When Dr. Ed Brinkley walked into her life at that charity luncheon, Linda had been starting to think that perhaps the life of a career woman without a family would suit her best. She had plenty of experience with men and none of them had thrilled her as a potential lifelong partner. Maybe she would best find fulfillment in the growth of the Davis firm which was thriving and changing Maple Ridge. The people at the Davis firm were like family, and watching the practice and her employees develop was important and satisfying for her.

But spending the weekend with Ed had ignited some new emotions. He fascinated her. His quiet depth and the fact that he had committed his life to caring for others, so different from her business world, was intriguing. And, unlike most of the powerful men who naturally attracted Linda, he seemed more interested in learning about her rather than telling her about himself.

His unusual arrival in Maple Ridge and his reluctance to describe how he got here bothered her. He must have experienced combat overseas that he was loathe to discuss. Perhaps that was common in returning soldiers, but it made her uneasy. How could she put her trust in someone who was so unwilling to talk about his experiences? That was part of what troubled her as she arrived at her office.

But he did attract Linda. She had a natural affinity for athletes, and Ed was lean as a whip and moved with grace despite his limp. His golf game was promising, and she would expect to enjoy golfing with him. She found his crinkly blue eyes and the graying at his temples irresistible.

And their weekend together was different in another way. He cared for her in bed. She felt his passion but also his friendship and his concern for her well-being.

In short, he was very disturbing.

With the good doctor firmly lodged in her mind Linda

parked at the office to join her team and discuss progress made with the Maryland litigators. The Sunday evening session stretched into early Monday morning, and Linda was grateful for the distraction.

CHAPTER 20: HQ

Sunday night, retired Master Sergeant Brooke Paltrig had been delighted to hear from Colonel Ed Brinkley even though the call had been unexpected, late in the evening and very unusual. It was however good timing for her. She had been out of the military for six months and had started up a cybersecurity consultancy with a couple of friends from the service.

When Colonel Ed called to ask what she was doing, Brooke told him about her new consulting work in cybersecurity and he responded immediately, "Perfect, we will hire you as a consultant for this project." Brooke's start-up had invested heavily in new hires and business development and a secure consulting gig like the Colonel offered was just what her fledgling company needed.

On that Sunday call, they spent considerable time discussing what she would require, and Brooke remembered that the Colonel knew how to listen carefully and then push her with his questions. It reminded her of why she loved working with the guy. He expected a lot from you, but then he ultimately trusted you to do your job. And, important for her new business, the terms he offered at the end of the call were extremely generous.

On arrival in Maple Ridge the next day, Brooke was impressed that Colonel Ed (or his organization – this was unclear, but he seemed to have some very deep pockets supporting him) had rented a large, vacant warehouse in an industrial mall about half a mile from his hospital. The Colonel told her that a commercial broker would meet her in the morning, and sure enough the broker had arrived in the mall parking lot just before Brooke. The broker provided her with keys to the space and told her that the Colonel's company had already taken care of the lease and the rent in advance. Brooke was puzzled by that. The Colonel had not mentioned a company being involved.

The Colonel had asked Brooke to source the IT and surveillance equipment that she would need for the task at hand, and she had emailed a list of the technology to an address he provided. He also instructed her to pick up a credit card that he would arrange to be left at a national bank branch on her way to Maple Ridge Monday morning.

The card was registered to Brinkley Enterprises and provided virtually unlimited credit. Brooke was also given a New York phone number that was answered by a very helpful woman who had received her email and promised that the gear that Brooke needed would be delivered to the warehouse by express courier Monday afternoon. When Brooke asked the woman who she was working for, the New Yorker sounded surprised.

"Mr. Brinkley of course." That piqued Brooke's curiosity because she did not know that Colonel Ed had a business in New York. "Are you referring to Colonel Ed Brinkley?" she asked.

"No, Mr. Benjamin Brinkley, CEO of Brinkley Enterprises. I believe the Colonel is his brother. I run all IT and technical services at Brinkley Enterprises and Benjamin told me that getting your project set up immediately is our top priority. I received the emailed description of the technology you need, and we have organized the first courier delivery later this afternoon." By Tuesday morning Brooke was extremely well equipped for the work the Colonel had assigned her.

Stephen yelled down from a small attic in the warehouse. After the Colonel's phone call Sunday night, Brooke had contacted Stephen early Monday morning on her way to Maple Ridge. Like Brooke, Stephen had recently left the Special Forces to join a consulting company focused on personal and corporate security. His business also responded quickly when offered the kind of money that the Colonel was paying. The two days were a whirlwind. Both Stephen and Brooke had worked through Monday night getting the project established.

Stephen sounded satisfied. "Brooke, the exterior security is all set. We have perimeter surveillance at the property limit as well as the parking lot, the roof and at the door. I am very comfortable that we can defend this site. I have sourced some ordnance, and more is on order. We should have it in the next forty-eight hours. And the Colonel is approaching the door."

Stephen was like a brother to Brooke. He had initially hit on her when he joined their team in Afghanistan. By that time Brooke had become expert in the art of gentle turn downs and she and Stephen became close friends. She was pleased when he joined the security consultancy in the Midwest after leaving the service and the two kept closely in touch.

Brooke checked the screens and sure enough the Colonel was walking up the drive approaching the door. She went to the entrance and welcomed the Colonel with a big hug.

"Colonel, it is so good to see you. Come on in and check out your new HQ."

Her immediate impression seeing him up close was that, despite a bruise on his face, the Colonel seemed much more serene than the last time she had seen him. Their team had taken bad losses in Helmand on their last mission together, and Brooke knew that the Colonel had felt personally responsible for two soldiers' deaths.

The last time she had seen him was about a year ago. At that time, she knew that he was in treatment, but he was looking very worn, with the weight of the world on his shoulders. Now he seemed five years younger.

It was a pretty big bruise on his cheek. But those brilliant blue eyes hadn't changed. It looked like he was enjoying whatever he was up to in this small town.

"You're looking good, Colonel," Brooke said, "except for that bruise. I guess that's why we're here, huh? We're getting all set up."

The Colonel looked over at Stephen as he entered the room. "It's been a while Stephen. Thanks for coming so quickly." Stephen came over and started to shake Ed's hand and then changed the greeting to a close hug.

"Colonel, I've been managing a security consultancy since I left the service. When Brooke called, I dropped everything else to come immediately. The rates that you are offering are much better than we are used to charging. In fact, Colonel, you are probably overpaying us. However, if you are offering it, my company is happy to accept, and you certainly got our immediate attention."

Then Stephen looked at the floor and his voice changed. "You know what I owe you, Colonel. I can never repay what you did for me. Any time you ever need anything, you can count on me."

The Colonel shook his head slowly from side to side. "Stephen, I may be paying too much, but you will learn that this gig may put you in harm's way. I want to be sure that I am offering fair compensation."

Ed turned back to Brooke. He remembered his surprise at their first meeting in Helmand province when she joined their unit. Brooke was willowy tall with soft, light brown hair, defined cheekbones, and striking eyes. You could more readily imagine her on a fashion runway than a Special Forces base in the desert.

But Brooke's talent in remote surveillance and her ability to hack through encrypted signaling became immediately evident as the team pursued their mission in Helmand. After their first two operations, Brooke was accepted as an essential team member by some of the world's toughest warriors. Virtually every soldier in the unit had hit on Brooke, but she readily resisted all advances with aplomb while maintaining her colleagues' dignity and friendship.

And now Ed planned to use her surveillance talents in responding to Tony Malto. "Brooke, you know from what we discussed Sunday and Monday nights that we want to find out everything we can about Tony Malto's operations. Do you also have the means to evaluate what law enforcement thinks about Tony and his gang?"

Brooke looked at him carefully. "I am going to assume that everything we discuss here is entirely confidential, Colonel." He nodded and she continued.

"Before I answer your question about law enforcement, let me say that since I left the force I have been working on the other side of the firewall, trying to keep people out. As you know, cybersecurity is a huge priority for corporate America right now. Cyberattacks that you have read about in the press can destroy corporate value within hours." She shook her head at the risk cybercrime represented to the nation's business.

"There is no one better at defending against hackers than hackers themselves. My partners and I have invested in building up our hacking team, recruiting from the military as well as finding young civilians. We have set up a Red Team hacking resource to test corporate cybersecurity by trying to invade it. Our start-up has been costly and to be honest, your generous offer to work with you here in Maple Ridge comes at a very good time for our new company."

She smiled thinking about the team she had set up. "You'll remember from our Afghan experience that I am pretty good at hacking, but these young kids have taught me a few new tricks. Of course, I have taught them a few things too."

She grinned again, thinking about the challenge of managing the Red Team. Hackers were notoriously competitive, and the guys Brooke had hired (to this point they were all male) were no exception. She needed to rotate membership on the teams working against each other to break into potential clients' systems to prevent permanent rifts from developing in the workplace.

"It's nice to be back using my skills against bad guys again like we did in Helmand. We all learned the power of hacking the Taliban cell and internet networks when we were in Afghanistan. I'm looking forward to using everything we learned overseas against some plain old gangsters here in the homeland."

Brooke enjoyed the uncomplicated objective of working for the good guys. Convincing corporate leaders that they needed her services by breaking through their cybersecurity was an important sales tactic for her new company. The ethical simplicity of helping Colonel Ed was appealing.

"Colonel, with your brother's company's help, we have put in some impressive spyware, and we have extremely good high-speed connection that is untraceable. I am always impressed by the degree of anonymity you can achieve when you have unlimited funds. And that credit card your brother established is just about unlimited."

The Colonel smiled. "Brooke, you are going to meet Benjamin soon. My brother runs our family business and this project has top priority for him."

"Well Colonel, it makes things easier to have the kind of financial backing that you have made available to us. In answering your question, it has allowed me to get into the local police records on this guy Malto." She picked up a couple of files that were already growing with hard copy from her investigations.

"It's interesting. The local police have quite a bit of information on Malto at a superficial level, but they often seem to give him a free ride. Occasional rough stuff where the assault charge is not laid, some suggestive stuff around drug dealing that is ignored. Quite a bit of low-level street stuff, but no really deep investigation into his gang has been initiated. They really seem to largely ignore him." It had been straightforward for her to get access to the local police files on Tony.

"The local police records certainly draw a picture of what Tony's gang may be up to Colonel. And I think that you are right in the suspicions that you mentioned Sunday night. The gang is suspected of dealing drugs and women, and of human trafficking, but nothing has really stuck to them so far. Despite indications that Malto is operating in a number of criminal activities, there seems to be very little if any real detective work investigating him. Either the local cops are blind, or stupid, or maybe they are giving Tony Malto a break for some reason."

Brooke already had suspicions that Tony might have some local protection in the police force. However, she had no idea what they would later discover about the extent of Tony's influence with the county police.

"Colonel, I have a lot more work to do but I am very comfortable that we are going to be able to gather a lot of information on Malto's activities. His guys are very lax with their management of passwords and keeping accounts protected. Surprisingly, they have very complete financial spreadsheets with regular daily entries that I accessed today. I also managed to hack into some of their businesses that really seem quite legitimate. It looks like Tony is a real authentic businessman as well as running criminal stuff."

Brooke had not expected what she was finding from hacking Tony's various online accounts. From her initial review of his records and public documents, it seemed that Malto owned a number of legitimate businesses across the state. "He has dry cleaners, laundromats, vending machines, diners, strip clubs, bars and car washes that I discovered late this afternoon from state corporate records. I was able to get into their accounts and it seems that they have enormous revenues for each of the businesses but also really high expenses as well. I am glad that you have Klaus coming to help me understand their accounting."

Brooke had been able to access Tony's numbers, but she knew that her accountant buddy Klaus was a genius at understanding what the numbers meant. Working together they would probably be able to figure out most of Tony's business records. The Colonel had approved getting Klaus as a consultant with the same very attractive compensation that had enabled Brooke and Stephen to arrive so quickly.

The pattern that Brooke was identifying was that Tony served as the middleman for a lot of illicit activity. She could trace money coming into Tony from what seemed to be prostitution, drugs, and other illicit activity. Some money would then be transferred back with a large cut remaining with Tony.

"You know Colonel, the one thing we should be thinking about with all Tony Malto's activities is whether he could be investigated and charged under RICO. He seems to be operating a criminal enterprise and that is what RICO is intended to combat."

The Colonel looked at her intently. "I have heard of RICO but to be honest I don't really know what it means. Can you elaborate?"

Brooke had not remembered just how blue his eyes were. "Sure, Colonel. RICO stands for the pretty dramatic title of Racketeer Influenced and Corrupt Organization Act and is meant to be used against gangsters who may violate any two of about forty state and federal offenses. Now I am not a prosecutor or a cop, but from what I understand and have read, the impact of RICO is that prosecutors achieve more power to bring charges against criminal organizations. And they can also freeze assets thought to be associated with the criminal activity."

Next came the important part about what Brooke was beginning to suspect about Tony's businesses. "This is especially important when gangsters are making use of legitimate cash businesses to launder proceeds of crime. RICO gives law enforcement the ability to investigate and close down those businesses even if the business is not directly engaged in criminal works. Prosecutors have used RICO very successfully to break up motorcycle gangs dealing drugs, as well as New York Mafia families, by identifying money laundering."

Brooke would need lots of accounting help from Klaus to make sense of the databases and records that she was uncovering but she was starting to suspect that dirty money was being washed clean in Tony's laundromats.

The Colonel was nodding his head in appreciation of what Brooke was telling him. "Brooke, my goal is to gain as much information as we can about the Malto gang, realizing that much of what we gather may not be useful for prosecutors because of the way we are accessing data. However, if Tony's security is not that sophisticated, it's possible that we will discover something that we legitimately can pass along for law enforcement to use."

Stephen had been quietly following their conversation. "Colonel, why are we focused on this guy Tony Malto? I am sure that there is no shortage of criminals who are operating in this region of Arkansas. What makes this Tony guy so special?"

Colonel Ed rubbed his bruised cheek carefully. "Yeah, good question, Stephen. I am here to practice medicine, not law enforcement. But Tony has made this personal. He and his guys have threatened me twice and have beaten me up once. Three times is enemy action that deserves an appropriate response. And I really don't think that I can rely on the county police for that response."

That was all the explanation that Stephen and Brooke needed. The Colonel was not the kind of guy that you should try to intimidate. They had seen his capability in action. He continued. "I like this town and I am really enjoying my medical practice here. However, I think that my conflict with Tony will eventually make it difficult for me to stay here. As you guys know, we are trained to act on this kind of tactical issue before it becomes a crisis. That's why I have asked for your help."

Ed turned to Brooke's colleague. "Stephen, tell me about our physical security team."

Stephen nodded. "Brooke and I discussed this at length and think that we should start with a team of about seven people including Brooke and myself. We understand that the Malto gang is bigger than that, but of course we have the advantage of our training and surprise. We are going to start by emphasizing protection for you."

Ed had worked with all the people that Stephen went on to name and knew how well-trained they were. If they were going to be involved in rough stuff, each of Stephen's team would equal four of the Malto gang – especially with the military kit that Stephen was sourcing.

Stephen continued. "Colonel, you will remember Bill from Helmand. Bill is here in the building testing perimeter security right now. He also brought the secure vehicle you requested from his firm on rental for as long as you need it along with the hybrid vehicles for the team.

"The rest of the team also worked with us in Helmand. Robert is in town with Frank and will be here tomorrow morning. They both left the force six months ago and have been doing private security work. They were delighted when I called them with your request, especially when they heard what you are paying. Henry and David are still instructing in basic training, but they are owed lots of vacation and will be here late tomorrow." Stephen smiled at Ed. "And you know how dedicated David is to you, Colonel." He gently punched the Colonel in the shoulder.

"It's a small team, Colonel Ed, but you've seen what we can do in combat. And I am assuming that Master Sergeant Brooke here will support us if needed." He paused.

"Believe me Colonel, everyone is very pleased to be back under your command."

CHAPTER 21: COUNTERATTACK

After his initial check on the preparations that Brooke and Stephen were undertaking in developing his new HQ, Ed went back to the hospital to see the clinic's patients. He left Sharon Malto until last. She was out of the ICU and had been transferred to a private room on the surgery floor. As Ed approached her room, he could see Tommy Lawsen and his friend Billy sitting in the hallway outside her room.

As Ed approached Tommy stood up and said, "Tony don't want you coming in here, Doc. You know what he told you Sunday night."

The doctor smiled at him. "Well, I am Sharon's responsible doctor, so unless she wants someone new, I am going to see her."

He stuck his head past Tommy and smiled at Sharon in her hospital bed. "Sharon, are you firing me as your doctor?"

"Hell no, c'mon in, Doc."

Ed closed the door behind him and could hear Tommy calling his boss. He checked over Sharon's abdominal wound that had resulted from her spleen removal. She had also broken a couple of ribs on the right side where she hit the car console, but he knew these would be fine. From a medical perspective she was doing well. But she definitely needed help with her domestic situation.

Of course, Ed knew that everything would depend on what she wanted to do. So many abused women decide that they would not leave their husbands and Sharon's choice was much more difficult given Tony's history of violence.

"Sharon, you are going to need to think about what you do with Tony Junior and yourself. Are you still thinking of staying with Tony, or are you ready to make a break?"

"Jeez Doc, after everything that happened the last few days, I know that I should leave Tony and take Tony Junior with me. That's what I want to do, but I just don't know if Tony is going to let me go." She looked frightened.

Ed put his hand on her arm. "Sharon, if you want to get away, I think that we need to start making arrangements for legal advice. It may not seem like the perfect time now, but I have a feeling that things may change in the next week or so."

"Doc, I don't think that any lawyer is going to want to help me. They are going to be scared about pissing off Tony. You know that he can be a real problem."

She looked closely at Ed's cheek. "Did you get that from Tony?"

"Yeah, but not to worry Sharon. I will find you a lawyer. And we are going to get you some protection from Tony."

Ed texted Stephen and Brooke and described what security would be necessary outside the hospital and for Sharon. He also explained the terms of engagement that they would need to follow given that this was a civilian security operation as opposed to a military mission.

He next called Linda on her private cell from Sharon's room.

"Oh, Ed, nice of you to call." Her tone echoed with sarcasm. Ed immediately realized that he should have called her yesterday morning. But, between being beaten up by Tony's gang on Sunday and getting Brooke and Stephen to town, and other arrangements being made along with running his clinic, he had just been seriously busy. He decided that the best course was to be honest with what he was doing, even if it risked worrying Linda.

"I apologize for not calling yesterday or earlier today, Linda. After I left you on Sunday, I went to the hospital to see Sharon Malto who had been injured in a car crash. Then I ran into Tony Malto and I'm afraid that we had a violent encounter. I am sore but basically fine.

"After that run-in with the Malto gang, I have been putting some security in place. And all that effort just kept me from calling you. I am so sorry not to have called." He could see that Sharon was eyeing him with surprise. This was not the phone call to a lawyer that she would have expected.

"Oh my God, Ed, are you okay? I told you that guy is dangerous. I think that you may have underestimated him." Ed could hear concern in Linda's voice replacing the sarcasm.

"You're right about not taking him seriously enough. But believe me, I am correcting that mistake even as we speak. I will need your advice however in helping Sharon."

Ed described the difficult situation that Sharon was in and the lawyer in Linda took over.

"Ed this is terrible. We are not living in the Middle Ages. I will have my team bring an injunction against Tony Malto keeping him away from Sharon and we will get her into a safe space when she is discharged from the hospital. I can cover some of her costs up front until we create some formal spousal support from Tony.

"But I am worried that anything we do against Tony will result in him trying to disrupt our arrangements or take it out on Sharon. We can't hide her forever."

"Yeah, I know. I am getting some assistance from very effective security services that will definitely help with Tony and protect Sharon. Some are already in place, and more are arriving over the next couple of days. I want you to be aware of them." He stopped and took a breath.

"And I would really like to see you. That was a very special weekend, and I am so sorry that I missed calling you like I should have. Can I see you tomorrow after work?"

By now Sharon was both puzzled and intrigued overhearing the call from her doctor to a lawyer. It seemed like much more than a legal referral.

Linda hesitated. What in the world was she getting herself into? "Yeah, I guess that would be okay, Ed. I need to finish off with those Maryland lawyers I told you about. We are tele-conferencing with them again tomorrow. We will probably be starting in court next week." And then her sarcasm returned. "I could get away tomorrow at the end of day, but this doesn't sound like a very romantic offer."

"Hot Springs was wonderful, Linda. But right now, I need to get everyone safe and figure out how we are going to neutralize Tony long-term." Sharon now turned away like she was embarrassed to be listening to the call. Ed looked at her and shrugged.

"Okay, Ed, you are worrying me. See you tomorrow evening. And stay safe for God's sake."

Before leaving the hospital, Ed called to ensure that Stephen and Brooke had sufficient time to set up the secure zone. As he walked onto the circular driveway leading to the parking lot, he was not surprised to see Tony's two dark Suburbans waiting with engines running. Tony had obviously responded to Tommy's call when Ed went in to see Sharon.

The Suburbans lurched into the hospital entrance driveway and Tony, Tommy, and three other bulky guys jumped out, all with handguns drawn.

Tony was out in front. "Dammit Brinkley, you just don't fuckin' listen, do ya? I told you to stay away from Sharon. After I finish with you, you are going to have trouble walkin' and talkin' to your patients."

But then, as the guys spread out to surround Ed, and Tony started a menacing advance toward him, three extremely bright lights suddenly lit up on poles that had been hastily erected surrounding the hospital entrance and Stephen's best aggressive voice came over a loudspeaker. "Freeze where you are Malto. Not. A. Step. Further. All of you put down your weapons."

Just as the lights went on, a heavily armored SUV came up the other side of the drive with Brooke behind the wheel. The SUV braked to a halt between Ed and Tony's gang. Suddenly shots were fired at the vehicle by Tony's crew, and Ed jumped in the rear driver's side door away from Tony. Tommy fired his pistol at the rear windshield but his bullets seemed to deflect from the tempered surface.

Stephen's voice came over the loudspeaker again. "I told you to put down your weapons. You don't listen very well." This warning was followed by several short bursts of automatic weapon fire quieted by suppressors that left four tires shredded and useless on the two Suburbans.

Brooke reversed out of the driveway and stopped on the perimeter of the driveway to pick up Stephen and Bill and their gear. Then they were off to their new HQ. Ed would be staying there rather than his apartment for the next few days and the team would be providing him with discreet security in the office.

The counterattack on Tony Malto in Maple Ridge had begun.

CHAPTER 22: RICO

When Linda picked up Ed at his office the next evening, he greeted her with a soft embrace and a slow, assured kiss. She thought that he seemed different somehow – less tentative, more confident. She couldn't quite put her finger on it, but it was different and somehow attractive.

He gave Linda directions to an industrial complex a short distance from downtown. They walked into a large open warehouse with unfinished metal siding walls that created an echo. And the space was indeed echoing with a noisy team gathered inside laughing and bantering together.

Ed introduced Linda to a lovely, tall woman named Brooke who was directing the organization of a pasta dinner while sitting in front of a long table loaded with technology hardware. Brooke was providing both insults and directions to a young man named Robert who was standing in a makeshift kitchen boiling water on a cooktop while chopping vegetables into a simmering sauce that he was regularly tasting as he added spices.

The two were trading good-natured barbs about each other's cooking skills while Brooke worked at a computer in the center of some rather complex electronic gear. They in turn introduced Linda to Stephen, Bill, Frank, Henry, and David. The entire group seemed well acquainted, and the cavernous space was filled with good-natured chatter.

As Linda evaluated this unusual group of newcomers to Maple Ridge, she made two quick observations. They were all very fit. Each one looked like an experienced triathlete. And they all seemed very fond of Ed who they referred to as "the Colonel." He seemed to be the target of their banter with one theme regularly repeated – that he should have organized their reunion in a more agreeable spot than this warehouse.

Linda could see that the open space was organized with washrooms and showers at the back. She also saw that the team had set up cots in a rudimentary barracks. They were set-tling in for the longer term here and Ed had mentioned that he was temporarily moving into the space for security reasons.

In the front of the space, Brooke was working with the so-phisticated-looking electronics. Linda asked her what she was expecting to do with this equipment. Brooke looked at Linda carefully, gave further directions and final insults about the dinner preparation to Robert and then linked arms with the lawyer and brought her over to two chairs adjacent to the tech equipment.

Sitting down, she gazed at Linda directly. "Linda, I want to be clear that there are some things that I am doing here that I am not going to tell you because I understand from the Colonel that you are a lawyer and an officer of the courts. There is noth-ing that I am doing that is strictly illegal but suffice it to say that in a couple of areas I may be bending privacy constraints."

She opened her arms to indicate the extent of the work that was underway. "The Colonel has hired us to gather all the in-formation we can find about Tony Malto's operation in this town. And believe me there is a lot to learn. I am not an ac-countant, and we will soon have a financial pro named Klaus, who used to be part of our team in Afghanistan, joining us. But I have been able to get into Tony's financial records and it is pretty straightforward to understand where Tony makes his money and how he hides and transfers his cash around."

Having worked on the project for three days now, Brooke was eager to talk about what she had learned about Tony's businesses. Linda guessed that Ed had explained to Brooke that Linda knew something about Malto. It seemed to Linda that

Brooke was assuming that Linda was a member of the team. Although Linda had not had much time to consider membership, this was looking like a pretty capable team to belong to.

Brooke continued. "Tony seems to have four major areas of business that bring in millions of dollars in cash every month. These are easy to recognize based on the entries to his accounts and his email traffic. He has nine different drug distribution networks around the state that seem to be managed on the street by a gang from Chicago called the Simon City Royals. Each of those nine drug networks has a record of how much cash is collected and how much is transferred to Tony.

"Similarly, in prostitution he has eleven groups of escorts and prostitutes that he has organized under various names and managers. I can actually now trace the names of the individual women and the proceeds that each collects and how much gets contributed to Tony from his spreadsheets. This appears to be run on the street by pimps associated with the Aryan Brotherhood."

Brooke shook her head in dismay about these women and the hoodlums who were controlling their lives.

"In gambling, I can recognize several different illegal gaming houses and sports lines that he is operating and again I can see lots of money coming into Tony. There also seem to be records for human trafficking. It looks like he brings in workers for his sex business and for undocumented labor maybe from Central America based on the names appearing in his records."

Brooke brought her hands together in mock prayer. "God bless him, Tony, or whoever is doing his bookkeeping, has organized his records very well and it's easy to track the money coming to him from all of these cash heavy businesses. As I said, he is collecting millions every month. The records are good, but his cybersecurity is terrible. With the spyware equipment that Colonel Ed's brother has organized for us, I was able to get through his firewall in less than an hour. I now have mirrored all his accounts, so I have a record of everything that gets updated each time someone opens Tony's books."

Linda was astonished at what she was learning. Ed had a brother? And this brother was organizing sophisticated spyware? Her potential doctor boyfriend, or colonel boyfriend, or whatever he was, was sounding more and more complicated.

"Brooke, can the police get in as easily as you have? This sounds like a slam dunk RICO case. He is making money from several activities that are against the law. All it takes to establish grounds for RICO is two offenses from a long list of federal and state crimes, and you have already described four different illegal activities."

Brooke nodded her head slowly. "I don't want to describe too much about what I know or don't know about what local and federal law enforcement has on Malto. They are certainly interested in Tony, and I believe they could have been building a RICO type case against him. However, I don't think that law enforcement has access to all the equipment that Colonel Ed's brother has helped us obtain. And two other factors are important."

She paused to organize her thoughts. "First, my training and experience as special forces master sergeant has given me the ability to invade the most secure data bases and not leave a trace. And since I left the military, I have recruited a Red Team of ethical hackers to work with some of the world's biggest companies testing their cybersecurity and trying to hack their data. Believe me, Tony's security offers minimal defenses compared to what our hackers have successfully invaded in industry."

She raised two fingers. "Secondly, I have reason to believe that Tony may have inside support in the local county police. There are some things that they should know that they are not following up on. I learned – I can't tell you how – that they may be protecting Tony from discovery, and they are certainly not turning over much information to the feds. But Linda, I really should not mention how we know about what is in the federal files."

Linda nodded slowly. "That doesn't surprise me. Tony is

a hometown boy, and his family goes back generations. He would have grown up with the guys who lead the county police in Maple Ridge. I would not be surprised if there are relationships that protect him."

Brooke went on. "For the next step in understanding Tony's businesses I am going to need my accountant friend Klaus to help me. The Colonel has put Klaus on contract, and he will be arriving soon."

She shrugged. "Every month, cash from the four primary areas of illegal business appears to transfer to about thirty legal businesses that Tony seems to own or somehow operate. These businesses are also cash heavy and I imagine that transfers are being added to the cash receipts that these businesses receive."

Linda was very impressed by how capable this young woman was and how much she had discovered in a short period of time. She made a mental note that when this was over she would get Brooke's Red Team to try and hack through the Davis firm's cybersecurity. She had ensured that her firm hired top notch outside professionals to manage their IT systems and it would be useful to have Brooke test whether her systems were as secure as Linda hoped.

Robert and Bill were starting to put the pasta out on a large conference table that was being used for dining when there was a knock on the door. Robert was reminding the team that he had created a delicious dinner despite Brooke's inappropriate interference while Bill linked his phone to speakers and cranked up some Metallica to set the dining mood. Bill winked at the Colonel who was covering his ears in mock dismay.

Frank was monitoring the entrance door camera in response to the knock. "Looks like a friendly at the door."

Linda had noticed Ed's casual ease in this rather chaotic warehouse and then saw him light up when he heard about the arrival at the door. He rushed over and as the door opened, threw his arms around a man several years younger with longer hair who was otherwise a spitting image of the man

Linda was learning was "the Colonel." Ed hugged him long and hard and then dragged him by the arm across the room to where Linda was sitting with Brooke.

"Benjamin, meet Linda and Brooke. Ladies, this is my little brother, Ben."

CHAPTER 23: LINDA MEETS BEN

Benjamin found himself facing two very attractive women. Stephen called for Brooke's attention about tomorrow's menu plan, and she excused herself to cross the room and confer with him. This left Ben attempting not to appear too obvious as he gave Linda the once over. Ed had never called his brother about a woman before. However, his recent messages and calls from Maple Ridge had become increasingly focused on this lawyer that Ed was clearly taken with. And looking at Linda, Ben could understand why.

She was dressed in a fine wool suit that looked both professional in its styling and attractive in its tailoring. She had ash blonde hair that almost reached her shoulder, combed asymmetrically so that it nearly covered her left eye. And those eyes – such a vivid green they could illuminate a dark room. No wonder his brother was intrigued.

"Linda, Ed tells me that you have provided the best of Southern hospitality in welcoming him to Maple Ridge and our family deeply appreciates that. I also understand that you may be offering some legal advice to help us deal with Mr. Malto." Ben hoped that he was not sounding too much like a corporate stiff.

And then Linda surprised Benjamin. She took him by the arm and led him over to where Robert and Bill were serving pasta. Getting them a couple of plates of spaghetti and plastic utensils, she told Ben to grab a couple of chairs and directed him to a small peripheral table set apart from the 'dining room' that the men had set up.

"Now, Mr. Benjamin Brinkley, you sit right here."

She then turned to Ed who was following behind them and pushed him away. "And you Colonel Ed, or Doctor Ed or whoever you are, you just go and give some orders to your commandos sitting over there in the dining room. I want some time alone with your brother to try and figure out who I may be dating."

Linda hadn't meant to say it quite that plainly, although in retrospect it probably came out about right. She could see Ed's team look at each other and smile. She could imagine they were thinking that their commander was dating a pretty bossy woman. But meeting Benjamin tonight was a great opportunity to learn about Ed and Linda was not going to miss it. She needed to know more about this man of mystery.

Ben smiled at Linda and sat down with his pasta. "Linda, it sounds like we both want to find out something from each other. Why don't you start with the questions?"

Linda examined Ben now sitting beside her. He had arrived with an expensive leather briefcase that he had casually tossed on the floor beside him. He was clearly dressed by a Wall Street haberdasher in a well-tailored, expensive suit and lovely complementary silk tie. Glancing down she noticed that his patterned socks matched his suit. Linda recognized the "dress for success" look from her days back east. She remembered that on the rare occasions when Ed had worn a suit he was very well turned out and again saw the resemblance between these brothers.

Ben watched her twirl her pasta around her fork thoughtfully. "Ed has never talked about his family and then suddenly all this equipment and military personnel magically materializes. I have a feeling that your family has brought some major resources to Maple Ridge." She paused and waited for Ben's response.

"Maybe the best way for me to start answering your questions is to describe Brinkley Enterprises. It is a private family firm that my great grandfather and grandfather started just over a hundred years ago as a shipping company focused on transporting oil from the Pennsylvania fields. When drilling started in the Gulf of Mexico in the 1930s and 1940s they expanded their focus to support underwater drilling operations." Ben glanced up to see those green eyes fixed on him.

"We became pretty good at the engineering aspects of drilling for oil. After my dad and his brother started leading the firm in the seventies, we added financing to drilling operations to become the full-service oil logistics organization. When the wildcatters and geologists thought that their exploration data suggested oil, they would come to us with the information, and we would decide whether or not we should borrow money from the banks or oil funds to support exploration based on our analysis of the information."

Ben paused to ensure she was following. Linda nodded as if to say *keep going.* "My uncle did not have any kids interested in joining the business. Our oldest brother is a drilling engineer. He joined the business with a mining engineering degree in the nineties and focused on developing the company's directional drilling expertise. He started us into fracking, and we have become expert at finding and developing tight oil and gas deposits in the western states."

He lifted his hands to show that this drilling expertise was foreign to him. "I have no idea how to find oil or how to get it out of the ground once we find it. I went to Wharton and became pretty good at raising capital and estimating risk. We figured out that instead of asking for financing from banks or funds, we could cut out the middleman by raising the money ourselves if we could match risk and potential return. And that has been my contribution to Brinkley Enterprises. Since I took over as CEO, we have become a resources fund company as well as a drilling and oil services enterprise. And we are just starting to develop renewable energy funds."

He leaned back in his chair. Linda thought again how much he looked like a younger version of his brother. "Our expertise in tight oil allowed us to develop some of the first funds devoted to fracking and these investments have been very successful for us and our investors. I am duplicating that approach now in renewables."

He pointed across the room to Ed, who was deep in discussion with Brooke and Stephen. "Our middle brother Ed was always interested in foreign countries. While Ed was doing his business degree in Boston, the Saudis wanted to ensure that they could empty their oil fields completely. Our experience in directional drilling made this a strong market for Brinkley expansion. Ed spent his summers and co-op terms during undergrad working in our Saudi office, where he became fluent in Arabic."

Ben looked at Linda. "After finishing his degree, Ed decided that he wanted more purpose in life than making money. I was still in high school at the time, but I remember my dad being initially upset when Ed told him he was enrolling in med school.

"Despite leaving the business, Ed remained fascinated by the Middle East and did several of his med school electives in Saudi. Ed is of course an owner of Brinkley Enterprises through our controlling family trust, but he always just signs his proxy over to me on any decision making. One of my major corporate goals is to ensure that my big brother stays a very wealthy man. Which he seems to have no interest in whatsoever." Ben looked over at his brother with an affectionate shaking of the head.

Linda said nothing but remembered wondering whether Ed could be interested in her because of her apparent wealth. How ironic that he was probably much better off than Linda could ever aspire to be.

Ben looked at Linda and paused. "All of our lives were altered on 9/11 but no one changed more than Ed. He was working in a hospital in Riyadh when the Towers fell. Ed was surprised by how many Saudis were proud of the destruction caused by their countrymen in Manhattan. We didn't have offices in the Trade Center, but we worked with several fund companies in New York. Ed had done business with these companies as an undergrad, and he lost several friends when the Towers came down."

He gave Linda a searching look. "And that's when Ed's life took a radical turn, Linda. He realized that America's place in the world was being challenged by radicals, and he knew from his time working in the Gulf that these terrorists were not going to help their fellow citizens in the Middle East. Ed's epiphany was that America needed patriots who understood the Gulf to join our armed forces and help lead our response to 9/11."

Benjamin was so young and earnest. Linda could see his older brother's engaging eyes in this younger man. "So, against our family's protests, Ed enlisted. He started in the Army Officer Candidate School, but it wasn't long before his language skills and experience in the Gulf region were recognized by our Special Forces. He quickly finished med school and was shipped out as a Special Forces medical officer in Afghanistan, fighting the Taliban.

"After some terrible injuries to his team, both Ed and Special Forces command recognized that modern combat in Afghanistan required an upgrade to surgical expertise in the field, and Ed became one of the Special Forces' first combat-trained surgeons." Here he looked over at his brother and Linda could readily sense the admiration Ben felt for Ed.

"He completed accelerated training that qualified him as a trauma surgeon. The program was developed for a few experienced Special Forces officers whose medical expertise and military training could support small teams of combatants deployed a long way from the closest hospitals." Ben paused to collect his thoughts.

"In 2010, Ed was posted in Helmand province in Afghanistan with a new Special Forces team. You won't find much written about his team's activities. Most of their work was covert. I believe that the people in this room were members of that team."

Ben and Linda both looked around at the young people

teasing each other over their spaghetti. It was easy to imagine them as a team of desert warriors.

Ben again looked over at his brother with obvious affection. "Although you won't find out much about Ed's team's combat role, you can learn about his work as a doctor with local Afghans. I understand that he established a new standard for helping civilian populations in Helmand.

"The doctors with his training were also expert combat leaders and his unit specialized in covert missions deep in enemy country. More than two years ago, Ed's team was dropped far from our lines in heavy Taliban country on a secret sortie. You cannot find anything official about their operational objectives."

At this point Ben shook his head slowly. "Ed never talks about it, but I have learned that on that mission, the Taliban attacked their unit killing their commander and second-in-command. This left Ed as the senior combat officer."

He looked around the room. "And I know that a couple of the guys here figure that they owe Ed their lives. He eventually led the team to a secure area for evacuation."

And now he looked again at his brother with what Linda could only describe as a bit of awe. "He was wounded badly himself. You may notice he limps sometimes?" He looked at Linda and she nodded. Of course, she had noticed his limp.

"Ed was devastated by the losses that his team had suffered and had probably just been in country for too long. He became very depressed and reclusive. Neither his Special Forces family nor our family could connect with him." Ben's concern for his brother showed in his eyes.

"He was finally diagnosed with Post-Traumatic Stress Disorder and went into a program run by the military. After quite a lot of treatment, Ed and his therapist decided that he was ready to start over. I know that they both thought that trauma surgery would be too intense for him, and that primary care would probably be the best practice for Ed to reenter."

Ben sat back and spread his arms motioning to the town

that surrounded them. "I am not sure exactly why he decided on Maple Ridge, but he has told me that there is something that Arkansas is doing for more complex patients that Ed believes in. I think that's what attracted him here."

Linda looked at Ben with those stunning green eyes. "Am I right in assuming that Brinkley Enterprises is paying for all the equipment and the people who are here to help Ed?"

Ben nodded. "It is actually a subsidiary of Brinkley, Linda, but I have personally ensured and will continue to make sure that Ed has all the resources that he will need here."

"I take it that you are pretty supportive of your brother?"

Ben looked down and when he looked up his eyes were glistening. "As you might imagine from what I have told you, Linda, Ed is my hero. I have been so worried about him over the past two years. It was just so unlike Ed to get down and with-drawn." He quickly rubbed his hand across his eyes.

"Every day that I sat in my office making safe decisions about growing our business, I gave thanks for Ed working to keep our country safe. It's great that he is having a chance to start over here. And our family and our company are abso-lutely committed to making sure that he has what he needs to protect him from this Malto gang."

Ben paused then switched gears looking at Linda with con-cern. "Just how dangerous are these guys, Linda? And why can't we just ask the local police to deal with the Maltos?"

Linda shrugged. "Our police are okay. But Malto's family has been in this community for generations. And I would guess he probably looks after some of the force's senior officers. Also, I am sure that Tony is telling the cops that Ed is interfering with his relationship with his wife. In our southern culture, that al-lows a man some latitude to protect his family."

As Linda continued Ben could sense a different tone. "Is Tony dangerous? Well, my family has some experience. My dad was in a real estate deal with Tony's father more than ten years ago. The deal was successful and allowed their partner-ship to expand their interest in a profitable business. Tony's dad wanted to buy out my dad and Dad refused. That was a few weeks before he had a fatal car accident.

"There was never any proof that the Malto's were involved in the accident. But their deal gave Tony's father the right to buy out my dad's share if Dad died. I have never been sure about what happened, but I do not trust Malto or his family. And yes, my experience suggests that they can be dangerous." Linda looked angry rather than intimidated as she related this information to Benjamin.

"I am really happy that you and Ed have brought this team here, Ben. And as a lifelong citizen committed to Maple Ridge, I think that it is past time for Tony Malto to meet his match."

Just then Brooke came over to see if the pair wanted more pasta. Linda realized that she was monopolizing Ben's attention and apologized to him. His quick response charmed her.

"Linda, I think that you may be the best thing that has happened to my brother in a very long time. I am really happy to start getting to know you."

CHAPTER 24: STANDARD OPERATING PROCEDURE

Brooke had noticed that Benjamin and Linda had been sitting with their heads together for quite a while. She went over and sensed that their conversation had become emotional. Ben's eyes were shining, and Linda was breathing deeply.

Brooke was intrigued by this Linda, whom she understood was a high-powered lawyer. Her presence in this unusual setting suggested that she had some sort of commitment to the Colonel. Brooke looked across the room at the Colonel and back at Linda. They could make a very attractive couple, she concluded.

Stephen was up monitoring the security cameras. "There is a guy approaching the door who looks like he may be an accountant. Brooke, this is Klaus, right?"

Brooke looked at the screen and let out a happy yelp. "Yeah, that's my money buddy Klaus. I'll let him in."

Brooke hugged the newcomer at the door and brought him into the makeshift dining room with her arm around his shoulders. Klaus had longish hair nearly to his shoulders and wire rim glasses. His khakis and tweed jacket made him look the part of a rather frumpy accountant.

However, despite this undistinguished appearance, Brooke knew his attributes. He was a very cool guy who worked like a madman and was known to be fearless. Brooke and Klaus had also spent some time relaxing together both in Kabul and in the States and she knew that this guy understood how to party.

Klaus smiled as he looked around the room at Ed and the team. "Hey, Colonel Ed, looks like you got some bad-asses working with you here. Are you guys planning to start a war? I thought that I was here to catch a crook."

Colonel Ed smiled. "Don't you worry Klaus, we gotta a job that needs your skills. And these guys are here to keep you covered. Let me introduce you to my brother Benjamin and my friend Linda."

Klaus shook Ben's hand. "I hear from Brooke that you are our quartermaster Ben, financing this op." And he gave Linda a broad wink. "And I hear that you may be keeping our Colonel happier than he's been in a while, Linda. Nice to meet you."

Brooke looked over at Linda and Benjamin. "Klaus and I started working together in Kabul. My job was to break through firewalls and his job was to figure out what the spreadsheets and accounts that I uncovered actually meant. Klaus showed the world that the Afghan government was robbing us blind."

Klaus shrugged his shoulders. "Yeah, except everyone already figured they were cheating us before I proved it. And nobody wanted to do anything after I demonstrated it because it wasn't politically correct to say our allies were thieves. But it sure taught me the various ways that warlords try to hide money. Who knows? That may come in handy in this exercise."

Brooke looked over at Benjamin. "Ben, you are supporting us here with some expensive resources and I want to make sure that Klaus and I will have something for you in the next twenty-four hours. I already know that we can get through the Malto firewall, and we've solved all their password protection. They are really sloppy with cybersecurity, thank goodness."

Brooke continued. "I have been able to mirror their databases and spreadsheets and they will never detect us. So, I have access to exactly what Klaus is going to need to figure out how the Malto gang makes their money."

And then she looked out at the entire team. "Now that we are all here, there's something I want to discuss with all of you.

I don't know how bad these Malto guys are, but I am going to follow our standard operating protocol and assume that they are really evil. So, I have to presume that they could target anyone on our team, including possible abduction. As your technical master sergeant, I am going to fix each one of you with an implanted GPS, somewhere impossible to detect like under a watch, fingernail or toenail.

"And I am going to program it to your cell phone GPS so that if you are separated from your phone or your sim card I will be alerted immediately. Usually if a bad guy kidnaps you he will throw away your phone or break your sim card. If he is too stupid to do that, just get rid of the phone yourself."

Brooke looked around the room. This was standard operating procedure for Colonel Ed and the rest of the Special Forces team. But she could see Benjamin's and Linda's eyes open wide at her announcement.

CHAPTER 25: TWO
MISSING YEARS

D r. Suzanne Fortis knew that her partner Lawrence Skalbane could be impossible to deal with. Lawrence would get an idea in his mind and be like a dog with a bone.

But in this case, the clinic group had to listen to Lawrence because they all recognized a major problem facing their town. Over the past few years Maple Ridge, like many middle American towns, had faced up to the fact that there was an opioid crisis in their community. And Lawrence was concerned that their group might be harboring an opioid addict in their midst.

As Lawrence had told the group repeatedly, they were not asked by management at the hospital or clinic to approve the appointment of Dr. Brinkley to their staff. One afternoon when Dr. Ed was away from the office working in the Emergency Room, Lawrence called an impromptu meeting of the clinic group at the end of the day.

As usual, the docs crowded around the boardroom table, sipping coffee, and chatting about recent events and cases that they were managing. Lawrence walked in and took his seat at the head of the table.

"Colleagues, thanks for meeting on short notice. I understand that we are all uncomfortable meeting without Dr. Brinkley who is the topic I want to discuss." He stared around the table ensuring they were paying attention.

"I am very concerned about Brinkley's record. We all know that there is a two-year gap in his record where he was not working. We are told that he had an honorable discharge from the military. But after his discharge, we have this gap of two years." Lawrence again looked around at his colleagues to ensure that they understood his point.

"I am concerned that the two years missing from his record may be an indicator that Dr. Brinkley was being treated for issues related to professional misconduct or competency. In particular, he may have been treated for opioid dependency. We know that addiction is common in ex-military types. If Brinkley was treated for opioid dependency, we need to know whether he is cured." Lawrence's hands curled into fists on the table in front of him, emphasizing the seriousness of his words.

"If Brinkley is still addicted, we are all at risk that he may not treat our patients appropriately when he is covering for us. He may be covering our patients while impaired by opioids. And he may not be concerned about creating addicts by prescribing excessive painkillers to our patients. This is a real concern for me and should be a concern for all of you as well."

Suzanne looked around the table. Her partners were surprised by Lawrence's accusations but concerned that their patients might be mistreated. She had to ask, "Lawrence, what do you expect us to do to sort this out?"

Lawrence responded immediately. "Good question Suzanne. I have asked the hospital about Dr. Brinkley's resume and health records, and they say that the missing time is personal information that Brinkley does not need to address. The hospital administration claims that there are no complaints or malpractice suits registered against him with any licensing authorities. That's easy for them to say at the hospital, they don't need to work with Brinkley daily, worrying that his addiction may put our patients at risk."

"Lawrence you are really assuming the worst here, I must say. If the hospital won't provide us with his records, what do you propose?"

He had figured that out. "I think that the only reasonable

path is for us to hire a private investigator to find out just what we are missing in Dr. Brinkley's resume. That is why I wanted us to meet tonight. I want the group's permission to use some of our reserve funds to hire a private investigator to report on Brinkley's missing two years."

Suzanne thought quickly. "Don't you think it is a little aggressive to hire someone to investigate Ed? Why don't we just ask him about those two years and see what he says?"

Lawrence was nonplussed and didn't respond. Suzanne looked around at the other docs and could see her partners nodding in agreement to ask Ed about his missing two years.

Suzanne followed up before Lawrence had a chance to respond. "Okay, team, does everyone agree that I speak to Dr. Brinkley and report back on what he says?"

Everyone nodded except for Lawrence. Suzanne promised that she would call a group meeting as soon as she had something to say.

Suzanne had actually been concerned that Ed seemed to be rushing out of the office at end of day lately. The next day she asked to chat with him and took him into her office.

"Ed, the group is concerned about the two years after your discharge from the military. To be very blunt, some of the group is concerned that you might have a substance issue and that you are going to put our patients at risk." She could see Ed's immediate discomfort with that allegation.

Suzanne added quickly. "Now, we don't all share that apprehension by any means. I want you to know that. But to answer any concerns, your other partners just want to know what you were up to for those two missing years."

Ed looked at the floor. "Yeah, I get it Suzanne. Well, I was in rehab off and on for those two years. I think everyone must suspect that."

"Drugs or alcohol, or both?"

"Neither. After the last action I saw in Afghanistan, having suffered terrible losses to our team in combat, and getting wounded myself, I needed some downtime. I was in physio rehab for more than a year and then therapy for PTSD. It took a while for me to realize how disabled I was. I don't really like talking about that time in my life and there's a lot that I cannot mention because it's restricted military information."

This was not what Suzanne had been expecting. She suddenly felt like she was intruding. "So, how are you doing now, Ed?"

"Well, I am trained as a trauma surgeon, but my therapist thought that it would be too stressful for me to go back to trauma work. I had some general practice training in the military prior to surgery, really enjoyed running a clinic for locals in Afghanistan and I have discovered here in Maple Ridge that I like primary care. It's very rewarding, and I get a sense that I am helping people."

Feeling sheepish at this point but remembering her promise to the group, Suzanne continued. "Ed, I hate to ask, but could I have your permission to call your therapist and confirm what you have told me today?"

"Well, that is rather embarrassing, Suzanne. Let me guess, it's probably old Lawrence who is convinced that I am an addict or something." Ed shook his head in disbelief.

Suzanne knew that she needed to settle this for Ed's sake as well as the group's. "Ed, let's put this behind us. If you give me permission to speak to your therapist and report back to the group at a very high level, we will put this whole issue to rest."

Ed reluctantly provided her with the number for his therapist and sent both the therapist and Suzanne an email that evening confirming his consent for the therapist to talk to her.

The next day Suzanne called Dr. David Romulus. She explained to him that Ed's practice group did not know what had happened during Ed's two "missing years." She further explained that a member of the group was concerned that Ed may have been treated for addiction and that he might put their patients at risk because of this addiction.

Dr. Romulus was initially sharp in his response. "Dr. Fortis, do you have any idea who Dr. Brinkley is or what this man has accomplished for his country?"

Suzanne responded that there were major missing pieces in her understanding of Ed and hoped that Dr. Romulus would help the group to understand him better.

"First of all, Ed comes from a very wealthy family and really does not need to work."

This was certainly a surprise to Suzanne. Ed had rented an apartment in a nondescript part of town close to the clinic and hospital. As far as everyone knew he had no car and was walking to work and around town.

"He joined the Special Forces just after 9/11. He is a very experienced trauma surgeon.

"As I understand it from Ed, the war in Afghanistan often resulted in our Special Forces going deep into enemy country in the Taliban controlled areas of the country. I don't know much about the role that these teams played. Most of their activity remains classified.

"Following combat, it could take several days to extract these teams and surgical services could be lifesaving on the battlefield. Ed was one of the first trauma surgeons to volunteer for this very dangerous duty." Suzanne could hear the admiration in Dr. Romulus' voice.

"This meant updating his combat skills as well as his field surgery skills. His last action apparently tested all of his abilities. He was supporting a team of Special Forces troops who had landed deep in the provinces, far from our lines. Although their mission was not admitted publicly, they apparently attracted pretty significant Taliban interest."

Romulus paused in his narrative. "I cannot tell you much more about this mission and Colonel Brinkley's role in it, Dr. Fortis. That information is heavily classified."

Suzanne heard a sigh on the line from Dr. Romulus. "But I did interview two of the people who fought with Ed, and they think that he is a hero. They are both certain that they are alive today only because of Ed.

"After this action, Ed became very depressed. He had just

seen too much and been exposed to too much stress, especially related to combat surgery." He sighed again.

"As I mentioned his family is extremely well off and wanted to get Ed access to private therapy. He refused, however. Said he wanted to be treated the same as any other grunt and came to our team for therapy through Veterans Administration. It has taken some time, but he is now fully functional and ready for all the challenges he could face in a primary care or office practice." Now there was a long pause as Dr. Romulus thought about summarizing his comments. Suzanne waited in silence on the line.

"I would not want Ed going back to Afghanistan. But then again I would probably not send anyone back to the role that Ed played in our war effort there."

Not hearing any questions from Dr. Fortis, Dr. Romulus concluded. "I would not want to expose him to the constant stress of trauma surgery. That could retrigger some of the PTSD symptoms that he has been treated for. But there is no question in my mind that he can readily manage the primary care practice that your group engages in, Dr. Fortis."

Suzanne responded, "Thanks, Dr. Romulus. I will keep the military parts of what you've told me confidential. I will report to our group that Ed had no history of substance abuse and that you strongly recommend that Ed is fit for work in Maple Ridge." She also said she would emphasize that Ed deserved his colleagues' deep respect and admiration for his military service.

Neither Suzanne nor Dr. Romulus could know that Ed's practice in Maple Ridge had retriggered his PTSD. And they certainly could not imagine how the former soldier was responding.

CHAPTER 26: SPECIAL FORCES OPERATIONAL DETACHMENT ALPHA

W orking with Colonel Ed unearthed memories for Brooke that had been buried for more than two years. She knew that the Colonel had gone stateside and was discharged after their last mission together and she understood that he had reacted badly to the stress of that mission. She could certainly comprehend that response – their last operation had been extremely difficult. But without the Colonel, Brooke knew that it would have been much worse.

The military was secretive about their Special Forces Operational Detachment Alpha, or SFODA, which was tasked with eliminating high value Taliban targets. Their mission was reliant on hacking Taliban networks and close electronic surveillance. The unit was generally operating very deep in enemy territory without immediate chance of evacuation. Accordingly, the usual twelve-man ODA structure was modified. Colonel Ed and Brooke both had roles that were added to the typical ODA team composition.

Brooke provided electronic surveillance, technology and hacking skills for the team. The Taliban military ops were coordinated through a cellphone and internet network in Afghanistan that relied heavily on encryption. Satellite surveillance gave a pretty good general idea of where targets were located. But eliminating high-ranking Taliban leaders cleanly required the team to get more information about the target's exact location than could be achieved from satellite information alone.

In the early days of the war, the allied forces would locate a target by remote surveillance and then attack by air or by drone. Those methods always resulted in tremendous collateral damage to civilians since the Taliban leaders were careful to hide out in populated areas. The goal for the SFODA was to bring surveillance and snipers within rifle distance to eliminate targets cleanly without injury to bystanders.

Brooke's task was to search for targets through close range surveillance, break their phone encryption and then identify the targets to the team snipers. Like every ODA member she also had experience as a rifleman. And since Brooke's particular responsibility was generally concluded by the time that combat started, she also cross-trained to assist in forward combat surgical care for wounded soldiers.

Colonel Ed was another addition to the typical twelve-person ODA, bringing the unit up to fourteen. Working with colleagues in the small Special Forces surgical group, Colonel Ed had developed radical new approaches to battlefield medical care. As Brooke understood it, this innovative treatment was called tactical combat casualty care. It was at the leading edge of military surgery and responded to the evolution of infantry protective equipment.

The use of body armor and enhanced combat helmets meant that soldiers were relatively well protected from head and body shots. However, maintaining combat mobility and functionality meant that the soldiers' arms and legs could not be as well protected.

For Brooke's ODA, the proximity to the enemy that was required to eliminate their targets meant that immediate evacuation from the battlefield was rarely possible. The team got in very close to enemy forces and their operational plan generally required a tactical retreat before chopper exfiltration could be expected. Rocket-propelled grenades were everywhere in Afghanistan – every teenager seemed to have one, and these RPGs were lethal for choppers. Bringing a helicopter in to evacuate their ODA nearly always required the team to retreat to a safe landing zone some distance from the site where they had addressed their targets.

If members of the team were wounded in the legs, the team's retreat to a safe helicopter landing zone became much more difficult. It took at least two soldiers to carry a wounded comrade, and in a small team this was a dangerous reduction of limited combat forces.

So, in order to reduce the impact of arm and leg injuries, Colonel Ed and his colleagues developed an approach to combat casualty care that took advantage of recent advances in bone fracture surgery. Part of Brooke's responsibility was to assist the Colonel in this battlefield surgery.

Utilizing very lightweight equipment, they would stabilize arm and leg injuries using a technique called external fixation. Working with industry, the surgical team developed battery operated portable X-ray machines the surgeons called 'fluoro,' which they would use to visualize the fractured bones on the battlefield. Then they would drill large, threaded stainless-steel pins into the anaesthetized soldier's bone above and below the fractures. These fractures were often complex injuries caused by high energy weapons. The surgeons would next connect carbon-fiber rods to these pins, attaching the carbon rods outside the skin to rigidly stabilize the broken bones.

Normally, an injured soldier with a fractured leg bone would be in terrible pain and unable to walk in the tactical retreat required to a distant landing zone. The team would either need to carry him by stretcher or leave him behind to be captured as a prisoner of war. And everyone knew capture would mean torture and death.

With Colonel Ed's treatment of fractures, the wounded soldier would be much more comfortable and able to move reasonably well on crutches. He would not be able to bear much weight on the leg but would be able to cover ground at about half his normal speed. The soldier with a leg injury would go from being a massive burden on his comrades to re-suming a combat role as a colleague who could move at reason-able speed and also return fire if needed.

Brooke's job in this battlefield combat casualty control sur-gery was to administer anesthesia and operate the fluoro unit while Colonel Ed did the surgery. During training, she had learned how to start and maintain intravenous lines and how to inject short-acting anesthetic drugs that would allow the Colonel to do his work. She also learned standard wound care and bandaging techniques. Her training and Colonel Ed's pres-ence allowed the ODA to replace the usual medic with another sniper.

And this medical care was essential in their last mission to-gether in Helmand province.

Satellite and phone surveillance suggested that a meeting of senior Taliban leaders was taking place in a small, remote village far from American bases in Helmand province. Sat-ellite imagery showed a heavy military brigade surrounding the meeting place. To reduce the risk of detection, the ODA members were dropped several miles from the village before daylight and spent most of the day hiking through hilly terrain to get positioned close to the village square. Brooke remem-bered that everything was going according to plan as the team arrived at their destination.

The ODA had been working together for more than a year and had run many successful covert missions without much enemy response. On this occasion, Brooke was able to identify the targets in the village meeting by breaking the encryption on their cell phone signatures. The team's snipers were posi-tioned less than 200 yards from the village square. Brooke had radio contact with the snipers to identify the two targets when they used their Taliban phones out in the open.

At the end of the day when the team deployed, the Taliban meeting broke up and the leaders who had spent the day in a wooden building wandered out into the center of the village. And as they walked into the village square, they immediately lit up their phones. This was a fatal error for them. Brooke used her sensitive directional equipment to identify the two targets for the snipers who immediately eliminated them without collateral damage.

Brooke shuddered when she remembered the chaos that followed. As the snipers returned to their meeting point, the surrounding Taliban troops determined the team's location and started a merciless attack with machine gun fire and mortars. The ODA commander was killed by a mortar and the assistant commander was killed by machine gun with further severe injuries to four of the team. This was the first time their team had sustained casualties. Brooke vividly remembered the sense that they were fighting for their lives.

The four wounded men were dragged back to a relatively protected knoll where Colonel Brinkley and Brooke were preparing for battlefield surgery. Two soldiers were bleeding heavily from neck wounds and two had leg injuries.

Brooke watched helplessly as one soldier with a neck injury choked to death while the Colonel tried to get a breathing tube down into his lungs. There was just too much damage to his airway from neck gunshot wounds for the Colonel to deal with. He was able to get a tube into the second rifleman and then worked furiously to stop the severe bleeding from his neck wounds. The soldier had sustained multiple injuries however, and despite the Colonel's best efforts, the rifleman just bled to death in front of Brooke and the doctor.

It was probably only seconds, but for what seemed like hours to Brooke, the Colonel just sat in despair holding their second dead colleague. However, he pulled himself together and turned his attention to the two soldiers with leg wounds.

Stephen, one of the team's snipers, had been hit by a bullet in the thigh and David, an explosives expert, had his shin shattered by machine gun fire. Suddenly the unit was down from fourteen to eight intact combatants with two wounded comrades and no hope of immediate evacuation. There were too many hostiles close to their position to bring in a chopper.

Any helicopter venturing this close to a strong enemy position would be destroyed by ground fire or an RPG.

Colonel Ed was now the ranking officer. He deployed his remaining six fighters to peripheral defensive positions but kept Brooke with Stephen and David in the protected knoll where he had unloaded his bone fracture surgical gear.

The Colonel knew that they would need to evacuate under darkness to get to the predetermined remote landing zone which was more than five miles from their current position. He also knew that they would never make that LZ if they needed to carry Stephen and David on stretchers through this rough mountainous country.

Working together Brooke and the Colonel started with Stephen's surgery. Brooke started an IV to provide Stephen opioids for immediate pain relief while his trousers were cut off to permit the cleaning of his badly damaged thigh with antiseptic solutions. Colonel Ed continued with sterilization of the leg while Brooke prepared for X-ray and anesthesia.

She inserted the lithium battery into the fluoro X-ray machine to ensure it was working. Then she slowly injected the milky anesthetic agent into Stephen's IV while carefully watching his breathing. As he fell unconscious, Brooke took care to minimize the injection of anesthetic drug that was necessary to render him unconscious but still breathing.

After Stephen was anesthetized, Dr. Ed instructed Brooke to pull on the foot of the broken leg to straighten the deformity resulting from the gunshot wound. Fortunately, Stephen's foot pulses were fine. The bullet had broken his femur thigh bone into several pieces but had not damaged his leg artery. Brooke then put the screen of the fluoro machine above his thigh with the X-ray generator below the sterile drape that his leg now rested on.

Stephen's thigh was already massively swollen from the injury. By rotating the fluoro back and forth to get right angle images of the femur bone, Colonel Ed was able to drill four large threaded stainless-steel pins into the intact bone – two pins above and two below the fracture. He then attached clamps to the pins and used carbon fiber rods to connect the pin clamps together. Brooke kept the anesthetic running and, with the Colonel's instructions, pulled hard on Stephen's foot to get the thigh as straight as possible before he tightened the pin clamps to the rods.

By the end of this forty-five-minute procedure, Stephen's leg had transformed from a floppy swollen mess to a reasonably straight and stable extremity. Brooke gave Stephen more opioid as the rapid acting anesthetic wore off and when the rifleman moved his leg on awakening, he was much more comfortable.

They then repeated the anesthetic, cleaning, and fixation for David's shin bone. Again, following the surgery, David was feeling much less pain and was ready to mobilize.

During this entire time, the Colonel and Brooke had exchanged few words. They had practiced this entire procedure on manikins together in training but never in combat. As they finished with David's tibia, Brooke felt suddenly drained. The intensity of both the combat and the two procedures was overwhelming, and she could feel fatigue washing over her.

The Colonel on the other hand seemed to surge with energy. "Brooke, I am going to check on the perimeter. Stay here with Stephen and David and get them up and moving on crutches. They are going to have to move out with the rest of us immediately after darkness."

The Colonel knew that they would have an advantage over their Taliban adversaries in the dark since the ODA team all had night vision equipment. They had at least one night's travel to the distant site for evacuation and he wanted them to be ready to retreat from their current exposed position immediately following nightfall.

As the Colonel disappeared over the ridge of the knoll, gun fire broke out and a couple of mortar rounds landed near the surgery area. Brooke kept her weapon close and started to get Stephen and David up on crutches. Their general toughness and intense physical training were essential in getting them mobilized along with some more opioid medication. Before long they were able to move reasonably well albeit slowly with the lightweight expandable crutches that Brooke had provided for them.

When the Colonel returned to check on Stephen and David, Brooke noticed that he was limping and that his fatigues were bloody. In response to her query about his leg, the Colonel responded, "Got hit with shrapnel from a mortar round. Not too bad and no bony damage – just my thigh muscle hit."

Brooke offered him painkiller, but he turned it down. He obviously wanted to remain sharp to lead the retreat since he was now the ranking officer left in the squad. Colonel Ed might be a doctor, but like all ODA officers he was a well-trained combat leader.

As dusk fell the unit set off on a complex, dangerous retreat. Although they had the advantage of night vision, there were at least one hundred well-armed hostiles all around them. And the team was limited by two team members who could only make slow progress over the rough terrain with their recent surgery and crutches.

Transforming from surgeon to combat commander, Colonel Ed spread the team out into a moving diamond formation. Two soldiers led the way on point and four men flanked in two groups about ten yards behind and to either side of the point. Brooke stayed in the middle with Stephen and David, and the Colonel protected their rear.

Brooke entered shared GPS coordinates into everyone's combat phones so that they could move in coordinated fashion in the dark, following the point soldiers leading their way to the predetermined evacuation point. Even using the night vision goggles attached to their helmets, it was difficult to see one another in camo gear at night. The GPS allowed them to monitor each other's position on their phones and ensured that they were moving as a unit maintaining the diamond formation.

It was the longest five miles Brooke had ever imagined walking. Their point did not encounter much resistance in front of them and the two flanking groups only experienced a couple of quick skirmishes. But the Taliban force was clearly tracking them from behind and Colonel Ed was busy protecting their rear.

The Colonel knew that it would be suicidal to allow the Taliban to follow them to the landing zone. That was the enemy's plan and if successful would result in the Taliban taking out the rescuing helicopter with ground fire and RPGs. The Colonel had been clear in ordering Brooke to stay with Stephen and David and to keep them moving in concert with the point and flanks. She could see from his GPS position however, that the Colonel was not simply following behind them.

Brooke could see the Colonel's GPS signal regularly stop as they passed areas with elevation and boulders he could use as cover to set ambushes for the following Taliban. His night vision gave him an advantage over his adversaries which he enhanced by using a suppressor on his rifle to prevent the enemy from locating his position through sound or muzzle flash.

She watched him set up on the GPS and then heard his muffled fire and the confused Taliban returning fire. She had counted four ambushes with gunfire lasting up to twenty minutes each time the Colonel attacked. And then after they had been walking for at least five hours she heard him whispering from about twenty feet away.

"Brooke, I lost my phone. I'm coming in. I need ammo."

Sure enough, Brooke's combat phone showed his GPS position at least a quarter mile behind them where he had obviously lost his phone during combat. If he had not announced his presence, she likely would have shot him.

"Colonel why don't you stay with the guys and let me take the rear? You have been plenty busy. You must be exhausted. Or we can send a couple of the guys back there to help you. Our point and flanks haven't been busy."

"We are almost at the LZ, Brooke, and I want to keep the formation tight and moving. I need magazines from Stephen and

David. There is a protected position here where I'm going to set up and make sure that the Taliban can't follow us through this pass." He lifted his arm to point out where he was planning to set up his next ambush.

Looking up, Brooke could see what the Colonel was planning. They were in a reasonably steep gully and anyone following them would need to walk through this pass. The Colonel was planning to shelter behind some boulders on the slope above the path and ensure that no one could follow them through the gully to the LZ.

"Colonel, lemme stay here with you. The boys can make it without me."

"Brooke, you need to make sure they get to the LZ. With the anesthetic and opioids, those guys could break down at any time and lose their way. I am counting on you to get them home."

The Colonel went over to Stephen and David and took half their magazines, loading his jacket pouches. He took grenades from David, gave both guys a hug and turned back to Brooke. "See you at the chopper, Master Sergeant." And with that he disappeared behind them, scrambling up the gully slope. Brooke and the two wounded soldiers pushed on using the GPS to guide them the last three quarters of a mile to the LZ.

Within minutes they could hear the muffled shots from their Colonel's suppressed weapon followed by a barrage of Taliban fire and screaming. Several grenades exploded and then all they heard was the Colonel's rifle firing.

Brooke stayed with Stephen and David and gave them a last dose of pain killer to allow them to move as quickly as possible. It was dangerously close to dawn as they reached the landing zone. Fortunately, team comms had been able to stay in contact with base through the night and as they approached the LZ, they could hear the rotors of a Chinook in the distance. Reaching the landing zone, they formed a defensive perimeter two hundred yards from where the helicopter would land.

As the chopper touched ground beside the smoke grenade

they had deployed, the force protection team leapt out of the chopper to join the unit's perimeter. Their sergeant organized return fire to some light Taliban resistance attracted by the helicopter.

None of the ODA team were going to board the chopper until they knew the Colonel had made it. Brooke told her colleagues that the Colonel had lost his combat phone and would be dependent on dead reckoning to find the LZ. Then suddenly, there he was, limping up the rocky path, waving the team to get aboard.

Colonel Ed actually tried to assist Stephen and David onto the loading ramp and then failed to climb aboard himself as the force protection team retreated up the ramp around him. At this point Brooke noticed that the Colonel's fatigues were heavily soaked in blood.

She watched him literally crawl up the ramp and collapse onto a bench in the chopper. He looked at her across the helicopter interior where she had settled David and Stephen onto some padding on the chopper floor.

"Great job Brooke. You got 'em here. That's what training is for, huh?"

Brooke wasn't thinking about their training. She was worried about his leg. Blood was dripping onto the chopper floor from his thigh. "Colonel, you have lost quite a lot of blood there. Let me have a have a look at that leg."

Using her scissors to open up his pant leg, she was shocked to see a massive open wound with extensive skin loss on the outside of his thigh, oozing blood with damaged muscle and contamination from dirt evident throughout the deep injury. "This is a bad wound, Colonel. I am going to clean it as best I can and dress it."

He looked up at her and grimaced. "We got 'em out Brooke. Thank God. Except those two poor guys with neck wounds. I should have been able to help them."

His voice sounded shaky and emotional. She started to tell him that there was nothing anyone could have done for those two soldiers as the Chinook started to lift off. But at that moment, Colonel Ed fell face first off the bench and passed out on the floor of the helicopter.

CHAPTER 27: DIXIE GANG

Klaus spent the day after his arrival in Maple Ridge studying the financial material that Brooke made available to him. Colonel Ed was in and out of HQ. The team thought that it was best that he sleep in their protected space, but he was busy at the hospital and clinic during the day. Klaus enjoyed catching up with the Colonel again and also liked meeting the Colonel's friend Linda. She dropped into HQ after work and announced that she had a snack for the team. It took three men to carry in all the boxes of pizza that Linda had loaded in her car. She smiled and said that she wanted to ensure that everyone had their choice of favorite toppings.

Klaus quickly discovered that the Colonel's brother Ben was exactly the guy they needed for logistical support. Any software Klaus or Brooke needed for analysis of Tony Malto's operation, Ben made it happen the moment it was mentioned. He also enabled Klaus to connect with the impressive finance team at Brinkley Enterprises to discuss some of his findings.

Klaus recognized this was quite a team assembled in the warehouse they fondly called HQ. Klaus knew these guys from Afghanistan and recognized that they constituted a formidable group of Special Forces soldiers. With Ben funding their purchases, the combat team had already gathered an extensive supply of weaponry.

Klaus had learned a lot about military firearms while in Afghanistan and was impressed with the armory in HQ. In addition to standard carbines and pistols, the guys had procured military electroshock weapons designed to substantially extend the effective range of the usual police weapons to nearly one hundred feet. These military electrical weapons delivered an enhanced incapacitating electrical shock compared to police models and also provided multiple shot capacity.

The explosive guys had sourced sophisticated "flash bang" grenades that could be useful in civilian settings. Klaus wasn't sure exactly what response the Colonel was expecting from the Malto gang, but he could see the team was prepared for just about every eventuality.

Klaus discovered that Brooke had done an effective job of penetrating Malto's financial firewalls and gathering intelligence on Malto's various criminal activities. And this evening, the whole team was gathered to listen to Brooke and Klaus describe what they had learned.

Linda was definitely part of the team gathering to hear the report on Tony Malto. Linda's legal expertise might be useful in determining how the team would proceed with their findings. And Klaus had heard something about the Malto family being involved with her father's death.

Brooke started the briefing. Everyone was gathered in HQ with chairs pulled up surrounding Brooke who was standing in front of her colleagues. Klaus thought she looked and sounded like a university lecturer. Some of the guys were taking notes and they were all listening intently. The usual continuous banter had ceased, and everyone was focused on the story that Brooke was describing.

"We have been able to penetrate Tony Malto's financial records, emails, and texts. This information, as well as some law enforcement archival records convince me that the Malto gang is the Arkansas outpost of the reborn Dixie Gang which terrorized law enforcement in the Southern states from the 1960s to 1980s. That Dixie Gang originally had its roots in the poor white communities of the Appalachian Mountains but reached prominence along the Gulf Coast of Mississippi and Louisiana."

Brooke explained to the team that the Dixie Gang did not have ethnic exclusiveness like the mainly Italian Cosa Nostra. Its reputation was characterized by intimidation of entire communities using violence directed against law-abiding citizens, police officers, prosecutors, judges, and other officials.

The Dixie Gang was responsible for spreading terror and fear through several Gulf state towns surrounding Biloxi, Mississippi. By the mid-1990s, the FBI and local law enforcement thought they had eliminated these criminals.

Brooke continued. "Federal and local law enforcement have reported that the Dixie Gang has probably been given new life by the massive amount of government reconstruction money that started flowing into the Gulf region following Hurricane Katrina in 2005. Those billions of dollars of relief money led to renewal and bolstering of the remnants of the Dixie Gang. Both criminal activity and money laundering became easier and very lucrative. The demand for drugs, women, gambling, and human trafficking all expanded significantly with the arrival of both redevelopment funds and outside workers in the Gulf.

"Police archival records show that Maple Ridge was always connected to the original Gulf Coast Dixie Gang. And now our monitoring shows the Malto gang is in constant electronic communication with partners who are operating on the Gulf. These communications generally refer to 'supplies' that seem related to drugs, women, and money."

Brooke turned to point at Klaus who was seated next to her. "My buddy Klaus has been examining the records of the money flow that comes into and out of Maple Ridge. In a moment he is going to describe the pattern of both local and regional crime and money laundering that he has identified." She then turned back to the room.

"As far as Maple Ridge is concerned, Tony Malto has eleven guys working with him. Tommy Lawsen is his number-two guy. Our mirroring devices on their email, text messaging and financial records have uncovered several patterns of criminal activity.

"They are running wholesale drug delivery to Arkansas

from Gulf Coast suppliers of meth, cocaine, Fentanyl and weed. They are importing illegal immigrants from Mexico and Central America who transition through Gulf states to come to various small enterprises in Arkansas. A lot of these immigrant women end up in prostitution. And they provide capital for loan sharking and gambling."

Brooke had the room's undivided attention. "Those illegal immigrant women go to several escort services in and around Arkansas, and I believe Malto partners with the Aryan Brotherhood as muscle to look after the escort business, which is big in Hot Springs and Little Rock as well as Maple Ridge. It also seems that the Chicago-based Simon City Royals gang run the drug business across the state for Tony."

Brooke paused and looked around the room. "Tony's team does not appear to operate the street-level retail stuff. They leave that up to the Aryans and Simon City guys, and that's how they stay under the law enforcement radar for the most part." She lifted her arms and eyebrows to emphasize the Malto gang's cunning at evading the cops.

"But the kingpin of all this activity in Arkansas is definitely Tony Malto. He controls the connection with the Gulf that supplies product. And his gang collects the cash proceeds of the criminal activities from the local street hoods. The real source of Tony's power and control comes from his money laundering. Less sophisticated small-time criminals run the pimps and prostitutes, the drug sales, and provide the muscle necessary to protect the money and product they are moving. But in order to use their money, they need to put it into Tony's highly effective money laundromat. And Klaus has figured out just how it works." Brooke then turned to the accountant.

Klaus felt obliged to stand and Brooke took his seat. "Brooke has given me total access to their banking and business records and their spreadsheets. Really, it's not too difficult to figure out what they are doing. As you know, dealing drugs, women, trafficking people, gambling, and extortion – all these activities require cash or prepaid, disposable credit cards. You are unlikely to pay for your hooker or your meth with a traceable credit card." Klaus looked around at his audience with a shrug.

"It used to be that criminals had little difficulty using that cash. They kept piles of cash 'under the bed' until they deposited suitcases of dollars in their bank accounts. But today's anti-terrorism and anti-money laundering rules in financial institutions have changed the rules of the game."

Klaus then provided a quick primer on money laundering. "You cannot deposit more than $10,000 at a time in most financial accounts without generating lots of questions from the bank and eventually law enforcement about where that money comes from. And even if you show up with $9,999 for deposit two or three times in a row, you will generate the same questions. So, criminals today need to do more than just generate cash from illicit activities. They also need to figure out how to get that money into legitimate bank accounts so that they can use the money with normal financial instruments like credit cards, checking accounts and electronic transfers." Klaus looked around the room to see if there were questions. Hearing none, he pressed on.

"Tony's team collects the cash from a number of different criminal activities that provide gross receipts of more than nine million per month on average. Tony keeps excellent records of all this cash transfer to show his criminal collaborators that he is not cheating them. Tony's gang takes this money in, subtracts their cut, and returns a portion of the laundered proceeds back to their criminal partners. Fortunately for us, they are good with accounting for cash flow, but really sloppy with cybersecurity." Klaus again paused to see if anyone had questions, but they were all following without comment.

"Malto provides two functions at the street level for this criminal activity. He bankrolls upfront 'product' delivery – drugs, women, capital for gambling and loan sharking, illegal immigrants – then he launders the profit. And he is keeping a substantial share of the proceeds for providing these services.

Part of the reason he stays unnoticed by police is that he is not engaged in the day-to-day street activities. Instead, he serves as the financial clearing house for a lot of drug dealers, pimps, loan sharks, gamblers and hoodlums." Klaus looked around the room before summarizing Tony's role.

"He's like an investment bank for gangsters." Klaus smiled at this, and the room returned his grin.

"To effectively launder this money, Malto mixes it in with real proceeds from a lot of 'legitimate' companies operating in cash-oriented business across the state. Restaurants and bars, carwashes, laundromats, concession stands, snack and soda dispensing machines – these are all excellent businesses for gathering legitimate cash proceeds that can be mixed with criminal cash that is then laundered into legitimate bank accounts.

"A bar owner may take in $25,000 in legitimate cash payments during a Wednesday night. However, if it's Tony's bar, this legitimate $25,000 will be salted with another $25,000 in drug or prostitution money." Klaus rubbed his fingers together in the universal gesture for cash flow.

"Tony's team have recruited a lot of legitimate businesses across the state. Looking at public corporate records, it seems that he may buy a business at what looks like a premium or he may go into partnership with the owner. Either way, he is taking it over for money laundering. He often keeps the original owner in charge. The Malto gang, however, undoubtedly looks after the banking and bookkeeping activities for the business. Tony's team keeps the books, and I am sure he pays the original owner well for managing the legitimate aspects of the business and staying quiet and cooperative."

Klaus paused for a sip of water. "That's the first stage of Malto money laundering. Cash from crime mixing in with cash from legitimate business and all the money becoming legitimate as the two cash streams flow together. However, it is obvious that all this extra cash will create a highly profitable bar, carwash, or laundromat. These businesses need to report their books to the tax man, and they naturally want to avoid paying tax as much as possible. They also want to keep their businesses from appearing abnormally profitable to avoid attracting attention from the law. They want these companies to appear just like regular operations – not massive profit generating machines."

The room was silent. Klaus really had their attention. "So, there is also a second level of money laundering where various services are provided at a big premium to these legitimate businesses that are laundering money. This might include business consulting services, construction and renovation, IT services, HR services. And these services typically take money out of the cash laundering businesses to reduce their profitability."

Klaus knew this could be complex for people without financial experience, so he summarized again to ensure everyone understood.

"To sum up, there are three levels working here in Arkansas. The first level is the street activity in drugs, prostitution, human trafficking, et cetera that generates lots of cash. The second level is where this dirty money gets mixed with clean profits of cash heavy 'legitimate' businesses that Malto either owns or engages as a partner. The third level is comprised of the back office support companies that massively overcharge the second level companies to ensure they do not look too profitable. It's a pretty sophisticated operation." Klaus smiled. He was feeling like he was in business school lecturing on corporate strategy.

"We think Tony has a unique partnership with the Gulf Coast elements of the Dixie Gang who provide services at the first and third levels. For example, the Gulf guys provide drugs to Tony's street guys. Tony does not pay directly for the drugs, but he collects the wholesale cost of drugs from the street guys after they sell them retail and turn all the money over to him. Based on email traffic from Tony's shop, the business with the Gulf may involve a guy named Gabriel Duquesne." Klaus looked over at Ed when he mentioned this name.

"Tony runs this money through his second level launder-ing facility, returns some laundered money in useable finan-cial instruments back to the street guys and keeps the rest in his companies. Then back office companies owned by the Gulf Coast guys provide services to the second level launder-ing companies here in Arkansas and charge them excessively, taking the payment for drugs and their own slice of profits back through this excessive invoicing approach." Klaus again turned to the Colonel.

"Just like in Afghanistan, you can usually figure out what's happening when you follow the money."

The whole operation was complex, but Brooke had rapidly achieved access to most of the first level and second level records. However, apart from some invoices submitted by the Gulf Coast companies, they were running into a brick wall try-ing to penetrate the third level of what seemed like an ingeni-ous criminal enterprise.

"Thanks to Brooke's mirroring techniques, we can readily trace criminal money to and from that second level launder-ing activity. The cybersecurity protecting the records of this activity is pretty elementary. But the guys on the Gulf have invested heavily in cybersecurity and we have not been able to get into their records to this point." Klaus shrugged his shoul-ders. He was not confident that they would ever be able to ac-cess information from the Gulf Coast element of this criminal conspiracy.

He continued. "I believe that we can provide this informa-tion about the Malto gang activity to the FBI as the foundation for a RICO charge. It has been so straightforward to access this information that I think Malto would have difficulty claiming privacy as a defense.

"However, we will then have a problem with the third level Gulf Coast guys. This guy Duquesne seems to have quite a nice business going with Malto and we will probably piss them off if we take Tony down."

Klaus looked directly at Colonel Ed. "Colonel, I do not know how far your rules of engagement go at present. I realize that we are focused on the Malto gang. But I think that we need to consider what we are going to do about the guys on the Gulf as well."

The Colonel nodded. He understood what Klaus meant.

To everyone's surprise, Ed's friend Linda spoke up next. "Klaus, I think that you and Brooke have described exactly what a prosecutor needs to bring these guys to account. It will need to be carefully described to the police with documentation. Law enforcement will need to add some evidence of street level drug dealing and prostitution to show what criminal activities Tony is financing. However, if we demonstrate that criminal activities are generating cash that is being laundered through these second level companies, then a RICO prosecution involving all these levels is definitely feasible. And you are right about the FBI, Klaus. The fact that the criminal conspiracy crosses state boundaries means the Agency needs to lead the investigation."

Klaus thought that he knew where she was heading with this but wanted to be sure that everyone understood. "Why is RICO important for us to think about, Linda?"

The lawyer joined him standing and turned so she was facing the team. "RICO pertains to anyone violating two or more of a broad set of federal or state offenses over a ten-year period. It allows us to tie Tony to ill-gotten gains by demonstrating that he has organized a criminal enterprise that shares illicit profits through multiple businesses as opposed to showing that he is personally involved in every example of prostitution or drug dealing. RICO will allow law enforcement to get Malto by tying him to the money flow, not individual acts of criminal activity."

She looked around at the entire group for questions. Klaus was pleased with her rapid grasp of what he was describing to the team.

"In addition to improving our chances to put Malto away

for this racketeering activity, it also allows the prosecutor to freeze assets derived from criminal activity prior to the criminal conviction. With the information you have gathered, prosecutors would freeze all the accounts of the legitimate businesses Tony uses for money laundering."

Klaus knew the lawyer understood the power of RICO prosecutions with her next observation. "This has convinced criminals in the past to enter plea bargains to avoid trial under RICO indictment because they lose everything if convicted under RICO. They also have difficulty defending themselves against RICO if their assets are frozen, thereby eliminating resources to pay for high-quality defense attorneys."

Klaus thought that they were likely at a decision point with respect to next steps. "Colonel, Brooke and I will work tonight on packaging up what we have discovered this week about Tony's operations. I think that we have plenty here for a successful prosecution. I do not believe that we can learn more about his connections to the Gulf Coast back office companies unless we can get into this guy Gabriel Duquesne's system somehow. Should we be approaching prosecutors and the FBI now?"

They were again surprised by the certainty of Linda's next comment. "This needs to be shared with the FBI immediately. With the inter-state aspect you have discovered with the link to the Gulf, this is beyond local police jurisdiction. You guys cannot take this any further without the Agency being involved. This will be a huge gift for them. It would take them years of hard slogging investigation to develop what you are going to serve them on a platter." Linda was extremely impressed with what Brooke and Klaus had achieved in just a few days.

She continued. "I have a pretty good relationship with the Little Rock FBI office. They have other offices around the state, but they cover our county from Little Rock. I know that they have lots of experience with anti-racketeering investigations into Little Rock motorcycle gangs and their anti-terrorism activity has given them expertise in recognizing money laundering when they see it."

She looked at Ed to explain her background with the Little Rock office. "We had a class action against an Arkansas headquartered bank that was shortchanging their employees on overtime. As part of our research for our clients, we discovered that the bank might be violating money laundering provisions and we brought the FBI evidence that we had obtained from our clients."

Linda smiled as she remembered the case. "I must say, involving the feds also helped us settle the class action very favorably for our clients. The bank realized that having a labor dispute with people who understood the bank's deposit and account history was not good business sense while you are undergoing a federal investigation for money laundering."

Linda looked directly at Colonel Ed. "I could open discussions with the Little Rock office based on what Brooke and Klaus have learned about the Malto gang.

"With the information that these two have developed, this is a very strong case to take to the FBI right now. I had planned to be in Maryland in the next week, but our case has been delayed. I could go up to Little Rock as soon as possible and have a confidential briefing with the Special Agent in Charge and describe what we have found."

Colonel Ed asked the question that everyone was thinking as Linda offered to brief the feds. "That sounds like a great way of engaging the FBI, Linda. But you do not have any direct role in the work to this point. Benjamin has hired everyone else in the room as consultants to work on this project. You are here as my friend. Are you certain that you want to get involved?"

They all noticed that Linda looked down before responding. They sensed that this was emotional for her. "Ed, there are a few things here that everyone should know."

She took a deep breath and looked around the room. "First of all, my family has lived in Maple Ridge for many generations. You have just arrived and have shown me that we have a very significant problem with Tony Malto. I am embarrassed that it took this remarkable little band just three days to discover something that we should have recognized years ago. Somehow, as Brooke and Klaus have described, Malto seems to have avoided police investigation in Maple Ridge. It is definitely time for us to end Tony's protected status.

"Secondly, Sharon Malto is now my client. Our firm has engaged a family law firm to help us represent Sharon but the abuse that she has suffered needs to be addressed. I want this information that we are discussing available to her family lawyer."

Then Linda paused and looked down at the floor. "Finally, I have mentioned to some of you that my dad died in a car accident. He was engaged in a real estate deal with Tony Malto's father just before his death and the terms of their partnership allowed Tony's dad to buy out the property from Dad's estate at very favorable terms after my father's death.

"With Tony's wife Sharon's recent 'accident' I am seeing similarities to my dad's traffic death. Certainly, if Sharon had not been protected by air bags and modern restraints, she might have suffered the same fate as my father. So, this is starting to feel very personal to me." Linda's green eyes were flashing at this point. Everyone in the room could feel her determination to deal with Tony Malto.

Colonel Ed brought the meeting to a close after asking for final comments from Brooke. She said that she was going to continue trying to access records from the Gulf Coast gang but thought that their security was too good for her current methods and equipment to breach.

The team got up and stretched almost in unison. They had absorbed a lot of information this evening but felt that they were certainly making progress on their mission – whatever their mission might be. Everyone agreed that they would meet again after Linda had visited Little Rock.

CHAPTER 28: PTSD

D r. Romulus was sitting in his office at the end of clinic with Colonel Brinkley's chart in front of him, documenting his conversation with Dr. Suzanne Fortis. Dr. Fortis's call had reminded Romulus about the Colonel and he worried about how Ed was making out in his new primary care role. It was absurd for his partners to assume that he might be addicted. However, Romulus could understand that the missing two years in his resume might seem suspicious to his new colleagues. The Special Forces were always very restrictive about disclosing combat operational details, and that limited what Romulus could say about the Colonel's injuries and his treatment.

He had become involved in Colonel Brinkley's case when mental health services were first consulted by the physical rehab team at the Veteran's Administration hospital. The physiotherapy team characterized the Colonel as being very flat in his emotional response to the world. Unlike most wounded soldiers, he did not complain about his injury, the way he was being treated, or all the various inefficiencies of the veterans' health system. The Colonel had no spontaneous complaints about his mental health. But on direct questioning from the mental health consultant, Ed admitted that he was not sleeping, had frequent nightmares, and was not recovering his energy and focus.

That was about a year after he had been evacuated back to the States and honorably discharged from the military. After his last mission in Afghanistan, the Colonel underwent surgical treatment and rehab for a terrible wound in his thigh. He had sustained this injury from a mortar attack during intense combat and the wound was not attended to for more than twenty-four hours.

Unfortunately, the Colonel developed deep infection in the leg, which required several operations with infected muscle removal and eventually skin grafts to close the wound. When his wound finally closed more than six months after his injury, he could barely walk. He had lost muscle from the infection and surgery on his thigh, and lost even more muscle from the rest of his body through atrophy caused by immobilization.

After his wound healed, Colonel Brinkley was started on intensive exercise and physical therapy. His therapists were sensitive to the risk of addiction in soldiers with severe injuries, but the Colonel came off pain killers quickly and fortunately did not seem to be at risk for opioid dependency. By a year after his injury however, his physical therapists were becoming concerned about the Colonel's emotional state and referred him for mental health consultation.

By now the Colonel was living outside the hospital and was attending the out-patient rehab department for two to three hours of treatment daily, focused on rebuilding his leg muscles and general strength training. Following his initial mental health consultation, he was seen by the psych intake team, and they documented features of sleep disorder, as well as finding high levels of both anxiety and depression on psychological testing.

This was all typical of Post-Traumatic Stress Disorder. The Colonel had been exposed to terrible battlefield stress and the PTSD diagnosis was not surprising. Dr. Romulus did not personally see the Colonel at this time. But as supervising psychiatrist, he approved the treatment course proposed by the mental health team.

Colonel Brinkley was started on three months of cognitive processing therapy led by a highly regarded psychologist. He was seen weekly for ninety-minute therapy sessions where his thought patterns related to the battlefield trauma were discussed and his emotional response to trauma explored. In addition to the one-on-one therapy sessions, the Colonel also had access to online resources and homework that focused on adaptation to battlefield trauma and better ways of managing his emotions around traumatic memories.

At the end of three months of intensive treatment, the Colonel's sleep and depression and anxiety scores had not improved at all. He was now at risk of developing chronic PTSD and long-term disability due to battlefield trauma.

Dr. Romulus saw the Colonel for the first time as a consulting psychiatrist at this point and agreed that mood modifying drugs were indicated. The team also changed his treatment to focus on desensitization to specific trauma memories. But three months after starting the drugs and the new therapy, the Colonel's psychological scores continued to show significant emotional distress.

Dr. Romulus knew that the eventual outcome with soldiers who had failed to respond after six months of intense trauma therapy was not promising. Most soldiers did well with their first or second rounds of treatment. Those who failed to improve after six months generally remained chronically impaired and were sometimes unable to return to work or a normal life.

As the psychiatrist responsible for leading the team providing the Colonel's treatment, Romulus decided to meet with him in a therapy session and explore other options for managing his condition. He had been aware of the Colonel's case for some time. He decided to do some prework in preparing for this second consultation session.

He called up two members of Colonel Brinkley's combat team as part of his clinical review. One was a female master sergeant who had responsibility for the team's electronic surveillance technology and had also participated in battlefield surgery with the Colonel. The other was a young rifleman who had been treated for a femur fracture on the battlefield by Colonel Brinkley.

The details of this battlefield surgical treatment were classified as a military secret, but it sounded to Romulus like the Colonel had developed important new methods for actually operating on wounded soldiers in very difficult battlefield situations. This was likely the first time that the techniques had been used in combat, but there were rumors that the Special Forces were now routinely deploying surgeons on high-risk missions to replicate the results that the Colonel had demonstrated were possible.

When asked about the Colonel, both non-commissioned officers responded in unusual fashion. Generally, Special Forces troops were understated in their admiration for their officers. They expected their officers to respond to adversity with bravery and resilience. But these two soldiers expressed surprising respect for their Colonel.

The rifleman clearly said that he owed his life to the Colonel's surgical skill and combat expertise. The master sergeant stressed the importance of the Colonel's rear-guard protection of the retreating team from the Taliban. She felt that the team's successful rescue would have failed without the Colonel's determined defensive action. She had not realized the extent of his leg injuries until the team was safely loaded on the evacuation helicopter.

"When I saw his leg after we boarded the Chinook, I couldn't believe that he had defended our rear all night the way he did. He saved Stephen and David by operating on their legs and then he protected the rest of us with his rear-guard action through the night." The master sergeant told Romulus that she had visited the Colonel once in hospital while on leave and mentioned to the psychiatrist that she had been very concerned about the Colonel's mental state on that visit.

Dr. Romulus had been involved with PTSD management for more than five years and had heard remarkable stories of bravery in the clients who came to him with mental distress from their battlefield experiences. But he was particularly moved with what he had learned about the Colonel. He opened his therapy session with the Colonel by simply describing what he had learned by talking to his Special Force's colleagues.

"Colonel, I have never been in combat. But I have spoken to two members of your team who explained to me how you saved lives for your team, first with surgery and then by leading them on a difficult retreat. I just want you to know how impressed I am by what you did on that last mission. You certainly have the gratitude of your team."

The Colonel seemed distracted sitting facing Dr. Romulus with a small table to the side between them. Romulus observed that the Colonel was a handsome man and from physio reports, Ed was recovering his physical capabilities with therapy and intense training. However, like many patients who were affected by combat psychological trauma, his thoughts seemed to be elsewhere, and he was clearly not fully focused on the therapist as they talked.

The Colonel looked briefly at Romulus without expression. "Who did you talk to?"

The psychiatrist explained that he had spoken to one of the soldiers that the Colonel had operated on as well as the technical master sergeant who also assisted him with surgery. He watched the Colonel take in that information. There was a long moment of silence and then Romulus was astonished to see the Colonel start sobbing wordlessly with tears streaming down his face.

The therapist simply sat in his chair wondering what this could signify. Ed's tears were quiet, his sobs remained silent as he continued to demonstrate what was for him very unusual behavior. Romulus decided that no questions were needed and gently pushed a box of tissues across the table. Ed did not touch the Kleenex but sat motionless expressing anguish without words.

Romulus knew that the next comment needed to come from the Colonel. And eventually the words came haltingly. "Did she... did she tell you about our two guys that... that I failed to help?"

The therapist lifted his shoulders in a neutral shrug. He had no idea what the Colonel was talking about but felt that his role at present was best served by silence.

And then it began. "I couldn't get a... get a tube down the first guy. His cords and throat had been damaged and when I tried... I tried to intubate him there was nothing to see to pass the tube. All I could do was hold him while he... he choked to death. It didn't take long, but I couldn't do anything... anything to help him." His sobbing increased and it took a minute or more before he could continue.

"I was able to intubate the second guy. But he was bleeding massively from his carotid and jugular on one side, and he also had multiple extremity wounds." The Colonel stopped and Romulus could see his eyes returning to Afghanistan. He was literally revisiting the battlefield.

"There was no time to check his blood pressure, but I could feel in his intact carotid that his pulse pressure was very weak. After intubating him I tried exploring his neck on the side of the damaged carotid but when I identified the injured artery it was completely destroyed."

For the first time in the session, Ed's eyes lifted to connect with Dr. Romulus. Romulus could literally see the pain in his eyes and could feel him beseeching the therapist for understanding that he had done the best that he could have done.

"I clamped it off, but I could see from the low flow in the damaged vessel that he had... he had just lost too much blood. He was unconscious and had probably suffered brain injury from the loss of blood flow through his carotid to his brain. But who knows, he might had survived if I had been able to stop... to stop the bleeding."

He now lifted his head and looked around the room like he was seeing it for the first time. "I should have saved those two guys. They had terrible injuries, but we owe it to our comrades to keep them alive if they get to the first doc with a pulse present. And I failed both... I failed both of them." Then he looked back to the floor and returned to silence with the flow of tears restarting.

Dr. Romulus realized the potential importance of this session for the Colonel's treatment. The mental health teams had understandably been focused on the trauma he suffered from the intense fire fights he was engaged in during his team's mission and tactical retreat. The reason for his lack of response to treatment was now perhaps becoming evident: they were feasibly treating the wrong trauma.

The Colonel was suffering not only from his combat experiences, but also from his inability to save the lives of two colleagues that the mental health team knew nothing about.

That interview started the Colonel's slow road to recovery. The treatment was complex because it needed to deal with a doctor's innate tendency to judge himself harshly when things do not go well. Dr. Romulus personally took over Ed's therapy and started bi-weekly treatment sessions where they evaluated his personality, examined his stressful profession as well as his intrinsic tendency to own responsibility for poor outcomes whether warranted or not.

They used multiple sessions of talk therapy to allow the Colonel to understand how his personality responded to perceived failure, as well as the risks that his personality posed when he was faced with insoluble surgical challenges.

After six months of treatment, the Colonel was sleeping better, he was off meds and his depression and anxiety scores had markedly improved. He and Dr. Romulus spent a considerable time talking about his return to clinical practice. The therapist was worried that returning to trauma surgery might pose a risk of triggering his PTSD. That could result in an emotional relapse and might even put a patient in jeopardy in the operating room.

The Colonel readily agreed with this assessment. "Dr. Romulus, my career as a trauma surgeon has been very rewarding. But let's face it, it's better suited to younger surgeons. I cannot imagine going back to battlefield surgery or even behind-the-lines trauma surgery with the Special Forces. I really need to think about starting over in a new type of practice."

He actually had already started practicing medicine again. He was working as a primary care doctor at the military hospital and the nurses and doctors that he was working with agreed that his clinical skills were outstanding. And then he came to one of Dr. Romulus's therapy sessions with a proposal.

"Dr. Romulus, I appreciate everything you and your team have done for me. I think that I understand myself much better and I know that I am ready to put my learnings back to work in clinical medicine. I have applied for a position in the medical home model in Arkansas. It's a new way of thinking about looking after patients with chronic disease and I think it is the kind of challenge that will help me to start over from a clinical perspective."

Dr. Romulus' admiration and respect for Ed had grown through their therapy sessions and he agreed that Ed now likely had the psychological tools to return to a primary care practice.

The psychiatrist had no idea that Ed providing care as Tony Malto's doctor was going to provide a stress test for his therapy. He did however think that his conversation with Dr. Fortis had likely solved a problem for Ed in Maple Ridge. The psychiatrist signed off on his brief note about the telephone call with Suzanne Fortis and put Ed's chart in his out-basket.

CHAPTER 29: LITTLE ROCK

One of the primary tactics used by defendants in class action lawsuits is to delay, delay and delay again. As time passes, memories fade, the class may get smaller through natural attrition and basically time is on the side of the defense counsel rather than the lawyers for the little guys who are suing. Linda's firm was expert in refusing to accept delays. However, in their Maryland case, the illness of a judge was forcing her to accept a pause in the tempo of the suit. She had been expecting to head to Maryland on the weekend but now her team was delayed for a week or two.

Linda was eager to get going in Maryland. She knew that they were going to win an award for her clients, but also recognized there would be important issues in contention during the trial. The first question was whether the other side would let the case go to the jury or offer a settlement during the trial. Linda knew that the recent work planning trial strategy with her Maryland litigation partners was powerful, and she expected that the other side would likely make an offer during the trial. Whether this offer would be sufficient for Linda's clients would depend on how the jury seemed to be responding after the first few days of testimony.

Another question was whether any settlement offer or jury decision would be available to all patients who developed disability after surgery, or only those who had already joined the lawsuit. The other side would try and limit access to any settlement and Linda's team would argue the outcome should cover all patients who eventually developed a severe complication from surgery.

These were important issues to Linda's firm as well as the various investors who were supporting the high cost of this class action suit. Class action is always undertaken on a contingency basis, which means that no one gets paid until the client gets paid. The Davis firm had been investing in this case for nearly three years, with their paralegals identifying potential clients, signing them up and then managing their concerns while they slowly moved toward trial.

There were also the high costs of filing legal documents with the courts to initiate the class action and having the class certified to go forward. Linda's team needed to engage in taking pretrial testimony from likely witnesses and also had to respond to the endless and sometimes frivolous motions raised by the defense team.

All these costs added to the expenses necessary to launch and advance a class action suit. Linda was careful to only accept cases where she could anticipate a positive outcome with payback to her firm through the contingency fees that she would receive when her clients were paid. To reduce the risk to her firm, she had also become adept in sharing expenses with partners like the Maryland litigation experts in this case.

Linda's firm also worked with financial leaders in Maple Ridge to syndicate financing for her cases with investors who were offered a later payback in return for upfront cash. Linda was pleased that these syndicated funds were now being offered to all communities in Maple Ridge. She liked the fact that a winning case would offer rewards to all citizens in the town. However, this also increased the pressure on Linda to achieve favorable outcomes – not only for her clients but also for her investors.

Each day of delay in the progress toward trial cost the Davis firm money. Counsel representing the insurance companies for the defendants that Linda was suing knew that her funding would only stretch so far. The other side's determination to delay was driven in part by understanding that if Linda was financially stretched, she might advise her clients to settle earlier for a lower amount of damages in order to stop the cash outflows needed to keep the case going. It was part of Linda's job to ensure she had sufficient financial backing so that she would not be forced to accept a settlement that was less than her clients deserved.

Everyone on Linda's side – clients, lawyers, and investors – were eager to get to judgment day and she was certainly looking forward to the trial starting. But it was impossible to appeal an adjournment due to a judge's illness and she would just have to accept this delay.

Although Linda had plenty to keep her occupied at the office in the meantime, she found the issue with Tony Malto to be all-consuming and she wanted to speak to the FBI as soon as possible.

Her office set up a telephone call with the Special Agent in Charge of the Little Rock office early Friday morning. Linda told the agent that she had information about a potential RICO cause of action and requested an urgent confidential interview that was granted for noon that same day.

Linda's driver was her only companion on the short trip to Little Rock for this meeting. She took with her summaries of materials that Brooke and Klaus had prepared. None of the documents mentioned Tony Malto or members of his gang by name.

The primary criminal enterprises and the first layer of money laundering were referred to cryptically. Linda did not plan to give the FBI everything she had to offer in a first interview. She wanted to protect the confidentiality of the people who had uncovered this information about Malto. Linda thought that this should be the first of several interviews and she wanted to determine how the Agency would respond to the information that she was providing.

Special Agent Sarah Bond oversaw the Little Rock office. She had the general air of competence that Linda had come to respect in the Agency. She led Linda into their boardroom and introduced her to the local agent in charge of racketeering investigations. But Linda was surprised and disturbed when she recognized another man in the room.

Sarah Bond introduced him as Bill Ashcroft, liaison officer between her office and the county police force in Maple Ridge.

"No offense to you Bill or to you, Sarah, but I was hoping to keep this discussion between myself and the Agency."

Sarah firmly shook her head. "I am sorry, Ms. Davis. After 9/11, the Agency's investigation into why we did not detect and prevent the attack on the homeland kept coming back to the fact that we tended to keep information in isolated compartments. Since that time, we have emphasized the importance of sharing information with local law enforcement."

She lifted her hands in emphasis. "In retrospect, leading up to 9/11, everyone saw a piece of the puzzle, but no one could tell what the overall picture showed because no one saw all the pieces. We are trying to avoid that mistake by ensuring that local police departments are engaged at an early stage in investigations that may eventually involve them. Bill was here on his regular weekly visit today and I asked him to sit in."

Linda thought long and hard and considered simply getting up and leaving. She was sure that Bill Ashcroft had been vetted by the FBI and was probably trustworthy. However, she also knew how the county police department worked.

The FBI agents were drawn from across the country and would regularly transfer between offices. For example, Linda knew that Sarah Bond was from Connecticut and that her most recent posting before moving to Little Rock was in Dallas. However, virtually all the members of the Maple Ridge police force, both leaders and officers, were lifelong residents of the county.

They would have grown up with Tony Malto and the rest of the gang, played ball and gone to school with them. Chances were, someone on the force would be related to a member of the Malto gang, at least by marriage. Did Linda feel safe discussing her information in front of a member of that force?

Linda resolved that she needed to gauge how the FBI would respond to the information and that she would have to take a risk on Bill.

"Special Agent Bond, I am working with collaborators who have gathered a substantial amount of information about organized crime headquartered in Maple Ridge that is active across the state and has commercial connection with out-of-state criminal groups."

She went on to describe what she had learned from Brooke and Klaus, including some details of the complex relationships between Tony's companies and the transfer of money from his retail criminal activity to his back office laundering operation and the connection to the Gulf.

She did not mention Tony's name nor make reference to any company that could be traced back to Tony and she did not mention Gabriel Duquesne. But she knew from the special agent's probing questions that basic information on Tony was likely present on their files and that they would quickly figure out who Linda was referring to.

After Linda had finished summarizing her information, Sarah Bond asked her to disclose her sources. Linda responded that she planned to describe how she came by this material but that she would want to understand what the Agency response would be prior to naming her sources.

Sarah nodded her understanding and said that she would discuss this with her team and with the Dallas RICO team that investigated criminal enterprise activity in Arkansas. She understood that Linda would want to know how the Agency would proceed with her information as soon as possible. Indeed, she had set up a call with the Dallas team after Linda had initially requested an interview.

Sarah suggested that Linda might take a late lunch break while she completed this teleconference with Dallas and that they could meet again later that afternoon to discuss next steps.

Linda sat outside the federal building café and called Ed

from the burner cell phone that Brooke had provided for her.

"Hi, I know that you are in clinic, but I hoped that I might catch you for a moment."

Ed sighed. "It's wonderful to hear your voice. Things have been simply crazy the past few days and I haven't had a chance to tell you properly how wonderful last weekend was for me. It seems like a lifetime ago."

"I know Ed. Hot Springs seems like a long, long time ago."

She heard a sigh on the other end of the line. "Linda, I need to get some time with you. We need time to sit together and get to know each other when we are not discussing gangsters."

Linda laughed. "You might say right now that we are truly partners in crime, or at least in crime prevention." She went on to tell Ed about her discussion with Special Agent Bond and that she would be returning later that evening after dinner. She was pleased when Ed suggested that they meet outside his increasingly crowded HQ.

"How about I pick up burgers to bring to your place and feed you when you arrive home? Doctor's orders that you need to eat."

Linda laughed again. "Do you realize that you are once again inviting yourself to dine at my home?"

She heard him groan on the line and she chuckled. "I'm teasing, Ed. That would be wonderful, and I really want to see you when we are not surrounded by your very impressive team. I will give you a call when I am approaching home."

Feeling excited about seeing Ed later in the evening, Linda returned to Special Agent Bond's office. This time Sarah was alone.

"Linda thanks for bringing this to us. The Agency thinks that we know who the perpetrator is in this case, but I understand and appreciate the care that you are taking around confidentiality. We also understand that time is of the essence to protect you and your colleagues who developed this information.

"We are going to work over the weekend to put together a

task force that can look at the data that you have described here today. We will have a special federal prosecutor assigned to the task force and I hope that we can meet with you and your collaborators early next week."

Linda breathed a sigh of relief. "Thanks, Sarah. I have known these guys that we are investigating for years but realize now that I have underestimated their reach and their danger. We have a rigorous security presence now, but it will make me feel much better to have you engaged as soon as possible."

"For the weekend, do you have security?"

"Sarah, you would not believe the security we have. It is quite remarkable."

Sarah hoped she was right.

CHAPTER 30: TOMMY'S TRANSCRIPT

Tony had been fuckin' impossible to deal with for the whole week before you guys got us. If I'm gonna tell you everything like I agreed, then I gotta tell you how crazy that week was.

Sunday night we beat up that mouthy doc and Tony thought he got some good shots on him. My voice was still hoarse after that bastard gets the drop on me and suckers me in the throat, so I was pretty happy Tony took him down a notch.

Then, that stupid bastard doctor comes back to see Sharon in the hospital. I let Tony know he is there, and Tony goes berserk and says he's gonna finish off this guy once and for all. I figure I am going to have to calm Tony down or he might hurt the guy too bad. He is a doctor after all, and it wouldn't be good to kill him.

So, Tony comes down to the hospital with most of the boys and is ready to kick the shit out of that doc and the bastard comes out of the door of the hospital and we go to surround him, and then these lights go on and all of a sudden, it's like we's in a war zone or something. Somewhere this doctor got military grade guys shootin' up our Suburban wheels and I am pretty sure he got picked up in an armored SUV. I seen bullets bouncin' off the windows after he got in.

Then, some guy who is scared to death drops some paper on Tony at his house before he comes home. It's from that damn woman lawyer and another lawyer and it says Sharon is filing for separation, wants custody of Tony Junior and tells Tony he can't come within one hundred feet of Sharon. Well Tony just freaks out and sends me down to the hospital to talk some sense into Sharon but when I get there, she was moved to another floor, and they won't tell me where.

So now I'm gettin' pissed at Sharon too. I mean I like her okay and I want to help her get back on Tony's good side and all but this is gettin' too much. So, I bribe someone at admitting to tell me where she is. I find out she's got private guards outside her room, two guys who are carrying, who tell me Ms. Laforge don't want no visitors and she has now got round the clock security.

And I think, "Who they talkin' about, this Laforge broad?" and then I remember that's Sharon's maiden name.

So, Sharon stays in hospital the next couple days and I am keepin' Tony from doin' somethin' really stupid like tryin' to break her outta hospital or somethin'. And each day he is more and more pissed. Like I believe he loves Sharon. But by the end of the week, I think he woulda cut off her head with a fishin' knife he was so pissed.

Then, I'm with Tony late Friday afternoon when he gets a call on a special phone in his office. Like I say, he was already pissed at what Sharon's putting him through. But then he gets this call and we are sittin' there and he don't say nothin', but he listens and gets like white in the face and then he gets red and like almost purple.

And then he says on the phone, "How the fuck does she know all that?" He listens some more.

"Where is she now?" And then, "You're sure that she didn't say my name? She didn't identify us?"

He listens some more and then he throws the phone against the wall. He looks at the ceiling for a minute and then says to me, "Tommy, get the black Chevy we use for a plain clothes cop car when we gotta chase kids offa the drug sites for the Simon City guys. And make sure that it's got the cherry siren to put on top and bring Billy and another car and bring some masks and some hoods and a buncha zip ties."

So, I wanna know, "What the hell's goin' on Boss? What are we gonna do?"

And he says, "We are going to pick up Linda fuckin' Davis the lawyer and we are gonna ask her how come she suddenly knows so much about our business."

I say to him, "What the fuck are you talkin' about, Tony?"

And he points to the phone he threw against the wall, and he says, "That's my guy on the inside of the county cops. He hears that bitch was in Little Rock today telling the FBI everything about us without using our names. We gotta convince her this is not healthy for her and get her to shut up."

So, me and Billy gets on suits like we is plain clothes cops and get the Chevy and drive out to that long quiet road along the Ridge where everyone knows the lawyer lives. One of the other boys follows in the Suburban with Tony.

Tony heard she was coming home from Little Rock tonight. And sure enough, fifteen minutes after we get there a half a mile before her house, her German car comes cruisin' by. We see she is on the phone in the backseat with her driver alone in the front.

Billy pops on the cherry top and siren and we pull the driver over. We walks up to the driver's side of the car in our suits and then at the last minute pull on masks and Billy drags the driver outta the car and tells him to shut up. He's an old guy I know has been driving for her forever.

Billy puts zip ties on the old guy and puts a hood on him and a gag and ties him to a tree off the road. The same time Billy takes him, I open the back door just as the lawyer woman is yelling something on her cell phone. I grab the phone and throws it into the bushes.

I put a hood over her head and put zip ties on her wrists and ankles. Then I pat her down, looking for another phone which I find in her jacket. I throw that down on the road and smash it with my boot.

Then I picks her up and throws her in the back of the Chevy. Billy jumps into the German car and drives it down a lane into the woods, so it won't be seen. The Suburban follows to pick him up after Tony gets out to drive the Chevy.

Tony is drivin' the Chevy and I am in the back with the lawyer broad who starts screamin'. Tony makes a circle motion around his head and I get it, wrapping a cloth I had with me around her mouth and tying it. She keeps on screaming and strugglin' for a while and then finally settles down cause it's hard to breathe through that cloth and shout. But then as she catches her breath every once in a while, she still keeps on trying to shout.

Me and Tony ain't saying nothing and I know she ain't seen us. I know Tony don't wanna kill her. He just wanted to scare the shit outta her and shut her up. And I think to myself while we are drivin', it's gonna be pretty tough to make this broad shut up. And I hoped right then that Tony knows what the hell he's doing.

CHAPTER 31: SADDLING UP

I t was around six p.m. on Friday night and Colonel Ed had just arrived in HQ after his day in clinic. He yelled to Stephen who was in the HQ kitchen, "Stephen, I'm going to take one of the vehicles to pick up burgers and meet Linda at her place when she gets home from Little Rock."

Stephen assigned two of the team to accompany him to Linda's home for security but then questioned Ed's decision with a smile and a wink. "Colonel we're having barbecue tonight. Are you sure that you want to join Ms. Davis and miss out on a great pulled pork meal with the guys?"

Ed was just about to respond to Stephen's comment when two of Brooke's computer alarms started signaling an urgent problem.

Brooke ran to her computer and opened the program. "Colonel, the alarms are coming from Linda's implanted GPS devices. I put one under her watch and one under a toenail and they are both signaling. And the program is showing that the signal was initiated because Linda is more than one hundred yards from both her personal cell phone and the burner phone I gave her."

At first Brooke figured that Linda must have forgotten the phones somewhere. But when Ed called the burner phone, it failed to ring. Ed then called her personal line, and it went immediately to voicemail. Ed called her housekeeper who said that she had been talking to Linda ten minutes ago on her cell when she suddenly screamed, and her cell service shut off. The housekeeper had called police and they were on the way to Linda's house, but the housekeeper had no idea where Linda was.

Meanwhile, Brooke was tracking Linda's GPS on her device. "Thank God that I insisted that everyone wear a personal GPS triggered by their phone. That worked for me in Afghanistan when our local contractors were abducted by the Taliban."

Brooke continued quickly. "You know the first thing kidnappers do is break their target's cell phone or tear out the sim card to make sure the victim can't be traced by cell phone GPS. This provides us a perfect proactive signal that we set up for all the team. If your personal GPS is separated from your cell phone, or if your phone is defunctioned, it activates this alarm here at HQ and also activates the implanted GPS to allow it to be tracked. The GPS power supply will let us follow the device for about twelve hours."

Brooke checked her computer and turned to Ed. "We need to assume that Linda has been abducted. We are getting a strong signal from her devices and that should persist for the next few hours. I have mobile tracking gear that we can use in the car to find her. Let's get going because there is a time limit on the GPS power."

Brooke could see Ed immediately falling into tactical mode. "Everyone but Benjamin and Klaus saddle up. Three cars, all weapon and explosive options. We'll figure out en route what terms of engagement will be. Brooke and Stephen lead in my car, Stephen drives."

Brooke grabbed her scanner. Her task would be to guide them in to Linda's location. And Brooke once again silently thanked her training that insisted she implant the GPS devices.

CHAPTER 32: TONY'S TRANSCRIPT

Now that I'm telling you guys everything, I gotta tell you I was a little nervous about takin' the lawyer. But what I heard from my man at the county police meant we was all goin' to jail forever if the FBI got us first or I was gonna get tortured and dead if Gabriel got me before you feds. The only way outta this mess was gonna be to make this lawyer shaddap. If we got ridda her on the day she went to Little Rock, we woulda had you FBI guys all over us. So, I figured we hadda make the bitch afraid about what her life would be like if she talked any more crap about me and my business.

I had heard from my guy on the police that she hadn't said my name yet. I figured this might be the last chance to make her shut up before she named me. If she knew we could grab her easy, and we scared the shit outta her – well that could be the best way to shut her up without killin' the bitch. Usually, I would call Gabriel for advice about this kinda thing. But if he knew what that bitch was sayin' I would be a dead man.

I left her in the backseat with Tommy on the way to the camp where we was going to hold her for a while. When we got her in the car, Tommy put a gag on her when she started screamin'. But even though that gag was chokin' her when she tried to scream, she kept on strugglin' and tryin' to shout through the gag. Her fightin' like that kinda told me that it was gonna be tough to shut her up.

There are lots of places around the Ridge where you can get lost in the forest and I have a coupla these places. I guess I can say now that we gotta deal between us that there are some un-marked graves on those places but like I say I wasn't gonna kill the bitch. That woulda brung you FBI guys down on me like ants to honey.

We get to the camp and takes her outta the back seat making sure her hood was in place. I told the guys to keep their masks on as well. We brought her into the main room of the camp and tied her to a heavy chair with zip ties. Even though big Tommy picked her up and tied her to the chair like she was a doll, she kept on fightin' and tryin' to yell through the gag. And I am thinkin', I gotta think of somethin' to scare her bad so she won't wanna ever piss me off in the future.

So, I let Tommy have a little fun to get her more scared. I mo-tion to him, and he uses his knife to cut off her clothes down to her underwear. She has a great lookin' body and I figured maybe I should have some fun with her. If I messed around with her and then let Tommy have her after me, then that would shut her up for good.

Her bein' a big-time lawyer, she won't wanna' admit a few guys had her – especially since she won't know who was doin' it. Tommy always had some rubbers with him and most times I don't like rubbers but that would keep us from getting found out with DNA or somethin'.

And then I would tell her while we are messin' with her that if we heard anything from the FBI, we would pick her up again to have some more fun with her. Then I looked at her sitting there with her legs held apart with zip ties on the chair legs and her fancy underwear, I started to get horny and figured this was all gonna work out for the best.

I already told the guys that I would be the only one to talk to her and I was gonna use a deep voice so she wouldn't recognize me.

So, I says to her using a deep fake voice, "Linda Davis, we know you was talkin' to the FBI today and we wanna know where you got that information. And then we are gonna have some fun with you tonight. And if you say anythin' more to the feds, we are gonna snatch you again and keep on comin' back here to have some more fun with you."

I motion to Tommy to take off her gag so she can tell us about how she got her information. And then, damn if the bitch don't pipe up right away, even though she still got a hood on, "Fuck you, Tony Malto. I know that's you and I'm going to put you away for a long, long time."

And then I started thinkin' maybe this wasn't such a good idea.

CHAPTER 33: TACTICS

The team was using hybrid vehicles, so they drove the last fifty yards down the camp drive in silent electric mode. They saw a Suburban and a Chevy parked in front of the camp and knew that they were in the right place just as Brooke's tracking device suggested. For the tenth time they silently thanked Brooke's foresight implanting the GPS devices on all of them.

Ed waved Stephen to the main window and the rest of the team spread around the doors and windows. The lights were dim in the room, and they all pulled down their night vision goggles. They could readily see that there were four masked men in the room including the big guy who was talking to Linda. Ed immediately recognized him as Tony despite the mask.

Poor Linda was strapped to a chair in the center of the room. Ed was furious when he saw that they had ripped off her clothes. Then the anger faded as Stephen hand signaled five seconds to flash and the Colonel went into his command oversight role.

Stephen had operational control based on the terms of engagement that Ed had described over comms as they drove here. As long as their assumptions remained correct, Stephen would continue to command. Ed could take command back any time if he felt the situation was changing. He would simply say "I'm taking command" into the comms equipment and Stephen would step back. However, Ed recognized that with his feelings for Linda, it was much better for Stephen to take control of the rescue.

This was a pretty elementary ODA mission with a well-established logic for selection of weapons. None of the bad guys in the room had weapons drawn that might endanger Linda and the gangsters' fate was determined by their holstered weapons. Anyone with a weapon drawn would have been dealt with using immediate lethal force to protect the hostage.

However, the fact that each of these men presented a risk of drawing a weapon meant that a strong electroshock disabling force was appropriate. Since the team assumed that the bad guys were all armed with a hostage under their control, they would not give the gangsters a choice of voluntary surrender. Linda's presence meant that Malto and his men needed to be disabled immediately and if for any reason they were not incapacitated by the electrical weapons, they would be terminated.

Consistent with these terms of engagement, each of Ed's combatants had their electric weapon dialed up to maximize its delivered electroshock incapacity. These weapons would deliver much higher current flow than standard police weapons. There was even a risk that these military weapons could deliver a lethal shock to a small or elderly target.

But the guys that they were taking out were big and young and presumably healthy. And at this point an inadvertent lethal dose would not be the worst outcome. In addition to the electric weapons, each soldier had chambered a round in their Glock 19s which would be used if any of the gangsters pulled a gun or if the current flow was not immediately incapacitating.

As Stephen's fist clenched, signaling ops starting, all the guys broke open the doors and windows with Bill and Frank shooting out the lights. David simultaneously threw two flash grenades into the room while everyone closed their eyes behind the night goggles and waited for the flash to fade. It was then elementary to shoot each of the four gangsters with the electric weapons and watch each of them collapse. The team stepped into the room through windows or doors and having delivered up a last shock to their subjects, dialed down the current and started zip tying the hands and feet of the gangsters.

It was over in less than ten seconds. Ed was standing beside Linda within that time, lifting the hood from her head and putting his jacket over her. He clipped her ties with a wire cutter from his belt and put his arms around her, helping her to rise from the chair. At first, she gazed at Ed with amazement. And then she astonished him.

She stood in front of him rubbing her wrists, looked right in his eyes, and said, "Thank you, Ed."

And then she looked down and slowly took the heavy baton from Ed's belt. Pivoting around she looked at the gangster who had fallen closest to her chair and removed his mask. He was still jerking slightly as a result of the electric weapon. On removal of the mask Ed could see it was Tommy Lawsen.

Her rescuers had not yet immobilized Tommy with zip ties and he was spread-eagled on the floor. Linda then carefully raised the weighted baton high above her head and swung it with both hands very heavily between Tommy's legs. And then repeated the blow.

She then spat on him and turned back to Ed. "Get me away from these creeps, Ed."

Knowing that the gangsters would likely remain disabled for the next hour based on the amperage settings used on the weapons, the team checked the security of their wrist and ankle ties and collected their guns which they left in a pile at the site. They then placed nearly all of Ed's team's weapons in two vehicles which departed down the drive with half the team, leaving Stephen, Brooke, and Ed with Linda and one car. Stephen kept his licensed Glock and two extra magazines just in case.

When the police arrived thirty minutes later in response to Ed's 911 call, they came upon four large gangsters who had been separated from their guns and zip tied seemingly without the use of force. Stephen showed the police his unfired, licensed handgun and told the officers that he had used a stun grenade to disable, disarm and cuff the hoods.

Tony and his men still could not talk and in any case would not be able to say what had happened to them. It had happened so fast and each of them had blacked out from the electro-shock. The electric probes had been shot through their masks and they had not felt them being removed from their faces or necks.

Waiting for the police to arrive, Linda and Ed held a quick conference. She was confident that her earlier conversation with the FBI had been leaked to Tony by someone at the county police. This level of local corruption was frightening and would need to be dealt with by the FBI. Linda therefore determined that her statement to the local police should only describe this as a kidnapping without any motive ascribed as to why the abduction occurred.

Linda asked the officers to send a patrol to the site of her abduction near her house and they reported back shortly thereafter that her driver had been located unharmed. Linda then described in detail with video recording by the police that she had been hooded and brought here but had recognized the voice and vocal mannerisms of Tony Malto.

She described being stripped, molested and sexually threat-ened while bound on the chair. There was nothing but icy fury in her voice throughout this recorded interview. There was none of the shame sometimes expressed by survivors of sexual assault, suggesting that they have somehow contributed to the attack. Linda was very clear. These gangsters had kidnapped her, ripped her clothes off and threatened to rape her, and she wanted them to pay for it.

After Linda's summary of the abduction, Stephen and Brooke and Ed spoke to their role in the evening's activities. Brooke and Stephen described themselves as security consult-ants and Ed said that he was a friend of Ms. Davis. The cops asked why Linda was engaging security and Linda simply said that the nature of her business required security precautions.

Brooke related the importance of personal GPS monitoring

in any approach to reducing corporate or personal risk and how her GPS directional tools had allowed the team to determine rapidly that Linda was abducted and then to locate her.

Stephen described the importance of non-lethal force in modern security and how his team had neutralized these armed men with a very powerful stun grenade. He agreed with the officers that it was taking a long time for the gangsters to recover from the grenade – but then again, it was a very powerful grenade in a small space.

The police nodded. They had no idea how long the effects of a stun grenade would last, but Stephen seemed extremely knowledgeable and competent. The cops did not think to ask why the gangsters were so disabled by the grenade while Linda seemed unaffected. And when Stephen suggested that he should drive Ms. Davis and Dr. Brinkley home, the police nodded their agreement.

CHAPTER 34: FALLING IN LOVE

Linda could smell that creep's breath and body odor all over her and the first thing she wanted was a shower. As they arrived at her home, she told Ed that she was going straight to the shower and he gently held her arm, "Linda, I didn't want to ask in front of the cops. But is there any reason that we should get a rape kit for you?"

And with that, Linda started crying her heart out and fell into Ed's arms. "No, those bastards did not rape me, but I am sure they were planning to. And they choked me and scared me and humiliated me. Ed, I cannot remember ever feeling this upset and angry."

Ed held her tight as they went into her bedroom and wrapped a towel around her as she undressed. And then he started the shower and held the door open, standing on guard as she let the hot water wash the stink of those disgusting men off her skin.

He waited outside the shower stall and wrapped her in a large, plush cotton towel as she emerged, and he kept on holding her as she continued sobbing. And then at least five minutes after wrapping her in his arms, he held her away from him by several inches and smiled. She pushed him further away in astonishment and anger.

"What are you smiling about, Ed Brinkley? I don't see anything worth smiling about in this." Her tears had stopped but she could not believe that he could be so insensitive as to smile at her like this.

He continued softly smiling at her. "I think that you probably broke both of Tommy's testicles. He was lying there paralyzed with his legs wide open when you hit him with that heavy baton. You could have broken a tree trunk you hit him so hard. And then you hit him again even harder the second time.

"Linda, you are an incredible woman and I have so much respect for you. But please remind me to never touch you when you don't want to be touched." And then he wrapped his arms gently back around her, looking straight in her eyes.

She stared back, at first still upset at his smile, but then started to understand that perhaps he was right. Those goons had assaulted her, choked her with that gag and then stripped her clothes off. But they had not violated her spirit.

The overwhelming emotion she was feeling apart from fear was unadulterated anger. With Ed's rescue and continued presence, that fear was starting to fade. And Ed was probably right. That horrible man was going to be a lot more uncomfortable than she was by morning.

She looked into Ed's eyes and imagined how she looked standing over that gangster, beating him with the baton. She could not muster a smile but allowed his arms to wrap around her mummified in her towel. And realized that this man was not just offering her protection – he was joining her in a terrifying moment and helping her to realize that it was over. He was trying to reduce the future harm that this night might cause by sharing the hurt with her.

And then he lifted her onto her bed and kept his arms wrapped around her in the towel while she cried again. Then her tears slowly stopped.

Keeping his arms cradling her, Ed looked at her directly and spoke slowly. "Linda, I have experience with trauma that I haven't mentioned to you before. I don't know how it compares with what you suffered tonight. I don't think you can objectively rank different sources of trauma and harm. But I do know from my experience that how you respond to this horrible event will determine whether it hurts you for years or instead can be left slowly behind starting tonight."

He adjusted his position beside her so he could continue to look at her eyes. "I won't trivialize the harm that has been done to you. But the most important thing I learned from my trauma is the importance of admitting that we need help when we have been hurt. Accepting help was really difficult for me.

"That help may need to be professional; we can sort that out in the next few days. But it's so important that people who love us know that we have been hurt and offer their unconditional support."

Then he kissed her softly on her cheek. "Linda, I don't want you to respond to what I am about to say tonight. But Linda, I know that I love you. No question in my mind. And I know the facts of what happened tonight, I share your fear and anger. I can understand the pain. I cannot know how this terrible event felt in your mind and emotions. I can only imagine. But you need to know that I will support you however I can in responding to this hurt – and I want that support to last forever."

Linda stared back at him. She started to speak and then stopped. And then she burrowed into his arms and just lay there, thinking hard to herself. *What was that he just said? "I know that I love you?" How could a night like this make him know he loves me?*

And then after many moments she pushed him back a bit to clear a small space between them to talk.

"Ed, I am struggling to understand that you decided that you love me tonight of all nights. I need to work on that for a while, I think. But thank you for sharing your experience with being hurt. I think that could help me to understand how I should cope with this. And maybe help me to understand you a little better, as well. Especially since you have decided that you love me."

She tilted her head forward and kissed him softly. "Thank you."

There was a moment of silence between them. Ed could see her thinking. And then Linda looked up at Ed with a hint of a smile. "Did you ever get those hamburgers that you were going to feed me when I got home from Little Rock? They must be cold by now, but I am starving. We can warm them up. I am starting to think that food may help trauma. What do you think, Ed?"

Ed hugged her, smiled, and apologized that events had prevented him from sourcing the promised hamburgers. He did agree however, that food was needed and might even be therapeutic.

Linda exchanged her towel for a thick robe, and they sat quietly in her kitchen eating comfort food – scrambled eggs, bacon and toast and brown beans. Ed had ensured that his guys would be guarding routes to her house for the foreseeable future, and Stephen was going to be installing military-grade security equipment in Linda's house in the morning. But for now, Linda felt very secure with this doctor sitting at her kitchen table.

"Linda, I am so sorry that you got caught up in this. It seemed so obvious that you were the right person to approach the FBI, but in retrospect, I should have done it."

"Ed, I know that I am going to feel violated by this evening's nastiness for a while," she said, carefully balancing beans on toast. "Can't help it, it was just so terrible. But you need to promise me that you are not going to feel guilty.

"Remember this is my town. You just arrived here, although I am starting to wonder how this town ever survived without you." She took a bite of the toast and set it down on her plate, grasping his hand firmly. "The depth of corruption demonstrated by Tony getting tipped off so fast today means that our civic leaders have a lot of work to do, and believe me I am up to that task. Heads are going to roll in that police department.

"Remember what I told you about my dad's accident? I have always harbored a suspicion that it was Tony's father who ran Dad off the road. There are plenty of reasons why I need to help you destroy this gang.

"But I have one favor to ask you, Ed. I know that we have elite troops guarding us. The efficiency and skill that your guys showed tonight was just incredible. But I do not want to be alone. Most important, I want you, just you, with me constantly for the next few days." She leaned over and kissed him softly. "In fact, I think that I may want you with me constantly for more than just a few days."

Ed lifted her effortlessly and carried her back to her bedroom. He held her gently, and she slept without dreams.

****

The next morning, Linda and Ed drove back to HQ. On the way out of Linda's house they met Stephen coming to secure her residence. Fortunately, it was Saturday and Linda had booked the day off work. When she entered HQ, the first person to see her was Brooke. She literally ran over and took Linda into her arms and hugged her and then they were both crying and couldn't stop.

"Those bastards will pay for what they did to you, Linda." She was drying her eyes with the back of her hand while she kept crying and linked an arm around Linda.

The lawyer gave her hands a squeeze. "Like Ed told me last night, that guy Tommy is worse off than me this morning. Ed thinks I broke both his balls – and it felt good, believe me. I can't say that no permanent harm has been done to me, Brooke. But I am going to try to keep it from worming inside me. The good Dr. Brinkley is helping me with that." And she looked over at the Colonel. Her eyes told Brooke that something had changed between the two of them.

"But I hate to think what might have happened if you hadn't implanted those GPS devices on me. You are amazing, girl. I know that I owe you big time." And then she looked around at the other guys. "And I mean all of you. I owe all of you for that rescue last evening. Thank you so much." Looking at her rescuers she started sobbing again, then stamped her foot. "Dammit, I have to stop this."

Benjamin came over to put his arms round Linda and

Brooke. "I am feeling left out," he said, "Big brother left me at home when the cavalry rode out last evening. I think that I am going to have to take basic training so that I can participate in rescuing women in distress."

Brooke responded for the group. "Ben, you let us take care of the tactical stuff. You just keep on providing us with all the gear that we used last night to free Linda and the other stuff we are using. *That* is your role, and you are the only one that can do it."

Ed had picked up coffee for Linda and they sat in the HQ dining room. He began, "So, let's think through where we are and what our next steps are. I think that we have probably closed down the Malto gang here in Maple Ridge. Kidnapping is a RICO offense, and with what we have on Tony, we can help the Agency and federal prosecutors put him away for a long time and confiscate most of what he owns."

Linda was carefully wiping her eyes. Then she remembered her lawyerly responsibilities and responded, "Ed, remember that we will need to think about Sharon Malto. She will be a lot safer with Tony behind bars, but the federal prosecutors are going to tie his finances up tight and it's going to be tough for Sharon and her son."

Ed nodded. "Thanks Linda. She's my patient and your client. I don't have a solution for her now, but you're right, we will need to think about her."

David turned up the sound on the television set that had been muted. "Looks like word is getting out about last night."

The county police chief was on television talking about how his force had broken up a kidnapping ring and taken the kidnappers into custody and rescued prominent Maple Ridge lawyer Linda Davis. The motive for the kidnapping was under investigation, but it was assumed that the kidnappers were preparing to demand ransom for Ms. Davis when the police intervened.

Shortly after that first report on television, Stephen rang from Linda's house where he was installing security gear.

"Linda, your housekeeper says that FBI Special Agent Bond has been frantically calling for you but of course your cell is dead. She called at your house and talked to your housekeeper. You should probably give her a call. She left a number."

Linda used Ed's phone to call Sarah Bond on the agent's private cell. Linda briefly explained the events of the prior evening. Sarah responded, "Oh my God, Linda, thank God you are okay! How did the police find you?"

"Ahh, good detective work I guess, Sarah."

"That bastard liaison officer must have tipped Malto – or maybe someone else in that damn county police force tipped him. You were careful not to mention his name during your briefing, but it must have been obvious to someone from Maple Ridge who you were talking about."

Ed's phone was on speaker and at this point, Ed joined the conversation. "Special Agent Bond, this is Dr. Ed Brinkley, a friend of Linda's. We think that we should keep this news quiet about Linda speaking to you yesterday to give you a better chance to figure out who the leak is in the county police."

For a moment there was silence on Special Agent Bond's end of the line. "I am sorry, who are you, sir? You are Ms. Davis's doctor?"

Linda laughed softly. "Sarah, Ed is my boyfriend." Linda could see eyebrows lifting in the room as she made this statement and she smiled at her words. "He is a doctor, but he has brought some interesting people here to Maple Ridge. You need to know that it was his team, not the county police who tracked me down and rescued me last night."

Again, there was silence on the line. "Linda, I think that I should come down to Maple Ridge and figure out what's going on. This is sounding... I don't know how it's sounding, but it's certainly unusual. I need to talk to you face to face. I will be there in less than an hour." And they texted her the address for HQ.

CHAPTER 35: SARAH IS PUZZLED

The FBI agent was puzzled about the events of the last couple of days and drove to Maple Ridge without regard for the speed limit. She arrived at the address she had received by text and found herself in a nondescript industrial mall. And then she noticed several security cameras surrounding the parking lot and the entrance to one of the buildings.

The door opened before she knocked. Clearly, she had been under surveillance from within. Sarah was greeted by a tall young woman who introduced herself as Brooke. Brooke then introduced Sarah to several young men who had military bearing and two guys named Benjamin and Klaus who seemed misfits in this group of what appeared to be seasoned warriors. Finally, there was Linda and a handsome older guy who Linda introduced as Dr. Ed. Sarah took it this was her boyfriend. They were a good-looking couple.

Sarah had to ask. "And why are you all here?" She looked around her. "In this Quonset hut?"

Brooke smiled and responded. "Most of us are security consultants, Special Agent." And then Ben introduced himself as CEO of Brinkley Enterprises and Ed's brother. He clarified that a subsidiary of Brinkley Enterprises had engaged all these consultants. Sarah shook her head suspiciously. "I am not sure that explains what is going on here."

"So, you are a doctor here in town, right?" she asked Ed. He nodded.

"And CEO Ben is your brother?" Again, a nod.

Linda then suggested that the team should describe what

they had learned about the Malto gang by way of explanation and Sarah readily agreed.

Brooke and Klaus walked her through their investigation of Tony's business and accounts. Sarah was progressively more and more intrigued. This information was clear evidence of racketeering and money laundering. If the Agency and prosecutors could get it admitted in court, they could put Tony Malto away forever. But she remained very puzzled by all this expertise.

Sarah turned to Klaus. Unlike most of the other members of this team, he did not look like he would be at ease dropping down a rope from a helicopter. "And why are you here?"

"I am hired as a consultant forensic accountant for the team."

"And how did you get involved with this team?"

"I worked with Colonel Ed and the team in Afghanistan."

Sarah was realizing that understanding what was happening here would require her to set aside the usual models of how the Agency gathered evidence from citizens. She looked back at Linda's boyfriend the doctor.

"So, you are a colonel as well as a doctor?" He nodded again. "I am retired now, Special Agent."

Sarah looked around the room. "Okay, let's talk about how you got all this remarkable information. Did you break into Malto's offices and access his computers?"

Brooke responded. "No, we were able to access his files, records, and accounts using passwords that we learned from the people engaged in the activity we are discussing."

"The Malto gang provided you with their passwords?"

Brooke explained carefully. "Special Agent, these passwords were readily available to the public since the Malto gang did not protect their passwords very well. I would say that the passwords were offered to members of the public who knew how to look for them and we simply took advantage."

"Do you think that we could use this evidence in a court of law?" This was the important issue for Sarah.

Brooke responded carefully. "I know that it may be a gray area. However, in this case, you did not receive this information by invading the Malto group's privacy without a warrant. You received the information volunteered by some civilians who gave it to you because they recognized that there was probably some illegal activity happening."

Brooke spoke again, holding her palms facing up and open. "Just imagine, Special Agent, that a private citizen was walking past an open door, and saw evidence of illegal activity in a room, and told you what they saw. That citizen's report would certainly be used in building your case."

She paused for a moment. "Sarah – can I just call you Sarah? This Special Agent stuff is tiresome." She asked this with a smile, and the FBI agent nodded, "Of course."

"Sarah, we have simply been looking in through Tony Malto's front door, which he carelessly left wide open. Now, Klaus and I do have some special skills which allow us to make sense of what is going on in the room. But we are able to look in the room, not because we broke in illegally, but because Tony left the door open. We have not broken any laws accessing this information because we simply used the same passwords that Tony would use to get to the files."

Brooke had been seated on the side of a desk. She now got up and started pacing. "Let's say a criminal leaves incriminating paper records on his desk in an unguarded room with an open door, and we can look into the room without breaking in or trespassing and take pictures of the records with a telephoto lens – well I think you would be delighted to use the photos of those records in court. They would clearly be admissible. And that's what we are giving you here. With some expert interpretation of the photos provided by my buddy Klaus here." And Klaus winced as she turned and punched him in the shoulder.

Sarah realized that this woman was whip smart and articulate. Even dressed in the plain khakis that most of the members of Doctor Colonel Ed's team were wearing, she was quite striking in appearance. She would make one hell of a witness.

"We certainly did not break any laws getting the information. And when we got it, we just did what any responsible citizen would do and gave it to you."

Being handed a virtually complete RICO case was just too good to be true. Sarah shook her head back and forth. "And you all are private citizens? You are not working for any government agencies?"

At this point the Doctor Colonel's little brother Benjamin chimed in. "I can assure you Special Agent, that everyone here except Linda and Ed is employed as a consultant on a special project sponsored by a wholly owned subsidiary of Brinkley Enterprises. Two of our consultants are on vacation from their military assignments and fulfilling security roles on their own free time."

Sarah thought to herself that everyone here was very certain of themselves and their responses to her. They were quite remarkable.

Ben continued. "During the time that they were working as consultants for Brinkley they became aware of information that might be useful for the FBI, especially in view of the kidnapping of Ms. Davis carried out yesterday. We are offering that information freely, and of course Klaus and Brooke would be willing to testify in court about how the information was gathered."

"You would not be concerned about intimidation from Malto's associates if you testified?"

Benjamin smiled and looked around the room. "Special Agent, do these people look like they would be intimidated by anyone?"

Sarah then went through the hard copy of the information that Brooke and Klaus had described to her. There was one puzzling element to her.

"You know, it seems clear that the perpetrators of prostitution, drugs, gambling, and human trafficking transfer money to Malto. And then it is clear that Malto is transferring money to his legitimate businesses, and some goes back to the street guys. But I agree with Klaus that a third level of business is taking most of the profits away from the second level. There are huge sums being spent on back office expenses."

"These second level legitimate businesses have enormous revenue lines. But their profits seem minimal. They appear to have very large ongoing expenses for IT, renovations, consultancy, and logistics. Do you have any idea what is going on with the companies providing these services?"

Now there was no rapid, highly confident response from Klaus and Brooke. Instead, they looked to Dr. Ed. Sarah couldn't figure him out. He was a doctor, a colonel and Linda's boyfriend? And it was becoming obvious that although his brother Benjamin might be paying the bills, this guy was really the leader that everyone looked to.

Dr. Ed looked around the room and then focused on Sarah, starting slowly. "Sarah, this is where we are dealing with unproven conjecture. We agree with you that there is likely another layer of criminality here. And we think the information we have to date points to the Gulf Coast. Have you heard of the Dixie Gang, Sarah?"

Sarah had of course heard of the Dixie Gang, which the FBI had largely broken up with anti-racketeering in the 1990's. They were said to be extremely violent mobsters who focused their activities around Biloxi, Mississippi. She had heard rumors that the rapid inflow of funds into the Gulf region after Hurricane Katrina had stimulated a renewal of Dixie Gang activity.

Ed saw the agent nod, and he continued. "We know that Malto is tight with a character from the Gulf Coast named Gabriel Duquesne. We are pretty sure that Tony sourced a lot of stuff – women, drugs et cetera – from Gabriel but we cannot find evidence of funds going from Tony to Gabriel in Tony's records." Then he turned back to Brooke and Klaus. "Tell Sarah what you are working on, guys."

Brooke took up the story. "We noticed a few of those third level of businesses have head offices on the Gulf Coast, Sarah.

And we are assuming that they may be owned by Duquesne or his associates. We are thinking that Gabriel may get paid for his contraband by providing legitimate but very high-cost services to Tony's second level of businesses.

"That way, Gabriel immediately launders the wholesale revenue from supplying women or drugs to Tony and Tony gets rid of some of the profit that he would need to declare on the vending machine operators, laundromats and bars that he is using as the first laundering layer."

This was getting really interesting. Sarah had heard of Gabriel Duquesne and understood that despite his elegant name, the Agency suspected that he was a cold-blooded killer. She knew that one of their paid informants had been discovered tortured to death after trying to obtain information about Duquesne.

She looked at Brooke and Klaus. "Do you have any financial records that we could use on Duquesne?"

Brooke shook her head. "Unfortunately, Duquesne is much more sophisticated than Tony Malto at protecting his records. We need to get invoices from Gabriel's companies to show that they are charging Tony's companies for phantom work or charging excessively for work. We cannot prove that from Malto's records. We need to get into Duquesne's records as well."

And then Brooke looked directly at Dr. Ed, or Colonel Ed, or whoever this mystery man was and said, "I can think of some ways that we could get access to his records. But I guess that would depend on the consulting arrangement that we are hired for here in Maple Ridge."

And Sarah thought to herself yet again, *There are layers here that I am not understanding.*

CHAPTER 36: GABRIEL PONDERS

A h'm so fuckin' confused by what the fuck is going on in Maple Ridge. Them Malto boys been doin' good bidness with us for years goin' back to Tony's grandpappy an' never no problem. They got that town tied up tight as a drum with lotsa cops on Tony's payroll. The nice thing about little towns like Maple Ridge is the cops grow up with the wise guys, so everybody looks after everyone else.

An' now they got Tony an' his crew thrown in county jail for some bullshit about kidnappin' a lawyer lady? That Tony, he does a lotta shit with women an' drugs an' stuff but he ain't no kidnapper. An' if he was gonna hoist someone, he sure woulda told me about it. Ah done rough stuff for Tony in the past an' he's a little squeamy when it comes to the wet work an' all.

It's good we got our own guys on the cops 'cause Ah hears this broad Tony hoisted, she was in Little Rock the day before an' she was telling a lotta shit about our bidness. So mebbe she was rattin' on Tony an' Tony decides to take her out. Sounds stupid with her bein' a big lawyer in town.

An' if he did hoist her, how come them county cops found him so fast an' took down his crew with that Tommy guy? Tony ain't no Einstein Ah know, but them cops ain't so smart neither an' findin' him so fast an' rescuin' that lawyer bitch so fast. It jus' don't make no sense.

So, Ah sends my fuckin' highest price lawyers in to bail out Tony an' his boys. An' they got FBI an' Federal prosecutors all over the place an' they holdin' Tony widout bail an' in segregation. So now Ah'm gettin' worried 'cause if the feds are there, they gonna RICO

Tony's ass an' if they threatens him with RICO, he gonna fold like a decka cards. In that posse there's only one guy who knows anythin' besides Tony an' that's that big Tommy guy an' he would sing too.

Ah got a real safe insurance policy here an' Ah figger Ah'm gonna use it. We got them Aryan Brotherhood guys in the county jail an' they can get anywhere 'cause they know them little jails inside an' out. Don't make no difference about no segregation or nuthin', them guys own them little jails.

An' right about now, Ah wanna make sure that Tony an' Tommy ain't gonna rat on nobody. And then Ah gotta figger out what we gotta do with that lady lawyer bitch.

CHAPTER 37: TRUSTING
YOUR LIFE

W hen Sarah let the RICO guys in Dallas know what she learned from Linda's initial interview in Little Rock, they were buzzing about the opportunity to take down Tony Malto. Even though Linda had been careful not to mention his name, the RICO squad knew all about him and had long considered investigating him for a possible racketeering charge.

So when he was picked up at the site of Linda's kidnapping, the RICO guys moved right in, got a federal prosecutor involved and made sure that Tony and his henchman Tommy were segregated to protect them.

When Sarah talked to the RICO team after her meeting with the Doctor Colonel's very unusual team, they were even more excited about widening the investigation to the Dixie Gang. Sarah had thought that the Dixie Gang was mainly of historic interest. All agents studied the cases in academy – how the gangsters along the Gulf Coast took over communities, influencing police forces, mayors' offices and legislators by a combination of violence and bribery.

Some of their history had been sensationalized in the media; how they murdered police chiefs and judges as well as ensuring that informants within their ranks were eliminated.

When the RICO guys in Dallas connected with the team in New Orleans, they realized the opportunity this might represent to learn more about the resurgence of organized crime on the Gulf and a chance to find out more about Gabriel Duquesne. Suddenly the county jail in Maple Ridge was a prime destination for FBI agents from several field offices as well as federal prosecutors. By their second day in custody, agents were riding both Tony Malto and Tommy Lawsen pretty hard. They told them that they had plenty of evidence to put them away for kidnapping and that in Arkansas kidnapping was a felony with potential life imprisonment and that they would make sure that they would never get parole.

They also pushed hard on what they knew about money laundering and told both Tony and Tommy that they were going to seize all their assets based on a racketeering charge. Their wives and children would be on the street, and they would have no access to money for lawyer's fees.

Sarah knew the RICO agent from Dallas who was leading Tony's interrogation. He called Sarah late on the second day to thank her for tipping them off about Tony and the Gulf Coast gang. He said that Tony had started talking and that his boy Tommy was independently confirming everything Malto was saying. They had both described how Tony had received a call about Linda being in Little Rock from someone in the county police. That tip led to them kidnapping Linda. Tony had admitted on tape that he was planning on raping Linda to keep her quiet.

When she heard what Malto was planning to do to silence Linda, Sarah was both disgusted and again impressed with Doctor Ed's rescue team.

The RICO agent wanted Sarah's opinion on whether they should offer Tony a suspended sentence with entry into witness protection for him and his family if he gave evidence on the Gulf Coast gang.

Sarah checked with Linda who responded quickly. "I don't know Malto's wife that well yet Sarah, but she is my client. I will check with her of course, but I am pretty sure that she would not want to follow Malto into witness protection. Really, Sharon Malto has been looking for protection *from* Tony, not with Tony. But I will get back to you right away after talking to Sharon."

The morning of Tony's third day in the county jail, Sarah got a call from the same RICO agent who was just seething. "These damn county jails. We had agents all over the jail, making sure that Malto and his henchman Lawsen were both segregated. And last night someone got both of them, slit their throats with a shiv.

"And no one knows anything of course. All the security cameras on the segregation run had their damn lenses taped over and no one in the monitoring center noticed it until morning. I know that they have a big Aryan Brotherhood population in that jail, and this looks like their work, but we'll never know. No one will talk.

"Sarah, I am worried about your witness. Whoever got rid of Malto so easily, they will not want your witness to be available for questioning. Should we be thinking about witness protection for her? Her name was all over the news the night that they broke up the kidnapping. Whoever wanted Tony dead will have no trouble figuring out that she tipped us off about Malto."

He paused to let his thoughts catch up. "Obviously no one cares now if she has testimony against Malto. But it will be assumed that she could have information about the other goons in this Dixie Gang thing. And, as they just proved with Tony Malto, they are brutal and relentless in eliminating people who know anything about their business."

Sarah was shocked about Tony and Tommy and needed to share her colleague's concern with Linda. Sarah called Linda's private line and was glad to learn that she had two 'security consultants' with her in the office and that they had rigged her office and home with surveillance equipment. Linda suggested that Sarah should meet her at home later in the evening.

When Sarah drove to Linda's home that night, she was pleased to see that tiger teeth between cement blocks had been installed at the gate of Linda's impressively long winding driveway. There was a voice box at the gate and the security forces checked Sarah's cell number as well as her name before lowering the tiger teeth.

Her door was opened by one of the discretely armed men that Sarah had met at "HQ" two days ago. And Dr. Ed was present as well. Sarah thought that he seemed to be a pretty permanent feature of Linda's life.

The three sat at Linda's kitchen table and Sarah accepted a coffee. "Linda, I am certain that you will not shed many tears about what I told you on the phone earlier. After what they did to you, no one here is going to mourn Tony Malto or his boy Tommy Lawsen. But the nature of their murder and the timing is worrisome."

Linda put down her coffee cup. "Sarah, Ed and I have been discussing this for the last hour since he finished clinic and I came home from the office. Although there were probably lots of people who disliked Tony Malto, we figure that the most likely beneficiaries from his death are his former business partners on the Gulf Coast. We are particularly thinking about the people who run with Gabriel Duquesne. Is that your thinking?" She and Ed looked at Sarah expectantly.

The agent chose her words carefully. The Agency had not figured everything out, but some things were clear. "As I mentioned to you, Linda, the RICO guys from Dallas and New Orleans were intrigued by Tony and the opportunity to turn him against bigger fish on the Gulf Coast. It was an obvious opportunity for our agents and clearly it must have occurred to the mob that Tony represented a risk to them."

Ed spoke up thoughtfully. "I obviously have never met this Duquesne character. But if I were him, hearing that Tony was threatened with what Linda knew to the extent that he was willing to take the risky step of kidnapping her – well if I were Duquesne, I would want to know what Linda knew about his relationship with Tony. Or better yet," and here he apologized with his eyes to Linda, "I would want to make sure that she could never tell anyone whatever she knew."

They all looked at each other knowing that what Ed was saying was both true and extremely worrisome for Linda.

Sarah broke the silence. "Linda, I want to mention the witness protection program to you. I am not sure if you can truly provide witness against anyone other than Tony Malto, but we would certainly extend the definition of entry criteria to include you if you wanted us to do that."

Ed and Linda were looking at each other long and hard. Linda broke the silence. "Thank you for that, Sarah. But the idea of slinking out of this town where my family has lived for generations because of some unknown threat feels kind of cowardly to me. And I think that I need to consult with my favorite doctor before I decide anything about what I am going to do.

"Apart from anything else Sarah, I have built something really special in my law firm here. A lot of people depend on me. And my boyfriend has a pretty good medical practice here in Maple Ridge." She took Ed's hand and Ed leaned over and put his arm around her.

Linda pushed back from the table and sighed. "And nothing against you Sarah, but I came to see you a couple of days ago for a confidential discussion. Within hours, I was kidnapped and now the Dixie Gang is probably out to kill me because of what I said to you.

"Sarah, I like you as a person and I am very sure that you are very good at your job. But Sarah, I am not sure that I would again trust my life to your organization's ability to keep a secret."

And Sarah looked back at Linda and slowly nodded.

CHAPTER 38: THE START
OF BEN'S PLAN

When Ed called the entire team together that evening, Benjamin appreciated that he was included. Ben's feelings were not hurt that Ed had excluded him when organizing the team to rescue Linda from her abductors. He had no operational experience and would have been a potential liability. But tonight seemed to be more about strategy rather than operations. And running Brinkley Enterprises gave Ben plenty of strategic insight.

Ed began by briefing the team on the demise of Tony and Tommy. To say the team was shocked by this news would be an understatement. Their whole focus to this point had been to eliminate the risk posed by Tony and his gang. Now it would appear that they were dealing with forces probably more sinister than Tony Malto and more difficult to understand.

Brooke spoke up first. "Let's think who was most at risk from Tony Malto when he was in jail. No question in my mind that it's Gabriel Duquesne. Klaus and I were not able to penetrate his firewall to prove that he was laundering money with Tony, but it sure looked suspicious."

Ben had discreetly arranged to sit beside Brooke and was enjoying watching her participate in the discussion. She was very good at technology but also great with people. And she was so attractive. He hoped his infatuation wasn't too obvious.

Klaus continued Brooke's train of thought. "Duquesne would know that if Tony started talking, he would incriminate the Gulf Coast guys pretty quickly. Duquesne would not know what we had on him in addition to Tony's potential evidence. But Tony would certainly be a risk to him. I would think that Gabriel had lots of reasons to eliminate Tony."

Brooke followed on Klaus' comments and Ben suddenly realized why they were discussing next steps. "Duquesne has pretty good cybersecurity, so we have nothing that definitely links him to Malto. But Duquesne would not know that he is currently safe from what we can prove. He would naturally suspect that Linda had information tying him and Tony together in a criminal enterprise."

Brooke concluded, looking at Linda apologetically as she spoke. "So, unless Linda is willing to disappear for a long time, we need to think about how to deal with Duquesne."

Linda slowly leaned forward capturing the attention of the group. "In the next few weeks, I expect to be on the front pages of every national newspaper when we win one of the most important class action lawsuits in our country's legal history. And after that, our Davis firm here in Maple Ridge will be considered a national asset for little people who have been harmed by big business. I have worked way too hard to quietly disappear. We need to figure out a different solution."

Discussion followed that focused on two issues: either making a deal with Duquesne to get him to understand that Linda would not implicate him or simply eliminating Gabriel by force.

After some debate, nobody really thought that negotiations with Gabriel would work. That would mean trusting a likely murderer with Linda's life. Trusting Gabriel had not worked out well for Duquesne's business partner Tony Malto. But none of the security guys wanted to eliminate him without trying other measures. There were so many unknowns. Taking Duquesne out just seemed precipitous and unpredictable with what they knew to date. As professional members of the military, they also realized that acting as accuser, judge, and executioner in killing Duquesne would be murderous.

Ben was intrigued by his brother's approach throughout this

discussion. Ed was clearly in charge but ensured that the entire team was involved in the brainstorming. Ben admired how his brother was attempting to get the maximum benefit from a group of smart people with different backgrounds thinking hard about their next steps. Ed kept summarizing what they currently knew and surmised. Then he would push the group to go further with their assessment and ideas.

Yesterday, Ben had listened carefully to the debrief that Ed led following the action to rescue Linda. Ben had initially thought it was risky to use electric weapons rather than simply using lethal force against Malto's gang. However, Ed was committed to terms of engagement that minimized loss of life or injury while accomplishing the operational objectives. The fact that Ed attributed value to the lives of Linda's abductors was surprising but meaningful to his brother.

That was the starting point for Ben's idea.

At first he was reluctant to speak up. But Ed had made this an inclusive discussion and gave Ben the floor when he cautiously raised his hand.

"Guys, I obviously don't have any operational experience. But the problem we are facing tonight is that we have not just neutralized Tony; instead, Tony is gone. And with Tony gone, Gabriel will likely move someone into his place. From what we know, Maple Ridge represents too good a business center for Duquesne to ignore. If Tony were not dead or put away in prison, but rather just neutralized, we would be in better shape."

Ben could see his brother and Linda were interested in this concept. Ed responded. "Ben, play this out for us. We are discussing eliminating Duquesne. What's the problem with that thinking?"

Ben thought hard about how best to express the thought that he was slowly developing. "I think that we need to assume that if we eliminate Duquesne, his place will be filled by some other hoodlum from the Dixie Gang. In the same way that Tony's death means that Gabriel will make sure someone takes his place here in Maple Ridge. And of course, that person will be gunning for Linda, one way or another."

And then his thinking crystallized. "If we eliminate Gabriel, no doubt someone from the Dixie gang will replace him. The other option is to think about neutralizing Duquesne so that he remains in place, but does not want to touch us. To gain information on him that provides him with a reason to protect Linda rather than threaten her.

"And something that we can use to make him fear us more than any FBI RICO thing." Ben was learning the jargon. But he felt momentarily embarrassed when a random thought crossed his mind – he wondered if Brooke would be impressed with his thinking.

Brooke and Klaus were speaking together softly. "If we could get into Gabriel's files, we could gather information that would put his whole empire at risk from the same type of RICO charges that were going to be brought against Tony. Maybe then we show him what we know about his money laundering and racketeering activities. And we threaten to release it all to the FBI if anything happens to Linda. Then he might have a good reason to protect us against any risks." Brooke looked straight at Ben. "Good thinking, Ben. I like this. Let's work on Ben's idea."

Ben felt like a kid when he realized that he actually got goose bumps from Brooke looking at him and saying that.

Ed followed up with Brooke. "How do we get into those files?"

"I wish I knew, Colonel. Gabriel and his team are very good at protecting their passwords. Their files are stored in a very secure cloud-based system and each file seems to have an individual password that is automatically updated by a leading-edge commercial system. I have tried several different ways of breaking into his files using artificial intelligence software that Ben's office provided to us. But Duquesne's system is really state of the art. It may be surprising for a gangster, but his firewall is leading edge."

Mention of the cloud-based commercial system started Ben thinking again. He remembered when they revised cybersecurity for Brinkley Enterprises. It was frustrating as hell because everyone had to stop using one password to access all their files. Suddenly, their security system insisted that each file needed a unique password that was constantly being updated.

But everyone needed immediate access to the same files to develop business cases, compare quarterly results or simply provide service to clients. And that is when Brinkley Enterprises went to a fully encrypted, commercial mobility solution that stored and continuously updated passwords on their executives' mobile devices.

Ben's mention of the importance of mobility solutions for cybersecurity at Brinkley Enterprises started shifting the plan to neutralize Gabriel in a different direction. As the discussion continued, Ben hoped that his experience, different as it might be from these remarkable warriors, was useful to their planning.

And although he would not admit it to anyone but himself, Ben was pleased to see that Brooke Paltrig was paying attention to his contributions to the discussion.

CHAPTER 39: GABRIEL'S THOUGHTS

Gabriel Duquesne was contemplating events in Maple Ridge and thinking to himself.

Ah was mighty happy those Aryan Brotherhood boys in Maple Ridge jail dealt with them turncoats Malto an' Lawsen real quick. Our family has a strong tradition of settlin' with stool pigeons. It surely needed doin' quick. Ah heard the feds were hangin' off the walls around that county jail an' they would have been offerin' Tony widness protection to rat me out.

And now we got ridda Tony, Ah need to think about that lawyer woman. Ah needs to be careful here. Ah hear she is important in the bidness world in Maple Ridge, an' it would be considered poorly to take her out. An' Ah don't know exactly what she was telling the FBI. Ah only got it third hand through Tony's buddy on the county police who told one of my guys what that lawyer was sayin' to the feds.

Ah'll never know what she knows an' that worries me. Tony was trying to shut her up through scarin' her. From what Ah know, Tony figured he better not take her out. An' look where Tony is now. Maybe that's the best proof Ah need to get ridda that bitch.

But she sure got some good security workin' for her. There's no way them keystone cops from the county woulda found her so quick when Tony took her. Ah heard rumors from the Ridge cops that there was some doctor who got some military heavyweights to find her an' them military boys handed Tony an' his posse over to the cops. Ah'm gonna need to think this through real careful before we do anythin'.

So, Ah was thinkin' hard about this lawyer woman an' how we gonna need to be careful with takin' her out. An' then, what happens today, Ah gets a call on my cell that nobodys got the number for. That's got me worried no end.

****

"Hello, is that Gabriel Duquesne?"

"What's it to ya'?"

"Mr. Duquesne, my name is Dr. Ed Brinkley, and I am calling about my friend named Linda Davis."

"What the fuck you callin' me for?"

"Mr. Duquesne, I have reason to believe that you care deeply about Ms. Davis's health and well-being. I also care about her health. For that reason, I think that you and I should talk. I expect that we can probably come to agreement about the best way to protect her health."

"Ah dunno what the fuck you are talkin' about. Ah ain't got no interest in that bitch's health."

"Mr. Duquesne, I am also interested in *your* health and well-being. I believe that your future health may be improved if you and I meet."

"You ain't my doctor. What the fuck do you care about mah health?"

"Oh, Mr. Duquesne, you should know that if things do not go the way I want them to go, then your health may be at real risk. It's always best to listen to the doctor about your health, Gabriel."

****

An' Ah'll be damned if he don't hang up an' next Ah getta text saying that Dr. Ed Brinkley will suggest a meeting place an' he hopes that Ah will be there for the sake of ma good health an' well-being.

And then later Ah getta a text sayin' that we gonna meet on a certain date at the Café de Paris at nine thirty in the mornin'. Now that bothers me a lot 'cause Ah go to the Café de Paris just about every mornin'. Ah have a croissant an' a café au lait an' most days me an' the boys are the only guys there at nine thirty.

So, whoever this doctor is he knows how Ah start mah days an' that worries me a little. Ah'm gonna text him back an' tell him okay we can meet at the Café. But Ah know Ah'm gonna have some extra boys there when Ah meets this damn doctor.

CHAPTER 40: GOING SOUTH AND GOING EAST

Linda had been surprised and impressed with the way that Ben had started the team planning for how they should deal with Gabriel Duquesne. Once the plans started to crystallize, Ed took over the operational planning with Stephen and Brooke. First off, Stephen said that the team needed more people and resources. Ed agreed and Ben immediately committed more funds from Brinkley Enterprises. Stephen signed on another ex-Special Forces security consultant group and assigned the new recruits to protect Linda with Bill leading.

Linda liked Bill and had become comfortable with having him around. The new guys seemed just as competent, polite and attentive as Stephen's crew.

The judge in Maryland had made an earlier recovery from his illness than originally expected, and Linda was expecting to start trial next week. She planned to be in Baltimore up to three weeks. The trial could possibly go on even longer, but Linda had a feeling that if things went as anticipated, the defense might be offering settlement fairly early in the trial.

So Ed was going south with part of the team, and Linda was going east with lots of protection. They made up for their planned separation while they remained in Maple Ridge. Ed was busy with his practice during the day and was also spending time connecting with his former Special Forces medical colleagues about something related to heart attacks. Meanwhile, Linda was prepping for Maryland at the office.

But at night there was only time for the two of them. Ed had moved into Linda's house, and she was pleased to realize how much she was going to miss him while she was away in Baltimore.

Ed made it clear to Linda that he had never known love like this. He'd had his share of relationships in school and in the army, but nothing like this, he told her. And she readily believed him because she was feeling the same sense of novelty.

When they were alone, Ed just completed Linda. He was tender and attentive when she needed it – she looked forward to his patented neck rub at the end of her office day. He was genuinely interested in Linda, her background, and her career. He was a great listener and a perfect gentleman everywhere except in her bedroom. There, he was a tireless and generous lover.

And his experience with the trauma he had suffered in Afghanistan provided insight to what Linda had experienced from Tony Malto. Ed knew the risks of triggering that recent hurt and explained to Linda how he had started to relapse the night that Tony had beaten him at the hospital.

Holding her softly as they lay together in her bed, Ed recounted his experience. "As I lay there on the ground after Tony had slugged and kicked me, the whole emotional pit of my PTSD just reopened and surrounded me. I was helpless, useless, and could not imagine getting out from under Tony's control and abuse. I felt so ashamed of my weakness."

Linda could see the pain in his eyes as he continued. "As I got up from the ground, I tried to go back to the cognitive understanding that Dr. Romulus had given me. How my personality made me vulnerable if I could not solve problems myself. How it was shameful for me if I couldn't entirely rely on my abilities to fix things. That all helped with the intellectual understanding of what was happening with that triggering event."

Now he slowed down and looked at her directly with a soft smile. "But the main thing that helped me that night was you, Linda. You remember that we had just returned from Hot

Springs, and I was starting to realize how special you are and what we might have together. It was that closeness that saved me that night, the feeling of partnership with you that had developed so quickly that weekend.

"I know it sounds crazy – we had really just started to get to know each other. But I felt a very strong sense that weekend that you were going to be part of my life, and that expectation helped me respond to the darkness triggered by the assault. It started me on the path to calling Ben and then Brooke to get help."

He concluded. "Linda, I think having unconditional love from someone who understands what you have experienced is an important way to deal with trauma. To have someone who knows what you have suffered and is willing to share the pain with you. And, who knows that pain can be countered by closeness." And with that he smiled and returned to being her lover.

Ed excited her much more than anyone she had previously been with. Making love to Linda seemed to put Ed into a trance that could last forever. And she needed his understanding and gentleness as she continued the work to put the events with Tony Malto into a healthier place.

Ed did understand how terrifying that night had been for her. After that horrible event he had been very careful, especially when making love.

Ed encouraged her to engage a therapist. They even considered connecting with Dr. Romulus. But as they continued to talk about that terrible event with the Malto gang, she realized that the trauma was a bond that she and Ed somehow shared. Talking to him about the impact it had on her seemed to deepen their partnership. And the residual from that terrifying night was slowly fading. There was just too much that needed her attention for her to focus on those disgusting creeps.

CHAPTER 41: MIGRATING DISCS

L inda was finishing a long day in the office doing final preparations for the trial. She had just concluded a discussion on jury selection with her team and was walking up the stairs in her dad's old office building. Linda had her main office and staff in the modern office tower she had acquired next door, but she still maintained her dad's adjacent, older building even though the space was not really needed.

Her dad's old office was on the top third floor of the heritage building, and she kept that space for herself when she was working alone. She often ended up going there just before leaving for home, quietly thinking about the events of the day and planning for tomorrow.

Ed was waiting for her at home, expecting to leave for the Gulf Coast on the weekend. Linda was in court in Baltimore on Monday. Her clients had been waiting so long for this case to come to trial and she was eager to get going. These poor people had been treated so badly and it was time for their day in court.

She settled in behind her father's heavy, old-fashioned desk. Visualizing how the court case would begin in Baltimore, Linda picked up a few summaries of clients' medical histories that she had brought to remind herself how these people found themselves in so much difficulty.

Each of their stories had started with back pain. They were all told after the usual MRI and CT scans that one or more of their spine discs were ruptured. They were all recommended to have the ruptured disc removed at surgery. However, each one of Linda's clients wanted to consider an alternative approach to simply removing the disc.

Reviewing the summaries on her desk, Linda realized how similar their stories were. Her clients were smart, did their research on spine surgery, and they all came to question whether an artificial disc replacement could be a better treatment than removing the disc.

Their questions led to referrals to a small group of spine surgeons who practiced around Baltimore. There, her clients all heard the same thing. That just removing the disc was yesterday's surgery. The Baltimore surgeons told them that what they really needed was an operation to implant an artificial disc that would restore their flexibility and back movement.

So over a five-year period, each of Linda's clients underwent surgery with artificial disc replacement. Leaning back on her chair and enjoying the peace that her dad's office always provided, Linda picked up the glossy product monographs that described the disc.

The device was designed like a sandwich with two layers of metal surrounding a plastic core. The outside metal parts had a rough, textured outer surface that was designed to allow the spine bone to grow into the implant and stabilize it. The plastic between the metal plates was supposed to compress and expand like the normal disc to allow spinal movement. It all sounded fine, theoretically.

However, these surgeons did not disclose that they were inventors of this artificial disc. So, the surgeons not only got paid for doing the surgery, they also took a cut of the money the hospital charged the patient to purchase the artificial disc. Linda's team would show the Maryland jury that these surgeons were making a lot of money from this operation.

Linda leaned back examining the plaster ceiling in her father's office. She had restored the office, maintaining the old cornices, but cracks were again appearing in the old plaster. She smiled realizing that renovating this office was maintaining the connection to her family's history in Maple Ridge, while the modern office tower next door represented the town's hope for ongoing prosperity. Linda was aware that this Baltimore case would be crucial to both her firm's legacy and its future.

The surgeons' hidden conflict of interest would probably have been acceptable if the artificial discs had worked. But as time passed, it became obvious that the artificial disc was not bonding to the spinal bone as planned. Far from anchoring to the bone, these things started migrating within the spine.

Paging through case summaries, Linda reviewed her clients' experiences after surgery. Most had continued to suffer from back pain, but their surgeons reassured them that the pain would stop once their spine bone grew into the disc and stabilized it. Eventually, Linda's clients got tired of flying to Baltimore to be told to be patient and went to see their local spine experts who had referred them to Baltimore. And that is when they started to realize that they were in serious trouble.

Linda flipped forward in a few of the case summaries on her desk. Within a year or two, it became evident that the artificial discs were migrating within the spinal bone. Sometimes the artificial disc moved forward in the spine toward the belly button and sometimes the disc migrated backwards toward the spinal nerves.

She looked at the consultations written by spine surgeons and neurologists her firm had contracted to describe the complications caused by artificial disc migration. When the artificial disc moved forward toward the belly button, it would compress the major veins located just in front of the spine. This pressure would block blood returning from the legs to the heart and cause massive swelling of the feet and calves.

Most of her clients with vein swelling would have to lie in bed most of the day with their feet elevated. Otherwise, their legs would swell like sausages and fluid could literally start leaking through the skin.

The few clients who tried to stay mobile despite the leg swelling usually ended up with deep ulcers around their feet and ankles. The pictures of these ulcers in her files made Linda feel nauseous each time she saw them. Some of those people had eventually needed amputations because of these terrible ulcers.

Despite these devastating complications, forward migration of the disc was probably better than when the disc moved backwards because this would put pressure on the spinal nerves causing paralysis and terrible pain.

The Baltimore surgeons refused to accept the extent of problems resulting from this operation and kept on implanting these discs. By four years after the first artificial disc was implanted, it was clear that most of the first patients the surgeons had operated on were suffering from severe disc migration complications.

As Linda's team signed up clients who had undergone surgery with the device, it became evident that the complications became more common and more severe the longer the disc was in place.

Linda closed her eyes reviewing her strategy. Her plan was to convince the jury that all patients treated with these discs deserved potential for full compensation because it was only a matter of time until most would get these difficult complications. It was apparently just about impossible to remove the artificial disc to fix the problem. On a few occasions, expert spine surgeons had attempted to remove the devices without success.

Over time, Linda had assigned forty paralegals to this case and each team member was managing at least fifteen clients who had signed up with the Davis firm to represent them in a class action lawsuit.

Linda was suing the surgeons who implanted the discs, the hospitals, and the manufacturer of the implant. The insurance companies that would foot the bill for any compensation that Linda achieved for her clients at trial had united in hiring one very experienced defense litigator to represent them.

Anticipating the argument that defense counsel would be present to the jury, Linda looked at the summary of the defense documents filed in the pretrial period.

Linda could tell that the other side had decided that their best defense was to argue that all these patients were severely disabled before surgery. They would agree that unfortunately back surgery could not cure everyone but would emphasize that many people were doing well with the artificial disc.

Linda smiled as she thought about one bombshell witness her team would present to the jury. One of the original four surgeons had stopped implanting the disc after using it for less than two years. At pretrial discovery hearings this doctor admitted that he had stopped doing the operation because he was concerned about disc migration. When Linda's team asked him if he had told his colleagues about his findings, he confirmed that he did tell them.

When asked why his colleagues had chosen to continue doing the operation, he responded, "Money. This is a very lucrative operation. We got very well paid for doing the surgery and we were also paid royalties on the disc implant because we invented it."

Linda knew that the defendants were going to fight hard to keep that testimony out of court, because if the jury concluded that the surgeons knowingly harmed people for financial gain, then she could probably achieve punitive damages for her clients.

Punitive damages would increase the compensation to Linda's clients because of the defendants' irresponsible behavior. Punitive damages were tightly constrained in Maryland law, but Linda had a feeling that when the jury heard her surgeon's testimony, the case would be headed to settlement on her terms.

Linda sighed and put the various paper files back into their appropriate folders. Things were so good in Linda's life right now. She had a case that was probably going to earn her clients and her firm a large amount of well-justified money. And she had a lover in her bed who was becoming her soul mate.

The only problem was that some gangster on the Gulf Coast

was probably planning to kill her!

So, Linda was getting ready to go and do battle in Maryland with Bill and his team providing security. And Ed was getting ready to go to the Gulf Coast and Linda was not exactly sure what he was planning to do there.

CHAPTER 42: BILOXI

Stephen remembered that the Colonel had been known as a very careful guy in Afghanistan, and he appreciated that Ed was cautious about the team avoiding recognition in Biloxi. They quietly rented three homes in different parts of town, and they all had different tasks in the reconnaissance initiated to learn more about Gabriel Duquesne.

Brooke was responsible for electronic surveillance, trying to get the information they needed about Gabriel's various business interests without physically encountering Duquesne or his gang.

Stephen's team was responsible for direct observation of Gabriel's various activities. It didn't take long for them to figure out that Duquesne was dealing in drugs, women, and illegal immigration. And the center of his operation was the rebuilt Café de Paris, a replica of the large establishment that had been a landmark on the Biloxi beachfront prior to Hurricane Katrina.

Before the historic hurricane struck in 2005, all of Biloxi's casinos were required to locate on coastal barges or buildings with piers on the water. The storm surge from Hurricane Katrina destroyed all the coastal gambling houses as well as most structures on the beachfront like the old Café. The gambling companies demanded that they be allowed to rebuild the casinos on land along the coastal road. This created prime real estate for smaller establishments like the Café which was rebuilt along the beach road amid the new gaming establishments, hotels, and condominiums.

The original Café had been on its site for more than seventy-five years and the new Café was built as a replica of the old building. It featured a country and western stage as well as an enormous saloon with three separate bars. The front of the Café facing on the beach was reserved for dining and featured booths along the windows facing the Gulf.

Stephen had a three-man rotation on his surveillance team, and it was easy to stay under the radar by dressing local with boots, jeans, and baseball or cowboy hats. Within days Stephen's team had learned about everything that was on offer from Gabriel Duquesne at the Café de Paris.

Gabriel's boys were in place at three or four tables in the Café by nine or ten at night. Customers were lined up at the bar waiting for them. The gang didn't bring merchandise into the Café, but Stephen's team saw plenty of cash changing hands and cell phone calls and text entries being made.

A few of the customers were retail – connected tourists or locals scoring a night of dodgy entertainment. But Stephen recognized many repeat customers who were clearly picking up various wholesale products to resell on the street. It was just like Tony Malto's modus operandi of generally avoiding retail street trade.

Customers sometimes picked up packages outside on the street, or they might leave the Café after paying inside to get into a limo with four or five women who would be taken to one of the local hotels where they would be marketed overnight. Stephen's team also overheard some intense conversations about needing people for various jobs – landscaping, housekeeping, and construction – and it was clear that Gabriel was carrying on an illicit employment service for undocumented immigrants out of the Café.

Everyone on Duquesne's teams had phones constantly in hand and they were constantly using them to make entries when money was exchanged as well as making calls and sending texts. It was clear that Gabriel's entire enterprise was mobility enabled and sophisticated.

Each day in the late afternoon, Ed's team joined up at the Colonel's rented home to exchange intel. They were all careful to cover their tracks, both in the Café and while getting to the Colonel's place. Stephen's team took care to rotate assignments for surveillance at the Café as well as constantly changing clothing, hats, and boots.

The Colonel's brother Ben had gone back to New York for the first couple of days that they were in Biloxi, but now he was back staying with the Colonel. The two of them stayed away from the Café, but when everyone gathered in the evening, the entire team pored over the surveillance photos Stephen's team had taken to familiarize themselves with the establishment's layout.

The Café dining room's front windows were its focal point, looking out across the beach to the Gulf. The dining area was enclosed with a three-sided partition that separated diners from the larger saloon. There were three bars along the other three walls of the rectangular interior with the bar opposite the windows only half as long as the room to allow for the stage that accommodated country and western bands. The live music usually started about nine p.m. and the place was then crowded until closing time around four a.m.

Stephen had also tracked how Gabriel Duquesne used the Café de Paris. He was never there in the evening, but it was clear that his gang members were constantly talking to and messaging him by phone from inside and outside the Café. They had observed that he was always at the Café for breakfast to discuss the prior night's business with a few of his boys.

On day six in Biloxi, Stephen led off the daily conference at the Colonel's place with what his team had observed. He described the various retail and wholesale criminal activities that Gabriel's team seemed to be running out of the Café de Paris, the muscle Gabriel had inside and outside the Café to protect his cashflow and the team on the outside that delivered his goods and services. Stephen felt that his guys understood Duquesne's operation reasonably well and emphasized that

Gabriel's entire enterprise seemed to run on the gang's cell phones.

Brooke followed Stephen and expressed disappointment with her own progress. "Colonel, all his records are mobility accessed, but their phones have the latest encryption and commercial secure password storage. We have not been able to penetrate the firewall of his main databases. He uses a cloud-based system that is very secure. We will need a physical way to interact with his system to have any chance of figuring out his passwords and entry protocols. We will probably need to break into his offices to gain access to his computers or maybe steal a phone to make progress. And even if we could get access to his phone or computers, I will not know if we can break through the security until we try."

And here she looked to the Colonel and then down at the floor. "I think we need to recognize that the FBI will never be able to use what we give them as the basis for a RICO charge in court. We are going to need to get into his systems through very illegal means. It will not be like the case with Tony Malto who just left access to his data wide open for anyone to see. We are going to need an office break-in or a phone theft to have any chance of getting into Gabriel's records."

The Colonel looked over to his brother Ben. Brooke found their relationship interesting. Ben obviously idolized his older brother, but the Colonel trusted his brother's intelligence and conceptual capabilities. If it was operations or physical stuff, the Colonel took charge. But in this complex process of planning to neutralize Gabriel, Ben was definitely an equal partner.

And it was Ben who opened the discussion that led to their eventual scheme. "Listening to Brooke, it's clear to me that we need a different strategy to protect Linda from this Dixie Gang. Even if Tony had not so stupidly kidnapped Linda, we already had information that the FBI would have used in bringing a RICO case against him. Of course, we all know how badly that turned out for Tony." Ben shrugged.

"But this Gabriel guy sounds much smarter. His lawyers

would probably be able to block prosecutors from using what we would give to the feds because, as Brooke admits, we will be obtaining it very illegally. And when you really analyze it, doing the same thing that we did with Malto might not be the best thing for Linda anyway."

Ben was clearly thinking hard while he talked. He stood up and started walking around the modest bungalow that was rented for him and the Colonel. The drapes were drawn, and the living room was dark except for a couple of lamps.

"If we were to take out Gabriel with a RICO charge based on information we gave to the FBI, it might end up just the same for Gabriel as it did for Tony. He might be murdered in jail to protect other Dixie Gang members. Or he might be put away for years with a successful prosecution."

Ben continued speaking slowly, considering each word, taking deliberate steps around the living room with everyone watching him walk, think, and talk. "If Gabriel were put away in prison or killed, we would be back to the same place. Someone in his crime family would take over and they would very likely connect Linda to Gabriel's downfall. Whoever succeeded Gabriel would be our new challenge."

He started pacing faster. "But what if we just convinced Gabriel that we had everything we needed to take him down? Let me think this through with you guys. Like we discussed at Linda's place the night we learned that Malto had been murdered, maybe we just need a different approach here."

Ben went to the fridge and took out a beer. He then sat at the large dining table that served as their conference table. "Let me tell you what I am thinking."

Some of the team followed his lead with a beer. Others just sat around the table. As Ben slowly started explaining what he was thinking, Brooke added her thoughts, and the discussion went on for over an hour.

The Colonel remained silent while the brainstorming was in progress. But by ninety minutes after Ben started, the Colonel started to summarize everyone's thinking. And then the Colonel added some medical thinking of his own to the plan.

Ed had remembered a sting operation on an Iraqi general that the Special Forces ran with the help of their intelligence agency. It had something to do with a heart recording that the Colonel did not bother explaining to the team. Before the Colonel left Maple Ridge, he had contacted some of his Special Forces medical colleagues who had participated in that operation. Those former colleagues had promised to help by sending some new equipment that they were currently using.

Colonel Ed said he had just received this medical equipment, and that he needed to work with it to understand whether it could help. The team had four more days to refine details before the Colonel was due to meet with Gabriel. Colonel Ed looked at Brooke and asked if she thought she could break into Gabriel's records if they got the gangster's cell phone. Brooke shrugged and responded that she would not know until she tried.

Brooke then reminded the Colonel, "If we can find a way to get his phone, we will also need to somehow disable Gabriel for a few hours. Otherwise, he will immediately just change all his security when he realizes his phone is gone."

The conversation continued and the Colonel offered some other ideas that Ben picked up on. Before the team broke up that evening, they had a plan that seemed almost outrageous – but just possibly workable. They christened the whole idea 'Ben's plan', and Ben didn't seem to mind.

CHAPTER 43: MAKING THE CASE

E veryone in the courtroom stood as the judge entered from his chambers and sat behind the traditional elevated podium. Although the federal district courthouse near the inner harbor in Baltimore was reasonably modern, the courtrooms were designed to look more historic. The dark wood furnishings, coffered ceilings and high, narrow windows would not have looked out of place in a gothic cathedral.

Linda returned to her seat at the back of the spectators' section of the courtroom and adjusted her dark wig. Most people would assume that since Linda was leading the legal team, she would command the presentation of the case in the courtroom. But she had learned that she should partner with expert litigators to do that work. Litigation lions who would tear opposing witnesses apart, outsmart counsel for the other side and make the jury love them. And of course, share in the financial risk and reward inherent in the class action lawsuit.

The Davis firm's responsibility was to identify harm caused to a group of people and then find and recruit the members of the injured class to start the lawsuit. And that took doggedness, compassion and empathy; Linda's paralegals were hired for and trained in those characteristics.

Linda's own special expertise became evident during the trial in assessing how the jury was responding. She always sat quietly in the back of the courtroom, usually wearing a wig to cover her noticeable blonde hair, and often sporting large, unflattering glasses. Linda tried to maintain a low profile in the courtroom, avoiding recognition by the jury.

Her assignment was to watch the jury as it heard the case, to determine if and when she should settle and how much the settlement should cost the defendants to adequately compensate her clients. Inevitably with the cases that Linda brought to trial, the insurance companies on the other side of the courtroom would make an offer at some point during the proceedings. And Linda's job was to figure out what the jury was thinking and how much the jurors were likely to award to her clients. She needed to assess whether the defense offer, when it came, was sufficient to match the jury award that she could expect.

Linda had worked for months with her Maryland litigation partners and their plan at trial was clear. After opening arguments, they would take testimony from two clients. Both these people were in wheelchairs four years after receiving the artificial disc. One had developed nerve paralysis that prevented her from walking and the other had terrible leg swelling that had caused deep ulcers, resulting in an amputation.

Just as they were to start taking testimony from the first witness, she received a text from Ed. The text read "Operation so far successful."

That message was pretty ambiguous. Linda knew that Ed and the team had a plan they were pursuing in Biloxi, but she did not really understand what they were doing. However, she had to feel that this message was a good omen for the days ahead in the courtroom. When this trial finished Linda was planning to be a very public figure. She hoped that she would not need a security detail following her for the rest of her life.

The first few days at trial went just as expected. The jury listened attentively as Linda's litigation partners explained what had happened to the plaintiffs as a result of surgery during their opening argument.

The jury could not take their eyes off the first witness's wheelchair nor the second witness's amputation stump. Naturally, Linda's team had their second witness come into court in a wheelchair without his artificial leg and with his pant leg pinned up to demonstrate the missing body part. By day four, Linda began to think that her expertise would be needed soon. She could feel a settlement offer coming.

Unbeknownst to the lawyers on the other side, one of Linda's paralegals had handed her a gift that was going to lift this settlement to an entirely new level. During the pretrial hearings where both sides had taken testimony from potential witnesses under oath, Linda's legal opponents had emphasized that although some patients had bad outcomes, many people who had received the artificial disc did well following surgery.

Linda was claiming that the results from this disc operation were so bad that it was only a matter of time until all patients who had been treated with the disc would have major disability. She was arguing that any settlement should include all patients who had been treated with the disc, not just her current clients. According to Linda's argument, patients currently doing well should be compensated in the future if they developed disability from disc migration.

This was an important and expensive issue for the insurance companies representing the surgeons, hospitals and manufacturers of the artificial disc. They wanted to limit any damages only to Linda's current clients by claiming that most other patients were doing just fine with the disc.

In the pretrial testimony, the other side relied heavily on a high school basketball coach from the Midwest who had decided on artificial disc surgery because he wanted to participate in workouts with his basketball team. His testimony was important for the other side because of the performance of his high school basketball team after his surgery. He had given up coaching while he was waiting for surgery. On his coaching return, the team had gone on to win the state championship.

The attorneys on the other side made a huge deal about this victory, almost suggesting that the artificial disc had won the trophy. They had prepared a professional, tightly edited video which they planned to show the jury during the coach's testimony. The film demonstrated the coach working out in practice drills with his team and the boys eventually winning the state championship with a dramatic, buzzer-beating jump shot.

Linda knew this would be compelling evidence for the jury. The implication was – *Sure, this disc had not cured everyone, but let's face it, back problems are complicated and difficult to solve. However, in many cases the disc has allowed patients to get back to a full and satisfying life.*

The other side would rely on the gym teacher's testimony to insist that at worst, any financial award should only go to people who were already suffering from symptoms today. It was a powerful argument and Linda knew that the coach's testimony would hurt her side at trial.

The other side had the coach scheduled as their first witness to take the stand after Linda's team had finished presenting their case. However, the skill and compassion of Linda's paralegals had paid off in letting Linda know that this important part of the other side's defense might be at risk.

CHAPTER 44: GABRIEL'S ARREST

Brooke wanted to wash her hands every time she touched something at the Café de Paris. The place just felt so sleazy. Although she had never been in the Café before this morning, Stephen's detailed briefings and photographs made her feel like a regular visitor.

The plan that Ben had developed with his brother was audacious, but Brooke knew that an unusual operation was needed to accomplish their goal of protecting Linda and Maple Ridge from the Dixie Gang forever. The Colonel and his brother had certainly developed an out-of-the-box scheme.

Ben intrigued Brooke. When she'd first met him in Maple Ridge, he had ensured rapid access to all the gear they had needed. At that time, he had stayed in the background. However, since they began planning for Biloxi, Ben had become an important member of the squad, demonstrating innovative thinking and effective leadership.

Ben was obviously smart and ran a large, successful family business. Brooke enjoyed working with him. And this morning, they were going to try and accomplish Ben's very bold plan. There was really no Plan B. In Afghanistan they usually had a Plan B, but here they all knew that they just had to make Ben's plan work.

Stephen's team had been watching Gabriel Duquesne for the past week, and his routine did not vary. For a man who practiced very careful cybersecurity, his consistent daily routine was a surprising weakness. The pattern of how he led his life demonstrated to Brooke how secure he felt here in Biloxi. And now, they were hoping to make him suddenly feel very vulnerable.

Stephen's briefing revealed that Gabriel went to the Café every morning between nine-thirty and ten-thirty. The Café staff had told Stephen's team that this had been his habit for years. He did not pay much attention to the waiters. If there was a cute waitress, he might call her sugar and try to grab her butt. But most of the wait staff were guys and he ignored them, even when giving his order.

In fact, most of the time he did not even order. Stephen had told the team that the waiters would usually bring him a platter covered with pastries and then return with a café au lait.

Gabriel spent his mornings with a few of his closest gang lieutenants who were running various activities out of the Café de Paris. Ed's team suspected that Gabriel likely had other partners like Tony Malto who would be engaged in criminal activities in other locations. However, from the number of people dealing with Gabriel's boys in the Café, this location was clearly a major focus of the Dixie Gang's business.

It had been no problem for Stephen to convince the usual Café wait staff to come in late this morning. There wasn't much work before noon anyway. In fact, according to Stephen, Gabriel was generally the only guest in the Café in the morning. There were usually four people working before ten a.m., mainly setting up tables for the day ahead.

Stephen explained to the usual staff that he and his friends were planning a celebration for a friend later in the day. Could they take over their work for a couple of hours this morning to set up the surprise event? When he sweetened his request with cash the usual waiters readily agreed and gave Stephen the details of their morning duties. Their manager would not arrive until eleven-thirty and by that time Stephen hoped his team would be finished.

On the day of the rendezvous with the Colonel, Stephen expected that Gabriel would come with extra muscle. He normally ate breakfast with two or three guys reviewing business.

They figured this morning that he likely would have at least four men with him.

Stephen had two men with him in the Café that morning, both dressed in waiters' dark slacks, white shirts, and black vests. They all had concealed weapons and plenty of ammunition. In planning the team's fire power, they did not count on the Colonel since they expected that Gabriel's boys would likely search him for weapons.

They knew the large table in the dining area of the Café that Gabriel inevitably used for breakfast. The Colonel got there at nine-fifteen and slid into the banquette with his back toward the window that faced out to the beach and the Gulf. There were five chairs on the opposite side of the table from the banquette.

They figured it would be a surprise to Gabriel that the Colonel was there first at his table and part of the plan was to destabilize the gangster with surprises and unexpected events. The team anticipated that Gabriel would initially underestimate the Colonel with Ed taking the banquette seat since that seat was difficult to exit. But they also had a plan to immediately undermine Gabriel's confidence with respect to seating.

Gabriel got there a bit earlier than usual at about nine-twenty-five. Brooke was acting as hostess and was dressed to distract with a short, low-cut dress, high heels, and patterned stockings. With the short dress, she needed to carefully conceal her thigh holster and was forced to use a smaller pistol than she would usually choose.

Gabriel noticed Brooke on entering the Café and asked when she had started working there. Brooke flirted with him as she answered, stroking his arm as she led him to the table, hoping that she would keep him from noticing that all the wait staff were new this morning.

Gabriel was being extra cautious with his muscle this morning. Stephen had told the team that he would usually eat breakfast with up to four gang members and sure enough, four well-dressed companions stayed with Gabriel as he headed toward his table.

However, there were four more men trailing the crew headed for the table and these extra four men spread out around the room, assessing their firing lanes professionally.

Stephen glanced at Brooke with concern, and she knew what he was thinking. If this turned into a firefight, they were badly outgunned. Hopefully things would go the way they had planned without weapons being drawn.

Duquesne registered surprise that the Colonel was already seated at his table. He and three of his four companions sat opposite Colonel Ed on the chairs across from the banquette. The last man motioned to the Colonel to stand up and expertly searched him for weapons. He then turned to Gabriel and shook his head.

"Y'all must be Dr. Ed. Mah name is Gabriel, Gabriel Duquesne. These here are my bidness associates," said Duquesne motioning to the muscle surrounding him. This was Brooke's first time seeing the mob boss in person and he was even more formidable than he appeared in Stephen's photos.

He stood about six feet tall and seemed nearly six feet wide. Brooke judged his weight in excess of four hundred and fifty pounds. He had a special reinforced chair in the center of his table and Brooke could imagine that he may have crushed a few regular chairs in the past.

"Nice to meet you. Please call me Ed." The Colonel sat with his hands quietly folded together in front of him. His usual stillness was evident as the five men across the table gazed at him intently.

"Well, Ed, Ah gotta say if Ah was you, Ah don't think Ah'd be sittin' back there in them banquette seats. If we have any disagreement my boys are blockin' your exit route."

Listening to their boss, Gabe's boys shifted their seats closer to the edges of the table, showing Ed that they could readily block his egress.

Ed nodded and let the tension build with his silence. After sitting quietly for nearly a minute, shifting his gaze to each of

NEW DOC IN MAPLE RIDGE

his five tablemates in turn, he separated his hands and rolled them over palms up, so that Gabriel and his boys could see the two small electric switches he was holding. He had taped the switches to the under surface of the table when he first sat down so that they would not be discovered when he was frisked. "You are correct, Mr. Duquesne, that if I wanted to run, your men could certainly stop me."

He leaned back and looked from one end of the table opposite to the other. He lifted his hands, holding the switches between his fingers so they could be readily examined from across the table. "However, there is really no need for me to consider running. You and your guys might all want to shift over a bit on your chairs – you will see that the fabric of all the seats you are sitting on has recently been cut open and sewn shut again. You may also notice that your seats may feel a bit lumpy."

All of Gabriel's men looked down and some felt their seats. Ed heard one of them mutter, "what the fuck?"

Ed again remained silent, allowing tension to build as all Gabriel's crew shifted to examine their chairs. Ed looked at each one of the guys and then settled his gaze on Gabriel.

"My guys are experts with C-4. They loaded those chairs with exactly the right amount of plastic explosive. They are just artists with that plastic stuff. I told them that I wanted them to blow off your genitals and your butts but that they could not break the glass behind me here. They have orders that they should not kill you, just damage you very badly so that your lives are changed forever."

He then rotated his hands, again demonstrating the two small electric switches. "If I push these switches, you will all be in hospital for a year and pooping in a bag for the rest of your lives."

The Colonel then shifted his hold on the switches to grasp the front of his sports jacket. "I wore an old jacket that I will just throw away rather than try and clean your body parts off the coat. But my guys guarantee me that they have simulated the blast from those chairs many times over. They promised me that I won't get a bruise or a cut on me."

The four gunmen who were scattered around the room were taking steps away from the table and had hands on their weapons while looking to Gabriel for direction.

Standing close to the table waiting to take orders, Brooke could see sweat appearing on Gabriel's upper lip. Clearly, he was realizing that he might have underestimated the man sitting across from him. Gabriel was a red-faced and fleshy man who looked like a heart attack waiting to happen. He had obviously never faced a situation like this and did not know how to organize his men against this unusual threat. He was flummoxed by the Colonel's quiet message about the C-4 explosive.

Being a bit of an operational pessimist, Brooke wished that they really did have C-4 plastic explosive in Gabrielle's chair. But she could see the impact that the Colonel's message was having on Duquesne. The gangster was not considering that the Colonel might be bluffing.

"You called me an' set up this fuckin' meetin'. What the fuck you wanna talk about? An' what the fuck you gonna do with that plastic bomb stuff?"

The Colonel smiled. "Well Mr. Duquesne, I wouldn't have mentioned the C-4 if you had not threatened me by suggesting that your men would block me if I tried to leave my seat." The two guys who had shifted their chairs to block the Colonel now quickly shifted back to where they had started.

Ed held up the small switches that he had implied controlled the explosive and ostentatiously put them in his jacket pocket. "But, Mr. Duquesne, we have gotten off on the wrong foot this morning and I apologize for that! Why don't we allow ourselves to experience that famous Southern hospitality I have heard so much about? Before we get down to business, how about we have breakfast together and get to know each other a bit better." He motioned to Brooke, and she hurried over to the table, looking every bit the tarty serving girl that Gabriel might expect.

"Yes sir, what can I bring for you gentlemen?"

The Colonel responded. "Why not just bring us some nice French pastries and café au lait to go around? Is that good for you and your boys, Gabriel?" The gangster looked up at Brooke and she bent over to give him a long, slow look deep down her dress. Despite worrying about the C-4, he couldn't take his eyes away. "Yeah, that's good for us."

Brooke was gone for no more than two minutes. She could see the gangsters all shifting uncomfortably in their chairs. Stephen's team were moving around the room cleaning cutlery and setting tables but also keeping a careful eye on Gabriel's squad. Brooke could see they were moving to try and achieve a tactical advantage over the four standing gunmen while maintaining firing lines to the table.

Brooke returned with a large platter of pastries that she placed in the center of the table. Gabriel looked at the pastries suspiciously. Seeing Gabriel's hesitancy to choose a pastry, Colonel Ed closed his eyes, spun the platter around, randomly selected a croissant and took a large bite from one end. Reassured that he was not going to be poisoned, Gabriel followed suit and his croissant disappeared in two large bites. He wiped the crumbs from his mouth with the back of his hand.

Gabriel's colleagues at the table were obviously wondering if they could get up and desert their boss or if they needed to stay seated on their presumably deadly chairs. They came to the obvious conclusion that leaving Gabriel would be much worse for their health than any amount of C-4. They remained seated and reached for pastries.

By now Brooke was back carrying a tray with two large latte cups, a pot of coffee and a second, smaller pot full of warm milk. She again bent deeply in front of Gabriel while slowly positioning his saucer, cup, and spoon in front of him. His eyes did not leave her cleavage. She then set the Colonel's cup and saucer on the table without the show.

Gabriel lifted his head, following Brooke as she poured aromatic French roast coffee into the Colonel's cup followed by warm milk. She then again bent low in front of the mob boss as she filled his cup.

Brooke smiled at Gabriel's men and promised, "I'll be right back with yours, boys."

As Brooke hustled back to the kitchen, nobody at the table thought it unusual that she was wearing long, white, cotton gloves which extended nearly to her elbows. The gloves were a bit dramatic but a fitting accessory to the short black dress and patterned stockings she was wearing.

Nor could anyone tell that she had two pairs of surgical gloves under the cotton gloves to protect her from the skin gel that she had generously applied to Gabriel's coffee cup.

As Brooke disappeared inside the kitchen, she wiped her fabric gloves free of any residual gel with a paper towel. Stephen followed her into the kitchen, put on his own surgical gloves and carefully rolled off Brooke's outer gloves. He then helped her to insert her surgically gloved hands back into an identical pair of cotton gloves.

The skin gel that Brooke had applied to Gabriel's coffee cup is used in external drug patches that stimulate drug absorption through the skin into the blood stream. The night before, Dr. Ed had fully saturated a large sample of gel with the opioid drug Carfentanyl.

This veterinary tranquilizer is similar to the drug Fentanyl which often causes street drug overdoses. However, Carfentanyl is much more powerful than Fentanyl, at least ten thousand times more potent than morphine, and is used to anaesthetize elephants. Looking at Gabriel's elephantine size, Brooke was pleased that they had decided to use the highest possible dose of Carfentanyl to mix into the skin gel.

There was enough Carfentanyl drug on Gabriel's coffee cup to tranquilize a herd of elephants. As Brooke returned to the table with coffee for Gabriel's men, she watched the gangster raise the cup to his mouth for a first sip after finishing off another pastry. She could imagine the drug being absorbed through the skin of his hands and lips and coursing through the bloodstream to overwhelm the opioid receptors in his brain. She saw that he probably felt something greasy on the coffee cup and possibly tasted something unusual as the cup touched his lips.

Brooke could envision him thinking that something was wrong with the cup, but she knew from the drug profile and the amount of drug they had applied to the cup that it was already too late for Gabriel. Within seconds of the cup contacting the blood-filled surfaces of his fingers and lips, he had absorbed enough drug to kill twenty men.

He turned his head toward Brooke, and she thought she heard him say, "This cup's..."

And then there was a loud crash as Gabriel's four-hundred-pound-plus body collapsed to the floor unconscious from the massive dose of Carfentanyl opioid he had absorbed. Gabriel also stopped breathing as his brain breathing control center was paralyzed by the drug.

There was a moment when no one moved. Then Colonel Ed shouted out, "My God, he's had a cardiac arrest, let me get to him. I'm a doctor. He needs CPR."

CHAPTER 45: THE OFFER

I n evaluating the other side's tactics at trial, Linda knew that their lawyers would focus on the argument that spinal surgery was complex and unpredictable. In making this argument they would insist that many people who had received the artificial disc were doing just fine, and that the operation had allowed them to return to their normal lives. Their best evidence for this argument would be the testimony of the high school basketball coach and the video showing his team winning the state championship after he had his artificial disc surgery.

More than a year before trial, one of Linda's paralegals had contacted the coach, sitting with him and his wife to describe what the class action meant and explaining that even though he was currently doing well, their clients' condition had often deteriorated dramatically after some initial recovery. The coach had been dismissive of any suggestion that he might get worse in the future. He insisted that he was entirely recovered, and he was sure that his team would be going back to the state championships again this year.

In the notes that the paralegal made after her interviews, mention was made of the coach's wife sitting quietly and listening, but occasionally reminding her husband that he had recently started having back pain again after practice. He made light of these symptoms, but his wife Judy seemed concerned enough that Linda's paralegal called her back after the visit.

"Judy, you have my contacts and if things ever change you can message me. I hope that George does as well as he is expecting, but if things change, let me know. If he is going to be disabled, it will be important for you to get compensation to protect your future."

And things had changed in the months between pretrial testimony and the trial date. Three weeks ago, Judy had called the paralegal to say that her husband was no longer coaching and could barely walk, even with a cane.

After hearing this from her paralegal, Linda herself called Judy back. "Judy, I can still represent George and add him to our case."

Linda could almost hear Judy thinking through the silence on the other end of the call. "Thank you so much, Ms. Davis. We really appreciate your firm's concern. You have been so helpful." She paused and then continued.

"But George won't join the case because he is hoping so hard that his symptoms will improve. But I see how much pain he is in. He can hardly walk around the house these past few weeks. I know he's in denial about his pain because he just wants to get back to coaching. It's his life's work."

Then Linda heard Judy's voice crack. "Ms. Davis, I am terrified for our future if George becomes disabled. We have no disability insurance, and our three kids are about to head off to college. I have never worked. I'll get a job if I have to, but I can never cover expenses the way that George's job has provided."

Linda responded, "Judy, if the class action is successful in protecting future disability, then George would be eligible for the settlement that we are claiming for all disc patients if he becomes permanently disabled. But, of course, we won't know if that claim is successful until after the trial."

However, Linda now knew that the other side's best defense against awarding potential future damages for everyone who had undergone disc replacement – the inspiring video showing a dedicated coach leading his team to victory because of the operation – would never be shown. She knew that the opposite side could not bring George, struggling to walk with a cane, into the courtroom to show that video to the jury. But the other side was not aware that Linda knew about their star witness's deterioration.

Linda now expected with virtual certainty that the other side's offer would come after her third and fourth witnesses testified. These two clients were in the early stages of migration complications from the artificial disc.

Sitting in her usual location at the back of the courtroom, Linda heard the jury mutter when the third witness explained that her doctor had told her that with her increasing symptoms, she would need a wheelchair very soon. The judge directed the courtroom to be quiet.

The fourth witness was a formerly active man who had mild back pain when he agreed to surgery. The disc was now migrating forward into his large abdominal veins and he was having increasing difficulty walking because his legs were swelling with any kind of upright activity.

The other side objected when Linda's litigation team asked the witness to roll up his pants to show his legs to the jury. But the judge denied the objection after argument from Linda's litigation partners.

When the judge instructed the witness to roll up his pant legs, the jury groaned audibly as they looked at the man's massively swollen ankles and calves.

These two witnesses were key to Linda's case because she wanted the potential for damages in every patient who had received this disc, even if their difficulties were just beginning. Her goal was to convince the jury (or the insurance company contemplating a settlement offer) that every patient with this disc implanted deserved potential compensation for major symptoms and disability, whether the symptoms were already fully developed at the time of the trial or appeared in the future.

Her Maryland litigation partners had done a wonderful job with their first four witnesses and Linda knew the jury was on her side. And lawyers on both sides in the case knew that tomorrow her surgeon would be testifying all day long. He would say that he had recognized these problems eighteen months after starting to do the artificial disc surgery and that he stopped offering the artificial disc to patients because he was concerned about the complications he was seeing.

He would testify that he had told his co-inventors of the artificial disc that it was not working the way they had all hoped and that they should all stop implanting the device. And he would say that the company and the other surgeons disregarded his advice because they were all making a fortune by selling and implanting the disc. He would even testify under oath that one of his former surgeon partners had told him, "That's why we pay malpractice insurance."

And Linda now knew that the other side could no longer rebut her clients' testimony by having George the basketball coach demonstrate that some artificial disc recipients were leading full and active lives.

Linda had arranged for the national and local press to be in the courtroom for tomorrow's testimony by the surgeon. She had called several reporters with "exclusive" tips about what tomorrow's testimony would entail and what her surgeon would expose about the company, the surgeons, and hospitals that had manufactured and implanted these artificial discs.

She casually met with one of the hospital vice-presidents monitoring progress at the trial and let her know that they could expect media the following day. Linda enjoyed watching the blood drain from the woman's face.

Linda also mentioned to the hospital VP that she had reserved accommodation for the visiting national journalists because several had mentioned that they might stay for the following days' testimony, when Linda's team was planning to put their expert radiologist, spine surgeons and neurologists on the stand.

The VP left the courtroom almost immediately after this conversation, pulling her cell phone from her purse. Linda ventured a guess that she was about to call her hospital leaders urging them to settle this case before their institution's reputation was destroyed in the national media.

Linda was reasonably sure that the other side would try and limit their losses by offering settlement before her surgeon had a chance to testify. Without any useful rebuttal from the basketball coach, it would be best to avoid having the surgeon testify that the defendants had been told that their device was dangerous. Especially since the defendants' dirty laundry would be discussed in front of a large media contingent expected in the courtroom for the next several days.

With the jury responding to the first four witnesses with the sympathy that Linda saw developing in the courtroom, she knew it was becoming obvious to the insurers that they would likely be facing a very large jury award.

The trial was reaching the moment when both sides would benefit from settlement. The insurers knew from Linda's surgeon's pretrial testimony that the award was only going to get bigger when the jury heard from her doctor. From Linda's clients' perspective, getting a settlement today instead of waiting for a jury decision and the possibility of endless appeals meant getting cash in hand immediately, rather than waiting for the deep pocketed insurance companies to lose interest in the case and stop appealing.

Linda's team was eating a late dinner in their hotel suite debriefing the day's courtroom activity when the call came that the opposite side wanted to conference that evening.

Linda and her team met with opposing counsel shortly before midnight in the boardroom the two sides had reserved in their hotel. The US District Court was in the redeveloped inner harbor area of Baltimore and their hotel was close by. The boardroom was well appointed, and the hotel promised to have staff available through the night for refreshments and any business support that the lawyers might need.

After some initial, interminable lawyer chit chat, the other side passed a sheet of paper to Linda. She smiled inwardly but maintained her well-practiced poker face when she saw their initial offer because she knew that this was going to be very,

very good. But she did not let up on her demands and negotiations continued through the night. Linda ostentatiously sent her Maryland litigation team to their rooms at one a.m., telling them in front of the opposing side that they would need to be well rested in the morning when she was looking forward to their surgeon testifying.

The next morning, they notified the judge that negotiations were still underway and asked for a recess until after lunch. During that morning, Linda's paralegals were in constant contact with their clients who were increasingly in favor of settlement as Linda pushed the other side very hard.

Linda's litigation partners were somewhat disappointed just after noon when they learned that their clients had settled for the largest medical class action award in the country's legal history.

The litigators would not get a chance to win a historic jury award. But Linda's clients would achieve a very generous outcome without risk of appeal. And the award would be extended to all patients who developed future disability after disc replacement, including George the basketball coach.

As the paperwork was being drawn up that afternoon, Linda called her lover on the Gulf Coast using the new burner phone Brooke had given her. She enjoyed thinking of him as her lover.

"Ed, I just got the biggest settlement in legal history for all our poor clients with those terrible artificial discs."

There was a pause on the line. For a moment she thought that the phone had failed.

And then he said quietly, "Linda I am so really proud of you. I am going to make sure that you will enjoy that success without ever needing to look back over your shoulder."

CHAPTER 46: SAVING GABRIEL

N ow, days after that triumphant phone call from Linda, Colonel Ed was trying to get out from behind the table in the Café de Paris to help Gabriel. After Gabriel collapsed, the café erupted in confusion. Gabriel's men obviously thought that if they let the Colonel get by their chairs to attend to their boss, their chairs might explode. They pulled out their weapons and yelled at the Colonel to stay in his place. But he showed them the supposed detonators and then put them back in his pocket.

Stephen and David, acting as waiters, both rushed to the end of the table shouting, "Let him help. He says he's a doctor." Ed then pushed past Gabriel's boys to attend to the fallen gangster.

Kneeling beside the stricken Gabriel, Ed started a classic first responder routine. He felt for Gabriel's pulse in the neck and then shouted, "Who knows CPR?"

Brooke immediately responded, "I do."

The Colonel instructed her, "Start compressions." He ripped open Gabriel's shirt and then started counting out the rhythm of one hundred pumps per minute for Brooke who dropped to her knees to start chest compressions.

He then told Stephen who supposedly worked at the Café, "Find the defibrillator. All restaurants should have one."

Brooke continued chest compressions on the massive inert hulk that was Gabriel Duquesne. Touching his blubber was revolting but she worked hard at it, pleased that all Gabriel's gunmen were shifting their position so that they could peer down her dress while she leaned low over their boss. It was now Brooke's job to keep them looking at her and she ensured that her dress slipped off her shoulders and that her bra straps followed.

Stephen returned rapidly to the scene after ripping something off the wall. Meanwhile the other two members of Stephen's team stood by attentively while keeping surreptitious watch on Gabriel's very confused gang.

The Colonel took the neat package that Stephen handed to him and unwrapped it with a show of familiarity and expertise. There were two sticky pads that he attached to Gabriel's chest. He then felt inside Gabriel's jacket and removed a cell phone which he placed on the table. "This phone could burn him if I need to shock him."

He instructed Brooke, "Continue compressions." She was pumping hard on his chest supposedly keeping blood circulating to Gabriel's brain. Gabriel's team were entranced watching her dress slowly slip off her shoulders as she continued chest compressions.

Colonel Ed picked up the clear greenish plastic bag attached to a mask that came combined with the defibrillator package. He passed the mask to Brooke who placed it over Gabriel's mouth and nose with her gloved hands. Ed instructed her, "Give him five big breaths."

Brooke squeezed air deeply into his lungs five times. She was still bent over Gabriel and his men's eyes did not leave her plunging dress.

The Colonel then pushed a button labelled "analyze" on the defibrillator. Brooke stopped ventilations and the device said in a weird computer-generated voice, "Bradycardia." Then a few seconds later it spoke again, "V Tach, apply shock."

The Colonel called out to anyone listening, "Call 911 for an ambulance. Tell them it's a cardiac arrest and we are shocking him. Everyone clear." Stephen used his phone to summon the ambulance. Colonel Ed checked to ensure that no one was in contact with Gabriel's body and pushed the button on the automated defibrillator.

There was a noticeable buzz and jolt and Gabriel's huge body jerked off the floor. The Colonel looked at the monitor on the device and said, "V tach still. Inject him." And Brooke pushed the contents of a large syringe that she had pulled out of the defibrillator packaging directly into Gabriel's leg through his pants.

No one was compressing his chest, but Brooke was again rapidly squeezing the bag to breathe for Gabriel. Colonel Ed again looked at the monitor. "We got him," he cried triumphantly, "He's back to sinus – but very slow. He must have a complete heart block. That's probably what made him collapse."

They could hear sirens in the distance and noticed that Gabriel was starting to move. Brooke continued to lean forward over Gabriel pumping the breathing bag. Her dress was barely holding on. All of Gabriel's men watched intently as she stopped compressing the bag while leaning over their boss.

With all Gabriel's men entranced watching Brooke, Stephen was casually sweeping everything from the table into a large, black plastic bag while wearing plastic gloves. He included the syringe, Gabriel's coffee cup and the cell phone that the Colonel had placed on the edge of the table after removing it from Gabriel's jacket breast pocket.

As the siren got louder, the Duquesne gang's attention turned from the front of Brooke's dress to the Café front door where the ambulance screeched to a halt. Brooke carefully wiped Gabriel's hands and mouth with a damp and then a dry napkin held in her gloved hands, putting the used napkins into Stephen's garbage bag.

And then the EMS technicians rushed in and took over. Colonel Ed told them that they had a witnessed cardiac arrest, and that the defibrillator tracing showed a profoundly low heart rate that went on to ventricular tachycardia and responded to chest compressions, ventilation, and a defibrillator shock.

The Colonel explained to the ambulance guys as he handed them the defibrillator case that he had repackaged. "I am an

ER doc. Take the defibrillator with you to the hospital. It will provide the hospital cardiologist with a record of what happened to Gabriel this morning. I will come to the ER to explain the treatment that he received. He's recovering but take him in with lights and sirens."

And then Gabriel was loaded with some difficulty onto a stretcher. The EMS techs attached him to oxygen, but he was clearly breathing for himself and looking around the room groggily. As they pushed out of the Café toward the ambulance, they could see him reach to his jacket pocket for his cell phone and realize that it was not there. He started to mutter about his cell phone, but nobody was listening to him as they struggled to lift his bulk into the vehicle.

And then Gabriel and the ambulance were gone as quickly as the vehicle had arrived. Colonel Ed turned to Brooke and said, "Great work. I will go down to the hospital and explain what happened."

Half of Gabriel's team were still rooted to their chairs, afraid of the C-4 explosive strapped under their seats. One of the guys looked at the Colonel, "Can we get up now?"

The Colonel nodded and said, "Yeah, you guys better get down to the hospital. Gabriel will need you. He and I will finish our conversation at a later date when he is feeling better. I think that he is going to make it just fine thanks to our waitress here."

Gabriel's gang had a final look at Brooke's dress and, then watching the Colonel very carefully, they got up and left quietly with their colleagues who had been standing around the Café.

The Colonel looked at Stephen. "Have we got what we need?", and Stephen nodded in response. The Colonel then looked at the team. "Time to leave."

Stephen carefully carried away the black plastic bag that he had filled. He had been wearing two pairs of plastic surgical gloves while clearing the material on the table into the bag. It had been Brooke's job to divert Gabriel's men so that they wouldn't notice Stephen and his gloves. This tactic had been entirely successful. In fact, everything in the Café had worked perfectly. Ben was going to be delighted to learn that his plan was a complete success to this point.

As Stephen led them out the rear door of the Café to return to the house rented for the Colonel and Ben, Ed was heading down to the hospital ER alone. Each of Stephen's team also carried away the chairs which were purported to hold explosives. These were placed in the vans for removal to the rented home that Ben shared with the Colonel.

Within a few minutes of arrival at Ben's house, everyone would be wearing two pairs of gloves and waterproof surgical gowns when the plastic garbage bag was opened carefully to recover Gabriel's phone. Although it was not likely contaminated by the Carfentanyl, they would wipe the phone carefully with damp clothes before touching it. Brooke had plenty of Naloxone, the antidote to the Carfentanyl, to administer to the team if needed. Just a tiny bit of Carfentanyl on the skin could be lethal if you didn't receive the Naloxone antidote.

As they were leaving the Café, Brooke had heard the morning manager coming in. He had seen Gabriel being loaded into the ambulance and one of Gabriel's men had told him that some doctor had saved the boss's life with a defibrillator in the Café.

The manager turned to one of the regular wait staff who were starting to arrive after their paid morning off, "When did we get that fuckin' defibrillator? The boss told me to get it six months ago, but I was slow ordering the thing 'cause he told me I had to pay for it from my bonus. Thank God it arrived before Gabriel needed it."

Brooke knew that the Colonel overheard this on his way out and she could see him smiling as he got into his car to head to the ER.

CHAPTER 47: VISITING HOURS

It had been three days since the fateful moment in the Café de Paris when big Gabriel had suffered his dramatic collapse. Ed knew that Gabriel would be going home tomorrow, thinking that he had been miraculously saved from his heart attack by Dr. Ed's timely action with the automated defibrillator.

During those few days, Ed's team had been working around the clock. Ed had extended his time off from the clinic, apologizing profusely to his partners. Suzanne's attitude to Ed had changed significantly since she had spoken to Dr. Romulus. But Ed could imagine that Dr. Skalbane was probably thinking that Ed was on a bender or drugged out in some flophouse.

Stephen's surveillance team was continuing to discretely monitor the Dixie Gang's activities. Members of Gabriel's team remained with their boss twenty-four hours a day in the hospital. He had plenty of visitors and most of them seemed connected to the Dixie Gang. Gabriel obviously thought he should have protection in his vulnerable state. Stephen's team observed and researched all the visitors, developing a detailed record of Gabriel's associates. The team reviewed this record nightly and it was apparent that Gabriel Duquesne's colleagues were very violent and dangerous criminals.

Brooke was under the most pressure. She and Klaus had been working non-stop since that morning in the Café de Paris. She was using the latest semi-legal and illegal software to try and break through Gabriel's phone encryption and secure password storage before he realized that his system was at risk and changed his security. The team figured that he would be too incapacitated in the first twenty-four hours in the hospital to alter his security.

Brooke worked feverishly to gain access to Duquesne's files within this narrow time window. And Klaus was ready to use any information that Brooke could obtain to build a forensic accounting analysis of what the Duquesne gang was up to.

About six hours after Brooke started working on the phone, the encryption and security yielded. Brooke suddenly achieved access to all of Gabriel's emails, texts, cloud-based records, and accounts and was able to copy everything she had discovered.

Klaus's expert interpretation of the exposed files showed that Duquesne was probably one of the wealthiest men in Mississippi. Like Tony Malto he was involved in multiple criminal endeavors and used money laundering to mask the profits of his activities. Brooke and Klaus gathered much more information than would be required in any RICO prosecution. If admitted in court, this information would put Gabriel behind bars for a very long time.

They also discovered messages and a large payment sent to members of the Aryan Brotherhood in Arkansas the day of and the day after the deaths of Tony Malto and Tommy Lawsen in Maple Ridge.

Ed knew that they did not need legally admissible evidence that Gabriel was involved in racketeering. The Dixie gang and Gabriel would know that if he was charged in a RICO case, he would be a threat to all his criminal partners. All members of the Dixie gang would be aware that Gabriel could provide information about their criminal enterprise to the prosecutors in return for lenient treatment.

If the Dixie Gang had reason to believe that Gabriel was under RICO investigation, they would almost certainly eliminate him to keep him quiet – just like Gabriel had taken care of Tony and Tommy.

Ed understood that the information that his team had gathered about Gabriel's criminal enterprise would never be used in court. Brooke had violated several federal statutes gaining access to Gabriel's records and she would probably be more at risk for prosecution than Gabriel if they took her new information to a law enforcement agency. And that was the reason that Ed now needed to visit Gabriel in hospital.

There were two reasons why Ed had staged Gabriel's cardiac arrest at the Café de Paris. The first reason was to obtain Duquesne's cell phone to gain access to his financial records. The second reason for faking Gabriel's cardiac arrest was entirely contrary to Ed's Hippocratic oath. But he was pretty sure that Hippocrates would forgive him when he fully understood what Ed was about to do.

The day before Gabriel's discharge from the private Gulf Coast hospital where he had been taken by ambulance from the Café de Paris, Ed arrived to see the patient just after visiting hours started at eleven a.m. Benjamin accompanied him carrying a thin, stylish leather portfolio. Ed brought an iPad with him that had been specially modified with help from Brooke and Ed's former colleagues in the Special Forces medical team.

They had phoned ahead to say they were coming. Gabriel's boys standing guard outside the hospital door had been warned that Ed and Benjamin were on the way and were puzzled as to the reason for their visit. The bodyguards searched the visitors for weapons. Ed then told them that he had private doctor business to discuss with their boss and pulled the door closed behind him.

Ben and Ed took seats on either side of Gabriel's bed. Duquesne's few days in hospital had not reduced his bulk. Various snacks – chips, donuts, pop, all bad for his heart – surrounded his bed. Ed remained silent in his chair and let the tension build.

"Ah'm guessin' that y'all are here to ask mah thanks for saving mah life at the Café." Gabriel sounded less confident than he had been when he and Ed first met at the Café.

"Well, Ah'm appreciative of you savin' mah life. But Ah figure that's your doctor duty anyhow. So, don't go askin' any special favors jes' for doin' your job.

"But mebbe Ah will give you a reward when Ah get outta here tomorrow. You let my boys know where y'all are stayin' an' Ah'll make sure you get somethin' delivered."

Ed nodded sagely. He could only imagine what that reward and delivery might entail. "You're absolutely right Mr. Duquesne that I don't deserve a special reward for saving your life. That is my job, and I am pleased that things turned out so well for you." Ed allowed a thin smile to cross his face which Gabriel returned with a look of intense suspicion.

"But I thought that, out of courtesy, I should explain a few new realities in your life. You do not go through an episode like you have just experienced without some big changes in your life. I want to make sure that you understand those changes."

Ed leaned forward and looked the gangster straight in the eyes. "First of all, you need to know who I am. Before starting practice in Maple Ridge, I spent more than ten years in the military Special Forces in Afghanistan as a surgeon and squad leader. For example, I was commanding the guys that put the plastic explosives in your seats at the Café de Paris."

Ed thought that Gabriel had probably been reminded about the threat of C-4. It was important that Gabriel should continue to think Ed capable of blowing off his backside.

"Now, let's talk about your heart. I saved your life when your heart started beating too slowly and then way too fast. The defibrillator device we used to shock your heart also recorded your heart's activity. It showed us a very slow heartbeat and then a very fast heart rate that required us to shock you to normalize your heart rhythm and save your life." Ed spoke slowly to ensure that Gabriel was following him.

"The doctors here in the hospital used the information that was recorded by the defibrillator to choose what type of permanent pacemaker they would implant for you. As you probably know, Mr. Duquesne, the pacemaker is that new bump below your collarbone."

As he talked, Ed stood and leaned over the gangster, putting his hand above his new pacemaker to show what he was talking about. Gabriel did not notice him dropping a tiny transparent plastic transmitter onto the chest of his hospital gown. At Gabriel's size it was hard to see down the front of his chest in any case.

"The pacemaker your doctors inserted also has a defibrillator. So, if your heart rate is too slow it will increase your heart rhythm and if your hearts starts beating too fast the defibrillator will automatically shock your heart to bring it back to a normal rate."

In telling Gabriel bald faced lies about what had happened to him in the Café, Ed took some ethical refuge in the fact that Gabriel was not his patient. Actually, Duquesne had not collapsed because his heart was beating either too slow or too fast in the Café. His heart had been just fine during the entire episode.

The real cause of Gabriel's collapse was the Carfentanyl drug that he had absorbed through his fingers and lips from the gel painted on his coffee cup. The Carfentanyl gel mixture was instantly absorbed through his skin to deliver a massive overdose of opioids that stopped his breathing and rendered him unconscious. His heart did not actually either slow down or speed up and he had never needed a shock from the defibrillator.

The abnormal heart rhythms that appeared on the defibrillator in the Café had been preprogrammed with the help of Special Forces military doctors who had used this technique on an Iraqi general that the Forces wanted to retire. Ed gave the prerecorded defibrillator information to the cardiologists in this hospital to ensure that they would insert the heart pacemaker that was appropriate for the plan to protect Linda.

What actually reversed Gabriel's so-called 'heart attack' was not the defibrillator, but rather the massive dose of Naloxone opioid antidote drug that Brooke had given him in the thigh injection through his trousers. Naloxone is the universal antidote to all forms of opioid, including Carfentanyl. Brooke gave him enough to reverse ten thousand overdoses.

Stephen had swept the Naloxone needle, the Carfentanyl-lubricated coffee cup, and the cell phone that Ed removed from Gabriel's jacket into the plastic bag that he removed from the Café table just before the ambulance sped off. Unbeknownst to Gabriel, the Naloxone had done a good job for the gangster, restoring his breathing, and saving his life.

Ed had rigged the defibrillator in advance to initially show a very slow heart rate that the cardiologists would think had been the cause of Gabriel's blackout, ensuring the cardiologists would insert a pacemaker. A very slow heart rate is often associated with blacking out symptoms similar to what Gabriel demonstrated when he collapsed from the Carfentanyl.

And Ed also programmed the defibrillator to show Gabriel's cardiologists that the big man had then developed ventricular tachycardia which is a potentially deadly fast heart rhythm. Ventricular tachycardia can develop when the heart is damaged by oxygen deficiency due to a very slow heart rate. With both slow and fast abnormal rates demonstrated on the faked defibrillator record that Ed delivered to the ER, Ed knew the cardiologists would implant a special defibrillating pacemaker.

The reason why this was important for Linda would soon become apparent to Gabriel.

But first it was time to educate the gangster about what they had learned about his criminal enterprise. Ed sat back in the chair at the side of Gabriel's bed.

"Gabriel before I explain to you any more about the health challenges that you will be facing, I want to introduce you to my brother Benjamin. He is CEO of one of the most successful energy companies in the country. You won't be able to find out very much about this company because it is privately owned by our family." Ed smiled and lifted his hand toward Ben.

"However, you do need to understand that our family has enormous resources, greater than you can imagine. And unlike you, because those resources are legitimate, we have friends in very high places who will be delighted to take the information that we have gathered on you and turn it into one of the biggest RICO prosecutions in history."

At the word RICO, they could see Gabriel get noticeably paler and Ed wondered for a moment if they might need to shock his heart again. Gabriel knew that even a rumor of RICO charges would leave him at risk from his partners in the Dixie Gang who would undoubtedly decide to silence him. Dixie Gang members would surmise that RICO would be used to get Gabriel to testify against his colleagues in return for favorable legal treatment. And RICO prosecution could leave Gabriel without funds to buy protection. Gabriel knew that he could be gone like Tony within days of rumors starting about a RICO charge.

At this point Ed again turned to Ben. "We have some interesting documents that we want to show you regarding your businesses and RICO, Gabriel." With that, Benjamin opened the thin leather folio he was carrying and turned over a summary twenty pages of Duquesne's accounts and transfers. The sources of cash revenue were clearly outlined as they related to drugs, women, gambling, and human trafficking as well as the transfers for money laundering that Gabriel had expertly organized. It also referred to invoices provided to the Malto companies for purposes of money laundering in Maple Ridge.

Importantly, it showed Gabriel that Ed had access to all of Gabriel's accounts. Ed wanted him to know that they could point a prosecutor to all of his assets if the feds wanted to seize his criminal accounts.

Ben now continued. "We obtained these documents using access to your cloud-based files. There is enough RICO-ready material here to put you away for the rest of your days, Gabriel. And it doesn't matter if you change all your security now because once we got in, we installed software that will allow us to keep coming back." Gabriel grabbed the documents and his forehead beaded with sweat as he flipped through the pages. The last comment about returning to his accounts through a newly installed security firewall was a bluff. But the next threats were not.

Ben pointed to a page that documented several messages and one transaction in detail. "Gabriel, the county police in Maple Ridge are still angry about Tony Malto and Tommy Lawsen being killed in custody. I am sure that they will be interested in this payment from you to a well know Aryan Brotherhood member who was in jail the day that Tony and Tommy were murdered as well as your messages to his colleagues on the outside. This payment and the messages demonstrate that you ordered and paid for his murder."

Ben paused to let Gabriel look at the details of the money transfer. "I can understand that you might be concerned that we are going to give this information to the authorities, which we both know would be a death sentence for you when they announced that they were pursuing a RICO prosecution. If your partners knew about a RICO investigation, your days would be numbered." Ben slowed down his delivery at this point. He had taken back the documents from Gabriel and carefully replaced them in his folder. He then handed the folder to Gabriel.

"You know that your colleagues would eliminate you to ensure that you did not rat on them to get the feds to go easy on you."

Here Ben took a sheet of typed paper from his pocket, unfolded it, and handed it to Gabriel.

"You also know that the death you arranged for Tony in jail would be gentle compared to the torture your colleagues would use to question you the moment they heard about RICO. And Gabriel, you can see from that paper I just gave you that we know exactly who you work with in your various criminal activities. Their names are written on that paper." This list had been compiled from Stephen's surveillance of the various gangsters that had visited Gabriel while he was hospitalized.

"You should also remember that Tony Malto is still remembered fondly by friends in Maple Ridge. Friends whose livelihood was hurt when Tony was murdered. It wouldn't surprise me if Tony's friends also came after you, Gabriel, when they learn that you are going to be weakened by the RICO prosecution and they discover that you organized the hit on Tony." Ben paused here as they had planned. He then concluded.

"Gabriel we could first release all this material to the Dixie Gang, to Tony's old colleagues and then to the FBI. There will be a lot of people interested in these documents, Gabriel"

Ed leaned over and patted Gabriel's arm below the hospital gown. It was clammy. Ed then took over from Benjamin.

"But you are going to be very happy when I tell you that Benjamin and I are not immediately taking this information to your Dixie Gang partners nor to the FBI. Instead, Benjamin's company is retaining two major law firms who will carefully archive this information. Those firms will ensure that this material can be rapidly mobilized for transmission to the FBI and federal prosecutors that we know extremely well."

Ed looked him directly in the eyes. "And Gabriel, we know who your Dixie Gang closest associates are as Ben showed you on that list. Before releasing these documents to the FBI, our law firms will also provide these materials with lots of explanation about what they mean to your business associates. And the lawyers will also provide evidence to the county police about Tony Malto's murder – and Gabriel, you know how leaky that police force is."

Now it was Ben's term to contribute. They had rehearsed this part carefully. "But these documents will remain confidential as long as no harm befalls us or members of our team including Linda Davis. If anything happens to any team member, or if a member of our team suspects they are at risk, our lawyers will immediately activate these archived documents.

"If there is any hint that you may be involved in threatening or assaulting a member of our team, these documents will be released to the FBI and federal prosecutors with a full explanation of why this needs to be a RICO prosecution. And we will make sure that your Dixie Gang partners also get the material along with information that the FBI is about to bring RICO charges against you.

"And Gabriel, as I said before, our lawyers will let the gang know several days before we notify the FBI." Ben paused, like his brother allowing tension to build.

"So, Gabriel you have a real interest in ensuring that our team remains healthy. You might say that your life depends on our health." Ben paused again. He had Gabriel's undivided attention.

"And now Gabriel, my brother the doctor is going to demonstrate another reason why you need to make sure that we do not get unhappy with you."

Ed picked up the iPad that he had brought with him. Brooke had modified it by adding a transmission antenna which they had received from Ed's military colleagues. The transmitter connected wirelessly to the tiny plastic relay device Ed had dropped over Gabriel's pacemaker when they had first entered his room. That relay was designed to connect remotely to the pacemaker to test or adjust the heart device. Brooke had also added software to the iPad that they had downloaded from Ed's military medical colleagues.

The Special Forces medical teams had figured out how to manipulate every pacemaker on the market. They very rarely used this knowledge, but sometimes the know-how was helpful to motivate foreign statesmen or military leaders who had implanted pacemakers.

"As you know through recent experience, your heart can suddenly slow down without warning and that can make you pass out and collapse. In order to prevent this from suddenly killing you, your doctors have implanted a pacemaker that will speed up your heart whenever it suddenly slows down."

Ed pointed to the cardiac monitor beside Gabriel that was recording his heart rate. "There is your heart rate displayed on this monitor. However, your pacemaker needs to be monitored and occasionally, settings need to be adjusted to ensure that it is working properly." He paused and smiled at the gangster.

"I have obtained access to the software that changes your pacemaker settings during check-ups. I have stored the identification codes for your pacemaker's telemetry address on my iPad and I am about to give you a brief demonstration." Ed showed Gabriel the iPad screen so he could see what Ed was about to do.

And here is the part where Ed definitely broke his physician's ethical code of conduct. After showing Gabriel the screen, he typed in a few new numbers.

"Right now your heart is pumping fine, and the pacemaker is not firing. However, if I turn up the rate on the pacemaker it will take over control of your heart. Watch that cardiac monitor screen, Gabriel, after I enter this command."

Ed showed Gabriel the screen as he tapped on ENTER and the gangster suddenly felt his heart rate accelerate. He turned to look at the monitor which clearly showed his heart rate speeding up.

He grabbed his chest, "What the fuck are you doin' to me?"

Ed turned up the rate to the maximum allowed by the device which gave Gabriel a definite sense of his heart pounding. He could also see his heart racing on the monitor.

And now Ed told the gangster a white lie. "And of course, I could double or triple the heart rate that you are feeling right now and then your heart would explode within minutes."

Gabriel's face was the color of the bedsheets. Ed continued. "One more thing we can do. You were unconscious the last time I shocked you. This is what it feels like when you are awake."

And Ed entered another command on the pad which set off the pacemaker defibrillator. A defibrillator shock for a conscious patient feels like a heavy, powerful, and painful punch in the chest.

Gabriel screamed and the boys outside pushed into the room with guns drawn. Ed showed the screen to him again with his finger over the ENTER key. "Tell them to get out Gabriel." Duquesne waved them out with one hand, his other hand grasping his chest.

"That was a little shock, Gabriel. If we shock you with five or ten times that strength, your heart will be fried once and for all time." Ed lifted the iPad as if he were going to use it again and then slowly lowered it. Gabriel looked frantic.

"But Gabriel, as you have already experienced with me saving your life, I am a doctor and I do not want to hurt you." He paused.

"Unless I have to."

Ed turned the screen away from Gabriel and closed its cover.

Gabriel's jaw was hanging slack and wide open.

Ben pushed a card across to him that demonstrated an email address. "We will be watching for you in the Café de Paris because we know that you go there six days a week. Every few months you may notice our team there in the Café, although you will never be certain it is us on any given morning."

"Any day but Sunday that you are not going to be in the Café for any reason you send a message to this email address to let us know."

Ed then rose from his seat again and stood directly over him, drawing up his best intimidating military bearing. "You will tell the Aryan guys and the Simon City guys in Maple Ridge that you are stopping doing business in the Ridge with Tony gone. Tell them that you do not want them working in Maple Ridge any longer."

Ed then slowly leaned over Gabriel and put one finger directly in front of his face. "We don't care if you carry on business anywhere else in the state – just not in Maple Ridge. And most important, you make sure that our people have protection. Because if anything happens to anyone on our team, the wrath of God will fall on your head Gabriel." Here he paused and then put his fist firmly on the mobster's chest.

"Or maybe I should say on your heart."

"And Gabriel, you are welcome. I am glad that I was able to save your life."

CHAPTER 48: MAPLE RIDGE

The weather cooperated beautifully on the night of the wedding. It seemed like the entire town of Maple Ridge had been invited to Linda's garden to celebrate with a night of dining and dancing under the spring stars. Standing to the side of the dance floor, Ben was watching Ed guide his very pregnant, very new wife around the dance floor as the celebration continued after dinner. A gospel group was coming on after the bride and groom's first dance and the party was promising to last until morning.

Ben looked over at his date who was approaching to take him onto the dance floor after the newlyweds completed the first few turns of their dance. Staring at that beautiful woman, Ben found it hard to believe how his life had changed since he first visited Maple Ridge.

Ben had been proud to stand up for his big brother as best man at an intimate ceremony with close friends and family in a small chapel earlier that day. He smiled as he remembered that, if it wasn't for him, Ed and Linda would have probably delayed their wedding indefinitely because they were both so busy.

In the months following Biloxi, Ed had overloaded his practice with complex patients and was proving that the medical home model kept his patients out of hospital.

He enjoyed working in the hospital and Dr. Bill Stanton had asked him to consider taking over as Chief of Staff when Bill's term expired in the next year. Collegiality in the clinic had improved after Dr. Skalbane stepped down as clinic chief and Suzanne Fortis took over his role. She and Ed had come to agreement on the benefit of the medical home model. She was here tonight enjoying herself with the rest of Ed's medical group. Even old Lawrence Skalbane seemed to be having a good time. And as the gospel group started, Esther Hightower was smiling full of grace as she swayed clapping with the music.

The clinic had provided evidence to state and federal authorities that they were saving Medicare and Medicaid money by avoiding hospitalization for their medical home patients. Based on these results, they were receiving funding to recruit more patients and expand the medical home team in the Maple Ridge clinic. The national Medicare office had recognized the Maple Ridge clinic as an early successful adopter of the medical home approach, and other physician groups from across the country were starting to visit the clinic to observe how the model could work.

Ed had moved in with Linda in her heritage home during the time that they now referred to as 'the problems'. The two were inseparable, notwithstanding the fact that Linda was in tremendous demand for her class action expertise. The results that she had achieved for her artificial disc clients were being talked about across the country's legal fraternity and the Davis firm was receiving almost daily offers of cases from around the nation. Linda was turning down far more clients than she was accepting and was busy creating a national network of class action firms to work on cases that she couldn't handle alone.

Although Linda was continually getting offers to take her practice to various locations across the country, she remained firmly committed to Maple Ridge. As she told Ben one night over a cup of tea when he was visiting from New York, "If I worked in New York or Chicago, I would spend at least an hour a day being driven to and from work, whereas in the Ridge it takes me about seven minutes to get to the office. There is nothing that I cannot access here in Maple Ridge, and I like how we are changing this town."

They were sitting in her kitchen that evening and she got

up to gaze through the window that looked out over the river. "You know, Benjamin, when your family goes back as many generations in a town as my family does – well you don't just pull out. You hope to leave a legacy. And I feel like that legacy is within reach. Maple Ridge is changing in so many ways."

Ed and Linda's legacy was the reason that Ben had taken on the role as organizer for their wedding and pushed them toward the altar. The need for nuptials became apparent to Ben shortly after Gabriel's momentous 'heart attack' when Ed was sharing a beer with Benjamin after the younger brother had flown in from New York to spend the weekend.

Ben had been looking forward to seeing Ed and Linda and was also anticipating checking in with Brooke Paltrig. A few weeks before, Brinkley Enterprises had contracted Brooke full time to establish a permanent security presence in Maple Ridge and Ben wanted to make sure that she had what she needed.

There was another reason for Ben's visit. On his last trip to Maple Ridge two weekends earlier, he and Brooke had finished negotiations on the contract to set up the security program. Brooke suggested that they should go for dinner to celebrate their new endeavor. Following drinks before dinner and an excellent bottle of wine, Brooke ended up in Ben's hotel room.

In the middle of the night, Ben awoke admiring her leg lying on the sheets. He started to say something about Brinkley Enterprises' corporate standards regarding intimate relationships and senior executives and contractors, but Brooke just rolled over to straddle him with those lovely legs resulting in Ben forgetting about his company's code of conduct.

Two weeks later, Ed and Ben were sitting on the patio outside Linda's kitchen, enjoying the early evening and the setting sun after Ben's arrival on the Brinkley corporate jet. Linda had sent Ben a text asking if he would mind if Brooke joined them for dinner. Linda always seemed to know everything about everyone before anyone else.

As the two brothers sat catching up on events of the past two weeks, Ed said out of nowhere, "Ben, you won't believe this, but

Linda is pregnant."

Ben stared at his big brother for a moment. When it became clear that Ed was actually surprised at his girlfriend's condition, Ben smiled, then started laughing and then could not stop. Linda heard Ben's laughter from inside her kitchen and came out smiling to investigate the source of his mirth.

"Benjamin, I know that you're always happy to see your brother after a couple of weeks away, but what's so funny?"

Ben caught his breath with some difficulty. "You two brilliant people. You, Colonel Ed – who fights off Taliban terrorists and mobsters and saves lives and you, Ms. Davis – who fights big companies on behalf of little people all across this country. With all your combined wisdom and expertise – could the two of you not figure out birth control?"

Linda blushed beautifully. "Oh, Benjamin, what the hell am I going to do. I am just too old to be having a first child. And our practice is just going crazy. Since that big disc case settled, I have hired twelve more paralegals and we are training everyone we can find. In fact, Tony Malto's widow Sharon has just joined the training program. I think that she's going to be great."

She shook her head slowly and crossed her arms looking out over the Ridge. "But Ben, I can't afford the time to be a momma, for God's sake. And you know your brother. He would be great with our child, but you know how much time he spends with his patients."

Benjamin held back his giggles. Here he was, younger than either of them, one of them a doctor, Ben not married and childless – giving them family counseling advice.

"Linda, I have heard you speak passionately about your family's legacy in the Ridge. Well, your family's history here is about to end abruptly unless you have a child. And Ed, I've seen you with kids in the office. You're like the Pied Piper. This is your chance, guys. You can afford lots of help." He motioned towards Linda's beautifully restored and spacious home. "And you certainly have plenty of room."

Ben recognized that they simply loved each other so much. Both of them had always been so independent and Ben was sure that they both had been initially concerned as to how they would cope with another person in their lives. But they were so in love, and just thoroughly enjoyed each other's company.

And, unlike some professional couples who could become competitive with each other, each was proud and protective of the other's success.

It really only took a few minutes for them to agree with Ben that they needed to have a baby to complete their relationship. For Ben, there was no question that this was what they had to do. It just seemed so right.

As Ed and Ben opened a bottle of single malt that evening to toast Ed's future family, the lovely Brooke Paltrig arrived in a rather stunning short black dress. And shamelessly provided Ben with a long and passionate kiss while Linda silently applauded behind her.

Brooke, looking at the open bottle of whiskey, wanted to know what the brothers were celebrating. Ed and Ben looked at Linda who gathered in Brooke for a close hug, and then held her at arms' length to announce, "Ed and I are going to have a baby."

And that started a memorable dinner with three of them enjoying wonderful food and wine and Linda ushering Brooke and Benjamin into one of her guest rooms at the end of the evening.

****

Winter was ending, the gardens were blooming and so was Linda. On his increasingly frequent visits, Ben loved watching Ed rub Linda's tummy as the baby grew. But he realized that if he left it to these two highly competent people, then his future favorite niece or nephew was going to be born out of wedlock.

So, Brooke and Ben started planning a wedding for the engaged couple and that necessitated more time for Ben in Maple Ridge. At first, he would fly in weekly and stay with Brooke at

Linda's. And then he couldn't stand spending five days apart from Brooke and decided to rent a place to serve as the Maple Ridge Brinkley branch office. Brooke recruited Stephen as a second-in-command of their security team to allow her to occasionally accompany Ben to New York.

Brooke and Linda became fast friends. Linda credited Brooke for saving her life with the GPS device that permitted her rescue from Tony Malto that awful night. So it was no surprise when Linda asked Brooke to stand up for her as maid of honor at the wedding.

In mid-April, with her due date in the not too distant future and Linda looking radiant, Maple Ridge was enjoying a wonderful evening wedding celebration and a night full of revelry.

Benjamin asked Stephen to take over security for the wedding so that Brooke could fully enjoy the evening. As dinner ended and the champagne flowed, Ben raised his glass to provide the first of many toasts to Ed and Linda Brinkley. He handed a glass to Brooke and was surprised when she demurred.

Brooke was stunning in a blue bridesmaid's dress that reflected her eyes. "Brooke, you know Stephen's working tonight. You can enjoy a glass or two this evening."

She looked up at him with those beautiful eyes, reached her hands around his neck and pulled him close. "Benjamin, I love you so much. We need to figure something out because we are going to have a baby too."

Ben's brother had come to Arkansas to start over as the new doc in Maple Ridge and now Benjamin was planning to join him permanently in his adopted home. Linda intended to subdivide her property overlooking the river if Ben and Brooke wanted, and it was intriguing to imagine their two future families living next to each other in this wonderful place with cousins using the ridge as their playground.

Brinkley's jet brought Ben back and forth to New York with a commute that he was doing less frequently. Brinkley Enterprises was moving its locus of operations westward as it concentrated on its American shale oil and gas business and continued its rapid expansion into renewable energy. Brinkley Enterprises needed to be in New York as a financial company and needed to be in the west as an oil and gas and renewables company. Maple Ridge put Ben midway between the two locations.

Brooke planned to give up her role to Stephen so that she could be full time at home with the baby. Ben had always been good at strategic thinking. And right now, he knew that the best strategy to enhance all their happiness involved him and Brooke raising a family alongside his brother and new sister-in-law, right here in Maple Ridge.

Stephen continued to ensure that every few months an elite team of former Special Forces warriors would visit Biloxi for a few days to remind Gabriel Duquesne that he was being watched in perpetuity. Gabriel regularly received time stamped images of himself enjoying breakfast in the Café and occasionally took delivery of a chair with plasticine sewed into the seat padding.

After Stephen's most recent visit, the brothers were told that Gabriel had lost about one hundred pounds in weight. Stephen said the team observed that Duquesne was working out daily with a personal trainer.

Ben's brother believed deeply that he could improve his patients' well-being by enhancing their health self-management skills. And it certainly seemed that Ed had changed Gabriel's commitment to improving his health – especially as related to the health of his heart.

ABOUT THE AUTHOR

Dr. Bob Bell

Robert Stuart Bell, MDCM, MSc, FRCSC, FACS, FRCSE (hon). Professor of Surgery, University of Toronto.

Dr. Bob Bell received his medical degree from McGill University in 1975. Following internship at McGill he worked as a General Practitioner outside Toronto. Bell returned to surgical residency at the University of Toronto and received his fellowship in Orthopedic Surgery in 1983. Bell then trained in cancer surgery and research at Harvard University and Massachusetts General Hospitals in Boston.

Recruited to the University of Toronto's Faculty of Surgery, Bell worked as a cancer and orthopedic surgeon for 19 years. During that time, he trained more than 30 surgical fellows in principles of cancer surgery and these former fellows are now surgical leaders on five continents. Bell collaborated with dedicated expert basic scientists throughout his surgical career and published more than 200 peer-reviewed, scientific and clinical papers. He has presented his research at scientific meetings around the world.

In 2005, Bell was appointed as President and CEO of University Health Network (UHN), Canada's largest research hospital. Toronto General Hospital, one of the hospitals in the network, was recently named the fourth best hospital in the world by Newsweek magazine. During his nine years as CEO of UHN, Bell led a substantial expansion of clinical and research programs.

In 2014, Bell was appointed Deputy Minister of Health for Canada's largest province of Ontario. For the next four years, Bell was responsible for the operations of a health system serving fourteen million people. While Deputy Minister, Bell was reacquainted with the importance of primary care as a crucial aspect of improving the health of both people and societies. He also became aware of efforts in America to institute the patient medical home model of care that is fundamental to Ontario practice.

Bell's experience as a GP prior to becoming a surgeon and an understanding of challenges in every modern health system provides a basis for "New Doc in Maple Ridge"- a medical thriller that will inform as well as entertain.

After resigning as Deputy Minister in 2018, Bell has focused on writing fiction, charitable activities and providing commentary on Canada's publicly funded health system. This commentary can be found at www.drbobbell.com and @drbobbell. Bell and his wife Diann divide their time between homes in Toronto and on Georgian Bay.

Proceeds from Bell's first novel "Hip" benefitted cancer research at Princess Margaret Cancer Centre. All proceeds from this book will be donated to serve primary care research at Toronto Western Hospital, a member of University Health Network.

BOOKS BY THIS AUTHOR

Hip: A Novel

Andrei Kovalov developed a biolayer for the super-B.I.G. hip replacement that shows remarkable results in dogs. He will soon receive $25 million when the hip is used in humans. However, Kovalov has destroyed evidence that some super-B.I.G. dogs developed bone cancer. If that gets out, the super-B.I.G. and his payday are finished.

Dr. Patrick Maloney is a lowly surgical fellow who notices cancer in a super-B.I.G. specimen and is concerned when this worrisome evidence disappears.

Patrick is warned he will be unemployable unless he ignores his suspicions since powerful medical forces will benefit from the super-B.I.G. implant. Patrick has also fallen in love with a scientist who studies the implant. Disparaging the super-B.I.G. will hurt her career.

This story focuses on the principle that a doctor must always uphold his oath to protect patients. Will Dr. Mahoney be able to honor his oath? Will Patrick's promising career be destroyed? "Hip" offers surprising answers to these questions.

Manufactured by Amazon.ca
Bolton, ON